-IN- DREAMS

THE DARK BEFORE
— YOU —

DALIA CLARK

First printed and published in 2020.
www.indreamsnovel.co.uk
Instagram: @indreamsnovel

Book cover design by Dalia Clark
Instagram: @daliaclarkdesign

In Dreams: The Dark Before You

Prologue

Having witnessed many magnificent spectacles throughout the centuries, he found it remarkable that this view never failed to impress him. High amongst the treetops, a wooden platform rocked in the gentle breeze. This peaceful viewing point had stood here since his childhood years, and he could picture the landscape it overlooked now without opening his eyes: the valley beyond these trees and the river that wound between it, the cherry blossom trees and red maples that lined the water's edge, the woodland in the distance, the luminescent flowers that flecked the ground like a reflection of the night's stars, and the mountain tips that reached up to the moon. Eagerly, he wished to see the morning touch this view, but it would be a long time before that would happen, and there were matters to deal with now that could no longer be ignored.

He opened his eyes. The view was no longer the one he so loved. This was not that place, and the *visitor* was here again. A shadow. Its lack of substance and air of arrogance had already begun to test his patience. Dealing with the same ones more than once was becoming tiresome, especially when their minds were this dull. He had decided it was best to get rid of it from here as quickly as possible. Technically, he was doing it a favour, and this was his only option now anyway. There had been too many shadows like this one lately, and he watched it with what could only be described as hatred. *Hate* was a strong word, but there was no denying its presence. This was unlike him, or at least it used to be. It was unsettling to feel this way already in the time since his return, eighteen years ago. Though this would probably seem a long time to *them*, it was nothing to him.

He specifically remembered returning on June 14. That day, he had woken with new energy coursing through his veins and fresh hope for the future. For a while, it had seemed like life was full of promise again. However, his days had become a train of endless, empty nights within the space of those eighteen years, and life's promises remained unkept. Shadows had done nothing but plague him. After tonight, it was time to take a break to go somewhere he would be left alone for a while. He knew just the place. But for now, it was time to act.

What name would he be known by tonight? he wondered. Within seconds, the answer surfaced in his mind. Not 'whom', but 'what'—a thing. *A demon.* That's how he would soon be known to this shadow. So be it. But, for a little while, he would hold on to being just an observing *stranger*.

This stranger now drew nearer to the oblivious shadow as it sat behind the driving wheel of a slick, black Porsche—its prized possession. The car appeared to be parked on a quiet suburban street while the majority of the neighbourhood slept. A cigarette bud was tossed to the ground as the ignition abruptly roared, breathing life into the vehicle. The shadow set the car rolling, unaware of *him*, the uninvited stranger, who now sat in the darkness of the back passenger seat. The Porsche sped out of town along an open road, into the lifeless night. The lights of the city faded rapidly in the distance behind. Dead, grassy banks and bowed, twisted trees now rose up at either side of the car, creating black looming shapes against the windows.

The summer's heat had made the night stale and stuffy. Something putrid lingered in the air outside. The stench of stagnant water, decaying vegetation, roadkill, or whatever it was, stung the shadow's senses. The window wound up. In that instant, the car radio started of its own accord. The shadow started fidgeting with dials and buttons in an attempt to turn off the station. Instead, the volume began to soar. The speakers let out a high-pitched tone followed by the blaring interference of static noise. The shadow smashed its hand into the radio with no result other than sore, bloodied knuckles. Louder the radio grew, blasting out from every rattling panel. The dashboard vibrated violently. Again the shadow's fist met the radio controls. But this unbearable sound could not be silenced. And still, it became louder. Piercing. Almost deafening.

The shadow spun the steering wheel sharply to the left and then flung both hands over its ears. The tires screeched as they skidded along the side of the road. The car came to a halt by the edge of some woodlands, throwing its driver backwards as the engine cut out and the radio switched off. The shadow hastily ran both hands through its hair, acknowledging the proximity of the trees beside the bonnet. With its ears still ringing, it glanced in the rearview mirror, wiping the moisture from its forehead. It froze as its eyes shifted to the reflection of the passenger in the back seat. The shadow's eyes met with his—*the stranger*—and so, observing time was now over.

The stranger edged forward with a dark, emotionless stare. His pale, gangly fingers reached out. The shadow gasped and scrambled to unhook its belt. Flinging the door open, it made a bid to run for the woods. The stranger followed, stepping out of the car in a slow, effortless fashion as the passenger door fell off its hinges to the ground. The shadow anxiously turned back, pausing briefly in time to see the car crumple like it was made of paper. The stranger stood in front of the vehicle, and following one hand gesture, the car burst into flames. The shadow cast a wary look at him, now sure that its initial fears were correct—this uninvited stranger was no ordinary man. His hands were long claws, and his sinister grin was dangerously sharp. He could be nothing other than a *demon*.

Black smoke began to swirl around the demon, picking up speed as it stirred up dust and dirt in a fierce, spiralling wind. It visibly grew with every step forward he took. The ground started to shake as broken trees and rocks flew up into the air, joining the growing tornado that had begun to form. The shadow's eyes widened as it backed up slowly, legs trembling, heart racing. Cracks appeared in the road and earth all around, threatening to swallow everything in sight. The shadow turned to flee, watching its footing as the ground crumbled beneath it. However, there would be no escape tonight. As the earth underfoot disappeared, the shadow plummeted down into the unknown. A scream filled the night for one brief moment. Then there was silence as *he*, once again, slipped away into the darkness.

Chapter 1
The Fog

Something was missing. What that was, exactly, remained a mystery, but lately, she was sure of its absence from her life. Day by day, it seemed to erode a small piece of what was once contentment. It niggled and played on her mind uncomfortably. It was almost like the ache that had begun to pulsate in her head this evening. Aarie sat nursing it as it throbbed stubbornly behind her temples. Managing to force a smile, she gazed back at the motley gang who sat around her in the small coffee shop.

Her closest friends.

They were the 'something good' and right in her life, something she couldn't imagine being without. They had known each other since they were small children, and she loved them now like family. It was hard to believe they would soon start a new chapter in their lives. Aarie examined them one by one, thinking up memories she had shared with each of them at various points in their friendship.

There was Jamie—an easygoing, carefree kind of guy who could never give a straight answer. He would always give a 'maybe' or 'we'll see' or anything that meant he could stay spontaneous in his decision. He 'lived for the moment', though many of those moments were often paused, adjusted, and then captured on his camera with great dedication. Extraordinarily, he could photograph the hell out of anything, always seeing an artistic angle and a potentially great story in places most people overlooked. As a result, a vast amount of Aarie's childhood memories had been preserved and digitally immortalised in their best light.

Jamie Saunders always looked like he had just rolled out of bed, with his tousled butterscotch hair that remarkably framed his face in an effortlessly masculine way. Aarie thought he seemed to have grown taller and bulked out slightly in the past two years. With his muscular physique, rugged good looks, and sizable ego to match, Aarie knew Jamie was the type of guy she'd be too shy to talk to if they were to have just met now. He was always the joker, the flirter, the confident one who never took anything too seriously. However, he was also one of the most kindhearted people she knew. Jamie always had time for her when it mattered, and he did not take kindly to anyone who so much as looked at her the wrong way.

A warm pair of hazel eyes met Aarie's gaze. Jamie winked at her, flashing his usual cheeky grin, and she smiled in response before moving her observations swiftly to another oblivious friend.

Angela.

Her long auburn hair curled over her shoulders like wildfire against her stunning black chiffon dress. No doubt, this was one of many exquisitely handmade pieces from the Angela Bennett *haute couture collection*. She had the figure of a goddess, the doe-eyed face of an angel, and a cheeky wickedness about her that drove guys crazy and made girls envious.

Bitch, Aarie joked to herself in her head, although she knew she loved her, really. Angela always revelled in a good story but 'never gossiped'. If something was not true, she wasn't interested. Of course, speculation about some truth being present, often qualified gossip as being a good story when actual good stories were scarce.

Ange had been a loyal friend who never failed to make her laugh. Her beautiful sage eyes would often light up at the mention of fun, but she was always there too when a girly chat was much needed.

And then there was Adam, her oldest and best friend who had stuck with her through thick and thin. They had been friends since the age of six and were very rarely apart. They told each other virtually everything and knew each other so well they could practically finish each other's sentences. As her eyes fell on him now, it was hard to believe he had been part of most of her life. This wide-eyed boy in front of her was now a man; however, if she was honest, he hadn't changed an awful lot since his early teens. His mussed, coffee-coloured hair swept across his forehead as it had always done, matching the colour of his eyes. He still had his boyish looks, slim frame, and a smooth babyface. His cheeks were still flecked with tiny adorable freckles that reminded Aarie of their childhood and that their friendship would never really change. They would always have each other.

Aarie had first met Adam when he and his mum, Mrs Guilford, had moved to the village of Thorndale and into the house next door to hers. At that time, Aarie's mother had recently passed away. Her father had thought a new friend would be good for her to help her through grieving. Aarie's dad had not told her that then, but looking back, she knew this was the case. It was the only time he ever introduced her to strangers and encouraged her to make new friends, especially boys. Anyway, it had worked. Despite his indecisive and unconfident nature, there was something that Adam had always been confident about: being good friends with Aarie. Right from the start, he had known they would get on well.

So with this in mind, Aarie knew that Adam was merely making the current conversation for the sake of some attention. He didn't really mean the words that flew out of his mouth as she zoned back into his voice. She tried her best to forget the pulse that still pounded in her head.

"But it's not going to be the same anymore, guys. This is the end of an era," whined Adam. "Who knows what the future holds for us all. We could all change. What if we don't get on anymore? University life can change people, you know. Friendships can just die. You all don't seem to care," Adam said, leaning back on his stool as he played with the cola can on the table in front of him.

Aarie rolled her eyes in his direction. "Stop being so melodramatic."

"I'm not melodramatic. It happens. How do we know we won't fall out? Living together changes people. Spending so much time together will mean getting to know all of each other's weird habits and any irritating things we never knew about each other. It can change things," Adam said, scanning over the small band of friends who sat around him.

"We already know all of your disgusting and irritating habits, matey," Jamie said with a snigger. "And we've tried to shake you from our gang many times, but you seem to be surgically attached to Aarie. We like her too much to do anything drastic about it. So, I guess we're stuck with you."

A faint chuckle broke from the two girls as Jamie smirked at Adam.

Adam scowled, casually throwing a scrunched up napkin at him. "That hurts, Jamie."

"I'm just keeping it real. It's what keeps friendships strong," Jamie nonchalantly replied.

"Adam, we all practically live together anyway," Angela piped up, playing with her hair as she glanced his way. "We all go to the same coffee shop together, eat the same fast food, go to the same gigs, the same movies, the same *everything*. We pretty much live at one another's houses from one day to the next already, for goodness sake. I doubt the fact we're going to university together is going to change much on that front. Just think of it as us gaining more independence and freedom without the disapproving, watchful eyes of our parents. We have to grow up sometime, you know. Though we don't have to rush and be too mature straight away. Think of all the fun we'll have! Come on, you know we'll get along just as well as always, Adam. Besides, you know too many of our dirty secrets for us to let you free from our gang. We could let you drift apart from us, but we'd have to kill you."

Adam laughed. "Yes, I do know many of your secrets." He narrowed his eyes at Jamie and flashed a mischievous grin. "And don't *you* forget it!"

Jamie smirked back at him. "Yes, but we also know all of yours," he said in amusement as his eyes briefly flicked towards Aarie, then back to Adam.

Adam quickly sat back firm in his seat, picking up his cola can to raise it in the air and change the subject with a toast. "Well, anyway... here's to future possibilities and a putting up with annoying friends that we can't seem to shake, for many more years."

Angela raised a hand in objection. "Or... here's to having three years of fun, freedom, and possibly the best time of our lives... ever!" Angela beamed.

Jamie's grin widened. "Yes, I like Ange's toast better. Let's toast to that," he boomed.

Adam pulled a face. "Okay, yeah, when you say it like that, it sounds bloody good to me too." He smiled in agreement. "Leeds, here we come!"

They scooped up their cups and cans, then clanged them together, letting out a burst of whistles, whoops and cheers.

"I can't wait," Angela said as they all slid back into their chairs and seemingly into their own happy thoughts and imaginings of their upcoming future.

Aarie sighed. "Well, I'm sorry to break up the gathering so soon, but I'm gonna head home," she said, pulling her stool from under the table. It made a little screech that sent shudders through her.

"Still got a headache?"Angela asked.

"Yeah, I can't seem to get rid of it. I'll see you all at Adam's tomorrow, I guess," said Aarie, pulling on a black leather jacket as she got up from her seat.

Adam got up immediately. "Aarie, I thought your dad's away this weekend? Why don't you stay over at mine? There's no point going home to an empty house."

"Thanks, but maybe tomorrow. I feel like this headache might be turning into a migraine, and I just want my own bed."

"Okay. I'll walk you to the bus stop then. There was something I wanted to talk to you about."

Angela and Jamie shared a glance, then stared back into their coffee cups.

"We'll see you tomorrow, Aarie. Take care, lovely," Angela said.

Jamie raised a hand in the air. "Yeah, we'll see you later, gorgeous." He nodded.

Adam threw one last glance back to the other two before following Aarie out of the door as he zipped up his green hoodie.

Their ears were greeted by a cacophony of people chattering, squealing car brakes and impatient horns as they left the cosy ambience of the coffee shop. The summer evening breeze brushed against Aarie's sun-kissed skin, gently blowing her dark chestnut curls over her shoulders. The sun had already set hours ago, and the inky night sky now held hundreds of tiny twinkling lights above their heads. The street was unusually busy with rosy-cheeked pedestrians all dressed in evening finery: men in fitted suits and tuxedos—women in cocktail dresses, gowns, exquisite hats and fascinators. They had all come to York City from all over the country for an annual festival at the local horse racing course. Thousands of people came flooding in every year to gamble copious amounts of money based on a whim or the compelling sound of a horse's name. It was the reason the loud hum of heavy traffic and alcohol-fuelled laughter filled the air tonight.

Adam tucked his hands into his pockets, fidgeting with some loose change. He glanced at Aarie beside him as they casually weaved in and out of the passers-by along the street. His mouth wavered, opening as if to speak but then closing again as he seemed to change his mind.

Aarie's eyes shifted to his. "You're staring again, Adam. What's gotten into you lately? Is something on your mind? And what was it you wanted to tell me?"

Adam blinked. "Erm, I'm sorry, I didn't mean to, I just—" He stopped abruptly, tugging his hands out of his pockets as Aarie came to a halt next to him. They pulled to the side of the street to let the crowds walk past.

"What is it? Is it important?"

Adam hesitated, fumbling with his hands as he looked down.

"Adam, what is it?" Aarie repeated. "You know we can tell each other anything, right?"

"Right, yes. It's just..." Adam looked up at Aarie as she waited for him to continue. He studied her face—the shape of her full lips, the curve of her jawline and delicate cheekbones. Her deep chocolate brown eyes focused on him intently, full of kindness and love. He was her best friend, and their friendship meant the world to both of them. His eyes dropped back down to his hands. "Oh, it's nothing really. I'm just getting sentimental and silly. I just wanted you to know that I'll always be here for you. You know that, right? I'll always be me. Uni won't ever change that. I was just acting daft before."

"I know." She smiled, leaning in to wrap her arms around him. "I know Uni's not gonna change anything, silly. So chin up, you. Uni can only be a good thing. You're stuck with me for a while. I promise."

Adam's arms slipped around her slim frame as he let out a long exhale. Over his shoulder, Aarie caught a glimpse of Jamie and Angela peering out of the coffee shop window in the distance. She focused back on Adam, pulling away gently.

"Unfortunately, you're stuck with us all. It looks like we have an audience for some reason, by the way," Aarie said, gesturing with a quick nod towards the coffee shop. "Anyway, I won't fuel Jamie's stories of us being surgically attached, so you should go back and finish your drink... preferably before this headache kills me. The bus stop's only a bit further. I think I can manage to get there just fine."

"Okay." Adam shrugged before turning back towards the coffee shop. "I'll see you tomorrow," he shouted over his shoulder.

"Okay." She watched the back of him as he hurried away, then turned, carrying on down the road.

Aarie thought back to Adam's voiced concerns about the future and realised she had mainly high hopes for university life. Deep down, she knew Adam did too. She imagined it would give her life more clarity and help her become more aware of the type of person she wanted to be. It was nice to believe it would steer her in a more purposeful direction and therefore, make her life more meaningful somehow. At present, she was finding it hard to get past that *missing something*; it felt vital somehow, and she hoped uni life would finally show her what it was. *It would uplift a fog*, she thought, and so, she didn't worry about the future. Although she appreciated the present, the future offered a new world full of possibilities. She was ready to embrace change. As frightening as that seemed, she believed it would be an exciting new adventure.

She always thought of herself as an adventurous person, but above all, she saw herself as a curious and creative-minded person. They all were— herself and her friends. It was like the glue that helped stick them all together. It made them *the same* despite their many differences. Adam had his love of fine art and music, and Angela had her passion for fashion and textiles. She was not necessarily a strict follower of fashion but rather a creator of her own.

Aarie and Jamie were true artists at heart, like Adam. They shared a love for design and photography and were both realists as well as dreamers. Half easygoing and laid back, half perfectionist with a prolific, creative determination. *A rare breed*, Aarie thought. They had both opted for the graphic design course at university, feeling a commercial world of design offered a more opportunistic road to keeping creativity part of working life in the future. It seemed so important for Aarie to believe creativity would always be part of her life. She felt it made her who she was. Also, Graphic Designer as an occupation felt reasonably respectable to say in her opinion, and, in a world of technology and media, it would surely always be in demand. Maybe she would never change the world with it, but she could use it to plant a subliminal digital seed in society's mind and make a small difference somewhere. Maybe one day, she would create something that really meant *something* to someone.

Or at the very least, she'd create the occasional cool logo here or there.
She sighed at the thought.

The bus stop seemed further than she initially thought, but she blamed that on her pounding headache and eagerness to get home. The pavements had emptied of people due to the crowds going in the opposite direction. Aarie could only just make out her bus stop across the road; the street had quickly become very dark, she realised. Glancing up, the street lamps above her appeared to be out. Strangely, the lights further down the road all seemed to be out too. Without the whizzing blur of white and red car lights, it would be pitch black on this street. She had never really been afraid of the dark, but still, she eagerly neared the edge of the busy road, glancing again at the empty bus stop on the opposite side. A dim light flickered beneath the shelter, offering a better lit temporary haven. Aarie waited for a gap in the passing traffic so she could cross. A thick smog of fumes wafted past as the cars zoomed by. She coughed.

An unexpected movement caught her attention. Her eyes flitted across the street and scanned down one of the dark alleyways from which she'd seen it. Just then, she noticed the road had gone quiet. No cars were coming either way, and this was her chance to cross quickly. She began hurrying across just as the same movement distracted her again from the alleyway. This time, she could make out a figure lurking amongst the shadows. It seemed to move in a creepy and unnatural motion. Aarie froze in the middle of the road as a glint of light reflected off what she knew were its eyes. They focused on her. Something was not quite right about the way they glared, and it disturbed her to know it had seen her.

At that instant, the screech of brakes and skidding tires filled her ears. A mighty thump shook through the whole of her body, taking all the air from her lungs and leaving her momentarily numb. The hard concrete ground laid beneath the grazed skin of her face and hands. She closed her eyes, dazed and unable to move. A distance scream cut through the confusion.

Aarie was unaware of how long had passed, but Adam frantically called her name in desperation now as she laid drifting into unconsciousness.

"Aarie! Aarie, can you hear me?"

Moments later, there were more voices. Then more and more sounds. They surrounded Aarie now: scuffling, gasps and sobs.

Adam's voice echoed in her ears again. "Jamie, where's the ambulance? She's not responding. She's not responding!" he shouted. "Aarie, please, you can't leave me. You're gonna be okay. You have to be."

For a moment, Aarie thought she felt Adam take hold of her hand.

"She just stopped in the middle of the road. I didn't see her," the driver of the car mumbled, but no-one seemed to be paying attention to him. They were too focused on the crumpled bleeding figure in the road.

A whirling high-pitched siren pierced through the voices, followed by a flickering blue light that penetrated through Aarie's closed eyelids. Still unable to move, a barely audible groan escaped her. All other sounds around her muffled into silence, and she was plunged into darkness.

Chapter 2
Amongst The Shadows

A crackling roar echoed through the dark, heavy clouds above. Aarie tilted her head up to the night's sky, blinking as the rain gathered in her lashes and trickled down her cheeks. Her mind whirled in confusion as she frantically spun around, scanning the unfamiliar surroundings.

She found herself stood at the bottom of some stone steps. They seemed to lead up to a large country manor house. Two huge pillars sat either side of an ivory archway that framed the grand entranceway of the building. Aarie turned away, exploring the surrounding gardens and the row of sculpted hedges that lined either side of the house's pathway. The luscious green lawn around her was rapidly transforming into a swampy marshland in the heavy rain. Gone was the warmth of the mild summer evening breeze she was sure had wrapped around her only moments ago. However, glancing down at her wet clothes, she couldn't remember how she had got here or what she had been doing before.

A flitting shadow grabbed her attention, and her eyes swiftly followed it until it disappeared. She scanned across the garden to a low stone wall that lined the edges. Beyond the wall led to the rustling trees of surrounding woodlands. Subconsciously, she had been drifting forward towards the woods while searching the darkness. Pausing briefly, she peered back at the house one last time before carrying on. Her body shuddered as the rain showed no signs of slowing. She knew it made more sense to try to take shelter back at this house and hope someone was in, but something seemed to draw her away from it. Curiosity guided her into the thick of the woods to find out what moved within its shadows. Deeper, she explored. She didn't know what she was looking for, only that something was in this woods that she needed to find.

Before long, the tallest trees loomed over her with twining branches that cast eerie shapes in the moonlight. Thunder roared once again in the sky, and Aarie shivered. She began to have doubts about delving this far into the woods. She pivoted around, trying to decipher the direction she had come. Unfortunately, the trees bore no significant difference to each other, and a dreadful realisation washed over her; she had no idea where she was. There was no hope of shelter now. She wondered what she had been thinking to have come here in the dark during a thunderstorm. It was not her best idea.

A sudden rustle startled her from the bushes behind. The snap of a breaking twig followed, and Aarie's ears pricked up. She spun around immediately. Her legs trembled, backing up nervously as she inspected every inch of the shrubbery. The leaves were still once again, and the night, for one brief moment, seemed unnervingly silent except for her quickening breath. It was so cold now that a small fog cloud unfurled with every exhale. Staring through the fog in front of her, she refocused her gaze. It landed on a pair of golden eyes that peered back at her through the leaves.

Aarie stumbled backwards but quickly turned around, forcing her legs to carry her deeper into the woods as fast as she could go. The trees blurred past as she ran, snagging her jacket on their stray branches as she went. She was aware that something had begun chasing her. Her head flitted over her shoulder to glance back again and again. Each time, she caught a glimpse of not only one set of golden eyes but a growing number of eyes that moved towards her. A faint cry escaped her lips. The terrifying uncertainty of what pursued her was amplified by the certainty that they were getting closer. Aarie pushed on, striding faster and faster until her surroundings became nothing but shapes speeding past. At that moment, the ground under her feet abruptly disappeared.

Aarie's back thudded against the cold, wet earth with the full weight of her body. Before she could catch her breath, she found herself tumbling uncontrollably down a steep muddy slope. Broken branches, stones and wet earth shifted beneath her. Blades of long, coarse grass and shrubbery scraped past her skin. Her arms frantically flailed in the air, desperately trying to grab anything that would ease her descent. Eventually, her fingers managed to weave around grass and wild vines, bringing herself to a slow. She finally slumped to a halt in soft, leafy undergrowth. Her head flicked up, and she scrambled to a crouch position. Aarie peered through the dense foliage and scanned the top of the hill from which she had tumbled, checking for signs of movement. She held her breath in anxious anticipation.

There was nothing.

The rain seemed to have come to an abrupt end. Aarie tucked her tousled, muddy hair behind her ears and then got to her feet quickly. A loud howl broke the silence. Her heartbeat thudded in her ears. "A wolf howl?" Aarie asked herself, still seeing nothing in the darkness. Then, confirming her fears, a chorus of responding howls bellowed as a row of golden eyes lined the top of the hill. They glowered down in her direction with snarling jaws that caught the moonlight. She was relieved that the long grass and leafy undergrowth hid her in the dark. Regardless, Aarie ducked down lower beneath the foliage, then backed up until she was out of eyeshot. After giving one last upward glance to be sure, she stood, turned in the opposite direction, and then ran further into the wood once again.

A clear opening in the trees appeared up ahead. Aarie's head flitted over her shoulder and back as she ran, checking again that nothing was following her. She worried that it would be harder to hide in an open space such as this. Before she knew it, the ground in front of her abruptly came to an end once more. This time, she skidded to a halt just in time to see the deadly drop that hid in the night. Frantically, her hands grabbed at branches around her. Rubble flicked under her feet and disappeared into the pitch blackness beyond the cliff. She hovered near the edge in pure horror of her near-fatal plummet. Sweat ran from her forehead as relief washed over her.

But this nightmare was not over. There was nowhere else for Aarie to run now. The low snarls of the wolves echoed through the trees in the distance, and it was just a matter of time until they got to her. The wild thump in her chest made it harder to think, harder to breathe, harder to make sense of anything, yet it was easier to believe that she could potentially die here. She twisted around desperately, unsure what to do.

A brief sob escaped her as she hid behind a large tree and slowly slid down onto the wet ground, momentarily defeated. Aarie didn't want to give up, but a sharp pain throbbed at the side of her head. She reached for it, feeling a thick, sticky substance coating her fingers. Aarie winced and realised this injury must have happened on the way down the hill.

The sound of another twig snapping instantly broke through her misery. Her head shot up with her eyes wide. Holding her breath, she glanced around the tree into the darkness. The wolves were not in sight, but she was sure something lurked in the trees behind her. Aarie couldn't see anything, but she felt like something was watching her. She craned her head further around the tree, expecting someone to be nearby, but she saw nothing.

"Who's there? I know someone's there," Aarie said quietly into the dark. "Please, is someone there?" Her voice broke to a faint whisper as she began to doubt herself.

Blood was now trickling down the side of her face from her head wound. The pain seemed to be growing, and she had begun to feel slightly lightheaded. More pain throbbed in her ribs, making her suspect she had done a lot more damage to herself than she had initially thought. She leaned back against the tree once more. Her eyes were slowly closing. They immediately snapped back open at the sound of footsteps unmistakably moving towards her now. Aarie's hands scrambled amongst the mud and shrubbery, searching for something to use as a weapon—a large branch, a thorny vine, a heavy stone. There had to be something. Her hands luckily settled on a large sharp rock; that would have to do. Aarie raised it in the air, drawing her arm back. She was ready. She would not give in that easy, and as the footsteps closed in, she swung around the tree, wielding the rock in her hand.

Aarie came up against nothing except a strange whisper carried in the wind. It caught her off guard as it seemed incoherent yet so near to her ears and almost tangible somehow. She gripped her rock as her eyes flicked up, noticing a figure standing a few feet ahead of her now. His dark clothing and hair made him a silhouetted shape in the night as the moonlight highlighted the edge of his profile. His sapphire blue eyes seemed to pierce through the darkness as he peered down, holding out a hand to her.

"Please, you need to come with me," said the stranger. "We don't have much time. I can keep you safe from the wolves, but we must hurry."

Aarie froze, startled by his sudden appearance from nowhere. She had no idea where he could have come from, but she was also very much out of options. The stranger seemed to sense her unease, but on noticing her head wounds, he stepped forward with more urgency.

"Please, trust me. I'm not here to hurt you, but we must go before they see us."

The complete sincerity in his eyes instantly made Aarie want to trust him—that and the fact that the wolves were coming down the hill. She nodded in acceptance but ignored his outstretched hand, opting to keep hold of her newly found weapon. She let him lead her quickly into the darkness of the trees from which she assumed he had come.

An arched fallen tree came into view. On reaching it, the stranger parted some branches and moved foliage to reveal a hidden tunnel within a cave. A single flamed torch lit the entranceway, casting a golden glow against the rocky surfaces. He stepped through, ducking his head down. Holding the branches from his face, he reached his other hand out to help Aarie. Her eyes focused intently on his as he pulled her through with such care. The branches crackled behind her, and her head shot around. She gasped in disbelief as the entranceway began to close on its own accord, concealing it from the other side. At once, she turned to face the stranger, who seemed to be studying her reaction.

"It's okay. They won't find us here," he said.

Aarie swallowed as she gazed back at him and then at the dark tunnel he had brought her to.

"Where is... *here*?" she whispered, clutching her rock tight in one hand.

The stranger did not answer the question, but his eyes scanned ahead and then back to her. The tunnel seemed to light up around her, and as though to answer the question of how, she noticed wooden lanterns fixed into the rocky walls; they were alive with golden flames.

"Tell me, how did you find yourself here?" the stranger politely asked.

"I don't remember," Aarie replied, trying hard to recall the moment before she had run into the woods. She reached up to touch the wound on her head, wincing again with the pain. The stranger shifted towards her, but she pulled back immediately, alarmed by his sudden movement.

"I'm sorry. I didn't mean to startle you," he whispered. "You seem to be hurt, that's all."

"Who are you? Why won't you tell me where I am?" Aarie replied, annoyed by the quiver in her voice.

The stranger seemed to be deliberating something in his mind as he hesitated to answer. Aarie's heart began to pound once again, picking up speed in the stranger's prolonged silence.

"Jaydon Onuris," the stranger replied. "My name is Jaydon Onuris, but most *people* call me Jay." He blinked quickly, then turned away from Aarie.

"I'm Aariella," she replied. "Well, just Aarie. No one calls me by my full name either." Somehow, knowing each other's name was a comfort to her. It seemed to take the dangerous edge away from being just strangers.

"Aarie," Jay said softly, turning back to meet her gaze. "If you do not recall how you got here, for your safety, I cannot tell you where you are. I am breaking the rules to bring you here, so please just trust that I am not here to harm you."

"Okay," she replied. She did not understand, but somehow, she knew Jay's words were the truth. "Is it your house? The house near the woods— do you live there?"

"Sometimes. I like the peacefulness. We don't get visitors. Not here, anyway."

"Visitors like me, you mean?"

"No, I mean 'visitors' full stop. We don't get *any*."

"Oh, that sounds quite lonely. I didn't mean to spoil the peacefulness. But what about the wolves? Aren't you afraid of them?"

Jay's eyes fixed on her now with a curious expression. "No. They won't harm me."

"Are they like your guard dogs?"

"You ask a lot of questions," he snapped, though no malice was in his voice. He watched as her brows creased and her mouth puckered slightly, unsure how to respond. Before she could say anything else, he continued to speak. "Anyway, you didn't spoil the peacefulness. To be honest, it can get quite boring at times, and no, they're not my guard dogs. My brother—" he broke off, hesitantly.

"They're your brother's wolves?" Aarie asked quickly, making an assumption.

"Something like that," Jay replied with a gentle smile.

"So, you live there with your brother?"

Jaydon shifted towards her suddenly, and for a brief moment, she thought she had pushed her luck by asking too many questions. He reached towards her head, holding a piece of cloth. Aarie realised that he must've torn it from his shirt sleeve as it was now tattered. She swallowed as he gently pressed the fabric to the side of her face. She winced as he began wiping away the blood that had run from her wound and down her cheek. Her eyes explored his face, observing his curious expression as he took great care to clean her wound.

"How come you are hurt?" he asked.

"I fell," she replied, continuing to study his face as it was so close to hers now. The flamed torchlight of the tunnel made his skin look a warm golden colour as it cast soft shadows under his deep-set eyes. She gazed at the deep blue hues that held a strange mysteriousness about them. Her eyes followed the shape of his almost straight brows and nose, his sculpted cheekbones, angular jawline, and the subtle natural pout of his slightly fuller bottom lip. His dark ash brown hair gently spiked out at the front and sides, subtly framing what Aarie thought to be a kind face. She could faintly make out mild crease lines at the edges of his mouth, and she could imagine him smiling.

Jay hadn't yet responded to her reply, so she continued to explain. "The wolves chased me, and I fell down the hill. I didn't realise I had hurt myself, but it must've been then."

"I saw you fall."

"Then you already know how. Why did you ask me?"

His forehead creased briefly. "Because I don't know why you're *still* here?"

Aarie's brows knitted together at once. "Sorry if I *disappointed* you. It was a steep hill—I'm shocked I survived it myself!"

"That's not what I meant," Jay whispered, still examining her wounds with a strange curiosity. "It's just that visitors don't tend to stay very long after the wolves come out."

"You sound okay with the fact that your brother's wolves nearly ate me. Believe me, I am working on getting out of here. I just don't know where 'here' is or how to get back home, that's all. And since you won't tell me, I suppose there's not much I can do about that for now." She huffed, hastily taking the cloth from his hand as she glared at him. "Besides, I thought you said you don't get visitors... ever!"

"We don't, not at *this* house. Look, I didn't mean to offend you. You just misunderstood my words, that's all. Though, I suppose that's understandable since I'm talking so cryptic. I'm not good with mortals. I'm out of practice talking to your kind, but it would never have been my wish for you to be injured. Just forget I said anything," Jay apologised, turning away from her again.

A twinge of guilt made Aarie regret snapping at him; after all, he had helped her get away. She wanted to apologise, but his words had triggered curiosity to take over. Something inside her couldn't help wanting to figure out why he talked so strange, why he was so cryptic, and most of all, she wanted to know more about who he was.

"Did you just call me a mortal?" she asked. "And what do you mean 'my kind'? You talk like I'm some kind of alien."

"You don't miss anything, do you?" he said, drawing in a long breath as he turned back to face her. "Nevermind, what does it matter anyway?" Jay said quietly as though to himself. "You're here now, and it's not like I can just let the wolves have you for supper."

Aarie's ears pricked up at that. "No, you can't. So, are you going to tell me where I am now?" she asked, puzzling over Jay's peculiar behaviour.

Jay slipped her an apologetic glance. "No. That I cannot do, I'm afraid. That is something that only you can work out for yourself, though, I urge you for your own sake, do not try. It is better that way."

"But you, you're not... human, are you?"

"Why do you say that?" Jay quickly replied, taken by surprise.

"I don't know, but there is something about you that I can't explain—like the way you move. You talk in an unusual way, and when I saw the entranceway to this tunnel, you made the branches move and lit the lanterns without touching them. You came from nowhere in the woods. When I shouted out in the darkness, you were already there, weren't you? I couldn't see you, but somehow, I knew you were there."

Jay raised an eyebrow. "Does that not sound a little crazy to you?" he asked as a curious smile softened his serious expression.

"Yes," Aarie replied.

"And yet you believe it and aren't afraid?"

"Yes, and 'question mark'. 'Question mark' meaning I'm still deciding."

"Because I do frighten you?" Jay asked.

"'Question mark' because I didn't actually believe it until you didn't deny it."

Jay mulled over her answer briefly as the corners of his mouth hitched up further.

"I never denied it because it sounds crazy. At least, it *should* do to you. But so be it, I will continue *not* to deny it," Jay said, watching Aarie's eyes widen. "So, if you have finally decided against hitting me with that rock in your hand, would you like to leave this awful damp tunnel for somewhere a little less dismal? If you are going to stay awhile, at least let me make your visit mildly pleasant."

Aarie glanced down at the rock still in her hand and blushed. She had forgotten she was holding it. She quickly let it slide out of her hands onto the floor and gave a nervous smile. "Erm... sorry. Yes, I suppose that would be better. Okay then, lead the way," Aarie replied, surprised at his casual tone and her acceptance of the situation.

Jay led their way along the rocky tunnel that was lined with lanterns all the way. The smell of damp earth and rock lingered in the thick, humid air that filled her lungs. As they travelled further, the pathway began to narrow and darken. Aarie wiped her clammy hands down the sides of her jeans as she stared at the back of the stranger she followed. Given any other situation where she was trapped underground with a stranger, she was confident that she would be terrified. However, though the tunnel was quite claustrophobic, she felt a strange comfort in Jay's company, even if her nervousness said otherwise.

Moments later, they came to a halt as they reached a dead end. Aarie threw a confused glance at Jay.

"So, what now? Did we take a wrong way?" she asked.

"No, but I must ask you to close your eyes just for one brief moment, I promise."

"Okay," Aarie said, and to her surprise, she closed her eyes without any other questions.

As soon as she did, she felt Jay's hands gently clasp around her wrists. Her eyes fluttered, but she kept them closed. A few seconds later, a gentle breeze brushed past her skin.

"It's okay," Jay whispered, "you can open them now."

Aarie squinted through her lashes at first. Then her eyes flew open to take in her new surroundings. She did not feel as though she had moved since her eyes had closed, and she blinked now in confusion. The sun was up. Though Aarie did not know how daytime had come so quickly, she was too in awe of the view to wonder about how impossible any of this seemed. She stood speechless on the edge of a red cliff that overlooked a vast canyon below. Across from this cliff, a mighty waterfall flowed into the winding streams below, sending the gush of running water echoing through the valleys. Aarie's eyes flitted from one direction to the next, trying to take in everything all at once.

Hues of green, red and gold covered the surrounding hillsides as though the colours of summer and autumn had merged and swept through the land. A variety of exotic flowers were scattered in exuberant clusters. Their blooms of gold, crimson and violet delivered vibrant bursts of colour in every corner, filling the air with a sweet alluring fragrance. They seemed to attract hummingbirds and exotic butterflies, creating miniature spectacles of their own. More colour hung from the large pink blossom trees nearby. Their branches arched around Jay and Aarie, swaying in the warm breeze and occasionally dropping soft petals that floated down around them.

"It's beautiful here!" Aarie beamed. A widening smile pushed uncontrollably at her cheeks as she whirled around in pure amazement. She turned to look back at Jay, who seemed to be observing her reaction as if it were a wonder itself. His full attention appeared to be on her and not the scene around them at all. *Perhaps it was all just too familiar to him*, she guessed.

In the clear light of the day, Aarie could see every detail of his smile and knew it was genuine. She took a moment to study him. He wore sturdy, fitted black trousers and a loose but smart-casual, black shirt that he had rolled up to hide its torn sleeve. His dark, ash brown hair complemented his smooth, bisque skin and his sapphire eyes, perfectly. Those intensely blue eyes now focused entirely on her. She had never described a stranger as handsome or beautiful before, but Jay was undeniably both. Aarie fidgeted self consciously. Unlike Jay, who looked like some kind of perfect vision from a movie poster, she was still covered in mud from tumbling down the hill earlier. Her hair was matted and filthy, and blood stained her face. She touched her head quickly as her injury throbbed and re-announced its presence. At that point, the ground began to spin. Her legs fell limp underneath herself as her vision faded to black.

Jay darted with such speed that he caught her before she could hit the ground. Lifting her, he moved her to a soft patch of grass beneath a blossom tree and then set her down gently. Aarie's eyes flickered back open seconds later. She peered up to see Jay leaning over her with grave concern etched on his face.

"What happened?" she asked, blinking in the sun.

Jay swallowed, taking in the new appearance of her wounds. "You passed out. Aarie, your wounds appear to be a lot worse than I originally thought. Or at least, they seem to have *become* worse. They also appear to be very real, which means you must be real too. You're not just a shadow— you're *really* here," Jay said, seemingly astonished but also horrified by some bizarre realisation she did not understand.

"When you talk, nothing you say makes sense to me. Do you know that?" Aarie whispered as she tried to sit up. She involuntarily cried out in pain as she moved. Jay was right; her injuries were severely worse than moments ago. Her ribs ached, and the pain in her chest felt like her lungs were being crushed.

"Aarie, you can't have acquired your wounds from the hill. That means something must have happened to you before you arrived here. I need you to think carefully because if you are really here, then you are not *there*. And judging from your injuries, you may *need* to be there. What I am trying to say is that you need mortal help, and fast. I'm not sure what to do," Jay panicked.

Aarie closed her eyes, grimacing in pain. "I feel like I've been hit by a—" Aarie broke off as a memory flashed up in her head.

A car's headlights were glaring as she laid in front of it on the road. Panicked voices murmured around her. A familiar voice shouted out to her, full of fear and urgency.

She opened her eyes again and peered up at Jay. "Adam was there. He was trying to help me, and the car... oh god," she said, remembering now with more clarity. She glanced down, startled to notice the black jacket and jeans she had been wearing moments ago, had transformed into what appeared to be a hospital gown. If the pain hadn't been so intense, she would have screamed, but as things were, she could only stare in horror.

"It was a car," Aarie finally murmured. "I was hit by a car. I remember now, but it doesn't make sense. I must have been taken to the hospital, so how can I be here?" Aarie's heart pounded, and her stomach knotted. Her eyes desperately went back to Jay. "Am I dead? Is that why you wouldn't tell me where I am? Am I dead, Jay?"

He flinched at her words as he eyed the gown she now appeared to be wearing.

"No, you're not dead, Aarie," he assured her before turning quickly to reach for something amongst the bushes beside them. Aarie couldn't make out what he was doing, and she was in too much pain to find out. A moment later, Jay turned back, carefully holding what appeared to be a folded leaf that cupped something inside it. He lifted her weight to him, enabling her to sit up slightly. "Aarie, I can't get you back home. I need you to drink this. It won't be pleasant, but it will help you. Please take it," he implored.

Gently accepting the leaf from Jay, Aarie bleakly eyed the thick dark liquid that filled it. It almost looked black against the deep green colour of the plant. Her brows furrowed, but Jay reassured her.

"It will help. Please, trust me," he said.

Aarie nodded. Closing her eyes, she raised the leaf and then poured it into her mouth. The warm liquid coated her mouth and throat with a bitter coppery taste. She bent forward fast, gagging. Jay moved to her quickly, instinctively lifting her face to check she was okay.

"What did you just give me?" Aarie asked as her eyes searched his.

Jay blinked, avoiding her gaze as he continued to analyse her bruises and head injuries carefully. She took note of how gentle his touch was to avoid causing her any more pain, but she also noticed how his mouth seemed to tighten whenever there was something he was trying not to say.

"Nevermind," she said, continuing to analyse his facial expressions. "I can see you don't want to answer that question either?"

His eyes met her eyes at once. "Has it eased the pain?" he asked.

"Yes, I think so," Aarie replied. Though she was still in great pain, it had very noticeably eased.

Jay let out a sigh of relief. "That's a good sign."

Aarie stared blankly, caught up in her thoughts of home.

"They'll all be worried about me. Adam thought I was dead on the road. I heard his voice calling to me. I need to get back, so he knows I'm not dead, not yet, anyway. I need to say goodbye, at least. I remember what happened, but what do I do now? How did I even get here? How is it even possible for me to have left the hospital? Wait—"

A sudden thought struck Aarie. She had no choice but to draw it as her only conclusion. "This place isn't real, is it? It can't be. Everything here must be just in my head. This has to be some sort of dream, and I can't seem to wake up. Obviously, I hit my head, so maybe that's why I'm so confused. What if I can't wake up because I'm in a coma or something? Wait—that's got to be it, hasn't it? Who knows what kind of injuries I've really got or what damage is going on in here," she said, reaching for her head. "And you, you're not real, are you? None of this is real, is it? It would explain why I feel like I know you even though we have just met, and why nothing here makes sense. *You* don't make sense because I made you up in my head. It just happens that I bumped my head really hard." She humourlessly laughed as a single tear began to roll down her cheek. Her laugh slowly turned into a quiet sob. Jay did not answer, but his sombre expression seemed to voice a silent and sympathetic apology.

He slid closer to Aarie, wrapping an arm around her shoulder to comfort her. She tensed for a moment but then gently leaned into him. Closing her eyes, she rested her head against his shoulder.

Seconds later, Jay felt her weight begin to disappear. He watched as her body faded and gradually became more transparent until she was gone. Uncertain as to what this meant, Jay stood still, momentarily in shock. He ran both of his hands through his hair as he stared at what was now an empty space.

Chapter 3
From Darkness Comes Light

Aarie's eyes fluttered open. An unnatural fluorescent light filled the small clinical room, but her vision was partially blocked by the oxygen mask over her face. She gagged slightly, realising a tube had been inserted into her mouth. Her hands flew to her face, removing both items from her face with sudden urgency. Aarie took a deep breath as she laid still again for a moment. A high-pitched sound pulsed to the rhythm of her heartbeat. She was instantly aware of a pain in her chest and head once again. Thinking back to her dream, she had been in excruciating pain until the stranger had helped her. She was glad the pain was not as severe now and wondered if morphine had been given to her to ease her pain. Her eyes followed an IV line from her arm to a drip by the bedside. A figure in the corner caught her attention, and she turned her head against her pillow.

Adam sat slumped in a chair with his eyes closed. Aarie noticed the dark purple shadows under his eyes as he slept. His hair was dishevelled and his t-shirt stained with dried blood. She knew it was hers, and she wondered how long he had been here. Her mouth and throat felt so dry as she tried to speak. A coppery taste lingered there, and she immediately thought back to her dream of Jay, the stranger who had seemed so real before she had awoken. Part of her felt a twinge of sadness in knowing that she would never see him again, but then, he hadn't existed in the first place.

Aarie finally managed a hoarse whisper. "Adam?"

Adam woke immediately and shot up to her bedside, eyes wide and disbelieving. A pained smile crept across his face. "Aarie, you're awake," he gasped as his eyes began to well up. "God, I thought I'd lost you. You can't imagine how good it feels to see your eyes open." He clasped her hand between both of his as he stared at her like she was a miracle before him, though grief and worry still contorted his smile.

"I need to call someone and let them know you're awake," he said, standing up quickly. "Don't move or do anything. Christ, why aren't they here already? You can't be completely out of the woods yet," he muttered, rushing to the door.

"The woods... " Aarie mumbled, thinking of the dark woods in her dream. She closed her tired eyes as she remembered running from the wolves.

Adam turned, hearing Aarie's muffled ramblings. "Stay with me, Aarie. Don't you go anywhere, you hear me? I'm going to get someone."

"Where would I go? We're surgically attached, remember?" Aarie whispered with troubled breathing.

Adam stopped in his tracks. "You remember?" Adam gasped.

Aarie's eyes opened again and noticed the clock on the wall that read 11:00 PM. She had been here a whole day.

"Is my dad here?"Aarie asked.

Adam hovered in the doorway as though unsure whether to get help or answer first. "Not yet. We haven't been able to get hold of him, but we will."

"No, you probably won't," she said. "He's out of the country. I remember. I'm so tired, Adam. If he does manage to come in while I'm asleep, tell him I'm okay. Will you tell him—" Aarie broke off as her eyes closed again.

Panic washed over Adam as Aarie appeared to be slipping back into unconsciousness. He turned back to the door, and as he did, a petite, dark-haired doctor came rushing into the room. Her dark eyes were bright and focused. A smile greeted Adam and softened what would otherwise be a serious face. Adam followed her back into the room.

"Aarie's awake," Adam announced just before his gaze fell on Aarie's closed lids. "Well, she was a second ago. They said that it could take days or weeks for her to regain full consciousness if at all—but Aarie spoke to me. She even made a joke. That has to mean things can't be as bad as we thought, doesn't it? It has to. She knows who she is and who I am."

"Did you move her?" The doctor asked, slightly panicked as she rushed to check Aarie. She glanced at the monitor beside her as Adam watched.

"No. Did you hear what I said? She was awake."

The doctor gasped as she looked at the monitor readings then back to Aarie.

"I don't understand—it's impossible," she said. "There seems to be a fault with this machine. We may have to get Aarie moved to one of the other rooms right away," the doctor informed.

"What's happening? I don't understand. She was awake a moment ago —"

"Adam, what's happening?" Aarie asked, opening her eyes again.

"Aarie?" the doctor said, turning immediately. "You're awake?" she gasped.

"Yes," Aarie murmured. "Is there something wrong? Am I going to be okay?" she said, looking at the doctor and Adam, who in turn, looked at each other.

Aarie thought to scenes she'd seen on casualty dramas where accident victims discovered life-changing injuries on awakening. She panicked and sat up abruptly. She moved her bedsheets aside, wanting to swing her legs over the side of the bed to stand and prove to herself she could do it. Pain in her head and chest throbbed as she moved, but she knew if she persevered, it was not impossible. However, Adam's face made her stop where she was.

"Aarie, no, you have to rest. You're going to be fine, but not if you don't stay in bed. Please," Adam said, hurrying to her side. His eyes flicked back to the doctor, who stood open-mouthed.

"Adam's right, Aarie. You need to stay rested. We were just surprised to see you awake and so well already, but that can only be a good thing. Aarie, we may need to reassess your injuries and run you in for a CT scan. I will be back in with another doctor soon. Until then, please just lie back and rest. Can you do that for us?"

Aarie nodded, laying back down on the bed as the nurse shifted towards the door, gesturing for Adam to follow. He did, and they left the room quietly.

"What's going on?" Adam turned to the doctor.

"Please wait here," she replied, gesturing to the waiting room. "I will let you know more when we know more ourselves."

"Okay. But, Doctor, this is a good sign, isn't it? I mean, she's awake. We worried she might never wake, but she nearly leapt out of bed. How is that even possible with her injuries?"

"That is what we're going to find out, but yes, this is a good sign that Aarie's injuries weren't as bad as we originally thought. We just have to be sure. We will let you know as soon as possible."

Adam reluctantly walked around the corner, following the coloured markings on the hospital corridor floor to the waiting area. He paced back and forth several times in this small space before finally sitting. He leaned forward with his elbows against his knees. His eye's skimmed over the many leaflets and posters pinned to the notice boards. The clicking of hurried footsteps echoed through the corridor, causing Adam to turn around. Two friendly faces hastily moved towards him, panicked by his presence in this waiting room.

"What happened?" Jamie fretted.

"Has there been a change?" Angela asked, urgently awaiting Adam's response as he got up from his seat.

"She's awake. She spoke to me. I think she's going to be okay," Adam replied, seemingly in shock.

"She did?" asked Angela.

Jamie's brows creased. "She's awake? But the doctors told us... Did she seem herself? Did she know what had happened?" Jamie asked with new hope.

"Yeah, she knew everything, Jamie. She wanted to get out of bed, and she nearly did if the doctor and I hadn't said she needed to rest."

"But how is it possible?" Angela asked.

"I don't know, but I saw it on the doctor's face, she couldn't explain it either. It's a bloody miracle! Either that or the doctors made a huge mistake. She mentioned something about equipment being faulty too. She was cagey about the whole thing. God, I don't want to jinx anything 'cos I don't think she's out of trouble yet, but there's no way she can be as bad as they said. She was our Aarie in there. She even made a joke."

"Can we see her?" Jamie asked.

"Not yet, I think they're going to do a scan or something to reassess her injuries, the doctor said. We have to wait here. They said they'd let us know as soon as they can," Adam said, sitting once again. Jamie and Angela let out a long sigh before taking a seat on either side of him. They slumped back against their chairs and stared at the walls.

A deep voice echoed from around the corner, breaking the silence.

"My daughter, Aariella Stone, was omitted last night. Please, I need to see her. You have to tell me she's okay."

A muffled voice replied from the reception area. Adam stood up again, crossing to the other side of the waiting room to make his presence known to the man he knew at the reception desk. Adam gave a gentle nod to Aarie's dad, who now hurried to the waiting room.

Lyle Stone was a proud man who seemed to exude a strange authority and respectful grace. He was a very calm and serious person at most times, but he always had a warm welcome for Adam. His broad shoulders and tall, muscular physique disguised his age. His dark chocolate brown eyes were the same as Aarie's, but they were bloodshot now. His skin had paled, and Adam thought his hair seemed greyer than the last time he had seen him. Adam greeted him with another nod and a slight tightening of his mouth. It was not the right time for a smile, and Adam could not deliver one now anyway.

"Hi, Mr Stone."

"I'm sorry. I should have been here for Aarie. They said I have to wait here, but I need to see her now, I can't just wait and be helpless like this— she's my daughter. Adam, they were vague about her injuries because there's been a recent change. They said she's awake now and that she spoke to you. How did she sound? Did she seem okay?" he desperately asked. His usual calm manner was temporarily shaken.

"She seemed incredibly well compared to when she first came in. She said to tell you she was okay if you came in while she was sleeping. I don't think Aarie would say that if she didn't really believe it. The doctor said it was a good sign. I'm telling you, they must have made a mistake when she came in."

"I need to see her. I can't stay here without seeing her, Adam," Lyle repeated.

"They took her to a different room, I think," Adam said. "I don't know where that is. It's probably best if we wait to hear what they have to say. We don't want to panic Aarie. The doctors will be here soon, I'm sure."

Time seemed to have stopped still as they all sat in the waiting room. The occasional nurse walked past, temporarily breaking the silence of the corridor. The small group of friends meaninglessly scanned over and over the leaflets and posters on the notice boards. Their eyes followed the coloured lines down the corridor floors, then back to the notice boards as though it would make them leave this room sooner.

Then finally, the doctors came.

******

Lyle swiftly walked into the hospital room. The doctors had assured him of good news in the corridor before he had come in, giving him full details of the CT scan results that had just come back, and a new assessment of her condition. Talks of miraculous recoveries, possible mix-ups and errors on the initial examinations, filled Lyle with both relief and doubt as he hurried to see Aarie was okay with his own eyes.

Aarie glanced up as soon as her dad entered the room. She tried to sit up gently.

"Dad, you're here."

"Aarie, my word, you look awful. Are you in pain? I'm sorry that I didn't come sooner. I didn't know. I would never have forgiven myself if... I daren't even think about it. I'm just so relieved that they say you're on the mend, though, if I had come a few hours ago, I hear I would have been getting a different story."

"I'm okay, Dad. I don't seem to be in too much pain now. The doctors said my injuries aren't as severe as they initially thought and that I seem to be making a fast recovery. Also, I think they must've given me some seriously powerful drugs because, when I woke up, I felt like a bus had hit me. Now, if I don't make any sudden movements, I feel like I just had a small run-in with, I don't know, a large dog or something, maybe a wolf or two," Aarie said, smiling to herself. "These guys have been taking good care of me too, the doctors told me," she added, glancing around the room at her friends, Adam, Jamie and Angela, who had come back into the room too.

Aarie's dad smiled, then leaned over her gently to place a kiss on her forehead. He took a seat beside her, involuntarily staring at his daughter's injuries. Bruises covered her face, masking it with swollen patches of blue and purple. Blood had begun to seep through the bandage wrapped around the top of her head.

"I can't believe this happened while I was away. I should have been here. I'm just so glad you have such good friends who were here for you."

"Dad, it's okay. It's not your fault. You're allowed time for yourself sometimes, and you hardly ever go anywhere anyway. It was just really unlucky that this happened the moment you did. Anyway, you're here now, and besides, there's nothing too exciting happening here. It's just me feeling sorry for myself with a few bruises, that's all," Aarie said.

"I'd hardly call this just a few bruises, Aarie," Lyle strongly disagreed.

"Okay, but I'm on the mend, Dad. I'm gonna be fine. So, nothing else matters, right?"

"Well, I'm not going away again for a long time, and I'm double paranoid Dad for a while, so I apologise in advance."

"Great, I can't wait." Aarie smiled, humorously rolling her eyes in her friend's direction. However, the same relief that was present on her dad's face was written on her friend's tired, drawn faces too. It spoke volumes, and she swallowed, quietly acknowledging that she had escaped a close encounter with death.

******

It had been a whole week since Aarie had left the hospital. She stared at herself in her bedroom mirror. Her bruises had faded significantly, and her bandages had been removed, revealing stitches at the side of her forehead. She was told not to do anything too strenuous as her ribs and lungs would still take a while to heal. She felt that the doctors must've made another mistake because, if she didn't think about it too much, it was easy to forget that anything had happened to her at all. Aarie didn't want her dad and friends to worry, so she tried to be seen taking it easy when they were around. Today had seemed to drag due to her being stuck in the house, trying to keep up appearances while everyone insisted on doing everything for her. They would not let her do anything that could potentially slow her recovery. It had begun to get frustrating. As a result, she had resorted to going to bed early to get away. However, she did feel tired this evening due to having trouble sleeping the past few nights. Her sleep pattern was messed up, and she had found herself waking before she could drift into a deep sleep. The dark shadows under her eyes were evidence that she needed some proper rest now. Pulling her duvet cover open, she climbed into bed and then switched off her bedside lamp. She tugged at the duvet, wrapping it tightly around herself before closing her eyes and nuzzling into her soft pillow. She gave out a content sigh as all her muscles relaxed for the first time since waking in the hospital. Tonight she welcomed sleep more than ever.

Not long after her eyes had closed, they opened again, but she was no longer snuggled in her bed at home. Instead, she found herself walking in her pyjamas through an all too familiar dark woods. She spun around, taking in her surroundings with a frantic blink as though hoping it would disappear.

"This isn't real. This isn't real," Aarie whispered to herself over and over. The wind began to pick up and rustled through the trees around her. Something scratched against her ankles in the darkness, and she glanced down immediately. She jumped, startled by something at her bare feet. Muddy vines had begun to surround her, seemingly trying to wrap themselves around her ankles. Grabbing at them in horror and disgust, she tore them hastily from her legs. At that same moment, a chorus of wolves howled, followed by the thud of several paws scrambling in the distance. She leapt over the vines that had begun to move towards her again, then darted through the woods. Faster and faster she ran, avoiding some of the trees around her which seemed to take on the shapes of haunting faces. Her feet hurt as she sped across a few sharp branches and stones.

At this instant, a white shape appeared in the distance. Aarie's eyes focused, and she could make out two golden eyes staring back at her. An enormous white wolf stood baring its sharp teeth as though ready to charge. She skidded to a halt, grabbing at nearby branches to steady herself. As she turned to switch direction, a shadow brushed past her, stirring up a cloud of leaves that whirled around like a small tornado. A black fog seemed to engulf her as she tried to flee. Her heart pounded as she felt she was being chased not only by the wolves but by something that lurked in this strange fog. It seemed to be everywhere now. She ran to hide behind the trunk of a large tree. Before she could reach it, something grabbed hold of her and pulled her beside another tree. An arm had gripped her from behind, holding her tightly around her waist as a hand covered her mouth. A familiar voice hastily spoke.

"Don't scream, Aarie. It's me, Jay. It's okay—you're safe."

"Jay?" Aarie gasped with relief as he gently moved his hand from her mouth. She looked down curiously at his arm around her waist before quickly turning to meet a pair of blue eyes staring back at her.

"Sorry if I scared you. I didn't know if you would be back. You were in pretty bad shape when you left, but you look like you're recovering well." Jay smiled, seemingly taking in every detail of her face.

"The shadows and the fog, was that all your doing?" Aarie asked, subconsciously analysing his face too.

"I didn't have much time to act. I haven't figured out if they can hurt you, so I couldn't risk them catching you. They can't see you now."

"Because of the fog?"

"Yes," Jay replied.

"And you're answering my questions now?" Aarie asked.

"It would appear so," Jay said, creasing his forehead slightly as he gave it some thought.

"But that's not going to last is it?" Aarie assumed.

"Probably not."

"Well, it doesn't matter anyway because you're not real, are you? Everything I see right now is in my head, isn't it?"

Jay looked down sharply as though Aarie's words had slapped him in the face. His jaw muscles flexed slightly, and his eyes narrowed for a moment.

"I should say yes as that would be the best possible thing for me to say and for you to believe, but somehow I can't. Somehow I don't like the thought of being 'not real' to you. Besides, surely, *no one's* imagination can be *that* inventive?" Jay said with a slight smirk.

"So, you're saying this is all real?"

"I'm not saying anything. I'm just *not* saying I'm *not* real." Jay's smile widened.

"Perfect. You're even more annoyingly confusing than the last time."

"Annoying? That's a little harsh considering I just saved you from the wolves... again," Jay protested, though his smile didn't waver.

"They're your wolves! Maybe you should have them on a leash. Besides, what kind of person has wolves guarding their home?"

"They are NOT my wolves. They're—" Jay paused, looking at Aarie's raised eyebrow as she waited for him to finish his sentence. "Nice try, but maybe I *will* answer that one. After all, it might keep you safe if you come here again. I don't want you putting your theory of 'things not being real' to the test, not when it comes to *them*. They're not my wolves. They're not even really my brother's wolves—he just has control of them sometimes. They're supposed to be illusions for you. They're not supposed to be able to hurt you, but something gives me the impression that this may not apply to you. As you appear to be very real, I'm worried that they are more than just illusions to you, which means it is very likely that they would hurt you if they caught you. Please understand that. I can't answer all your questions, and I know that my words don't make a lot of sense to you, but please trust me on this—while you are here, they are as real as am I," Jay said firmly.

"So why not tell your brother to stop these illusions?"

"I can't. You're not supposed to be here. It's dangerous for both our worlds and for you. I'm breaking the rules, and I can't seem to stop myself."

"And what if I *do* put my theory to the test?" Aarie asked. "I'm not the kind of girl who likes running away from things, and I most definitely am not ready to become some kind of pathetic damsel in distress."

"You never struck me as the type. In fact, I'm pretty sure the last you came here, you were giving it serious thought to face the wolves with nothing but a rock in your hand."

Aarie nodded in agreement. "Yes, and if I do see the wolves again, maybe I should stand my ground, try to fight them off."

"No. I'm asking you, please don't. These are not your average wolves, though the average regular kind *should* be enough of a deterrent for you. For your safety, just trust me on this," Jay replied with the utmost seriousness.

"You don't know me. We're *apparently* not even from the same planet. Why do you care?"

Jay's forehead creased as his eyes appeared to search hers for the answer. "I don't know," he whispered. "But the last time you were here, you had severe injuries and left so suddenly. I didn't know if it was because you had died back in your world. I didn't know and... I didn't like it."

Aarie blinked, breaking away from his stare. For a brief moment, she was glad of the darkness as heat flushed through her cheeks. She knew she was blushing. She hadn't expected the answer Jay gave, but she couldn't help thinking back to how he had helped her the last time she was here.

"I think I did nearly die," Aarie said, breaking the brief silence. "It's what everyone keeps telling me, anyway. My friends and Dad keep telling me that I'm so lucky and that it's a miracle for me to be healing so fast. I can't lift a finger to do anything for myself these days. Everyone's so scared that I might do myself more injury or slow down my recovery, but the truth is I feel fine. I hardly feel like I've been in an accident at all. They said when I first came to the hospital, it hadn't looked good for me. It doesn't make sense that I am as well as I am, so no one will believe what I say. They think I just don't want sympathy or to be a nuisance or that I'm just stubborn. Now, I can't help but wonder if me being so well is due to whatever it was you gave me that day, and that somehow it may even be the reason I am still alive." Aarie gasped as though she had just had this revelation and was thinking it out loud. "Is it true?" she asked.

"Aarie..." Jay paused as his jaw tightened again.

"Don't tell me—you can't answer that. It's okay. Jay, you told me before that knowing too much about this place would put me in danger somehow, but when I ask you certain questions you shouldn't answer, does it put you in danger too?" Aarie asked.

"Not in the same way, but I suppose the answer is yes," Jay replied.

"Then, I'm sorry. I didn't know. I won't ask you any more," Aarie said, feeling a rush of guilt.

"Look, don't worry about me. You don't even believe I'm real, remember?" He smiled.

"But the wolves are *still* definitely real?" she asked, unable to resist grinning back.

"Yes!"

"Sorry, that was another question, but I was kind of joking, and I already asked that one before anyway, so it doesn't count. So, if I can't ask you questions about this place, or about what you are, or anything that involves some strange, mysterious things that aren't possible—can I ask you normal questions that *normal* people ask *normal* people?"

Jay rolled his eyes. "I see this no questions thing lasted well."

"No, you have me wrong. You don't have to answer anything that you can't. I just want to make conversation. I thought it would be nice to have a conversation that doesn't involve wolves eating me; me dying; me drinking weird stuff—stuff, I might add—that tasted a lot like blood; and finally, a conversation that doesn't remind me that I'm stuck in some weird place that I may or may not have conjured up as a result of going very insane or possibly due to some kind of irreparable brain damage that I've incurred in the past few days." Aarie took a long deep breath.

"Have you finished?" Jay said, visibly failing to suppress the smile that was now turning into a massive grin.

She nodded. "Uh-huh."

"You can't ask me questions that normal people ask *normal* people because, as you have probably gathered, I'm not *normal*, and so, we may have a little problem."

"Sure I can. How about... how old are you? What do you do for fun? Do you have any weird habits?"

Jay sighed. "Answer number one would blow your mind. Answer number two would blow your mind or frighten you. And answer number three—all of my habits would probably seem weird to you, hence the not being normal!"

"Oh—really?" Aarie asked in a high-pitched voice. She couldn't help wondering about potential possibilities to Jay's answers, had he answered her questions properly. She especially pondered at Jay's age. From looking at him, she would have guessed he was in his early twenties though he exuded the confidence and presence of someone much older. She grumbled, having to stifle her curiosity this time.

"So, what do you wanna talk about?" she finally asked.

"Maybe we just talk about you," Jay replied, looking quite pleased with his suggestion.

"Me? I guess I could," Aarie said disappointedly "What do you want to know?"

"Hmm, how about, what do you do back in your world? What is your purpose, your interests or role in your world? Basically, what do you spend most of your time doing?"

"Erm, well, I don't know about my *purpose*. It's something I'd like to figure out myself, to be honest, but I like art and photography. I sketch a lot. I'm going to university to study graphic design in a few weeks."

"Ah, so you're a visual person—creative. You create imagery, is that right?" Jay asked.

"Yes, I love creating things."

"Hmm, I guess you could say we have that in common."

"Really? So, not all of your habits are too weird then." She smiled.

A cold breeze rustled through the trees, and Aarie shivered, remembering she was still only in her pyjamas. It was chilly in these dark woods, especially with bare feet.

"Are you cold?" Jay asked, taking off his black jacket before she could answer. He placed it over her shoulders.

"Thanks," Aarie said, wrapping the jacket around her tightly. The warmth left from Jay's body heat was pleasantly comforting. It was also a very nice blazer jacket she noted: smart but light and well-tailored. She felt a little self-conscious now as she realised, on both occasions she'd seen him, he looked well dressed even though he had managed to hold a casual and easygoing presence. He wore a black shirt and what looked like smart, black fitted biker jeans and leather boots. She wondered if she looked scruffy to him, but then, she hadn't exactly been expecting to be wandering around the woods.

"Shall we get out of here?" Jay asked, interrupting her thoughts. "Somewhere a little warmer and less gloomy, perhaps?"

"That would be good."

"So," Jay continued, "why don't you use your creativity and describe to me where exactly you would like to go. Anywhere—I'll try to take you there. Let's see how inventive and creative your *insane* mind really is," Jay said enthusiastically.

"Anywhere? Because... you can do that?" Aarie asked, in disbelief.

"Yes." He nodded.

Aarie's forehead creased slightly. "You see, that's what confuses me. You say you can't answer my questions, and then you tell me things like *that*—like that is a *normal* thing."

Jay's mouth twitched to the side slightly. "Okay, fair point. It's hard to remember what is and isn't normal sometimes. I guess you could say that's one of my weird habits," Jay admitted. "But I've said it now, so we might as well have a bit of fun since I can't take it back. Besides, I can't let you shiver to death out here, can I? So, go ahead, be inventive," Jay said with a gleam of excitement in his eyes.

A curious smile spread across Aarie's face as she thought about it for a moment. "Hmm... inventive? Okay then. I had a dream once about a place when I was a child. It's always stuck in my mind because I'd never seen anything like it. I used to think it was a real place then, and every day I would ask my mum if I could go there one day. Of course, I couldn't because it was just a dream. The place hid within a valley surrounded by mountains covered in trees of gold, red and green. A little like the ones near the waterfall you took me to before. There were bright red maple trees and blossom trees that grew along a long winding river, leading to a wooden bridge. The bridge crossed the narrowest part of the river beside an old stone cottage. It wasn't any ordinary cottage though—trees grew through the centre of it with winding staircases that wrapped around them. The stairs led to rope bridges and many more trees outside. You see, behind the cottage, it was like a wooden village in the treetops. It had a collection of tree-houses joined together by the rope bridges and more winding staircases that wrapped around the trees, higher and higher. There were platforms right at the top of the trees with turrets and balconies but no stairs or bridges that led to them. I always wondered how anyone could get to them. When I woke, I used to daydream and imagine that they were used by great winged creatures, angels, fairies and... unicorns. Well, I *was* five—I loved unicorns." Aarie cringed. "Anyway, I remember in my dream there were markings on the cottage door. Symbols that looked like—"

"A moon and stars," Jay whispered, finishing Aarie's sentence in complete astonishment.

"Yes, that's right. How did you guess? *Come on*, that was pretty inventive, don't you think?"

"Aarie, you didn't invent it. It *is* a place, a place that exists here. I know it well, but the question is, how do you know it?" Jay said, utterly bewildered and amazed by her clear description. "Is it possible that you could have been here before?" he whispered as though thinking out loud to himself rather than asking Aarie. She chose to answer it anyway.

"No, I don't think so, and what do you mean it's a real place? I dreamt it up when I was five! How can it be a real place?" Aarie implored Jay to answer.

Jay rolled back his sleeve, revealing a black pattern and symbols that wrapped around his right wrist. They reminded Aarie of intricate henna tattoos. She gasped, recognising the symbols within the design; they were the same from the dream she had just described.

"What does this mean?" she asked.

"I don't know. The place that you described is a place I spent a lot of my childhood. My father built it for me because I loved spending time around here so much. It's not far from here. It's near the place I took you to before. The trees that you said looked similar were not just similar—they were the very same trees. Close your eyes, Aarie. I will take you there now."

Without a word, Aarie closed her eyes. Immediately she felt Jay take hold of her wrists as he had done before. A gentle breeze brushed her skin and then a comforting warmth, like the rays of summer, surrounded her once again.

"Open your eyes, Aarie," said Jay.

She did so nervously, looking straight at Jay for several moments before she dared look around. He was still holding her wrists she realised, but as soon as she moved, he let go.

"Is this the place you described to me?" he asked.

She turned her head slowly over her right shoulder, and her eyes widened. Her body automatically spun around as her eyes followed the row of cherry blossoms and red maple trees that stood along a riverside. The wooden bridge was nearby. Beyond it, Aarie could make out the mountains of gold, red and green in the distance. Straight ahead stood a large stone cottage. More cherry blossom trees dotted the cottage's garden, which looked very well maintained, as did the building itself. The white window frames gleamed as though new; they were even more pristine than she had remembered in her dream. The immaculate slate roof sloped upwards, meeting three large glass domes in the centre of the building. Out of the tops of the domes shot an enormous golden beech tree, a green cedar tree, and a giant red maple tree. Intricate wooden staircases wound around them like giant spiralling strands of DNA. Platforms and rope bridges joined them together, swaying gently in the warm breeze. Aarie's eyes followed the bridges to more platforms and large wooden structures within other surrounding trees. Some looked like separate little houses, each with a spiralling staircase around the trunk that held them up. Others had swirling domed roofs made of glass and gold. She glanced up toward the tops of the trees where she could only just make out tiny platforms with turrets sticking out above the branches. She gasped at how accurate her memory had been. However, being here now, everything about the place seemed so much more alive, and every detail caught her eye.

Tiny floating lights filled the air now like hundreds of fireflies, though Aarie had always thought fireflies only came out at night. She held out a hand as the tiny specs of light floated down, briefly landing on her palm then floating off again. From where she stood now, the wooden village in the trees looked like a giant floating palace. She laughed in pure elation as she took in the full view of this magical land. It was the only place she had dreamed about for years. Secretly, she had never stopped wishing she could visit this place for real.

It had always been a mystery to Aarie why people referred to having 'butterflies in their stomach' until now, and as her heart skipped a beat, she felt like she had swallowed a hundred butterflies. She turned to Jay, who was watching her reactions with the same intrigue as he had on the clifftop. There was something new in his eyes that she just couldn't fathom.

"Jay, this is incredible!" she beamed. "*You're* incredible. You don't know how much I've always wanted to see this place again, for real."

Jay walked towards Aarie slowly, stopping close in front of her. "So, you think this is all definitely real *now*, but the last time you saw it, it was just a dream?" Jay quickly asked as though urgently curious to know her answer.

Aarie's smile wavered a little as she thought about it for a moment. Her confusion was evident on her face, and it slowly engulfed her radiant smile, replacing it with worry.

"I... I don't know," she replied finally. "All I know is, if this is a dream, I don't want to wake up for a very long time."

"Don't say that," Jay whispered, reaching to move a strand of hair from Aarie's eyes as it blew in the breeze. His touch surprised her for a second, but she was too distracted by what he had said, to react.

"Why not?" she asked immediately.

"Because you don't know how dangerous that sounds to me."

Aarie puzzled at that comment and at his lingering hand that still held a strand of her hair. Jay's hand moved from her hair and gently stroked her cheek as their eyes locked. She closed hers very briefly, surprised again by his touch and how gentle it was. She opened them again at the sound of his voice, and he gently dropped his hand back to his side.

"The last time you were here, you said you felt like you knew me, but somehow I feel like I know you too. I'm not under any illusions, Aarie. I know we barely know anything about each other. My mind can only guess at what you really make of things, and I... I don't even know your full name. There's just something about you, and the fact that you've been to this place before—a place only I ever go to these days—makes me wonder if there's a reason why you are here and why I can't seem to ignore you. But none of these things can change the fact that I know it's dangerous for you to be here, especially if you *want* to be here."

Aarie's eyes searched his as she tried hard to make sense of the way he was looking at her now. She couldn't stifle her curiosity any longer.

"I know I said I wouldn't ask any more questions but—everything you just said—is that why sometimes when you look at me, it is like there's something you really want to tell me, but then you don't? I don't know for sure if it's because it'll *break the rules* or if I just simply imagined it, but it drives me crazy or crazier, and I'm not sure of anything anymore."

"That's the problem, Aarie—*anything* I do that involves you, breaks the rules. Furthermore, I want to tell you everything. I shouldn't because anything I tell you can only make things more dangerous for you. The worse thing is those aren't even the main reasons why I don't tell you. I don't tell you because I fear you may discover what I really am, and somehow, I don't want you to see me as a monster."

There was a sudden sadness behind Jay's eyes that made Aarie's hand instinctively reach for his. She held it loosely in hers.

"I don't think I could ever think that," she whispered. "If you were, you wouldn't have hidden me from the wolves or brought me here. I'm pretty sure I wouldn't even be alive after the accident if it hadn't been for you."

There was a brief moment of silence, and Aarie worried that she shouldn't have reached for his hand, but as his fingers closed gently around hers, she instantly forgot that worry.

"You even lent me your nice jacket," she added, "which I'm pretty glad of because I'd feel a little ridiculous in just my pyjama's right now."

He smiled gently, looking down briefly at their hands as he spoke. "It *is* a nice jacket, and your PJ and blazer combo is working just fine."

Jay glanced away, and his smile soon began to dissolve. He turned suddenly and moved away from Aarie. He rubbed his face as if trying to ease some pain behind his eyes.

Aarie took a step to him. "Jay, I don't care what you are. Don't tell me if it matters to you what you think I'll think. Just don't tell me. Don't tell me anything else that I don't need to know from now on. I don't *want* to know if it puts you in danger, and I don't *want* to know any of it if it makes you want me to leave."

He turned around instantly. "I don't want you to leave—that's the biggest problem of all. You are such a mystery to me, Aarie."

"*I'm* a mystery? Believe me, you are the biggest mystery that ever existed, and I think that is really gonna test my curiosity, but a mystery you can stay if that's what it takes. At least for now, anyway. That also goes for any unusual things or happenings that I come across. As far as I'm concerned, I'm just having a very imaginative dream, one that happens to feel very real. How does that sound?" Aarie asked.

After a long silence, a subtle smile tugged at the corners of Jay's mouth. He raised his eyebrows ever so slightly. "But *I* am still real, and the wolves are still real?"

"Yes, you are still real, and the wolves are still very, very real. Okay?" Aarie smiled back.

Jay swallowed. "Okay. Man of mystery I am," he agreed. His attention immediately went to her muddy bare feet as though noticing them for the first time. "And maybe I should lend you some boots from the house to go with that combo of yours."

"Erm, yes, please. I'd really appreciate that. Thanks," Aarie replied. "So, now that everything is kind of okay again, and while I am happily enjoying this pleasant dream with a very real you—are you gonna show me around this amazing treehouse properly or what?" she asked with a childlike gleam of excitement in her eyes. "Oh, and my name is Aariella Stone, Jaydon Onuris."

At that, a gentle laugh escaped him. He placed her hand in his to lead the way towards the cottage.

Chapter 4
Palace In The Sky

Aarie stopped a couple of steps behind Jay as they reached the cottage front door. She whirled around in awe at the magnificent red and green maples and pink blossom trees that decorated the garden. Red and green leaves flecked with tiny white flowers covered vines that climbed around the windows and hung over the arched entranceway. A sweet fragrance like jasmine drifted from them in the gentle breeze.

Aarie's gaze moved to the markings that were carved into the heavy wooden door—the same pattern and symbols that she could see again on Jay's wrist now as he reached his right hand to push the door. The door clicked and creaked as though being unlocked. Then it began to open. Aarie's eyes widened as she realised there had been no door handle on the door; Jay's marks on his wrist appeared to be what had unlocked and opened it. She wondered if this was just a very cool way *his kind* secured their homes or if there was more to these patterned markings. Other questions began to pour into her head, but she shook them off, wafting a hand in front of her face as though to bat away the curiosity that filled her mind. She blinked and stared back at the opening door.

Jay turned and gestured for Aarie to go inside. "After you."

She stepped through the door into a large open-plan room. The combination of natural woods and rusty red and ochre soft furnishings made the room feel cosy and inviting despite its grand size. To the right of her weaved a rustic wooden stairway with a bannister made from wild tree branches. It twisted and turned upward, meeting a mezzanine that led to several solid wood doorways.

Back on the ground floor, three large leather sofas and a coffee table sat in the centre of the room before an open fireplace. Wild wooden beams ran through the walls all around, curving up to the ceiling at the room corners. An archway sat underneath the mezzanine. It led to another open space where natural light flooded in from above.

On the left, the room led into a rustic kitchen area that was slightly partitioned off with a high breakfast bar. It curved around in the same wild wood fashion as the rest of the room.

Jay stepped in behind her, closing the door. "Welcome to my childhood home. This is where I spent most of my time when I was growing up."

"It's amazing, Jay. This is like something from a fairytale. You must have had such a wonderful childhood."

"Yes, I suppose I did," he said nodding. "This place holds many fond memories for me. That's why I still come here."

They walked further into the room. Aarie's face beamed as her eyes darted everywhere, unsure where to look first. Lanterns hung on all the walls and in the centre of the ceiling, and she imagined that at night they would cast a warm, golden glow that would fill the room. She curiously scanned over tapestries on the walls. They depicted various images of winged silhouettes, wolves and magical landscapes. After musing over them for a long while, her eyes fell upon something else; a small framed pencil drawing sat between the tapestries. She moved closer to get a better look. It was a detailed drawing of the cottage and the incredible treehouse palace that ran through and around it. Jay came up behind her at that moment, mildly startling her as he spoke.

"I drew this place when I was a child. I used to make up stories about a magical place in the sky and tell them to my father and brother. My father used to say that I lived in my head so much that he couldn't wait to see what wondrous imaginings it would bring me as an adult guar—"

Jay abruptly paused, consciously aware of his mistake as Aarie turned around to look at him. He closed his eyes and held a palm up, predicting Aarie's next question and stopping her asking it. "Please, just forget that. It's hard this mystery thing," he said.

"Please, go on without the details you can't reveal," Aarie replied, turning back towards the drawing.

"On my seventh birthday, my father surprised me with this place. He built it from my drawing and the stories I had told him. Obviously, not on his own—he had a lot of help."

"Wow, that's incredible. What a gift. I can't even imagine how any child would react to receiving something *this* amazing, but Jay, how old were you when you drew this?"

"Six."

"Six?!" Aarie shrieked in pure astonishment as she stared at the intricate drawing. It looked like a drawing by a professional architect rather than that of a small child. "Were you some kind of child genius? Don't ever ask me to show you my childhood drawings, that's all I can say on that matter."

Jay smiled. "I always loved to draw. It was one of my favourite things."

"I loved to draw as well, and after I dreamt about this place, I drew it too, but believe me, it did *not* look like this even if I may have thought it did at the time."

"You drew this place?" Jay asked, intrigued.

"Yes. Don't worry though—I never showed it to anyone except my mum, who thought it was just the silly imagination of a five-year-old."

"I'd like to see it one day," Jay said.

Aarie shook her head. "Uh-uh, that's not going to happen."

"I'm sure it can't be *that* bad. Besides, I'm sure if you had drawn it at the age of six, it would have been even better. You can improve a lot within a full year."

"Anyway, what else are you good at?" Aarie asked, changing the subject as she grew ever more curious to learn more about him.

"Um... mystery bit and mystery bit and... fighting."

Aarie's mouth fell open in surprise. "*Fighting?*"

Jay shrugged. "Because of who I—no, scrap that bit. Because of certain *mysteries*, I learned various fighting skills from a young age. We... *mystery people* learn these skills as part of our culture and old traditions. We think of it as sport or meditation but also a very beneficial and necessary life skill."

"Kinda like martial arts—karate or judo or something? So, it's more for fitness or maybe self-defence, rather than just hurting people?"

"Yes, I suppose so."

"Oh, okay, and you're good at that?" Frowned Aarie.

"You disapprove?"

"No, not at all, I'm just trying to picture it. Though, if you're good at it, maybe that explains why you're not afraid of the wolves."

"That's not why I'm not afraid of the wolves," Jay instinctively replied. "That is another *mystery*."

"So is there anything that you're bad at?" Aarie asked.

"Being convincingly human around you," he said as though thinking out loud. "...and being able to decide if that is or isn't a bad thing."

"It's not a bad thing," Aarie whispered.

Jay didn't reply; he just glanced down.

Aarie casually leaned against the wall, examining her nails as she spoke. "Anyway, so far we have a man of mystery who was a child genius, ninja artist that designed complex architectural structures and lived in the most magical place I've ever seen. What do you like to eat?" Aarie asked, smirking as she looked up at him through her lashes.

Jay looked up. "Erm... mystery... and pretty much any kind of meat."

"Mystery? Oh come *on*—what possibly could you eat that's a *mystery* thing?"

Jay shrugged at her. "It's a hard one to explain without mysteries unravelling here and there, I'm afraid."

"I think you're enjoying this mystery thing a little too much, and possibly maybe even inventing a few mysteries now. Maybe to add, say, *more* mystery!"

Jay laughed. "Are you insinuating that I'm a liar, Miss Stone?" he said, shifting closer. He playfully loomed over her, casually leaning an arm against the wall behind her shoulder. Aarie's heart skipped as Jay was almost close enough to kiss her. His blue eyes were mesmerising up this close, and she could do nothing but look into them. For a second, Aarie thought they seemed to darken a little, but she was now conscious of staring. Her heart thumped so loud that she worried he could hear it.

"You have nice eyes," she said out loud, to her own surprise. To her relief, she realised Jay was staring back at hers.

"You have nice eyes too," he whispered as all humour was now gone from both of their faces and replaced by something else. Aarie swallowed as a strange tension began to build between them. Jay's eyes darkened more this time, only for a brief moment, but this time she was sure of it.

"Do you know they change slightly, your eyes? It's almost like they flicker," Aarie said.

Jay blinked suddenly, then stepped back, turning away quickly from her.

"I'm sorry," Aarie blurted out. "Did I say something wrong?"

"No. *I'm* sorry. I'm just not used to being around—"

"—Mortals," Aarie sighed, finishing his sentence.

He slowly turned back around. "No. I'm not used to being around... people that make me feel like how I feel now." He closed his eyes briefly, then re-opened them. "I'll get you some boots," he said, disappearing into another room around the corner. He came back a few moments later, holding a pair of small brown boots out to Aarie. "These are the smallest in the house, but they look about your size."

"Thanks," Aarie said, taking the boots and then slipping them on. They seemed to fit just snug, and Aarie couldn't help but wonder whose boots they had been in the past.

"Okay, let me show you the rest of the place," Jay said.

He led Aarie through the archway and into the other large room. It had three large tree trunks growing out of the ground, each with intricate patterns and symbols carved into their bark. An ornate spiral staircase wound around each tree. Aarie's eyes followed them up to three opened glass domes above her head. Daylight was slowly fading, but the glow of the moon was gradually taking its place. The trees and staircases carried on outside the domes to where she could make out wooden structures through the glass.

Jay gestured to the three staircases in front of them. "Take your pick, Aarie."

She looked carefully at the three trees and the different symbols carved on them. One showed moon and stars, the next had wings and flames, and the last one displayed a curling serpent amongst thorns. Aarie's eyes immediately rested on the second one. She glanced up at the glorious fiery red leaves above it, through the glass.

"This one," she said, walking to the bottom of its spiral staircase.

"Good choice."

Aarie waited for Jay to lead the way and followed close behind him in silence. She couldn't get that moment they had shared out of her head. His eyes and his face had been so close to hers. Her heart was still pounding at the thought of it... and from the moment outside when he had touched her cheek and held her hand and...

"Aarie, are you okay?" Jay asked, breaking her out of her reverie as he called down from the top of the glass dome.

"Sorry, what? Erm, yes...I'm fine."

"You don't look fine. Look, I'm sorry if I frightened you before, or stepped out of line, or did something that's not... *normal*. I didn't mean to make you feel uncomfortable. I'll be—"

"—You didn't, frighten me that is. Not in a bad way anyway, and I don't feel uncomfortable. If anything, I feel too comfortable around you, considering we practically just met. I'm just not used to feeling how I do now either, that's all." She blushed, unable to keep her words from spilling out of her mouth. She hurried up the steps and followed Jay out of the top of the dome. It led onto a wooden platform to the first rope bridge. Jay looked as though he wanted to say something in response to Aarie's reply, but whatever it was, he kept it to himself.

Warm lighting shone from inside the domes now, illuminating the bright colours that soared above them. Aarie's eyes scanned up and around to the other rope bridges and wooden structures that mingled between more treetops. Her mouth held open in pure amazement. She walked past Jay and then leaned over the platform railings to see the ground below. The hundreds of tiny lights still floated in the air, but since the day had rapidly faded from dusk to darkness, they seemed all the more magical. It was baffling how day and night could come and go so fast here, but she supposed this would have to remain another mystery. She flashed a smile back to Jay before bravely stepping onto the rope bridge and briskly crossing over to the next platform. The following wooden structure looked like a tiny house except it had no doors on either side of it. It had two viewing point windows inside with comfortable seats beneath them. Sitting on one, she stared out at the incredible landscape in front of her. It was lit up by the brilliant moonlight that cast dramatic shadows and shapes across the valley. From here, she could make out the mountains and waterfalls in the distance. Jay came in and sat beside her.

"Do you like the view?"

She turned to face him. "How do you do anything else but just be here?"

"Sometimes, I don't. Let me show you the other spots. There's so many, and the views just get better the further you go." He stood, holding his hand out to her. She jumped up, sliding hers into his, letting him lead the way once again.

For hours they explored the many little wooden houses and structures within the trees, each with unique views and quirky features. There were secret doorways, passages and hidden tunnels; gold and glass spiralling dome rooftops; intricately carved archways and pillars; glass tunnels; see-through bridges; and staircases that wound higher and higher above the trees, offering a clear view for miles. Rope swings and hammocks were placed high between branches. So too were many balconies and ledges that felt like being on the edge of the world.

Aarie and Jay sat together now on one of the highest reachable platforms, gazing out at the clear night sky. Lanterns hung in the branches above, casting a soft golden spotlight on them. The calls of tropical birds echoed faintly in the night from distant branches. The tiny glowing specs still floated all around them, illuminating the trees like golden fairy lights. Aarie gazed up at the even higher platforms that rose above them—the narrow ones that had no stairs to get to them. She wondered at the possibilities explaining their absence as well as the lack of any safety railings.

Jay followed Aarie's gaze. "What are you thinking?" he asked.

"Just pondering about platforms that only mysterious people can reach," she answered, smiling.

Jay bit his lip. "A decorative design feature? Or rather a design flaw—I was only 6, remember?"

"Of course," Aarie replied. Her eyes were heavy all of a sudden, and she closed them for a brief moment.

"Are you tired?" Jay asked.

"Yes, I feel exhausted. Then, I suppose that's because I should be sleeping right now. Instead, I'm having this very realistic dream where I don't actually sleep. But I feel like I *could* sleep. Is that even possible—to sleep while I'm asleep? Then again, I guess I'm not really asleep, am I? This is so confusing. Anyway, if I end up *here* when I sleep, what happens when I fall asleep here? Do I wake up back in the woods or back in my bed?"

"I don't know, Aarie. I honestly don't."

"Well, I'd better give you your jacket back and these boots, just in case," she said, taking off the items and then putting them to the side of her. "I don't want my dad to think I snuck out and stopped out all night with some random mystery guy when I'm supposed to be recovering."

"But that's kind of what you did." Jay grinned.

"I didn't sneak out. I have no control over this, even if I do happen to like being here—" Aarie finished abruptly with a yawn.

"Whatever happens, you're eventually going to have to sleep for real because you can't stay awake forever. That means, if you wake up in your bed, you may have to cancel your plans for the day."

"Oh no, I think I may be in trouble then," Aarie said.

"Why?"

"I said I'd meet Adam first thing in the morning."

"Adam? You mentioned him last time you came. Is he your mortal partner?"

Aarie looked puzzled. "My what? Oh—no, he's my best friend. He's more like family. My friends—Angela, Jamie and Adam—are all like family, really. I wish you could meet them. But you may need to stop calling people mortals," she whispered, casually leaning into him to use his side as a pillow.

Aarie half closed her eyes, peering down at Jay's arms as he stretched them out in front of him. She could just about make out the dark patterns on the inside of his right wrist as he fidgeted with his hands.

"Jay, if this is the last time I ever come here," she began to muse glumly, "I just wanted you to know that I'm really glad I spent this evening with you and that we spent it here." She reached her hand out and placed it in his. His fingers automatically closed around hers as he glanced down at her resting against him. Her breathing had already begun to slow, and her eyes were now shut.

"I'm really glad too," he whispered. "But something tells me you'll be back again... if nothing but to pleasantly torment me with all your questions."

Part of him was sure she *would* be back, but a small part also worried that there was a possibility he was wrong. The pain of it began to linger in his mind as he leaned his face against her hair.

"Sleep well, Aarie," he said as she fell silent. She slowly began to fade once again, gradually becoming transparent until she had disappeared entirely. Jay was left staring at the night sky on his own, and for the first time, he felt the loneliness of it.

Chapter 5
Goodnight

Aarie pulled her pillow over her head, trying to block out the buzzing sound coming from her bedside table. It had interrupted her sleep. After several minutes the noise stopped. It was soon replaced by knocking that echoed from the downstairs hallway. A few moments later, there was a clicking sound of a latch followed by a creak and then a murmur of voices.

"Aarie, Adam is here. Did you oversleep?" her dad called from downstairs, signalling game over for Aarie's attempt to get more rest.

"I'll be down soon. Just give me a few minutes," she groaned.

"Okay, no worries," Adam called back.

The muffled sound of her dad and Adam talking moved from the entrance hall through to the kitchen. Aarie sat up. Her tousled hair fell into her face as she rubbed at her eyes. She had gone to bed early yet somehow felt as though she'd only had a couple of hours sleep. She moaned as she stood up and caught a glimpse of herself in the mirror on the wall. Stopping for a second, she noticed that her pyjamas seemed to be muddy.

"What the hell?" Aarie murmured to herself as she caught sight of the scratches and mud on her arms and legs. Her feet were filthy too. She wondered if she had been sleepwalking outside. After all, she had done it once or twice as a young child, according to her mother. Images popped up in her head of dark woods and running. Aarie jumped, startled by the memory of the white wolf that was ready to chase her. More images from her dream came to mind, including the tall stranger who had helped her again. *Jay.* He had first helped her in the dream that she'd had at the hospital. Aarie thought of the magical land he had taken her to. She had called it her place when she had first dreamt of it as a small child. However, on the last visit, it had been his place, and he had shared it with her despite having so many secrets that he couldn't tell her. She touched her cheek, remembering Jay's hand on her skin and how soft his touch had been.

I don't tell you because I fear you may discover what I really am, and somehow, I don't want you to see me as a monster.

Jay's words echoed in Aarie's mind as she recalled the sadness in his eyes when he had said this. She thought about them being together in the cottage as well as the time they spent in the treetops. Her chest fluttered slightly. She sighed, feeling the heavy weight of disappointment that it had all just been a dream, one that had probably seemed so real because she had been sleepwalking in the garden. She wanted to go back to sleep. Her body physically needed her to go back to sleep. Her reflection stared back at her from the mirror. The bags under her eyes looked purple and sore.

A sudden knock on the bedroom door startled her.

"Aarie? Are you okay?" Adam asked.

"Erm, one moment, Adam."

She reached for a long dressing gown quickly, worried about what he would think of her muddy clothes and scratches. As she put it on, her mind wandered back to her dream. She had worried about having a man's jacket on when waking because of assumptions her dad and Adam might have about her stopping out all night with a mystery guy.

But that's kind of what you did.

Aarie laughed out loud to herself at the memory before rushing to open the door. A confused Adam greeted her.

"Were you just laughing?"

"Erm, maybe. Is there something wrong with me laughing?"

"Nope. Feel free to share the joke if you like," Adam said, walking in casually. He sat on Aarie's bed as he re-registered her appearance. "Aarie, you're not even dressed or showered or—is that mud?"

"Erm... I overslept. I can't have heard my first alarm. Look, I'm just gonna be honest with you. I didn't sleep very well last night," Aarie said. She wanted to say that she had had the best night's sleep ever, but it did not explain why she was so exhausted.

"Oh. Bad dreams?"

"Yeah, and I think I was sleepwalking this time, hence the mud. I vaguely remember being outside. I might have to hide the house keys from now on."

Adam's eyebrows raised. "Whoa, that sounds nuts. Though, you did that as a child a few times, didn't you? But you feel okay, right? You're not suffering from any memory loss or any other strange things, are you?"

"No, I'm just tired. Sorry, I know we said we could do something fun today, but I guess I'm still not up to it after all."

"It's fine. I really don't mind. To be honest, I was a little worried that you might be overdoing things by being up and about too soon. And I'm not sure if what I came up with is much fun anyway."

"What did you have planned?" Aarie asked.

"Well, after getting you some breakfast somewhere nice, I thought we could maybe go to this graffiti exhibition in town. I can't guarantee it'd be great, but it's next to this new shop that I think you'd like. It sells loads of cool stuff I thought we could look at getting for our uni house, seeing as we'll be housemates soon. It could be good to plan what kind of pad we're gonna have. They've got these nice retro record players and great sound systems. I thought we could get something for the house, you know, for all those house parties were going to have." Adam grinned. "But we can do this kinda stuff anytime. I'm just glad you're still around and able to do anything, to be honest. You really had me scared. I know I keep saying it since the hospital, but it's true. I'm lucky to have you back and so quickly on the mend. I couldn't care a less if you just wanted me to cook waffles and let you sit in your pyjamas all day."

"Hmm, well now you've said it, that does sound good." Aarie smiled. "I may still nod off at some point, but at least you'll get to eat most of them."

"Well, that sounds like a good deal to me. I'll get started. You just bring yourself downstairs when you're ready. I'll get you some juice too. Good old vitamin C and all that business," Adam said, disappearing out of the room.

Fifteen minutes later, Aarie wandered into the kitchen in her dressing gown. She rubbed her damp hair with a towel and then wrapped it into a neat bundle on top of her head. The sweet smell of sugary waffles and chocolate sauce filled her nostrils, making her mouth water. She was exhausted, but there was always enough energy to eat waffles.

"Hey there," Adam said, sliding a plate under her nose. She perched on a stool at the breakfast bar and glanced down at the chocolate-covered waffles and icecream.

"Mmm, nothing like a healthy nutritious breakfast to start the day, hey?" She grinned.

"Ah-huh," Adam said, taking a stool beside her. "We've got dairy, nuts and protein—a healthy balanced diet if you ask me."

Aarie's dad, Lyle, sat across the room at a dining table. He shuffled a newspaper as he read it by the window. "Hmm, looks like you've got another visitor, Aarie," Lyle grumbled as a figure passed the glass. The doorbell rang, and Aarie turned to get up.

"I'll get it, you sit back down," Lyle said, already crossing the room. A minute later, he wandered back, resuming his position by the window with a newspaper. Jamie strolled in soon after, holding a bunch of flowers and grapes.

"Hey," he said to Aarie, then eyed Adam sat beside her.

Aarie smiled. "Hey, Jamie. We're having waffles. You want some?"

Adam turned, waving a hand as a silent hello. His gaze wandered over the flowers in Jamie's hand as he chewed on a mouthful of waffle.

"Mmm, well, now I've smelled them—yeah," Jamie said, sniffing the air. "I brought you flowers and grapes. I think the law of nature says they're supposed to help people heal faster or something, so, you know, I got some for you."

"Oh, thanks, Jamie. They're lovely, and I should probably be eating more fruit too."

"They're not as tasty as waffles though," Jamie said, breaking a tiny piece of waffle from Aarie's plate and then placed it into his mouth. He perched on a stool to her left and set the grapes and flowers down on the breakfast bar.

"Dad didn't want any, so you can have his if you like?" Aarie said, reaching across the breakfast bar to an untouched plate of waffles.

Jamie's eyes widened. "Mmm, well, if you insist. I wouldn't want to let them go to waste," he said, taking hold of the spare cutlery before he dug straight in.

Adam leaned forward. "So what are your plans today, Jamie? Are you just passing through?" he asked.

"No plans. I just thought I'd come to see how Aarie was keeping. Why, are you two planning to go somewhere? I don't wanna ruin your plans if you are. I should've phoned, but I kinda... you know, spur of the moment thing."

"No, we don't really have plans," Aarie answered.

"Well, Aarie didn't sleep well, so I don't think she's up for going anywhere or doing much," Adam added.

"Oh, that's cool. I just came over to chill anyway. I'm not fussed about going anywhere. Oh, that is, unless you mind me being here, eating your spare waffles and stuff?"

"Course not," Aarie replied. "As long as you don't mind that I'm probably gonna be rubbish company and not quite with it today."

"What's new?" Jamie smiled, giving Aarie a gentle shoulder nudge as she laughed.

Lyle shuffled his paper from across the room, and Aarie turned.

"Anything interesting in the news today, Dad?"

"No, not really. I don't know why I bother reading the papers sometimes. It's all nonsense." Lyle sighed. He folded his newspaper and placed it on the table. "So, are you three pottering about the house today then?"

"Possibly. Is that alright?" Aarie answered.

Lyle nodded. "Yes, it's fine, but make sure you do get some rest if you need it, Aarie," he said as he stood up. "Adam, take care of her. She doesn't listen to me sometimes, and I have to pop out for a little bit,"

"Will do, Mr Stone," Adam replied.

"Okay, I'll see you kids later. Help yourself to whatever food and drink you want in the cupboards," Lyle said, throwing one last glance at them before he left the room.

"Your dad's so nice," Adam said.

Jamie frowned. "Hmm, I think I may have done something to offend him somehow," Jamie muttered. "Have I done something in the past, Aarie?"

"No, how do you mean?"

"I don't know—I just always get the impression he doesn't like me."

"Don't be silly. He's like that with everyone that comes round to visit me."

"He's not like that with wonder boy over here. *'Adam, take care of my Aarie for me'*," Jamie said in a mocking voice.

Adam smirked. "Well, I am a perfect gentleman."

"A perfect prick, more like. One who kisses ass." Jamie smirked back before tucking into more waffle.

"Shh, you two," Aarie said, gently nudging the boys either side of her with her elbows.

Two weeks later:

The taxi pulled up a few yards from Aarie's house. The headlights lit up the quiet, muddy village road as moths hovered in the beams. Two doors shut as the engine continued to purr. Jamie leaned in to pay the driver and exchange pleasantries. He turned, and the window slowly wound back up. Loose stones crunched beneath the car as it gently rolled away, leaving Aarie and Jamie with just the moonlit night. Aarie linked her arm into Jamie's as they began walking up the road toward her driveway.

"Are you sure your dad won't mind me staying over?" Jamie asked.

Aarie shook her head. "Nope, not sure at all, but I live here too. We're going to uni soon. He has to get used to me living in the same house as you, so what's the difference? Besides, it's late, and that taxi would have cost you a fortune at this time.

God, I'm so tired. I think you wore me out on the dance floor, Saunders," Aarie grumbled, though she was smiling.

"Saunders is it? You haven't called me that since we were eleven."

"Haven't I?"

"No. In fact, the last time you did was not long after you punched me in the face for kissing you."

"I didn't punch you."

"Erm—you did! I think my nose has never been quite right since."

"Well, I was only eleven, and you asked for it. I mean, jumping on me like that outside the school gates, Jamie. I didn't even know you. You startled me, and all for a silly dare with your friends. What if my dad had seen you? Hey, maybe he did. Maybe that's why he doesn't like you," she said.

"I didn't jump on you. I was just a stupid kid back then. And I apologised to you the next day, didn't I?"

"Yes, and that's why we're here today."

"Anyway, it wasn't a dare. I never told you that, did I? I think I lied to you. So, tonight I'm setting the record straight. I didn't kiss you for a stupid dare with friends—I just fancied you. I didn't seem to be able to get your attention any other way. You just never seemed to want to talk to me."

"Is that the truth?"

"Yeah," Jamie laughed. "It's only taken me seven years to tell you that."

"Well, I didn't talk to you because all my friends fancied you, and so I found you too intimidating to approach. I mean, how could little me talk to the boy whose name every girl seemed to have scratched into their pencil tins? They were all jealous when we became friends, do you know that? That's why Cheryl and Victoria started tagging around with us for a while. I think it's why Adam didn't like you at first—because you had a fan club."

"At first? Sometimes I think he still doesn't like me," Jamie said.

Aarie gave in to a massive yawn as her hand came up over her mouth.

"Boring you, am I?" Jamie mischievously laughed. He bent down, abruptly lifting Aarie off her feet and into his arms. She giggled as he carried her to the driveway. "Nobody falls asleep on me till the night's over, and you are not home yet, so I'll have to carry you there just to make sure!" Jamie boomed.

"Put me down, you idiot," she laughed.

As they approached the gateway, a shadowed figure stood at the gate next door.

Aarie's face scrunched up. "Adam? What are you doing up and outside at this time?" she asked as Jamie set her down gently.

"I was out with friends. I only just got back, then I heard you two laughing," Adam said in a huff. He glared now at Jamie. "Are you staying over then? I thought you had a date? Isn't that why you didn't want to come out?" Adam hissed at Jamie.

Jamie frowned. "Actually, I said I was out with a girl. Aarie is a girl, just in case you hadn't noticed."

Aarie frowned. "Hey, come on guys, what's with the tone?"

Adam shot a glance at Aarie. "He lied to me, Aarie. If you guys wanted to go out and didn't want me around, you should've just said. You didn't need to lie."

"Didn't want you around? What are you talking about, Adam? I didn't even know you wanted to go out. I didn't even know I was going out until Jamie turned up on my door."

"But Jamie *did*. I asked him, and he said you were busy tonight too."

Jamie groaned. "God, Adam, we just went to that new club in town that I know you don't like. I just decided to go at the last minute, and I asked Aarie 'cos I knew she wanted to go too. It's no big deal. Sorry if I didn't ask permission, but I didn't lie—I just couldn't be arsed to explain it 'cos I knew you'd be like this. I knew you already had plans with your other mates, so what's the problem?"

"What's the problem? You *know* what the problem is!" Adam spat, shoving Jamie with full force in the chest.

Jamie stood up straight as his fists clenched by his sides. He hastily moved back towards Adam, gritting his teeth. "Don't sodding do that again, Adam. I'm getting tired of your bullshit, and I'm not putting up with this crap tonight!" he said, aggressively raising his voice. "You're spoiling Aarie's night," he hissed.

Adam's face washed over with rage as he flung himself forward. Aarie hurried between them, holding her arms up at their chests. Adam almost knocked into her but righted himself just in time.

"Stop it! For god's sake," she shrieked. "My dad's gonna be out here in a minute. What are you doing? Adam, what's gotten into you? Have you had too much to drink? We didn't lie to you, okay? We didn't leave you out purposely. We just went out—that's all. Look, just go home, Adam!" Aarie shouted.

Adam fell silent. Aarie very rarely lost her temper with him, but she was furious now. He glanced down at her. "Aarie, I'm sorry. I'm sorry if I've ruined your night. I never meant to. You're right—I'm drunk. I'll go."

Aarie sighed, softening her expression. "Look, just forget it. We'll talk about it later. I'll see you tomorrow, okay?"

Adam nodded. Seemingly abashed, he turned and then disappeared down the driveway next door. Aarie and Jamie shared a glance before turning to make their way to her house. Security lights came on as they neared the front door. Aarie rattled her keys out of her bag and then opened the door. Switching more lights on through the house, they wandered to the kitchen.

Jamie cleared his throat. "I'm sorry, Aarie. You know I didn't mean to lie to him, I just—"

"—I know, I know. Adam can be just so over the top sometimes. I don't need to tell him everything I do anyway, and neither do you. Still, I worry about the two of you. Tonight, you both seemed like you were on the brink of just kicking the hell out of each other. It's not the first time either. I wish you'd just quit it 'cos we're all supposed to be moving in together soon. I don't want us falling out before we even get to uni."

"I know. I'm sorry. He just winds me up sometimes. I can't help it."

Aarie grabbed two glasses from a cupboard and then filled them with water from the tap. She passed one to Jamie, then took one large sip as she looked up at him.

"I had a good night tonight, by the way. Thanks for taking me out."

"I had a good night too. A great night, in fact. We should do it more. Though, maybe I'll check if it's okay with Adam next time so that he can book it in his diary," Jamie said sarcastically.

She waved a hand. "Stop it. You know he's just had too much to drink."

"He's always bloody like that, Aarie. Don't blame the drink. You're too bloody kind to him, and he's too bloody clingy sometimes. He needs to let you breathe."

"Well, you two better patch things up in the morning. I mean it, Jamie," Aarie said, resting a hand on his arm. "You're both important to me, so it's not nice to see you at each other's throat. I don't want you two acting like kids competing for attention, or whatever the hell it is that's got into you both lately. You're not eleven anymore. You're both my best friends, and Angela too. I know Adam likes to take that title 'cos he's known me the longest—and maybe I go along with it because it seems to matter more to him than you and Angela—but you're all my best friends, really. You're all as close as family to me."

51

Jamie gripped Aarie's hand briefly. "I'll apologise to him in the morning... well, later today anyway, and to your dad too for making noise, okay?"

"Okay. Thanks," she said, moving back to the door. "Anyway, you know where everything is. The spare room should have fresh sheets. Just help yourself to towels when you wake up. I'll see you then." Aarie smiled.

"Aarie?" Jamie said, causing her to pause in the doorway.

"Yep?"

Jamie looked at his watch. "Did you know we met seven years today?"

She gasped "Really? Today?"

"Yeah." He nodded.

"Wow, seven whole years I've had to put up with your shenanigans," she said with a smirk.

"And you know you bloody love 'em." Jamie smiled. "Goodnight, Aarie."

"Goodnight, Jamie," she replied. With one last glance, she disappeared around the door, leaving him drinking his glass of water alone.

Chapter 6
Ghosts And Shadows

The room that Aarie found herself in was so dark she could barely make out anything around her. Her foot kicked a metal object that made a tinny clatter against the concrete floor. She paused immediately, worried that someone would hear her if someone were here at all, but there was only silence now.

It was instantly a relief that she had fallen asleep before having the chance to get changed for bed; somehow pyjamas had made her feel so much more vulnerable in a strange place than the good sturdy jeans she had on now. She was also glad that she'd kept her boots on too. However, the slinky black cami top she wore offered little protection from the cold chill of this room.

Slowly and gently, her hands felt their way around until she bumped into a storage unit that seemed to hold rows and rows of sealed cardboard boxes. Running her hand along the metal edge of the unit's framework, she followed it until she finally came to a wall and then a door. Scuffling around, she found a cold metal handle. The door subtly creaked as she pushed the handle down, easing it open as slowly and quietly as she could. Peering out of this room, she spotted a dim lamp that hung on the concrete block wall in the distance. She poked her head around the corner to scan either side of the doorway. Two more dim lamps hung on the wall at either side. As her eyes adjusted to the low light of the room beyond this one, she could make out the outline of several large square objects stacked on top of each other on wooden pallets. It appeared to be a room filled with wooden crates, pallets and cardboard boxes; Aarie guessed it was a storage warehouse of some kind.

She stepped forward into the room, staying close to a row of crates at all times. She felt it would hide her if anyone were to come into the warehouse. Weaving in and out of the wooden boxes, Aarie kept peering around to make sure no-one was around.

A voice instantly made her freeze on the spot. It was a man's voice, but she did not recognise it, nor could she work out what he was saying; he was mumbling. It seemed to get louder as did her racing pulse. She ducked down into the shadows of a large open crate. The voice sounded nearby now, but glancing either side of her, she saw nothing.

There was silence once again.

The light in the distance flickered slightly. Aarie couldn't be sure, but she thought something had passed in front of it briefly. Her clammy hands pushed her hair out of her eyes as she frantically scanned the room, but still saw nothing.

Suddenly, she caught a glimpse of movement in her peripheral vision. She hesitated to move as she could now make out a pale, gangly shape that stood beside her. The voice mumbled again, but this time it came from the ghostly figure next to her. She forced back a scream as she slowly turned to face it. In the dim light, she could only just make out a gaunt, elderly man. He was looking in her direction but seemingly through her. He was no monster or animal, just a man, but his ghostly looking appearance alarmed Aarie, as did his unexpected presence. She leapt up at once, scuttling out into the open and away from him. But as she fled, he also began running in her direction at high speed. She abruptly spun around to confront him, but he carried on coming towards her with no signs of slowing. There was not enough time to move out of his way, so she braced herself, throwing up her hands as she closed her eyes.

A split second later, she was sure that a collision of some kind should have happened, and she squinted through her lashes to see the man passing straight through her. Her eyes flew open and followed him. Gasping at what she had just witnessed, she could not help staring long after the man had passed. He seemed to be running from something and, for whatever reason, had not acknowledged her existence in any way.

Out in an open space, the man moved to a stack of large boxes, then frantically started to climb them. Before he could get a decent grip on them, a strange black fog surrounded him. It seemed to coalesce into a monstrous serpent-like creature. Aarie couldn't make out what it was, but it seemed to glide and float as though made of smoke. It appeared to change its form, continually whirling around the man. Wrapping its body around him, it threw him to the ground. It changed shape once more, becoming more menacing with demonic-looking eyes and clawed arms. The serpent-like body now spiralled into a tail with a razor-sharp point. This deadly spike raised above the man as the creature let out a piercing roar that sent shudders through Aarie. The beast now towered over the man, baring fangs as he cowered on the floor. The tail momentarily held firm, poised for attack. It thrust down to strike the man. His hands instinctively came up to protect his face. However, there was no impact; before the tail struck down, the man immediately vanished into thin air.

Aarie froze as her ears filled with the pounding of her heartbeat. Her throat had turned dry, but she dared not even swallow. She was out in the open and could not move to hide without drawing attention to herself.

Too late.

The demon smoke monster spun around, and its gaze met Aarie's with widening eyes. It studied her, and Aarie could do nothing else but stare back. Her pulse seemed like it was going to break out of her chest, yet she could not will herself to move. She felt on the verge of hyperventilating, but before she did, the demon turned around. In an instant, it disappeared.

Aarie whirled around to make sure it had gone, then clambered towards some more crates to hide. She leaned against them to catch her breath but soon heard footsteps coming from the end of the passageway between the wooden boxes. She worried about what else could be lurking in this room, and her mind explored a hundred dark possibilities. To her relief, a familiar figure now approached in the darkness.

"Jay?" she whispered.

He approached her cautiously. "Are you okay, Aarie?" he asked, standing in front of her now.

"No, Jay, we need to get out of here. There's something in here. I saw it just now. I don't think either of us is safe this time. We have to go—now!" she panicked, sounding almost hysterical.

"Aarie, you're safe, there's nothing here. You are safe with me—you know that don't you?" Jay calmly said.

Aarie worried at his calmness as he didn't seem to have heard her, or if he had, he didn't react.

"You don't understand, Jay. These weren't the wolves I saw this time. This was something else—a demon or something. It could change shape. And I saw a man who ran straight through me. I don't know what this place is, but maybe I'm not *real* this time, because he didn't see me. But I was out in the open after the demon creature attacked him, so it must have seen me before it left. I don't know, maybe I'm wrong, and it didn't see me because I'm not real or... or... maybe it did, and it's coming back—I don't know. Whatever its reason, I don't think either of us is safe this time. It was huge! We have to go. *Please!*" she begged, trying to tug at Jay's arm as she looked around frantically.

"Aarie, you're not in danger, and I can assure you I definitely am not."

"Jay, please, you didn't see this thing—"

"—Aarie, listen to me," Jay said firmly now. He reached out holding her by the sides of her arms. "There are things I can no longer hide from you, and I don't want to lie to you. I know what you saw and, trust me, it saw you too. You are still very real, but there is *nothing* else here but us. There was *never* anything else here except you and *me*," he stated, empathising his last words.

Her eyes frantically searched his, trying to take in and comprehend what he had just told her. "But... I don't understand?" she whispered.

Jay stared back at her with a pained seriousness about him. "I think you do, Aarie," he said as sudden realisation sparked in her eyes. Letting go of her arms, he turned away. "I didn't expect you to come here. This is such a long way from the house and the woods."

"But what about the man?" Aarie asked, unnerved. "What happened to him? Is he dead? He just disappeared."

"*He* was the one that wasn't real, Aarie. We call them shadows because they're not really here. You were just witnessing his *nightmare*. He was not harmed. He simply woke up safe in his bed, that's all." Jay turned back to her. Her small frame trembled slightly, and it stung him to acknowledge that it was because of him. "When the shadows come, they don't always get nightmares like that," he added, lowering his eyes. "In this realm, they're often dreams—*pleasant* dreams, Aarie. Or at least, they used to be. The shadows minds often seem darker these days, and dreams rarely seem to be enough to keep them away for long. Maybe we no longer understand your world anymore, I don't know, but my purpose is to keep this world and yours safe. This is who I am, Aarie," he said.

There was no change in Aarie's body language as the room fell silent.

Jay sighed. "Aarie, I will always keep you safe when you come here. *Always*. However, I don't have to be around when you do. I understand if you would prefer me not to be. I don't want you to be afraid and especially not of me."

"Where would you go?" Aarie quickly replied.

"Anywhere. You never have to see me again if that's what you want."

There was another silence as Aarie's mind flooded with the images of moments ago, of unanswered questions, and above all, of the thought that Jay could disappear forever.

"No, Jay, I don't want that. Why would you think I would want that?"

"Because I'm a *monster*. Wasn't that what you said? A 'demon'. I don't want to be *that* to you, Aarie. I can't change what I am, and I don't want to be the reason you have fear in your eyes. And don't deny that you are afraid, because I can hear your heartbeat," he declared, not taking his eyes from hers, and seemingly not hiding anything from her now either.

"Of course I'm afraid... or at least I *was*. I'm just in shock now, that's all. What just happened was a lot to take in!" she blurted out.

She took a deep breath and then exhaled, leaning back against the crate behind her. She glanced down at her hands, fidgeting with them to avoid Jay's intense gaze. "I'm not from here, okay? Everything I see here is new to me. When I come here, I don't even know where I will find myself, or with who, or *what*, or what danger will be waiting for me when I get here. All I can do is hope *you* will find me first. I've never liked having to be reliant on anyone or having to hide, but I trust my instinct, and if the things I've seen in this world are real, then I know they're a lot stronger than the average human. You know it too, and despite it not being the simplest option for you, you still chose to protect me. What I called you—I didn't *know*, Jay. I would never have said... How could I have known? I don't understand any of this," Aarie said.

She thought back to the old man cowering as the demon's tail was about to strike him. During that moment, she had felt Jay's presence and had immediately worried about what would've happened if it had been Jay caught in the creature's grip, instead of that man.

Her eyes flicked back up to Jay again. "I could feel you were here, but all I could think of was that *you* might be in danger this time. I was afraid, yes, but I was afraid mainly for you. Afraid that you would get hurt trying to protect me. I don't want you to disappear, Jay. My mind keeps telling me that's not the smartest thing for me to say. I know that it makes no sense, but somehow, I don't care. I don't know what you are, and I barely understand what is happening to me or why I keep coming here—if *here* is even still where *here* was. All I do know is that the last time I was here was the *best* bad night's sleep I've ever had... and it was because of you. So no, now I know the truth, I'm *not* afraid anymore, because I know you wouldn't hurt me," Aarie said firmly.

Jay had subconsciously moved closer to Aarie. He stood right in front of her now. Gently cupping her face in his hands, Jay brought his closer to hers. He paused as she trembled under his touch, but they held each other's gaze.

"Aarie," he whispered so gently as though her name meant something else entirely, "you're trembling."

"Because you make me nervous," she quickly replied, placing her hands over his before he could move them. "When you're close to me like this or when you look at me how you're looking at me now, it's like I can't think properly. I had planned all these things I wanted to say to you when I came back, and now I can't remember what any of them were. I haven't been able to stop thinking about you, and I know I've said exactly all the wrong things. I don't understand everything you are, but I *don't* think you're a monster, Jay. That couldn't be further from the truth," she said blushing.

"And I make you *nervous?*" Jay asked almost in disbelief.

"Yes, and now you've also made me pretty paranoid about what my heart rate might be doing."

"I make *you* nervous." Jay laughed in astonishment. "Aarie, I've been trying my hardest to be *normal* so that I don't frighten you, but it has suddenly occurred to me that you are the furthest thing from normal a mortal could get!"

"Is that a good thing?"

"To me, it is." He smiled. "You are simply a mystery to me, a unique and pleasantly baffling mystery, and you have no idea how hard it is for me to be around you. I'm not used to having certain *emotions* around people, and it is hard to conceal them when I have never had to conceal anything before," Jay confessed.

"But you don't have to. I'd like to know what you're thinking. I want to know the real you. Whatever rules you would be breaking, surely it can't be bigger than the ones you just broke, can it?"

"Aarie..." Jay began in an apologetic tone.

"It's alright. I understand. You don't have to reveal any more about yourself if you can't," Aarie said, sounding disappointed even though she had meant her words. Jay had already given up so much information, and she worried at what cost.

"I want you to know the real me too, Aarie, but I'm afraid you won't get to if I tell you everything all at once," he said, moving his hands back to his sides. "This place can do things to the human mind—" Jay paused, studying her expression. He rubbed his eyes as he shook his head briefly. "You're right, I have already broken most of the rules. Besides, I'm convinced that you can't be an ordinary mortal, so certain laws probably don't even apply where you're concerned. You're just simply too... *weird*."

Jay studied her reaction carefully as he brought his arms around her waist. She was slightly caught off guard but smiled as he pulled her closer. Her arms rested against his chest as his heartbeat thumped against her skin. It was as fast as hers. She lost herself in the eyes that explored hers like she was a wonder they couldn't fathom, observing their flickering of different blue hues—from ice blue to dark navy and very briefly, almost black. Leaning her head against Jay's chest, she listened to the comforting rhythm and then wrapped her arms around him too. Never had she felt such a strange mixture of emotions. She wondered how it was possible to feel so instantly complete and as though nothing else mattered in the world except being here. It was like a painful ache had been soothed immediately, though she had not been aware of any pain until now. As they stood holding each other in silence, Aarie wondered if he felt the same strange connection that she did.

She reluctantly broke the silence, feeling the burden of something else that now played on her mind. "I lied to you. Because I *am* scared," Aarie admitted. She felt Jay look down at her, but she didn't move from his chest. "Not for the reasons you think I should be, but because I know the longer I stay here, the harder it will be to accept that one day I may just wake up and never return. If that happens, you will become nothing but a dream to me. I know it, yet I can't save myself from the pain because it's already too late. It seems so cruel, and I cannot work out why fate or the universe or whatever the hell is to blame, why it would do that. Why would it let me come here if I shouldn't be here?"

Jay tightened his arms around her and then leaned his head on hers. "I don't know," he whispered, closing his eyes. "But maybe it won't happen. I don't know all the answers. Like I said before, you're not like the others. There are things you know and have done that no other mortal has ever done before. Maybe that means something.

My father used to tell me old stories when I was a child. Most of our kind think them to be just like your fairytales or mythology, but there are some of my kind who believe they're prophecies—predictions from oracles gifted with the sight of time. Anyway, there was one story that has always stuck in my mind. It spoke of a dreamer from your world who would come here. They would have the power of our kind in their veins but the mortality of their own world. In the story, their arrival represents a time of significant change for us. It is supposed to be a time of peace amongst my world, one in which the damned will be reborn and freed—" Jay broke off abruptly. "Don't ask about that last bit too much. That bit needs to be kept a mystery for now. Basically, the mortal is supposed to signal new beginnings and prosperity, bringing light to all darkness."

"And what else happens in this story?"

Jay cocked his head to the side. "It's quite abstract. I don't think it's supposed to be taken literally. It's more about what that mortal represents, and that is something good."

"Jay, are you trying to tell me that the reason you're telling me stuff now is that you think I'm part of some prophecy?" Aarie tilted her head up to him.

"No. I don't know. Maybe... at least partly." Jay sighed. "If I'm honest, I've probably let my emotions get the better of me and simply said too much. After what you saw, I was afraid you wouldn't trust me anymore or wouldn't want to. Also, I don't want to be a *stranger* to you, but how can I be anything else if I don't tell you anything about myself.

Aarie, if I'm wrong, the dangers are still there, I won't lie about that. I seem to be fighting hard to convince myself that they're not because I don't want to accept that you will just wake up one day and never return. But I really *do* believe there is something about you that makes you unlike any other mortal, and maybe because of that, we have some kind of link too."

"Jay, I'd like to believe it too, I really would, but you're talking about *me* here. Doesn't it sound a little crazy to you?"

"Crazy? You can believe in monsters, dream worlds and giant wolves, but this you can't? How is this any crazier than any of that, Aarie? Think about it. It just doesn't make sense how you found me here. You are on the very edge of this realm. Any further, I would not have been able to keep you safe. Outside this realm, there are others of my kind who would not greet you with any kindness. Do you realise how far we are from the house right now? Oh—sorry, I guess you wouldn't, but it's the equivalent of being halfway around your world, on a remote island where a select few go. Is that not a coincidence to you? It is almost impossible that you were able to find me, yet you did."

"Everything here seems impossible to me," Aarie said. "Maybe I *am* just dreaming you and everything after all." She groaned, utterly confused.

"Don't *say* that," Jay said in a melancholy tone. "I know you don't really believe it. Otherwise, you wouldn't have said what you did before."

"But I thought this was the way you wanted me to think about things?" she asked.

"That was before you came here and we'd had this conversation. It was before I knew you were so addictively... *weird*," he said, giving in to a gentle smile as his eyes flickered between a multitude of different shades. "Besides, I said I am *always* real, and so are the wolves, remember?"

Jay's smile was so infectious, and Aarie couldn't help it spreading to her own lips as he still held her. "Of course. How could I forget. Sorry, Man of Mystery is always real, and so am I."

Jay took a glance around him. "We should go. There could be others nearby. Let's get out of this gloomy place."

"Ready when you are," she replied, taking one last look at the dim, bleak surroundings of the seemingly very mundane human warehouse. She closed her eyes without Jay even asking, then leaned into him. A moment later, she felt a gentle warm breeze on her skin and knew she would be somewhere else as soon as her eyes opened.

She was correct.

Chapter 7
Chiaroscuro

Aarie peered up at Jay as his arms around her slipped away. She whirled around as the sun flickered between the branches above. Pink cherry blossoms fell from the overhanging trees and floated around in the gentle breeze. Aarie and Jay stood in the centre of a wooden bridge, looking directly across a river. A haze of pink and vibrant red lined either side of the water's edge, and she recognised it immediately. To her right, across the bridge, stood the stone cottage with its magnificent glass domes. The spectacular wooden palace that floated amongst the trees rose up behind it. Jay turned, leaning his back against the side of the bridge.

"Aarie, before you go to sleep in your world, I'd like you to picture this place. This is the safest place for you to come. I don't know if it will work, but it's worth a try. No one else comes here but me, not even shadows. It is ro—" He broke off suddenly to reword his sentence. "It is forbidden for any of my kind except my family to come here. Because of that fact, it is also impossible for anyone else to come here without an invitation. It should have been impossible for you to have come here those many years ago. However, as you did, it means you are somehow immune to the family seal that protects this place from being found by others. It also means you should be able to come and go even if I am not here. The door will open for you."

"'The family seal' meaning the marking on the door? Like the one on your wrist?"

"Yes, and the one that protects this whole place."

Aarie bit her lip as she shot a glance towards the cottage. Her brows and forehead creased slightly, imagining opening the door on her own and making herself at home without Jay there.

"What are you thinking?" he asked.

"I can't imagine letting myself into your home if you weren't here. It'd feel strange—like I was trespassing or something."

"You can hardly trespass if I *want* you here and invite you here, though you don't technically need my invitation at all. It's the safest place for you, and it would put my mind at ease. I'd feel a lot better if I didn't have to worry about all the potential dangers you could appear in front of at any time. So, will you try to think about it the next time you sleep?"

"Okay," she said, smiling nervously, "but why do I feel weird? I mean, I know you didn't, but it kinda feels like you just gave me the keys to your place... and in the mortal world that would normally be a big deal. I know it's not the same thing in this case," she said, suddenly looking sheepish.

"I didn't give you anything, Aarie. It was already yours..." he replied, pausing as though pondering over something. "But if it weren't," Jay continued, "I would have given it to you anyway. As for this being a big deal, it is the same in this world too, if not more so. Trust me, *Oneiroi Guardians* do no make such decisions lightly," he whispered.

Aarie gasped, unsure which part of his statement justified her surprise the most. Her eyes searched his as his fixed on hers.

"That's what I am, Aarie," he confirmed. "I don't want to keep that from you anymore. *I can't.* All I ask is—if you don't know what that is and have never come across the word in mortal fiction already—don't look it up. Don't *'Google it', 'Wiki it'* or whatever else you get tempted to do. Don't believe any mortal fiction that mentions us, because that's all it is—fiction. Nonsense and fabrications that have been embellished by human imagination over time. At the very most, they are fragments of partial truths based on vague dreams, so-called ancient 'visions of the future', or encounters with other shadows and dreamwalkers. If you want to know more, *I* will tell you the truth one day. Just trust me on that. I promise if I can tell you everything one day, I will."

Aarie's mouth hung open. "Jay... I don't know what to say?"

His lips twitched at the corners. "I'm sure it probably ends with a question mark."

A deep blue coloured his iris's now, full of emotion and longing. They reflected what she knew was present in the dark brown depths of her own. Her heart skipped, and she wondered if he noticed.

"What's happening between us?" she asked suddenly.

"I don't know, Aarie, but I don't want it to end."

"I don't want it to end either," she quickly replied.

Jay took a deep breath. "Aarie... you need to know that I can't offer you normal," he said, bringing a hand up to touch her cheek.

"Normal can be very overrated," she said, reaching up to place her hand on his. "But I'm willing to settle for extraordinary if you are?"

He laughed gently as he laced his fingers through hers.

"No pressure then," he said, glancing down at their interlocked hands.

Jay began walking them across the bridge towards the cottage. This place was so stunningly beautiful and magical, but Aarie's mind was too occupied with thoughts to appreciate it right now.

Her head sprung up to look up at Jay. "You said 'Google'. Do you have the internet here?"

His brows raised. "Seriously? Do you want to 'Google' me now?"

"Ha-ha," she said sarcastically. "No, I just wondered how you know of stuff like that if you've never been to my world?"

"I never said I hadn't ever been," Jay replied.

"Then... couldn't you visit *me*?"

"No. It would break the most important of all Oneiroi rules. It is forbidden, Aarie, and unsafe from watchful eyes. I can only go when absolutely necessary or in very exceptional cases, such as life or death situations—that kind of thing. The law for such a serious and dangerous crime otherwise, is death. Death to *all* involved, unless there is just cause. The law would not make exceptions for dates, especially ones between Oneiroi Guardians and mortals."

"Oh, so it *is* something that's frowned upon, dating a mortal?" Aarie asked.

"Telling them secrets, letting them into your home, doing *anything* that makes them acknowledge our existence, and yes, definitely dating," Jay confirmed.

"I don't like your laws," Aarie said glumly.

"Yes, well, I've recently begun to dislike them too, if that's any consolation, but they are there to keep both the mortal world and my world safe."

"I don't want you to call me a mortal anymore, even if that is what I am. Every time you say it, I wonder what that makes *you*, and I know if I ask, you won't want to reply or can't reply, but I will still wonder. So, can we just be called people? We are still people, aren't we? I am just a girl from now on, okay?"

"I don't think you could ever be just a girl, Aarie, but yes, we are people, you are right. Sorry—another one of my 'weird habits'.

Anyway, speaking of you, I definitely think it is time to talk more about you. You always seem to find a way to make me spill all my secrets, and I never seem to find out any of yours," said Jay.

"That's because I don't keep any." Aarie smiled, making a halo gesture above her head. "You can ask me whatever you like?"

"Alright. How about, how come you're not wearing your sleep attire?" he said, eyeing her fitted, coal grey skinny jeans and black silk cami top. Her eyes seemed even more mysterious with the smoky shimmer that darkened her lids. "Did you even go to sleep before you came here this time?" he asked.

Aarie nodded. "Yes, I did, just like the last time I found myself here. But this time, I didn't get home until late. Then I had loads of stuff going on. I fell asleep before I had a chance to get changed."

Jay rubbed his face. "Hmm... I think you left out a good story somewhere in there and replaced it with 'stuff'. Who knows, maybe you left out secrets," he teased.

"No, I just didn't think it would be that interesting to you, that's all," Aarie insisted.

"Everything is interesting to me," he replied, but then shook his head. "Hmm okay, no that's not true. There are some mortals—I mean, *people*—that could send the sleeping to sleep, but you, on the other hand, interest me a ridiculous amount."

"Well, if you must know, I went out to a nightclub," Aarie said, watching Jay's response closely.

"By 'nightclub' you mean a place of dancing, possibly drinking and loud music—that kind of thing?"

"Yes."

Jay's mouth quirked up to the side. "So would you say you're slightly intoxicated right now, Miss Stone?"

"No, I would not," Aarie denied. "Well, not enough to affect anything I have said to you tonight, anyway. I really didn't drink much at all," she said, trying to portray the face of pure innocence as she casually examined her nails. Jay laughed, and though Aarie smiled in response, she seemed to drift off into her thoughts for a moment. A glumness seemed to reshape her face as her mind wandered. Jay turned, stopping them from walking on.

"What is it? Did you not have a good night?" Jay asked.

"No, it's not that. I had a great night. At least, most of it was good. It's silly, really. It's just my friends, Adam and Jamie—they had a stupid argument that's all. That's why I was up so late. Well, no, that's not true. It was already late when we got home, but their falling out really bothered me afterwards, so I didn't really think I'd sleep much after that."

"So what did they argue about?"

Aarie shrugged. "You tell me. I really have no clue. Adam's been acting weird lately. They kind of both have. I think Adam might have drunk too much, and he always finds a way to wind up Jamie at the best of times. They've always had stupid little arguments in the past, but nothing like this. They seem like they're always competing for something lately, and some days it's like they just really hate each other. It worries me because I don't want us to drift apart before we've even made it to university. We're all supposed to be becoming housemates soon."

"So did they quarrel early in the night?" Jay asked.

"No, it was just me and Jamie that went out. Adam didn't come. Adam lives next door and just happened to get home when we got back to mine. When he saw Jamie and me together, he just went nuts. I mean, literally— he went crazy. I've never seen him act like that."

"Didn't he want to come out with you both? I thought he's your best friend?"

"Well, it was kind of a spontaneous thing. Jamie just turned up on my doorstep, and we just went out. Jamie told me Adam already had plans."

Jay cocked his head slightly. "So, have I got this right—you didn't invite your best friend, but you and Jamie spent the night dancing together, and Adam didn't seem to like it? Is that the general gist?"

Aarie frowned. "Erm... no, I don't think that's what I said. I never mentioned anything about us dancing together—"

"—But did you?" Jay asked.

"Well—using 'dancing' as a very loose term, seeing as I can't really dance—yes, we did a little. It *was* a club. To be honest, we mainly chatted in one of the quieter areas for most of the night, but anyway, it's not really relevant—Adam simply got angry as soon as Jamie appeared at my doorstep. He never even asked about our night, and he wouldn't have cared about something like that anyway."

"I'm starting to think he might have," Jay said under his breath.

"What?" Aarie asked, failing to hear his last words.

"So, was Jamie staying over at your house too?" Jay asked.

"Yeah."

Jay's forehead creased slightly. "And you don't think maybe Adam got worked up about that?" he asked.

Aarie scrunched up her face. "I... I don't think so. I don't see why he would—"

"—Actually, is that something I should be worried about?" Jay interrupted in a slightly uneasy tone, though he tried to disguise it with a gentle smile.

Aarie blinked. "What? Why?" she asked, confused. Then the penny dropped. "Oh," she said, blushing slightly. "No, Jamie was staying in the spare room—of course, in the spare room. He's just a friend, Jay. It was two in the morning. Adam and Angela—they've all stayed over plenty of times. We have enough spare rooms. It's not a big deal. Trust me, my dad would really make a big deal if he felt there was a reason in *his* house.

But back to Adam, he was simply not making any sense. I think I should pretend it didn't happen and never bring it up with him again. He'll probably be embarrassed about it because he must have just been drunk. I can't see any other reason for why he would act like that. Can you?"

Jay thoughtfully studied Aarie's expression. The sincere puzzlement in her deep brown eyes revealed an innocence and a naivety where her male friends were concerned. His gaze traced over the delicate features of her face and lingered briefly on her lips.

Jay swallowed. "No. I can't see another reason either. You're right— maybe you shouldn't mention it again. It must have been the drink talking," he said weakly. "What other reason would there be to drive a man to act so unlike his usual self," he whispered too quietly to be heard. He squeezed her hand gently, then they continued walking.

They reached the cottage, stopping in front of the entranceway. Jay let their hands fall away from each other's as his eyes flickered to the symbols on the door and then back to Aarie.

"I like the way you look tonight, by the way. Though, I always like the way you look," Jay said suddenly, clearing his throat again.

"Thanks," Aarie whispered, glancing up at him, but Jay already seemed to be examining the door.

"Aarie, I want you to try something. Give me your right hand."

She held her hand out to him, and he placed it on the door over the engraved symbols.

"Now, I want you to imagine that you're opening the door. Will it to open as you would by simply pushing it, except you don't need to push it."

Aarie cleared her mind of all other thoughts and then focused on the door as Jay asked. To her surprise, the door immediately made a clicking sound as though unlocking. Then it opened.

"Was that me?" she gasped.

"Yes. Incredible, isn't it? No mortal—sorry, I mean, no person can do this. Apart from my family, not even other Oneiroi Guardians can do this without an invitation. And though I verbally invited you, an actual process has to be followed out to make it official and physically possible. I guessed you didn't need that."

"Maybe you invited me officially in your dreams? Wouldn't that be weird if you visited me in my world when you went to sleep one day?" Aarie smiled at the thought, as did Jay.

"I wish I could visit you, Aarie. If I could I would," Jay said thoughtfully. "Shall we?" he asked, gesturing to the open doorway.

Aarie stepped in as Jay followed close behind. The scent of oak, firewood and freshly cut flowers filled the air. A vase sat on the table in front of the leather sofas in the centre of the room. Vibrant red and gold lilies reached out from it, complementing the soft furnishings and tapestries around the room. Aarie tried to imagine Jay arranging them there. She wondered if he always had fresh flowers here or if he had placed them there just for her benefit. She hadn't noticed flowers the last time she had come. They were beautiful, and their tantalising fragrance welcomed her as she took in this wondrous place for the second time. So much detail caught her attention once more: the twisting wooden beams, the wild branches that wound up the staircase, and the fireplace that was well-stocked with freshly chopped logs. Beyond the archway that lay under the mezzanine, the light flowed in from the wondrous glass domes she knew were there. She took a deep breath, soaking it all in.

"Your place is definitely the best guy's place I've ever been to," she gasped, thinking out loud and immediately regretted it sounding dumb.

"And do you make a habit of visiting guys' places often?" Jay teased.

"No," she insisted. "I just meant my friends really—Adam and Jamie. I don't actually know many other guys... I guess it's not as good a compliment as I meant it to be when I put it like that. Anyway, their places —or at least their rooms at their parent's places—are quite often a mess. They don't make an effort to make their place look so magical and perfect. But then, I suppose that's teenage boys for you. The only other man I know who does is my dad. I think you and him would get on... if you weren't galavanting around with his daughter, that is."

Jay scoffed. "*Galavanting?* Is *that* what I'm doing?"

"That's just what he'd probably say," she nonchalantly replied. "I like your flowers, by the way. They smell really nice."

"They're Aneiros Dream Lilies."

"Aneiros?"

"Aneiros is what we call this world, Aarie," Jay replied, watching her silently mouth the word to herself. "Anyway, the lilies are meant to be good luck. They represent new beginnings and prosperity for the Oneiroi, amongst other things. Their petals have a natural luminescence that can be seen clearly at night. It's a magnificent spectacle when you see many growing together in the wild. However, they are a lot rarer to find these days, but they can bring light to any darkness."

"Like the mortal in the old story—the prophecy one?"

"Yes, exactly like that. The lilies' fragrance is believed to invoke the mind's most inner creativity, bringing the true beauty of one's soul to the surface."

Aarie scrunched up her face. "Really? That sounds a bit like pot to me." She chuckled. "Not that I would know anything first hand about that, of course."

"Yes, well, it's just a myth, but I like the idea," Jay said.

Aarie raised an eyebrow. "So, if my inner soul surfaces for all to see, what happens if you don't like it? Maybe I have a dark, dark soul." She smirked.

Amusement twitched on his lips. "I suppose I could just have the locks changed."

Aarie's bottom lip slumped into a sulky pout as she thought about his reply. He stepped forward, immediately wrapping his arms around her waist to gently pull her to him; he couldn't stick by his comment for a moment longer even though she knew it was a joke.

"Though no one's soul could be darker than mine, so I guess it's something we could work on. And the darkest shade of black is my favourite colour anyway." He smiled.

Her brows knitted together as she tilted her head up to his. "Really?"

"No," he laughed. "I don't really have a favourite colour. What's the point? What good is one without another?"

"That's what I've always thought too," she agreed. "What good is blue without green or black without white? What good is light without darkness? Alone, neither have much meaning—they would create no image or beauty. They would simply exist," she said thoughtfully.

"But together, the possibilities are as infinite as the wildest imagination," Jay added, searching her face as he held her.

"Exactly," she whispered, getting lost in his eyes as she gently bit her lip. "You look good in black, though." She smiled, running her hand down the collar of his shirt.

"So do you," he replied as his irises took a turn for a much darker shade. Jay blinked, releasing Aarie from his arms as he turned away. "So, can I interest you in some more galavanting, or are you feeling tired from all of that dancing, partying, boozing and pot smoking?"

"I do not booze or smoke pot," she objected, though her smile never wavered. "But yes, 'galavanting' sounds good to me."

"I'm glad you say that, because I prepared a surprise for you."

"You did?

"Well, it's nothing really. By the way, can you swim?"

"Yep. Are we going swimming?"

"No, but I was thinking back to when I asked you to think up a place in your mind—when I asked you to test how inventive you could be."

"And?"

"Well, I never did really get to see your version of this place. So, I thought you could describe it to me. I know it was similar to how it is now, but you said that you daydreamed about it and made up extra details. I'd like to see them."

"Alright. I'm not entirely sure how, but I'm sure you'll show me. I have to warn you—I *was* five at the time. It'll probably seem stupid to you and even to me now."

"On the contrary, children can have some of the most interesting and creative minds when it comes to imagination. There's nothing stupid about it."

"So what has this to do with swimming?"

"Well, just a precaution really, you'll see. Come, let's go out this way." Jay gestured to follow as he led her through the archway. Aarie followed as he turned left, under the glass domes and passed the grand tree trunks beneath them. They came to another smaller room. The same twisting wooden beams lined the sides of the walls. A large chandelier hung in the centre of the ceiling, made from strange horns and sharp antlers that were not from any animals she'd ever seen before. They twisted into spikes and spirals, appearing transparent at the tips, with tints of gold. A large ornately woven rug laid on the wooden floor beneath the chandelier. It reminded her of expensive Persian rugs she had seen in stately homes, except this one had wolves and strange figures weaved into it with a surrounding border of symbols. A long L shaped leather sofa sat to her left with a couple of armchairs and a small table opposite. Brilliant streaks of white light cast across the rug from the large glass French doors that stood across the room. They overlooked a small lake that led to a winding river through the woods in the distance.

Aarie strode across the room towards the glass doors where Jay stood looking out. A small wooden rowing boat caught her attention as it bobbed up and down the water's edge, tugging at the mooring ropes that held it in place. As it gently rocked back and forth into view, she tried to read the inscribed golden letters that decorated the panel on the side. A flicker of some kind of recognition widened her eyes as she read. Jay followed her gaze to where it had landed.

Morpheus

He took a deep breath as his own eyes narrowed at the word. The boat had been here for many years, and it was so familiar to him like everything else here. It was the reason Jay had forgotten about the name even being there. Words hovered on his parted lips, but before he could say any of them, Aarie spoke first.

"God of Dreams," Aarie whispered.

Jay cleared his throat as his head tilted down to the floor. "Aarie, remember what I said about mortal fiction. It is *just* fiction."

"I know," she replied, turning to him. Apprehension had crept onto his face, making his features tense and unsure. She reached for his hand, and he gently took hers in his. "It's so beautiful out there, Jay. Are we getting in the boat?"

"Yes. That is if you want to?"

"I'd love that."

"Do you have another question for me, Aarie?" Jay asked.

Her eyes searched the deep blue hues of his and traced the tension in his jawline. Muscles twitched at the side of his face as he swallowed.

"No. Except... I can't row. So, I'm hoping you're going to do the rowing, right?"

Jay's face immediately softened as a gentle smile re-emerged. "Yes. I can do that. It wouldn't be very gentlemanly of me otherwise."

He gently pushed the glass doors open, leading the way with his hand in hers. The warmth of the sun rested on Aarie's bare shoulders as she stepped out onto the stone path, towards the boat. Birdsong and tropical calls echoed through the surrounding treetops as the steady sound of flowing water drifted in the warm breeze. The scent of lilies, blossom and fresh pinewood filled her lungs as she took a deep breath, then looked at Jay. He offered his other hand out to her as he stood on the swaying boat. Taking it, Aarie steadied herself as she stepped down into a space in front of Jay. She settled down onto the wooden seat behind her legs as Jay finished untying the mooring ropes. After quickly dropping the ropes behind him, he sat down and then took hold of wooden oars by his sides. Leaning back slightly, he pulled his arms back with smooth rhythmic strokes, moving the boat forward and away from the path's edge.

Chapter 8
Awakening

Aarie's head turned to watch the cottage slowly drift into the distance. She leaned back, briefly closing her eyes as the sun's rays warmed her face. It felt so good on her skin as she took a moment to listen to the soothing sounds around her. There was the gentle rocking of the boat, the splash of the oars as they dipped into the water, the creak of the wood as Jay rowed, and the echoes of exotic wonders that breathed life into the surrounding woodland. The light flickered against the back of her lids at that moment, and she opened them again. The sun peeped in and out from behind the treetop branches as Aarie and Jay moved further into the woods. The lake narrowed as it flowed gently into the winding river. The trees now stood tall at both sides of the boat.

Aarie glanced at the face that she knew had never left hers.

"Do you do this a lot?" Aarie asked.

Jay's brows went up. "What, rowing you mean?"

"Rowing, preparing flowers, being very gentlemanly, wowing girls with your amazing everything—is it something you do a lot?"

"Are you asking me—an Oneiroi Guardian, I might add—if I'm... a bit of a *ladies* man?" Jay asked, reaching a pitch higher than his usual tone.

"In my defence, I don't know what *is* normal or customary for Oneiroi Guardians in these situations. For all I know, maybe they're the biggest *players* in the galaxy?" she said.

A fit of laughter burst out from Jay. The boat rocked and came to a slow as he released the oars, cupping his face to contain himself. Aarie's mouth hung open, and her brows raised in response to his reaction. He caught his breath for a moment as a few more eruptions of laughter escaped his lips.

"Sorry, is that really the vibe you're getting from me?" he chuckled.

Aarie's face beamed. She was unable to control the enormous smile spreading across her face as she'd studied the pure amusement on his.

"*No*. Not at all, in fact, but it's just that you're so *good* at it. It makes me wonder."

His eyebrows shot up again. "I am? Really?"

"Yes," she answered, trying for a more serious tone.

Humour slowly faded from his face, though he still held his smile. "What part was good? The bit where I nearly scared you half to death; or when you called me a demon, and I worried you'd never trust me again; or how I constantly worry that it's just a matter of time before I do something that makes you not want to be here with me?" he asked.

"The part where you made me want to always be here with you," she replied.

Jay blinked, but his gaze refused to leave hers. "I don't *ever* do this Aarie. I've never brought anyone here but you.

Oneiroi Guardians, especially ones such as my family, have certain responsibilities and duties. Sometimes those duties make it easier to choose a lonelier path, at least for a long while, anyway. I'm not saying that all Oneiroi Guardians live a reclusive life of misery and celibacy—we don't. We are all still men like any mortal, but there has never been anyone else that I've wanted to bring *here*... or to 'wow', as you put it. This place is special to me. Does that answer your question?"

"Yes, and I didn't mean it to come out the way I said it. Or to pry," Aarie said blushing.

"I know." Jay smiled. "And you didn't. Anyway, it is time for the proper wow factor part. You were going to show me how inventive your mind can be, remember? Though, I know you've already demonstrated an amusingly creative imagination regarding me," he said with a laugh.

"And how am I supposed to share my five-year-old self's vision of this place with you, exactly? Do I just describe it to you?" Aarie asked.

"Yes, you could. Or..."

"Or what?"

"Your mind must be linked to this world in a similar way to the shadows. It is why you come here when you fall asleep, as *they* do. The only difference is, you know you're here, and it makes you real. Anyway, my point is, I can look into a shadow's mind's eye. It's how Guardians decipher what type of dream is required to keep them safe and draw them away from this place. Sometimes it can even be used to inspire a bit of creativity of their own, back in their world. But I am sidetracking now. What I'm trying to say is that, because you have that same link the shadows have, I could pluck the images straight from your mind if you let me. You are real, so you have to open your mind up to me voluntarily. You have to willingly want to give up those images to me and bring them forward in your mind."

"But you can't get images from me now, without me letting you see them?" Aarie's brows anxiously creased.

"No."

"But would you have looked into my mind if I *had* been a shadow?"

"Definitely. You're far too interesting to pass that up."

"Jay, if I ever do come here as a shadow, I want you to promise me that you'll never delve into my mind. EVER! I don't want you digging around my private thoughts and memories. There are some things that a girl wants to keep to herself," Aarie said, slightly startled by the thought.

"Ooh, intriguing. Like what?" Jay said with a mischievous smirk.

"Private stuff. Private thoughts," she said, fidgeting with her hands.

"Private thoughts about what? Or should I say... whom?" he teased.

Aarie blushed. "Are you going to promise me or what?" she said, finding it hard to look him in the eye.

Jay sighed. "Alright, if I must. I promise I won't. I'm pretty sure you'll never come here as a shadow now anyway."

"Good," she said satisfied. "So, if I bring images up in my mind now, how do I know you'll see them... and just the images I want you to see?"

"Just think back to how you opened the door. Think about how you just concentrated and willed it to happen. All you have to do is think of the images you want me to see, and then will them to be transferred to my mind. You have to concentrate hard on them. The clearer you see them in your mind, the easier it is for me to pick them up. It's as simple as that. I will only be able to see what you want me to see, I promise."

"Right. I guess, okay then," Aarie said, closing her eyes.

She focused hard, drawing up the old memories of this place from her dream as a child. It was very much as it stood now, though some of the details had been lost over time. Now, she concentrated on the extra things she had invented in various childish daydreams and games she had played. Over and over, she ran the images through her mind, offering them up on an imaginary plate for Jay to take. She opened her eyes as Jay did now too. A smile had taken deep root on his face.

"Did it work?" she asked.

"You tell me. Give me a moment," Jay replied.

He picked up the oars and started rowing again. The boat began to float forward once more. Aarie watched as the oars rose and dipped back into the water, again and again. A sudden gold shimmer flickered in the water, and she leaned over the side to get a closer look, rocking the boat slightly. A shadow passed beneath them, leaving a shimmering trail of gold and silk behind. Aarie gasped as her gaze followed it up ahead. In an instant, a hazy blur of gold, aqua and coral leapt out of the water, sending a delicate spray over Aarie and Jay. A beautiful being—half woman, half sea creature—gracefully looped in the air. Her long golden locks and silky drapes clung over her feminine curves as she arched into a dive. Aarie's jaw dropped as a shimmering tail of gold scales disappeared back into the water. She stared at the circular ripples where the creature had vanished, watching as they smoothed back to the river's natural waves.

Something else flickered in the corner of Aarie's eye, and a high-pitched hum now filled her ears. Her brown curls brushed against her face, and she soon became aware of something caught in her hair. She wondered if it was a bug and immediately ran a hand through her locks to find out. She came up with nothing. A toy-like laugh came from her shoulder, startling her slightly. Aarie turned her head immediately as a tiny winged figure floated around her. Her eyes widened in awe as the delicate creature smiled at her, giggling with a childish playfulness. She reached out to touch it, feeling the flutter of its wings against her skin as it gently floated away. She shot a glance back to Jay, who was leaning back, studying her with a curious smile. Before Aarie could say anything to him, something else caught her attention, and she turned to the side.

A black panther now weaved through the trees along the bank, following alongside the boat. Its thick silky coat glistened, highlighting the frame and power of this predatory creature. A deep roar rumbled in its throat, but Aarie felt no danger from it. Its emerald eyes caught the light as it bounced playfully towards the water's edge and then stopped to take a drink. It stretched with a great yawn, displaying an impressive set of jaws before curling up as the boat carried on drifting past. Branches broke in the treetops above, causing Aarie's head to flick up to follow the sound. A shadow swooped by and disappeared into the trees. As the boat wound around the corner of the river, she could just make out one of the tallest platforms of the wooden treetop village. It was hidden behind these trees in the distance. She gasped again as a winged humanoid figure landed on the platform and stood seemingly looking in her direction. Her eyes narrowed, straining to focus on it, but before she could, it jumped off the edge to glide through the sky, then disappeared behind the trees once more. A flock of birds flew past briskly, with golden and neon pink feathers. Their long feathered tails trailed behind, sprinkling shimmering glitter.

The boat moved on again, and Aarie focused now on the bank in the distance. A mass of white fur was lined up amongst the trees. A row of golden eyes shone amongst the brilliant white coats, and they all looked at her now, though, once again, no danger seemed present, nor did Aarie fear them.

Her eyes flicked to Jay. "I used to dream of wolves all the time, even before I came here. I dreamt that they were always watching me. They featured in random dreams. Most of the time, they were just in the background. I always thought they were beautiful. Though sometimes, when I had nightmares, they came out of the background and chased me home." She shuddered briefly, thinking back to the woods and the hill she had tumbled down before Jay had helped her.

Aarie's gaze flickered back to the trees, but the wolves had vanished already. Random blocks of colour littered the floor now, making up hundreds of giant pixelated toadstools and tropical flowers. More and more sprouted from the ground. She looked closer, realising that the pixelated shapes were made of tiny plastic building blocks. Little round stumps protruded from their tops, each with four-letter words etched on them.

Aarie laughed at the memory as she turned back again to Jay.

"Jay, this is amazing. You actually took this from my mind. It's just as I imagined back then. You caught it all."

"Not all of it. There was something else you mentioned the last time you were here," Jay replied.

Before Aarie could ask, a distance thud echoed through the trees. Her eyes flitted from side to side, trying to decide the direction of the sound's origin. She tilted her head, unsure what she was hearing. As it got louder,

Aarie finally recognised the train-like rhythm as a set of galloping hooves beyond the trees. A whining neigh cut through the air. Aarie's head shot up to her left as a white horse raised up on its hind legs. It kicked its front legs forward just before settling back down on all four legs, giving its mane a shake. As its face came into clear view, a large horn glimmered upon its forehead, spiralling to a sharp point. Aarie's eyes widened as her heart fluttered in her chest.

"I don't believe it. Jay, it's incredible. How are you doing all of this?" She abruptly stood up. "Can we get off the boat and follow him?" she asked, nudging her head in the creature's direction.

"Sure," he replied.

Jay steered the boat to the bank, then stepped out, pulling it onto the embankment. Aarie jumped out, throwing a smile at him as she ran past, following the sound of trotting hooves. Jay finished knotting the ropes of the boat around a tree as he heard her faint laugh in the distance. Aarie had disappeared out of sight now, but Jay followed, scanning through the trees for her. It wasn't long before he caught up with her. She was stood still with her back to him.

"Shhh," she whispered to him as he approached. "He's just behind those bushes. Do you see?" she pointed.

"Yes."

Jay could make out the flash of white between the branches and leaves up ahead, but something seemed different about the creature he had conjured up. It was bigger somehow as he got brief glimpses of it through the branches. A horse-like whine came from behind the bushes. Then a swooshing sound ripped through the air. A strange flapping noise immediately replaced it, and Jay's eyes narrowed on an opening in the bushes. The creature had seemed a lot bigger because it now had wings— incredibly large ones that he had not given it.

A moment later, the horse-like creature reared back and then began charging forward. It jumped over the hedge with heavy hooves pounding towards them. Two glorious white wings spread out over its back. A rainbow of coloured feathers lined the underneath of them as they flapped, and the creature continued to speed their way.

Jay urgently pushed Aarie out of its path, knocking her flat to the floor, then covering over her with his body. The creature leapt up, soaring over them as it took to flight. They both glanced up, watching with awe as it disappeared over the treetops.

Jay looked anxiously back to Aarie. "Are you okay?"

"Yeah. How did you know?"

"Know what, Aarie?"

"Exactly how the unicorn in my vision looked? I never showed you an image or described him to you."

"I didn't, Aarie," Jay said, seemingly bewildered as his eyes searched the sky. "But if I didn't give the creature wings, who did?" he whispered so quietly that Aarie did not hear.

"Are *you* okay?" Aarie asked, taking in Jay's baffled expression. She glanced at the fallen leaves and earth around them. "Was this part of the illusion?" she asked. "Because it definitely added drama," she said, struggling to move as Jay's full body weight still pinned her to the ground.

"Sorry, did I hurt you?" he replied, shifting his weight to his elbows.

"No, I'm fine."

"Aarie, the unicorn—its wings... I didn't—" He paused, unsure what to tell her.

Aarie's chocolate brown eyes bore into Jay's as her heart raced against his chest. The sweet floral scent of her perfume lingered in the air as a gentle breeze brushed past her skin. Jay's gaze shifted, following the delicate curve of her nose, her fine brows and soft ridges of her cheekbones. His eyes moved along the smooth skin of her jawline and stopped at her lips. Aarie noticed how his irises began to darken from a warm blue to a deep navy and continued to darken. He looked away quickly, moving his body from hers as he sat up abruptly.

Aarie sat up too. "You don't need to turn away from me, Jay. Whatever it is you try to hide from me, I don't care. I'm not afraid of you."

"I know," he whispered without turning back. "But I'm afraid of myself. Sometimes when I'm around you, I don't feel in control of certain *emotions*, not quite yet. I just need time, Aarie. It's harder than I thought it would be and I don't know why. I'm not human, but you *are*, and because of that fact, I need to know for sure what this means. I know that doesn't make sense to you right now, and I'm sorry I can't explain it to you, but I know *this* would definitely frighten you."

"No, I don't think it would. Whatever it is, you can tell me, Jay," she said, reaching out to touch his arm.

Jay turned to her, still with his eyes closed. "Yes, Aarie, this *would*," he insisted firmly. Her hand came up to touch his cheek. His lids slowly opened, and Aarie already knew the warm blue would have returned. His brows creased, but his face softened.

"Aarie, I would never hurt you, you know that, don't you?"

"I know," she reassured him. "Thank you for bringing me here, Jay. Did my old vision of this place, amuse you?"

"Very much," he replied, gently smiling once again. Rays of sunlight escaped through the trees, warming the skin of Aarie's face and making the edges of her dark brown curls, golden.

Jay took a deep breath. "You're so beautiful," he whispered unexpectedly, tucking a loose curl of hair to the side of her face.

Aarie blinked slowly, unsure how to respond to the compliment. She could see his eyes darkening once more and didn't want him to turn away again.

"I wish I came here in the day and not when I sleep. Then I'd have longer with you," she said glumly. Her lids felt heavier now as they took another long slow blink.

"Are you tired?" he asked.

"I want to say no..."

"I'm sorry, I forget sometimes," Jay quickly said. "Where are my manners? I haven't even offered you something to eat or drink since you've been here. We should go back to the house."

"Okay," she agreed, unable to deny that she was a little thirsty. She had been awake for a long while, but she had no idea what time it was. "Jay? How come it's still light here? The sun is still shining, but normally it's dark here by now," she asked, suddenly curious.

"It *is* dark," he replied nonchalantly.

Aarie's forehead creased as she eyed the golden rays of sunlight streaming through the trees. At that moment, the sky turned an inky black before her eyes, and she blinked in disbelief.

"I just wanted you to see this place how you pictured it in your dream," Jay explained casually, as though explaining the reason for flicking on a light switch.

Everything he did amazed Aarie, and she sat momentarily wondering if she would ever get used to witnessing things she couldn't explain. Jay almost seemed as though he'd given up trying to hide his unfathomable abilities from her now, though there were still many mysteries she knew would remain just that.

"Should we head back to the boat?" she asked.

"No," he replied, helping her up as she brushed off loose leaves from her clothes. "I know a quicker way. It will save time."

Aarie scanned the trees. "A shortcut? Which w—"

Before she could finish, Jay scooped her up in his arms, lifting her off the ground.

"This way." He beamed as he carried her. Aarie gasped as their surroundings began to blur. She closed her eyes, unsure if Jay had just forgotten to ask her to. A moment later, she felt a sudden change in temperature, and the scent of oak and lilies filled the air again.

"We're here, Aarie. You can open your eyes. Make yourself at home," he said, gently putting her down.

"Thanks," she replied as her eyes widened, taking in the cottage living room from the doorway. She was almost sure she would never get used to this form of transportation.

Aarie eased off her muddy boots, setting them down next to the door. The torches on the walls were ablaze with golden flames that licked the glass cylinders that contained them. A warm glow filled the room, bouncing off the wooden beams and making it homely. She wandered over to the sofa and then sat in front of the log fire. As soon as she sat, flames arose from the fireplace, adding a finishing touch to the cosy atmosphere of the room.

The glow of the fire reflected off her face, warming the skin of her cheeks to a rosy pink.

"Is this all real or in my head—the fire and the warmth?" she asked, staring into the flames.

"Yes, it's real," Jay replied, wandering into the kitchen area on the left. "Most things are. Even things that may seem unlikely to be. The things from your imagination before, they weren't—they were just illusions mixed with some real elements for effect, but the daylight was all real even if it was not natural."

"So how do you to that? How do you make flames appear?"

"I can control certain natural elements—manipulate them. Fire, water, light, weather, plants and certain materials."

"And here—how did we get here, from the woods?"

"That's a little more complicated, and I'm not sure it's safe to explain that one to you yet. Is that okay?" Jay asked.

She nodded. "I guess so. To be honest, I'm still pondering over the stuff you have told me, and getting used to you actually telling me things, full stop."

Jay paused, looking back at her. "Aarie, you must tell me if you ever feel different somehow whenever you visit here, especially after I reveal something new to you. If you ever get confused, disorientated or if you just feel stranger than usual when you're here, you must let me know, okay? It's important. Will you do that for me?"

"I will, I promise," she agreed.

"Are you hungry? Thirsty?" he asked.

"I could drink something, maybe. What do you have?"

"What would you like?"

Aarie pictured a hot chocolate in her mind and placed it on a mental post-it note for Jay.

"One hot chocolate coming up." He laughed.

"Really? You have that here?"

"Well, something near enough to that, if that's okay?"

"Hmm, who am I to be fussy?" She smirked, wiggling her feet in front of the fire.

A few moments later, Jay sauntered over to Aarie, holding a metallic-looking glass cup. A whirl of fluffy cream sprinkled with tiny golden petals floated above the chocolate coloured liquid. Aarie's eyes widened as the delicious chocolatey aroma wafted under her nose.

"Wow, this looks amazing." She grinned as he gently placed the cup down on the coffee table in front of her.

Stepping around the table, Jay settled down beside her on the sofa. He quickly sucked a smudge of golden powder and chocolate off his fingers. "The gold flowers are edible. They taste a little like what you call marshmallow, I guess," Jay revealed.

Aarie lifted the drink to her mouth. "Mmm, this is divine," she said as she took a sip, then licked the cream from her lips. "This is pure heaven, Jay. Seriously, are you not having one?" She dived in for a giant gulp, letting it quench her thirst and soothe her dry throat.

"Nah, I'm good. I'm glad you like it, though."

She eyed his relaxed position on the sofa—one arm strewn on the armrest to his right and the other on his lap. He leaned in the corner at an angle with his feet propped up on the edge of the coffee table. She nursed the warm cup in her hands as she swallowed another mouthful of chocolatey goodness.

"This feels slightly surreal, being here with you like this," Aarie whispered.

"Doing something slightly normal, you mean?"

"Uh-huh." She nodded. "I like it."

"Me too."

"Though, I'm not sure I can picture you drinking of one of these here by yourself," she said, waving her cup at him.

Jay turned. "Why? I have it in my kitchen, don't I?"

"Well, it's just—"

"Just what?" he said, raising an eyebrow. "An Oneiroi Guardian can like chocolate too, can't he? We are people just like you, remember?" Jay teased.

She laughed. "I know... but I still can't picture it."

Jay's mouth quirked up at the corners as he reached a hand out for her cup. "Okay, pass it here," he demanded.

She pushed it to him, and he took a long sip. With an exaggerating sigh of satisfaction, he wiped his mouth.

"Can you picture it now? Was that convincing enough?"

"Not really, but I believe you... if you say so." She grinned, taking the cup back as he leaned back in his corner.

"Well, I also drink alcoholic substances, if that comes as a bit of shock to you too? Though, I'm not sure mortals—I mean *people*—can quite handle the Oneiroi alcohol I have in my cupboard. Therefore, I won't offer that up to you tonight, but maybe I should cook you dinner next time and bring out a milder bottle of Oneiroi wine. That is customary for people of your world, is it not?"

"Is it for you?"

"Yes, but also, I'd just like to."

"Then, that'd be great," she said before finishing the last sip of her drink.

Aarie pushed her cup onto the coffee table. She curled her legs up and leaned her head against the sofa back. Her eyes fought sleep as she gazed up at Jay. "There's something I wanted to try. Since you can't come to visit me, maybe I bring little snippets of my world to you. So, like for example, you can't meet my friends, but I could show you a memory of them, if you want, that is?"

"I'd like that," he replied.

"Alright, well here goes."

Aarie closed her eyes, focusing her mind back to a time with all of her friends at her house. She made sure to focus on enough detail to give Jay a good overview of them, trying her best to select a moment that showed them in their best light. Her eyes opened again, and she waited for a response from Jay. His brows twitched as his eyes flickered underneath his closed lids. They blinked open and went to hers immediately.

"So who's who?" Jay asked. "You mention no names in your memory. Though, I think I can guess who Angela is."

"Adam is the dark-haired one, and Jamie's the cocky one. So, you saw them?"

"Yes. This was just after the accident, wasn't it?"

Aarie nodded. "Yes."

"It's good to know you had people around you after you left here. I'm glad you have friends who care about you. You all seem so *close*."

"We are," said Aarie.

Jay stared briefly into the distance as though replaying the memory again. Aarie wondered which part he was thinking about as she watched his face; it was as though he was analysing details thoroughly.

"What is it?" she asked in his silence.

"Nothing," he replied, sounding glum. "I just wish I could see you for longer. They're so lucky that they get to be with you all the time."

Aarie shuffled across the sofa. She curled up against Jay's chest as his arm lifted up and wrapped around her. Her eyes were painfully heavy now, so she closed them to stop the aching. She listened to the sound of Jay's heart as the gentle rise and fall of his chest soothed her.

"In the arms of Morpheus." She breathed a content sigh. Jay's muscles tensed slightly, but she ignored it, nuzzling closer to him. "That means to sleep, back at home. And though I can't fight sleep for much longer, I've never felt this awake or this alive before, Jay. I just wanted you to know that."

Jay's head tilted down to her in his arms. Aarie had known the name on the boat was his, and she had not cared. Her breathing now slowed, and her arm around him slackened.

"Goodnight, Aarie," he whispered as her body began to disappear before him. He clung to her, pulling her closer to him, but within seconds she was gone.

Chapter 9
Here To Dream

Several weeks had passed, and the summer had begun to draw to a close. Aarie and her friends had moved to their shared house in Leeds to start their new university lives. Life was exciting in so many ways. These days, she found it a rare thing not to be smiling to herself or humming along to a tune that had somehow found its way into her head. As it had turned out, Aarie and her friends made great housemates, and it made it handier that they were always nearby. There were so many good times lately: fun days, lazy days, drunken student days, busy days, and even on occasion, long, studious days. On quieter days, she always found herself daydreaming about another world and sketching it in private; her secret place, she called it. After new revelations between her and Jay, and the memorable boat trip, Aarie found herself now returning to her special world every second or third night of every week. Though it seemed no more than an incredibly realistic dream most of the time, it was one she had become very much attached to. She found herself thinking of the cottage in her mind before she closed her eyes on most nights, hoping the dreams would come again. She had also convinced herself that it made the dream far better if she weren't wandering around barefooted and in her pyjamas. As it happened, the only way she seemed able to change that was to go to sleep in whatever she wanted to be wearing in the dream. Her new bizarre habits of getting ready for bed had gotten some strange looks from her new housemates. Angela, in particular, had teased her about sneaking out in the middle of the night for *secret rendezvous*.

Soon after closing her eyes and drifting to sleep, Aarie would often find herself wandering under the cherry blossoms and maples at the edge of a familiar river. She had become accustomed to claiming a spot on the grass beneath them since the night of the boat trip. While glancing across to the cottage every now and then, she would wait for Jay. He had invited her to his home to come and go as she pleased, but something was charming about *him* letting her in. Also, she liked watching him in the distance, drawing nearer as he strolled to meet her by the riverside. It gave her time to take him in fully. She did so now as he strode across the grass towards her. His black shirt fluttered against his chest in the gentle breeze, briefly outlining his strong frame beneath the fabric. He was always so immaculately dressed in fitted, dark trousers and a tailored jacket. The style, colour and cut of his clothes varied slightly from day to day; today, his jacket seemed longer and more robust than usual. As he drew closer, it seemed—from a mortal point of view—to have an almost military look to it,

Aarie thought. His trousers were ribbed and slightly padded at the knees. Straps and buckles hung from the sides of his waistline, and his tall, heavy boots rode up to his lower shins. Aarie had seen him in similar attire before, but today they looked more hardwearing and purposeful somehow. It gave Jay a strangely new presence. She knew there must be a specific reason he wore the clothes he did. *Then again, maybe he just knew he looked good in them,* she thought. There was always a timeless and sophisticated air about him, mixed with a mysterious edge that spoke of danger. However, the kindness present within his eyes and smile formed the perfect package that made Aarie contently sigh as he stood in front of her now.

"Miss Stone, though I love watching you in this picturesque setting, I wish you would feel that you can just let yourself in. My home is your home."

"I do. I just like it out here, and the weather's nice. But I am sure you have something to do with that, don't you?"

"The weather can sometimes be mood-dependent around here if I don't think about it too much."

"You must always be in a good mood then."

"Whenever you are here, yes."

Aarie got to her feet, shaking loose pink blossoms from the white slip dress she wore. As soon as she straightened up, Jay caught her by surprise as his hands took firm hold of her hips, moving her body gently closer to his. Her arms immediately wrapped around the back of his neck as his settled around her waistline. Jay's black clothes contrasted with her white dress as they curved together like a yin-yang symbol. Their faces stopped just short of each other's as they smiled. Aarie took note of his darkening blue eyes, anxiously remembering back to one time she had come here a few weeks ago.

Jay had cooked for her, and they had drunk Oneiroi wine. It had started like any proper date. A normal, could-pass-as-human date. Though, when it came to Jay, the standard of what counted as 'normal' was very high. Jay's 'cooking' could more accurately be defined as 'a gourmet chef's culinary masterpiece', in Aarie's opinion. He had been right about humans and Oneiroi wine; it had definitely begun to go to her head slightly faster than she had thought at the time. However, she was sure Jay had been slightly merrier than usual too. If anything, maybe it had been the reason for his 'slip up in caution', as he had put it. That night, they had come close to their first kiss. In a heated embrace, their lips had almost touched, but Jay's eyes had changed dramatically in colour. They had nearly turned black before he had abruptly turned away from her. He had suddenly become panicked by something and had refused to explain to Aarie why. Nor would he come as close to her again for most of that evening. All he would say was the same thing he had told her back in the woods when he had closed his eyes to her then. He had been more cautious with her since that night, always keeping a little more distance between them... until now.

She could feel the warmth of his body against hers, and a glimmer of hope sparked within her. But as his eyes closed slowly, hiding a glint of black behind his lids, Aarie's hope faded.

Jay's head tilted up suddenly, and his lips brushed against Aarie's forehead as he placed a lingering kiss on her skin. His face moved to the side of hers as he whispered in her ear. "I missed you."

The softness of Jay's breath briefly caressed the skin of her neck, but after one lingering moment, his face moved back to hers. Their foreheads pressed together lightly as his eyelids opened once again. Sapphire blue.

"I missed you too," she said.

"It's so good to see you, Aarie." He smiled "Are you okay?"

"Yes. More than okay, actually."

"There's something I wanted to show you, back at the cottage," Jay said, taking hold of her hand.

"Okay," Aarie replied, letting him lead her back to the cottage as her mind wandered, rendering her in a brief daze. Before she knew it, they were stepping through the cottage doorway, and her curiosity sparked up at once.

"Alright, so what do you want to show me?"

"Up here," Jay replied, already heading up to one of the doors at the top of the winding, wooden stairway. She had been in many of the cottage rooms, but never any within the mezzanine area. Aarie didn't know what they were used for as she'd never been in the house without Jay, nor had she ever seen him go in one until today. It was almost like she had forgotten they were there altogether.

Jay opened the door to reveal a spacious bedroom with a tall window that overlooked the gardens to the left side of the cottage. Aarie wandered past him as her eyes scanned over the elegant furnishings of this luxurious room. It reminded Aarie of five-star hotels she'd only seen in films. A mixture of timeless, exquisite detail and modern simplicity. A large wardrobe stood in the corner beside a chest of drawers. A dresser stood across the room. In the nearest corner sat a king-size bed.

Jay followed Aarie's gaze. "I thought, since you seem to fall asleep before you leave this world, you should probably have somewhere you can sleep more comfortably than on my sofa. There's plenty of wardrobe space in this room too, so you could bring some of your belongings here when you come. That way you don't have to worry about wandering around barefoot or in your pyjamas. It might save your housemates thinking you're sneaking out on at night, anyway," he said. "And maybe you would feel more at home when I'm not about if you had your own space and some of your own things. You can do it up how you like and make it feel more like your home. Though, I don't mind if you want to make any part of the house feel more like your home. I just know that if I'd said it just like that, you wouldn't, so I thought I'd start small. Oh, and it's got its own ensuite, as you would probably call it," Jay said, gesturing to another doorway in the furthest left corner. "What do you think?"

Aarie's mouth dropped open as she turned back to him. "Jay, I don't know what to say..."

"Is the room okay? There's another five to choose from if you don't like it, though this is one of the bigger ones."

"I love it. It's great! But are you sure about this? Are you sure you don't mind?"

"Of course I don't mind. I don't even use half of these rooms."

Her brows lifted subtly. "But you *do* have a room? A bedroom, I mean —where you sleep?" she asked, eyeing the bed again as she continued. "I've never seen you sleep before, and I've suddenly realised, I don't even know if you do or not."

"Yes, of course I sleep. Admittedly, I don't always need to sleep, but I do. My room is next door. Speaking of which, I need to go change, shower, get out of these dirty clothes. Are you okay here for a bit? The view from the window is a good one."

"Dirty clothes? What are you talking about, they look immaculate?" Aarie said perplexed as she eyed his pristine outfit.

Jay waved a hand over himself. A wave rippled over him, peeling back the illusion that had hidden the damage of his shredded garments; they were covered in mud and grime in reality.

"Hmm, well, I could hardly show up to meet you like this, could I?" He grinned, gesturing to his filthy clothes. "I wouldn't have wanted to alarm you. This, by the way, was just a result of immature Oneiroi fun. It seems I have yet to 'grow up'—don't ask." Jay laughed. "I'll be right back in five minutes, is that alright?"

Her eyebrows raised in mystified amusement. "Sure, I'll be fine exploring my new space," she replied, reluctantly letting her curiosity slide about his reply. She stepped towards the window to take in the view. Jay was right; it was magnificent. The treehouse palace wrapped around the cottage a little way off in the distance. It was like a magical floating illusion within the trees. Aarie glanced down below at the beautiful floral displays of vibrant reds and golds. They decorated the garden around the cottage, gently spilling over a low stone wall.

"If your room is next door, is your view like this one?" Aarie asked. There was no reply, and Aarie turned to realise Jay had already left the room. She moved to the doorway of the ensuite and flicked a switch that lit up the room. Her eyes opened wide. She scanned the polished granite tops and complete white marble bathroom suite. An elaborate self-standing marble bath stood proudly in the centre of the dark slate floor and a large shower in the far right corner. Everything about this room and the whole of Jay's place, in fact, displayed an eye for beauty and quality. It also subtly hinted at affluence that Jay never boasted about nor could Aarie imagine him regarding it as something worthy of mentioning. Aarie wondered if this was something distinctively Oneiroi or something that only resided with Jay and his family. Even without this in mind, Aarie could not believe Jay had practically suggested she move in with him. Her visits were often short, and she wondered if this had made it easier for Jay to make his decision. Whatever his reason, she knew this was a big deal. *Undoubtedly, this was another big step for them as a... what were they? Were they officially a couple?* Aarie thought. She didn't know if Oneiroi counted themselves as boyfriend and girlfriend. Jay had mentioned dates before, but she wondered if dating qualified them for the other titles.

But then, they hadn't even kissed yet, not properly, she thought to herself glumly.

Aarie wandered out of the room to the next door, eager to clarify things with Jay. If she was going to bring more of her belongings here, surely she should know where she stood with him. Maybe she would bring it up subtly or perhaps she would just outright ask him.

"Jay?" she said, pushing the slightly ajar door fully open.

Jay looked up nonchalantly as he was in the middle of picking a towel out from a cupboard in the wall. His torn dirty shirt and jacket had been cast aside on a chair, and Aarie flushed slightly at seeing the bare skin of his upper body. She had never seen him without a shirt, and somehow felt she had intruded. She glanced away briefly, blushing as she cleared her throat.

"Um, sorry. I should have knocked," Aarie mumbled.

"It's okay," Jay said, unfazed or seemingly unaware of Aarie's unease. "What's up?"

"Oh, erm, nothing. I just—"

She realised she was in his room and had never seen it before. Her eyes scanned around with uncontrollable curiosity. It was immaculate just like the other room, except he used this one all the time. Clearly, he was not a teenage boy; Adam's and Jamie's room was never this neat. It just looked like royalty lived here. Maybe it was an Oneiroi thing, or maybe it was just a Jay thing. This room had the same luxurious quality and layout as the other room, though the bed sheets and throw were white and grey. A more masculine tone asserted itself in this room.

Jay's gaze followed hers as his eyebrows raised. "Did you just come to check if I was lying about the fact I sleep, or was there something on your mind?" he asked as an amused grin took form.

"Sorry, I just came to chat really, nothing important. I forgot you were, you know, about to have a shower. I just wanted to say, the room's amazing and thanks, but I'll come back in a bit," Aarie said, hovering in the doorway as her eyes slowly wandered back to his bare skin. At that moment, her gaze fell on two red slash marks on his side. Parts of it looked like fresh wounds, though parts seemed to have faded where it had healed. She puzzled at what could have caused them.

"Jay, you're hurt. What happened to you?" she panicked, instinctively moving towards him. She reached out to him to get a closer look.

"It's nothing. Honestly, don't worry about this," he said, registering her concern. "It'll be healed up and completely gone by the time I'm out of the shower."

"Really? But how? What happened?"

"My brother and I had a little catch-up, that's all."

"What? He attacked you?" Aarie worried.

"Not exactly, not like *that*, anyway. We attacked each other. We were training—fighting. Fun stuff, really."

"Fun? Does it normally look this dangerous when you catch-up?" she asked, delicately examining his skin with her fingertips.

Jay laughed. "*This* is not dangerous. Trust me. You should see him."

Aarie's anxious eyes flitted back to his. "And this is the fighting that you're good at?"

"Yes, despite appearances. Unfortunately, so is my brother," he replied, taking her hands gently in his. "Look, don't worry about this. You'll see. This will be gone soon. Okay?"

"Okay."

"And you don't have to go. I'll only be five minutes, make yourself comfortable if you like," Jay said.

Wandering barefoot to the ensuite, he closed the door. Aarie sat down on the edge of his bed, pondering about his wounds as a sudden patter of rushing water faintly echoed through the door. Alone in the room, Aarie felt the inevitable wave of tiredness that always hit her. Today it hit her much sooner than usual. She was exhausted but had tried so hard not to show it or admit it to Jay. It felt like they never had enough time as it was. The last thing she wanted to do was waste it. Her days had been spent writing essays and delivering coursework assignments; the past couple of nights in her world had been late ones. Aarie decided that it wouldn't hurt to rest her eyes, even if only for five minutes while Jay was busy. She slid her sandals off. The bed was so soft as she laid upon it and curled her feet up. Gently resting her head on Jay's pillow, she took in the faint scent of him as her arm wrapped around it. Then she closed her eyes.

Five minutes later, Jay strolled back in, dressed now in a pair of loose grey trousers. His wound on his side had entirely healed as he said it would, and no traces of it remained. He glanced across to a very much asleep Aarie, curled up on his bed. A smile inched its way onto his face as he took in the content and peaceful expression on her face. She was asleep, but she had not left this world yet. He wondered if it was just a matter of time before she disappeared if he did not wake her. But he couldn't do it. She must have been exhausted to have fallen asleep so soon. He came to sit on the bed beside her, leaning his back against the other pillow. As he did, she stirred and then her body flinched suddenly. Her eyes shot open.

"Sorry, I didn't mean to wake you. Did I startle you?" Jay worried, sitting up slightly.

"Erm, no," she blinked, rubbing her eyes. "I did that weird thing where you feel like you're falling, then you wake up."

"Oh."

"Sorry, I didn't mean to fall asleep. At least I'm still here. I just closed my eyes for a second. Hope you don't mind me taking over your bed?"

"Of course I don't mind, you're welcome to sleep wherever you want as long as you're comfortable."

Aarie's gaze fell on Jay's side, acknowledging with relief the unmarked skin where his wound had been.

"All gone, see? Nothing to worry about," he said.

She couldn't help but scan over him once more in disbelief, but immediately noticed a silver chain hanging from his neck. A rectangular pendant hung from it. Engraved on it was a short inscription next to a looped symbol that had a subtle violet shimmer to it.

"What do the inscription and symbol on your neck chain mean?" she asked.

"The inscription means to keep someone safe. The symbol is what we call The Seal of Semper Sodales. It is the mark that represents the bond of two special Oneiroi souls. My mother gave it to my father. He asked me to look after it for him until he returns."

"Your mother—I've never heard you talk of her before?"

"She died a while ago, Aarie."

"Oh. Jay, I'm sorry."

"It's okay."

"And your father, when did he leave?"

"He's been away for a while, but he will return one day. When my mother died, it almost drove him to madness with grief. You see, she was his Semper Sodale."

"Is that like a wife?"

"She was his wife, yes, but there's more too it. Semper Sodales are something else. The only other word for it that you may understand is soul mates."

"What, like *real* soul mates? They exist here?"

"As near to that as could be, yes. By 'soul' I mean someone's immaterial essence—the thing that makes us who we are beyond our physical selves. When two matching Oneiroi souls meet, a bond can be formed that goes beyond love. Their Oneiroi bond is so strong and so real, it creates a visible violet symbol on their skin—like this one," he said, touching the pendant lightly. "The Seal of Semper Sodales is thought to be the greatest blessing amongst the Oneiroi, but also, some would say a great curse. For, once a bond has formed, each Guardian may be much stronger, but they are also each other's weakness. If a Guardian's Semper Sodale dies, it quite often means the destruction of the other in some way. For a while, I thought this would be the fate of my father, but a long time has passed now, and I know he is strong. He will return."

"And do all Oneiroi Guardians find their Semper Sodales?"

"No, not at all. Most don't, in fact. They are extremely rare. So rare that some Oneiroi don't even believe they exist. They lead perfectly happy lives with partners as in your world. Whereas some would never take a permanent Oneiroi partner for fear that they may one day have to turn their back on them if they ever were to meet their Semper Sodale.

"Would they really do that?"

"It has happened in the past. The connection between Semper Sodales is very strong, and it is a highly regarded Oneiroi phenomenon.

"And what do *you* believe?" Aarie asked, as her forehead creased ever so slightly.

"I know they exist, Aarie. My mother and father were Semper Sodales."

There was a brief silence as Aarie glanced down. She knew she would never be Oneiroi and therefore, that meant she would never be able to offer Jay a relationship as special as the one he knew his parents had once had. Jay examined her expression as though trying to read it.

"What was it that you really came to ask me before, when you came into my room?" he said suddenly.

"Um... nothing," she lied. She couldn't ask *that* now. Not after what he had just told her.

Jay took a long exhale of breath as he watched her face. Aarie could not hide her emotions or the fact that her mind wandered now. Her brows furrowed. The corners of her mouth uncomfortably twitched as they fought to stay pulled up straight.

"Aarie, I may know they exist, but I also know how destructive they can be... and also how very very rare—as in, one in a billion. Maybe I shouldn't have told you about them, but you asked, and I don't ever want to lie to you. I want you to know that I don't care that your human, but I *do* care about *you*. I've worried these past weeks that you may think I didn't due to me being slightly distant and cautious around you. I don't want things to be like that forever. Trust me, I am working on it. I want to be with you, Aarie. Believe me, what's between us is rarer than any Semper Sodales. If there's something I've learned in the past few weeks, it's that ordinary Oneiroi rules don't seem to apply to you and me. And I would never... I shouldn't have mentioned them," he whispered, lowering his head. "It was too soon. I should've realised it would upset you. I'm sorry. I just didn't think. It's just that it's not important to me, Aarie. Maybe there was a time when I thought it was, once. It's not important to me now, but you *are*."

"Jay—" Aarie glanced up at him, but no more words would come out. He had answered her unasked question. He cared about her, and that's all that mattered to her. She wanted to tell him how she felt, and she wondered why it was so hard to say it. Then again, no words could reflect the happiness she felt inside at this moment. Rubbing her eyes, she tried to ease the ache. They fought so hard to stay open so she could have more time with Jay. Now was not a good time to leave.

"Aarie, I don't mind if you need to sleep," Jay said. "You're human, and you can't stay awake for full days at a time. I understand. We can do something together the next time you come. Let's talk again properly then. There *will* be a next time. Besides, if it makes you feel better, I could actually sleep right now too. Training can be very draining."

"Really?"

"Really."

"Okay," Aarie resigned, glancing at the door and thinking of the room Jay had shown her next door. "I do really need to sleep. Do you want me to leave so you can sleep too?"

"No," he whispered as his eyes searched hers. "Do you want to leave?"

"No." She turned her sleepy gaze back up to him, cradling her head with one hand on the pillow.

He pulled his knees towards his body, pushing the bedsheets from under him, then gently slid beneath them. "Lift up then," he said, tugging gently at the covers at her side.

Aarie did the same, sliding beneath the sheets and then pulling them over her shoulders. They laid mirroring each other from their separate pillows; one hand cradled the side of their head, and the other hid under the sheets as they faced one another in silence. Jay slowly reached out a hand for hers under the covers, and she took hold of it.

"Goodnight Aarie," Jay whispered as his gaze lingered for a few more moments. Then he closed his eyes. A subtle smile crept in from the corners of his mouth. She examined the shape of his face as he laid there. The hazy daylight from the window still flooded in, though she knew it would probably be dark soon. Her heavy eyes gave in, and her lids finally closed too. Her smile completed the mirrored reflection once more.

"Goodnight, Jay."

******

Aarie woke. The bed was warm and comfy, and she pulled at her duvet, tightening it around herself. But it wasn't *her* duvet, and they were *sheets*. She peered through her lashes as the morning sun filtered through the trees outside and through the window. A shimmering light danced on the sleeping face beside her.

Her lids flew open as she realised where she was. She scanned over Jay's closed eyelids, his slightly ruffled hair, the relaxed peacefulness on his face, the delicate natural pout of his lower lip, and his slow, gentle breathing as he slept. His right arm was spread over his pillow, revealing the bare skin of his muscular shoulders and top of his back. Aarie could make out the tips of what looked like two black swirls below his shoulder blades. Another marking, she guessed. Its colouring was similar to his mark on his wrist, but she was sure this one was part of a larger pattern that hid beneath the sheets.

Jay stirred.

She drew in a long breath in anticipation. His eyes flickered, slowly transforming into a blink. Then open. They immediately went to hers with the same surprise.

"You're here," Jay whispered in amazement.

"Uh-huh." Aarie nodded. "It would appear there's no getting rid of me. I'm like Goldilocks, but maybe more... Brownilocks."

"Hmm, well, I definitely don't have any porridge here, and there are no bears in these woods... unless you want there to be?"

Jay gave out a warm chuckle as he slid towards her. Wrapping his left arm around her beneath the covers, he pulled her closer to him. Aarie gasped at the warmth of his skin as it brushed against hers. The fabric of her loose slip dress had rucked up slightly while she had slept, and she was immediately aware of his body being so close to hers. Her head tilted up to meet his gaze as her heart beat wildly in her chest.

Jay leaned his head back slightly, taking her in. "Sorry, am I making you uncomfortable?" he asked.

"No. Not at all," Aarie said with a reassuring smile. "I'm just not used to *this*," she whispered, stroking her fingertips against his bare chest. "And being here, like *this* with you."

"Oh—but you're okay?"

"Yep. I'm definitely not complaining."

His eyes were beginning to darken once again, and she watched, unwilling to move. This time he did not turn away or close his eyes. The navy hues of his irises flickered to black but then back to blue once again. They continued to switch between the darker navy hues, gradually lightening until they fixed on the natural warm sapphire tone that Aarie knew well.

"You're getting better at that, aren't you? Controlling whatever it is you need to control," she asked.

"Yes. Being around you more seems to help."

"So, do you think—whatever it is that you *think* makes you a danger to me—that maybe, it's not so much of a danger anymore?"

"Soon it won't be, I'm sure of it."

After one more lingering glance, Aarie leaned her head on Jay's chest, and his arms tightened around her. "Good," she sighed. "Because, it's driving me crazy being around you—being so close to you, but not being at the same time."

"Me too," he replied.

A metallic clanging echoed from outside, breaking them from their embrace. Jay quickly pulled away, leaping out of bed to move to the window. He peered out of the glass and glanced down below. His eyes narrowed at a figure clashing two long metal objects together in front of the cottage.

"Aarie, stay here," Jay cautioned, as he turned back to face her. "Whatever you do, don't leave the room or come too close to the window. I have to go. I'll be back soon, but it's not safe for you to be seen."

"What is it? What's out there?"

"Not what—who. It's my brother, Phelan. We were supposed to be training again today, but he's early. Remember what I told you the first night you came here—he can't see you here, Aarie. It's not safe for you to be seen by other Oneiroi Guardians, not even him. Trust me."

"But he's your brother. Can't you just explain things to him? Surely he'll understand if you tell him everything?"

"No, Aarie, he won't."

"How do you know if you don't try?"

Jay stepped towards the bed. He touched her face gently as she sat up. "I know because he's just like me before I met *you*. He *won't* understand, Aarie. I wish it were that simple. I can't risk that he might hurt you. He doesn't know you're really here, and he may think you're still part shadow or worse. I have to go. I'll be back soon, alright?"

What did he mean by 'worse'? Aarie thought, but now was not the time to ask. She reluctantly nodded.

Aarie slumped back onto the bed, propping herself up against the pillows as Jay swiftly shifted across the room. Throwing one last anxious and apologetic glance at her, he left. She pulled the covers over herself. There was nothing else she could do except lie here wondering what would be said and what would happen if Jay's brother found her here. Aarie closed her eyes and tried to imagine what Jay's brother would look like in her mind's eye. She wondered if he had come from the big manor house she had once seen. *What would that house even look like inside? Would it be anything like this one?* Her thoughts drifted.

Images now flickered in her mind: *the steps, the pillars surrounding the house entrance, and the ivory archway above the door. Only the moonlight lit the night's sky as it moved in and out of the clouds. A warm golden glow flooded the doorway from inside. Music, chatter and laughter greeted her ears as she drifted through a montage of blurry scenes—a grand hallway, corridors and rooms. A ballroom appeared with faceless figures and their meaningless spoken words. They placed demonic masks in front of their faces, filling in their missing features. The warmth of the atmosphere slowly began to dissolve as a string quartet began to play a new tune. Jay held out his hand to her. The music itself was pleasant, but Aarie's heart somehow could not help sinking. A crushing pain stuck deep in her chest. Confusion and despair followed, gripping hold of her tightly. Then more pain. Excruciating pain. Fear now engulfed her, but still, she dreamed on.*

Chapter 10
Dreams Of Flying

The sun warmed the fresh morning air, and the smell of fresh pine and jasmine lingered as Jay stepped out from the cottage doorway. He squinted through his lashes as the sun's low rays glared at him from the sky. A tall figure stood ahead of him just beyond the cottage, and Jay briskly walked to him. It was Phelan, his older brother. His profile matched Jay's with subtle differences: tall with the same broad shoulders, though Phelan looked ever so slightly stockier as he wielded two large swords around in a casual manner. He wore a smoky black shirt, jacket and trousers, similar to those Jay often wore. He had the same dark ash brown hair, though Phelan's was longer with slight curls that flicked out in small wisps at the sides and behind his ears.

Up close, the Onuris family resemblance was very apparent in their facial features, especially their sapphire blue eyes. Phelan's features seemed just that little sharper and harsher somehow. Phelan's eyes were narrower; his brows were slightly thicker but more raised in the centre; the arch of his nose was more defined; the angle of his jaw was more pointed; and unlike Jay, who was always clean-shaven, Phelan had a rugged layer of stubble that coated his jawline and upper lip.

The corner of Phelan's mouth quirked up into a smirk as he greeted his half-dressed younger brother. "Did I wake you, little brother? That is a first. Did I do more damage than you made out yesterday? I am a little early. Do you need more recovery time?"

"No. How about you—are you sure *you* don't?" Jay grinned back, but as quick as it had appeared, his grin faded. "Phelan, I'm not training today. There's something I need to do. Let's do this some other time, okay?"

Phelan raised an eyebrow. "Another first—are you sick?" he joked, but his smile also seemed to fade in the humourless air that graced Jay's presence today.

"No. I'm fine." Jay rubbed his temples for a second and then looked back at Phelan, who appeared to be scrutinising his every movement.

"What is it, Jay, is something wrong?"

"Why does something have to be wrong?" he huffed a humourless laugh. "In all honesty, I simply just don't want to train today. Is that allowed? Does that bode well in the Oneiroi Guardian rule book?"

"Jay, of course that's fine, but *you* do not seem fine. What is it that's troubling you?"

Jay pictured Aarie's face as he left her in the room. He wondered why he couldn't just tell his brother. *Why were they so bound by the law that his own flesh and blood could not be trusted with something this important to him?* He wanted to tell Phelan. He didn't want to hide Aarie away like she was something he should be ashamed of. Over his shoulder, Jay glanced briefly at the window of his bedroom and then back. His fingers rubbed his temples again as he let out a groan. "Nothing. Please, just let it go, Phelan. I just don't feel like it today, okay? We'll do it tomorrow or whatever day you want, but just not today."

Phelan's eyes flitted to the cottage behind Jay, looking over the windows and then back to his brother. "Do you have company? Is that it?"

"What?" Jay panicked. "No, that's not it. I just want to be left alone. Why can't I have that without being quizzed?"

"Because you *should* have company, Jay. It's not good for you to be cooped up here alone all the time. You've not seemed yourself for a while, especially these past few weeks. Even yesterday, you seemed slightly distant. Why don't you come back to the old house with me, instead of being here on your own with old memories? It's not good for you."

"There are memories there too, and there's nothing wrong with old memories, Phelan."

A glint of light reflected off the chain around Jay's neck, and it caught Phelan's attention.

"You know, he doesn't expect you to wear that all the time. You can just keep it safe," Phelan said, pointing to the pendant.

"This is the safest place for it."

"Look, why don't we go back to the city for a while. We've got some free time these next few days. Why don't we have some fun? Guardians do get to have a break sometimes, you know? We don't have to train—we can socialise. Mingle. Maybe it'll be good to be around others for a while. After all, how else do you ever hope to find your Semper Sodale?" Phelan grinned, trying to lift Jay's spirit with a common joke they'd shared many times in the past.

Jay's jaw tightened, and his lips pursed into a fine line. "I don't ever *want* a Semper Sodale, Phelan," he said firmly and with such resolution that it shocked himself as well as his brother.

"Jay? What's brought this on? Why can't you just tell me what is troubling you?"

"Because I can't!" Jay blurted out. "Because no matter what I say to you from now on, you're going to want to try to figure what the problem is that's causing me to act the way I am. You're gonna preach from the Oneiroi handbook and tell me how I should be acting, accordingly to the rules of Aneiros. Then you're gonna try to fix me and erase the problem, but I'm afraid it won't work, Brother. Moreover, I won't let you because I don't want to be fixed!" Jay warned, bitterly.

Phelan stood dumbfounded. "Jay? What's gotten into you? Have you been drinking? What are you talking about?"

Jay blinked. Too many words had spilt from his mouth, and he knew he was coming undone. He turned away but instantly paused as a hand gently rested on his shoulder.

"Jay, wait. I'm sorry if you thought—I'm not even sure *what* you thought I was trying to say to you. I'm worried about you, that's all. I've never seen you like this before. I had thought you were not yourself simply because it's this time of the year and you would be thinking of Mother, but it's more than that, isn't it?"

"Yes," Jay admitted as he turned back around. He pressed the sides of his own face with both hands, then raked them hastily through his hair.

"And you can't tell me?" Phelan glumly asked.

Jay creased his forehead, and for a brief moment, he knew pure agony masked his face. "Phelan, I don't even think I could tell *her*—our own mother. Do you know what it feels like to not have someone to turn to? I will have eternity, but I will have nobody. Because I know I will *want* nobody ever except—"

"Except what, Jay? You're making no sense."

"Nothing," Jay snapped abruptly. "Please, Phelan. Just leave me in peace, just this once. Maybe you are right. I've been drinking. I'm upset, and I'm not myself. Look, just give me until tomorrow. I just need more time alone. I'll be fine. We can talk again then."

Phelan fixed his bewildered gaze on his brother. He was oblivious to where Jay's outburst had come from but did not want to cause him further distress. Reluctantly, he nodded.

"Alright, Jay. I'll go for now, but I'm your brother—please, don't forget that."

Phelan pressed on Jay's shoulder again lightly, patting it as he turned. He stepped away and disappeared in an instant. Jay let out a long, drawn-out breath, hunching over with his hands on his knees. He turned, looking up to the bedroom window again, then hurried back to the cottage.

Stepping back into the bedroom, Jay found Aarie tossing and turning in troubled sleep. Moisture trickled from her forehead as she murmured something incoherent. Her eyelids flickered as her brows creased, and Jay was sure tears laced her eyelashes. He hurried to sit by Aarie's side and then gently reached to wake her. Before he could, she thrashed around, then abruptly woke up with a scream. Aarie quickly pushed herself away from Jay, startled by his proximity. She backed up against the headboard as tears rolled down her face. Jay's heart sank to see her like this, and what was worse, for a brief second, he thought she looked afraid of him.

"What is it, Aarie? What happened? Was it a dream?"

Her breathing was staggered, and she sighed with great relief. "It wasn't real. It was just a dream," Aarie murmured, wiping her eyes hastily.

Jay propped himself up beside her. He slid his arm around her shoulder, pulling her into him.

"Are you okay?"

"Jay, how can I have dreams here? Where did I go?"

"It wasn't real, Aarie. You didn't go anywhere. There is only here or your world."

"But I won't be able to tell my dreams apart. When I wake in my world, this world *still* feels like just a dream. Do you know that? This still feels like a dream. If I ever leave here for good, that's what I'll believe. Do you understand? You won't be real to me. Now, when I dream here, I can't tell if I am really here or somewhere else. I can't let these places get mixed up, especially if bad things happen in them. I don't want to be here to dream, Jay. Not like I just did," she said in a wavering voice.

"What did you see? What happened in your dream?"

Aarie shook her head against his shoulder. "I don't want to talk about it. I don't want to think about it anymore because the more it's in my head, the more it might get mixed up with here and now. I don't want to wake up in my world and think it was part of *this* reality."

"But was it something to do with me or the wolves? What was it?"

"I can't tell you, Jay. I'm really sorry. I just can't. I need time to sort my head out. I'm confused. I'm so confused," Aarie whispered into his shoulder as she held him tight and closed her eyes. Jay helplessly watched as she began to disappear while in his arms.

"No. Not now," he whispered desperately, but she was already gone.

******

Aarie woke with a start on her bed. Her dream was so lucid in her mind as she wiped away the moisture from her cheeks. There was also something else. *A dream within a dream?* she wondered. But she did not want to think about that part. Somehow, that part had not seemed as real as the rest, and she was glad; it threatened to taint the rest because it was more a nightmare than a dream. Jay had come back to find her having this nightmare. She couldn't bring herself to tell him what it had been about and had tried to push out the images from her mind.

When I wake in my world, this world still feels like just a dream. Do you know that? she remembered saying to him, and she knew at that moment, she had truly believed she was there. Now, back at home, she wished so hard that she could still have that belief. Her dreams had become such an essential part of her life and, as insane as it made her feel, it was as though she was somehow letting herself down. She could still feel the warmth of Jay's arms around her, imagine his scent, his touch, and his infectious smile.

"What are you grinning about?" said a voice from the slightly ajar door. It was Angela's.

Aarie looked up. "Hey. What are you doing home? I thought you were away this weekend, like everyone else?" she said as Angela's face poked around her door.

Aarie was still getting used to having her friends so close by since they had all moved into a shared house together, but it felt nice having company whenever she needed it.

"Hmm, Lori cancelled," Angela replied. "She's not well. Anyway, I thought *you* were supposed to be home all weekend too, but *somebody* wasn't home last night and snuck in very early this morning without me seeing, didn't they?" Angela grinned as her brows raised and eyes lit up.

"What? But I was here last night," Aarie said puzzled.

"Oh, come on. I know you didn't sleep here last night, Aariella. You left your door open, and I needed to borrow your straighteners. The cat's out of the bag, so you may as well share. So, who is he? Tell me all about it," she beamed, rubbing her hands together as she scurried into the room. She plonked herself down on the bed beside Aarie, whose mouth dropped open to form a perfect o.

Aarie wondered for a moment if she might have truly been there with Jay. She *was* wearing the same clothes, and she must have left her sandals at Jay's because they were nowhere to be seen in her room. The thought filled Aarie with excitement, and she could no longer keep herself from wanting to tell someone all about him. Dream or not, he always felt very real to her.

"Okay, he's called Jay," Aarie blurted out, pulling her knees up as she backed up against the headboard.

"Ha, I knew it! You dark horse," Angela squealed with excitement. She leaned back against the pillow beside her to get comfy. "So, what's he like? Is he a student?"

"No. He's a lot older."

"How much older? Not like *old* old, right?" Angela said, pulling a face.

"No, I just mean he's not a teenage boy. He's not an old man either!"

"But he's sexy, right?"

Aarie looked thoughtful for a moment before answering. "'Sexy' wouldn't be my choice of word but—"

"What? Are you telling me he's not hot?"

"No, that's not what I'm saying at all! He's incredibly hot if you must know. In fact, he's ridiculously, unbelievably hot. Sometimes I find myself just staring at him, literally getting lost in his incredible blue eyes... I can't believe I just said that out loud. God, that sounded so cheesy. It's just that I've been dying to tell someone for weeks, but 'sexy' isn't the word to describe him, Angela, even though he is. He's just more than that to me. He's—"

Angela held up a hand. "Hang on a minute—weeks? You mean this has been going on for weeks, and you haven't told me?"

"Well, it's complicated."

"Complicated? Is he married or something?

"No! Angela, what do you think I am?"

"Well, you *have* been sneaking out a lot."

"I have not been sneaking out."

"If you say so." Angela shrugged. "Anyway, so what does he look like apart from the '*incredible blue eyes*'?" Angela said, mimicking Aarie's voice as she fluttered her eyelashes.

"Tall, dark brown hair, a really kind smile—"

"—And his body? What's that like?"

"Well... that's pretty hot too if you must know, but—"

"Ah-ha! So you have *seen* his body then?" Angela smirked wickedly.

"Well, we all have one, so I guess it's hard not to notice."

"You know what I mean. You *did* stay over, after all."

"Ange it wasn't like that. He's a perfect gentleman. Besides, I said it was complicated. And anyway, we simply fell asleep. It was late, that's all. Nothing happened—not what you think, anyway."

"So why all the grinning?"

Aarie rested her chin on her knees as she glanced up to Angela. "Because he really makes me happy, that's why. I've never felt like this before, Angela, but I'm worried it could all just disappear just like that," she said, clicking a finger for effect.

"Because it's complicated?" Angela asked.

"Yes. That's the real reason I haven't told you or anyone, and I'd prefer it if you didn't say anything to the others. Not yet, anyway."

"Do we get to meet him?"

"I don't know if that's possible right now, but one day, I hope."

"Hmm, he's a criminal on the run, isn't he?" Angela joked.

"That would probably be simpler."

"But he's good to you, right?"

"Always."

"Well, that's good. That's the main thing," Angela said as she rubbed her hands together once again. "Oooh, this is so exciting. I hope we get to meet him. I'm a little disappointed that you're not really telling me the juiciest parts of this whirlwind romance, but I've got time to work on you now I know." She pulled a sulky face. "Unfortunately, I've got to head out now, which is really annoying 'cos I want to know everything. I'm running late, and I said I'd pick up some cough medicine at the shop for Lori. I won't be long though, so don't you dare go anywhere. Do you want anything getting?"

"No, I'm good thanks."

"Alright, well I'm not done with you yet. I'll be back in an hour or so. Then you can tell me more." Angela grinned as she shuffled off the bed, then made her way to the door.

"Okay, I'll see you in a bit."

"Yeah, laters."

Angela disappeared around the door, and Aarie sat for one more moment, gathering her thoughts. It felt unbelievably good for her to have told someone about Jay. It made him more than just a dream. For this moment, he was real to her. *Angela had surely proven that, hadn't she? What else could explain it? Sleepwalking?* She thought back to when she had woken up—if that had even been what she had done. The thought of leaving Jay at *that* particular moment made her anxious. They could have spent the day together for the first time. She had been so confused and upset from her 'dream within a dream', or more accurately, her nightmare. However, she felt that things were so much clearer now. She had realised the nightmare had been the only part that wasn't real. The part where she had woken up with Jay (and all the other times she had spent with him) had all really happened.

Aarie wanted desperately to get back to tell him but wondered how. She had always gone to sleep thinking of the cottage before waking up there, and so, that's what she would do again.

But first...

She got up from the bed, then scurried across the room to the door. Pushing it closed, she turned the key that was in the keyhole before springing back to her bed. Settling back down, she closed her eyes and relaxed. She was glad that sleep seemed to find her easily.

A moment later, Aarie stood in front of the cottage. Without even thinking about it this time, she hurried to the door. It opened instantly at her touch, and she bounded into the living room. There was something strangely unfamiliar about the place, but she just couldn't figure out what it was. Nothing seemed altered, yet it somehow felt strange to be here now. She wondered if it was because Jay had not let her in. *No, that wasn't it.* However, she knew that he wasn't here. She could somehow sense it as well as another thing; there was someone else here. Her eyes scanned the room —past the kitchen, past the fireplace and sofas, through the archway, and...

A sudden creak startled her, and her eyes darted to the top of the stairs to the mezzanine. Her gaze stopped at the doorway next to Jay's room. A figure stood there now. A tall man with dark ash-brown hair. At first glance, her mind told her it was Jay. The blue eyes that met hers were like his. But they were not his. Her jaw dropped, and she gasped. Aarie knew who he was but wondered what she was supposed to do and what would happen now. He was Jay's brother, but Jay's warning voice echoed in her mind. *I can't risk that he might hurt you. He doesn't know you're really here, and he may think you're still part shadow or worse.*

Phelan's brows knitted tightly together, then his eye's turned black. A snarl rumbled deep in his throat as he grimaced, baring sharp white fangs. Aarie knew she was no longer welcome here. Her heart throbbed in her chest as her whole body began to tremble. She backed up slowly, but before she could get far, a cloud of black smoke whirled around the room. Jay's brother now stood scowling beside her. A scream shrilled deep from within her throat as she dashed for the door. Hopeless panic swept over her as she knew he would be able to reach her; he could move as Jay could move. He could be anywhere he wanted to be if he let his mind take him there. If she was going to escape, she needed to be able to do the same. Another cloud of smoke surrounded her, whirling round and round. Something wrapped around her ribcage, and she cried out in pain. At that moment, images came flooding into her mind of faraway places—the clifftop that Jay had first brought her to and its view of the canyons and desert lands in the very far distance. Aarie thought of them harder and wished Jay was with her to take her there now, but he wasn't. As the grip on her squeezed the breath from her lungs, she wondered if she would ever see him again. Within a sudden blur of motion, she found herself transported.

Ripples of dry, red sand and dust surrounded her, flecked with patches of dead grass. It was a vast barren wasteland. Whirling around, she assessed the area. To both her relief and dismay, she was alone. She had never stepped foot here before but had seen it in the distance when looking down from the clifftop. The sun beat down on the ground and was harsh against her skin. Her shoulders could already feel the sting of its heat as she breathed in the dusty, dry air and remoistened her lips.

Movement on the blurry horizon caught her attention. A cloud of dust travelled along the ground, and Aarie's eyes narrowed. She could make out several shapes that sped along, kicking up the dry dirt in their path. One shape seemed to take the lead. Aarie eyes widened as she took in the four great paws, a coat of grey-white fur, open jaws, and golden eyes that rapidly moved towards her. The wolves were here.

Aarie's heart picked up its pace once again as she frantically looked around her. There would be nowhere for her to hide this time. No direction would offer refuge. There were no trees, just acres and acres of sand, dirt and dead grass. *Would Jay come for her? Hadn't he always arrived in time?* But this time felt different. She knew she had to buy herself time at least. After all, that's all she could do.

Aarie swiftly turned and began to run. The dust flicked up as her bare feet pounded the ground. She was glad it was soft with no stones or sharp branches to slow her as she propelled herself faster. Of all the times in her life Aarie had ever run anywhere, this was the fastest she had ever travelled. She knew it because she was sure her life depended on it. Her head flitted back and forth to look over her shoulder as the wolves drew closer. Small beads of sweat trickled down her neck and back, soaking into her damp white dress. Her breathing became heavy as she gasped to the rhythm of her strides. A coppery taste filled her dry mouth, and she swallowed as she surged on. She was tiring. Panic filled her mind as fatigue spread through her limbs.

I will never see Jay again, and he will never know why I didn't come back, she thought to herself. Aarie's could hear the snarls up close now, and could almost imagine the wolves breathing down the back of her neck. She cried out involuntarily as she frantically glanced over her shoulder once more. Her feet suddenly lost footing as she stumbled on something large beneath the sand. Her hands flew out immediately to break her fall, but before they could, her head struck something that sent a shock of pain vibrating through her skull. Then she dropped to the ground.

Cliffside view

A winged shadow cast onto the red dusty cliff edge, gliding and then coming to a halt. A whirlpool of grit swirled around and resettled again just before the soft thud of footsteps touched the ground. A lone figure now stood amongst the rocks of the cliff edge. His attention was instantly grabbed by something happening in the distance below. Amongst the dusty wasteland, a large moving dust cloud trailed along the ground.

Jay's eyes narrowed, focusing on it. A group of wolves were the cause, and he wondered at the reason for their numbers. Horror immediately struck. Jay's eyes focused again, this time looking ahead of the wolves to a lone runner with long dark hair. It was *her*. It was Aarie. She was back, and so soon after she had left.

Loose stones flew forward from underneath Jay's feet, tumbling off the cliff as he moved to the edge. His knees bent. Abruptly, he lunged forward as though to fling himself off the cliff and towards to scene below.

******

Dazed, Aarie reached a hand to the side of her head. Her hair was wet and sticky, and her fingers were coated red. A dizziness came over her as her face laid on the baking ground. Her half-closed eyes gazed through her lashes. She blinked as sand flicked towards her, and a horde of heavy paws moved close by. Her vision began to fade, then her lids slowly closed.

Before Aarie could slip into unconsciousness, she found herself being scooped up into the air. Strong arms held her tight, and her body immediately relaxed, strangely comforted by their skin against hers. She felt a strange sense of being lifted higher and higher as the unsettling cacophony of howls slowly faded into the distance. Her head fell back slightly, letting her get a quick glimpse of the clear blue sky above.

"*Up*," Aarie whispered with a smile, witnessing the escape route she had prayed for. She momentarily wondered if she was rising to heaven.

With that in mind, Aarie could have sworn she had seen a pair of brilliant white-feathered wings beat above her head just before her eyes closed.

A little while later, Jay carried Aarie gently in his arms as he stepped onto the clifftop and then jumped down to the clearing. He was still half-dressed, wearing only the loose grey trousers that he'd had on when Aarie had left less than an hour ago. His body tensed now as he focused on the other man who awaited him there. Tightening his grip around Aarie, Jay pulled her closer to his chest, shielding her with his arms.

Phelan stepped forward, scowling as his eyes flitted from Jay to Aarie and then back to Jay.

"It would appear we need to have that talk NOW, Brother. Some secrets should not be kept or, as you know full well, should not even be created in the first place!" he scolded.

Jay's gaze drifted to Aarie, avoiding the intensity of Phelan's judgmental stare. Her head was still bleeding, and though he could hear that her heartbeat was strong, he still worried about her injury.

"Phelan, not here," Jay whispered. "I know what my duties should be as a Guardian, believe me, *I know*. Therefore, I know what yours are too. So, I ask you as your brother, please, don't act upon those duties now, for my sake. There are things you don't understand about her and about me. Please give me the time to explain. Let me meet you back at the house. I'll follow you there soon, but please, let me have a few moments here with Aarie first. That's all I ask," Jay implored. His eyes glazed over as his mind wandered to a hidden, tortured place.

Jay knew a pained expression now shaped his face, and Phelan would not fail to notice; he was analysing everything. Phelan's gaze raked over Jay's protective stance. For every small movement that Phelan made, Jay warily adjusted his position. Jay was guarding Aarie. Blood had trickled down her face and now dripped onto his skin.

"*Please*, Phelan," Jay pleaded again. Jay, who had never asked or begged for anything in his life. There was a new fragility about him that he had never revealed before, and Jay knew he could no longer conceal it. Phelan's harsh scowl seemed to soften suddenly.

"Is *this* what you wanted to tell me but couldn't? The thing that has troubled your mind for the past few weeks—it is *this*?" Phelan asked, nudging his head towards Aarie.

"Yes."

Phelan examined them both for one more long moment. Then abruptly, he turned, shouting back to Jay. "Very well then, Brother. I'll wait for you, but don't keep me waiting too long."

Then within seconds, Phelan was gone. Jay's attention immediately went back to Aarie, who had begun to stir in his arms. He delicately inspected her head wound before she woke. To his relief, it appeared to look worse than it was, though it had been enough to knock her unconscious. Aarie's eyes opened and went straight to his.

A sudden warmth coursed through her. Only moments ago she had been in a potentially life-threatening situation, but now she was here in Jay's arms, nothing could dull the happiness that radiated from within her. She took a deep breath and then reached her hand to his face.

"You came. I was afraid I would never see you again. I was afraid that you'd never know what had happened to me or that I came back. I thought you would think I didn't want to come back because of my stupid dream. But I *did*, more than anything," Aarie whispered. Her eyes had started to well up, though a smile formed on her dry lips.

Jay glanced down at her in his arms. Pure adoration shone on his face, yet something else now lingered there too. His brows pulled together, and his face looked strained. "I didn't think I'd ever see you again either. Your dream was a nightmare, wasn't it?"

"Yes," she replied.

"I thought that it might have been enough to stop you coming here forever. I thought you had finally realised I'm no good for you."

"Don't say that. You know I would never believe that."

Jay glanced away briefly. "Do you feel okay to stand?"

She nodded. "Yes, I think so."

He set her down gently, releasing her from his arms. His body was still tense as he leaned against a large flat rock. Aarie leaned against another rock opposite from him. His mouth was set tight, and his forehead still creased as he stared down at the ground.

"What is it, Jay?"

"My brother knows, Aarie."

"I know." She swallowed.

Jay's eyes shot up "Did he hurt you? I saw the wolves and how you hit your head, but before that, did he hurt you?"

Aarie thought back to the cottage, to the black smoke that surrounded her, and how it had begun crushing her. "No," she lied. "But he was at the cottage when I came back. He scared me, but somehow, I ended up here. I don't know how. It's all a blur, and I don't really remember much. What happens now, Jay?"

"You're no longer safe here, Aarie. I can't keep you safe anymore. Phelan knows, and he is bound by law to do his duty."

"But he's your brother!"

"I know, Aarie. That's why I can't expect him to ignore the law. It would put himself in danger too."

"What are you saying, Jay?"

"There are things about me that I haven't told you, Aarie, details regarding my family. There are things expected of me—of us all. Laws are not meant to be broken and especially not by Guardians like me. It does not sit well with the Oneiroi. Because of that fact, if certain Guardians found out about you being here, they would make an example of me, but more importantly, they would make an example of you because of your involvement with me. You can't imagine what they would do to you, Aarie. I can't bear the thought of that, do you understand? I can't let that happen."

"Are you saying you want me to leave?" Aarie asked.

"No. You know that's not what I'm saying, but—"

"—Because I can't control coming here, not usually, you know that."

Jay pondered for a moment. "But how did you come back, Aarie? How did you do it so soon?"

"I somehow forced myself to sleep, and I made myself think of coming here."

"That means you are still linked to this place through dreams, like the shadows," Jay whispered as though to himself.

"Jay, back in my world, you felt real for the first time, even when I was wide awake. I even told Angela about you. I never mentioned anything about this place but—"

"—Aarie, I have to meet my brother," Jay said, cutting her off. "He's waiting for me now. He granted me only a little time to speak with you, but I saw it in his eyes, he will not let you stay here. Don't you see? It would have been better for you not to have come back because there's nothing I can do now. I'm helpless, and all that awaits you here is inevitable danger or worse—"

Aarie heart sank. "Is that what you would have wanted—for me to have never returned?" she asked as her voice tapered off.

Jay glanced down at his hands, pausing before he answered. "It doesn't matter what I want, Aarie. It won't change anything. You will still be in danger, and if anything happened to you, it would be my fault."

"That's not true," Aarie said.

"Yes, it *is!*" Jay insisted. "I always knew the consequences, but I was too selfish. I wanted to believe it would be alright, but it *won't*, Aarie. It won't, and I know that now. As an Oneiroi Guardian, I have responsibilities. I am supposed to protect you and your kind as well as my own. It is my duty to make things right. I can't forget what I am, Aarie, and so, I cannot forget my duty. That is the main purpose of my whole existence."

"Your duty," Aarie repeated, in a disbelieving and detached whisper. The world around her seemed to be becoming a meaningless blur. "So, what happens when I come back here? I don't think I can stop it, Jay."

"I know, but you have to try. You have to stop thinking about this place... and me. You have to believe I'm not real and that I'm just in your head. Earlier this morning, you said this place still felt like a dream when you woke in your world. You have to believe that now, Aarie. While there's still a chance to."

A tear began to roll down Aarie's cheek as she stood momentarily speechless. Her heart ached, and her insides seemed hollow as though all life had drained from her body. She could not reply straight away; no words would come out. *Was this it? Had the dreaded moment finally arrived?*

Jay moved to her, wrapping his arms around her waist. Her arms came around him as she leaned her head against his chest.

"I know it will take time, Aarie. I will make my brother understand that you can't control reappearing here. I will buy you time. I will keep you safe, always, but you must try to stop, for your own good. Promise me, please."

For your own good? She repeated in her head, wondering how this could ever be that; surely, this could have no positive impact on her life from this point. *How could he not see that?* As the tension built within the silence, she had no option but to reluctantly surrender.

"I'll try. I promise I'll try not to think of this place when I sleep," Aarie said as her voice broke. "But, Jay, *I know* I can't stop myself thinking of you. I know I can't do it. I'm sorry. I just won't be able to do it," she cried.

The ache in her chest was suffocating, and her heart seemed as though it no longer beat. She wondered if Jay felt any trace of what she did now or if he would just be fine. *Would he simply go on as he had before she came here? After all, he was letting her go, wasn't he?* Uncontrollable sobs broke free from her. She stifled them as best she could as her body shook silently against him. His body tensed, but he did not say a word. Aarie hoped there was something he could say that would console her, but it was eventually exhaustion that stilled her.

"I have to get back to my brother," Jay whispered, adding to Aarie's misery. "He won't wait for me for too long, and I must take you back to the cottage. You will be safe there for a while until I return. I don't want to leave you like this, Aarie, but I have no choice."

"I understand," she replied without looking up.

Before she could blink, she was back at the cottage in the living room. The fire was burning, and the smell of lilies filled the room, inviting as ever. Everything that had transpired earlier had not affected this place in any way. She wondered if it would be like this when she no longer came here— as though she had never been here in the first place.

"I have to go now," Jay said. "I'll come back as soon as I can, I promise." With one glance, he turned and was gone.

Aarie's mind played back the look in his blue eyes, over and over, and she knew her time here was truly coming to an end. She sat down on the sofa, staring into the fire as the wild flames slowly consumed the charred wooden logs. They crackled and hissed as cinders sparked from them. Inch by inch they crumbled to a powdery, lifeless ash.

Chapter 11
Oneiroi Guardians

Dim grey light seeped in through a large bay window, subtly highlighting Phelan's side profile. The muscles of his face were tight as he stood staring out at the gardens of the old manor house. He scratched a clawed hand along the paintwork of the window frame as tension began to fill the atmosphere of the large white room behind him.

Abruptly Phelan turned, directing his agitation and anger towards his brother. Jay was sitting across the room from him at a large, old wooden table. Jay's shoulders hunched over, and his gaze followed his fingers as they scored up and down the rough wooden panels in front of him.

"The mortal does not belong here!" Phelan cried out as he paced back and forth in front of his brother. "You have purposely concealed her from me. She is the mortal that came to this house weeks ago, isn't she? The one that got away twice. I recognised her. What were you thinking, Jay? You know the rules and the dangers!"

"I don't believe Aarie is just another mortal. She can't be. There are things she knows and can do. I can't explain how or why, but I'm telling you, there has to be a reason she is here."

"There is *no* other reason except that you have let her be here, Jay!" Phelan snapped. "She is just another shadow. By the looks of things, she may make the transition to dreamwalker soon, and *you* will have been responsible for it. These things you think she can do—they are nothing special—they're just signs that she is becoming a permanent dreamwalker. I've seen it with my own eyes. At the cottage, I tried to wake her. I could feel her fear as I surrounded her. She gasped for air in pain as if she thought she was genuinely here, mind and body. This place seemed so real to her that she truly believed I was killing her, yet she did not wake. Instead, she transported herself to somewhere you would find her. Tell me, Brother, how can you think this is not the sign of a dreamwalker?"

Jay's hands had balled up into fists on the table as he glared at his brother. Images surfaced in his imagination of Phelan hurting Aarie. She had denied being harmed, and Jay knew now that she had lied to spare his feelings. His lips were drawn to a fine line, and his brows had knitted tightly together.

"This place is real to Aarie because she is real to it!" Jay snarled. "When you tried to wake her, you weren't giving her a nightmare—you were really hurting her, Phelan. I know, or at least, I *want* to believe that you didn't know that and that you thought she was just a shadow who was unable to be hurt. I want to believe that because I don't want to hate you, but you have to know now that she can be hurt here, even killed. You saw her head wound earlier. I can't let anything happen to her, and I won't. She wasn't a shadow from the first night she came here. I found her bleeding. She had been injured in her world, and she had come here dying. Does that sound like something ordinary shadows do?"

Phelan took a moment, seemingly processing his brother's words with deep thought. "It doesn't matter how it sounds, Jay. It doesn't change the fact that she is mortal and you are an Oneiroi Guardian. She cannot be here!"

"But she cannot help being here. She isn't in control of it."

"They never are, to begin with. Jay, why am I telling you things you already know? What is this mortal to you?"

Jay did not reply. Instead, he stared at the wooden beams of the table.

"I won't let you destroy yourself over this," Phelan continued. "You know the Alinoy family will not let this slide if they find out, and that's if they don't already know. They'll kill you, Brother, and that's summing it up lightly. You know it will be even worse for her. You're endangering her by letting her stay here. You *know* that."

Jay flinched. "I know," he whispered as his eyes moved back to meet his brother's. "I *know* if she dies, it is my fault, Phelan. Don't think I don't already know that. I wanted so much to believe something would happen to make things okay. I wanted more time to find a way to make things right, but I have run out of time, haven't I? Maybe there was never a way anyway because I can't change what I am."

Phelan frowned. "Would you want to?"

"Yes."

Phelan growled. "You don't mean that. This mortal has messed with your mind. Jay, you need to wake her up and fast, or I swear I will do it for you now!"

"No!" Jay roared, slamming his fist on the table.

"Jay, it needs to happen. These wounds you think she has, they're not real, they're in her head. She's making them look real, but they're not. She will wake like all the rest. I can see you have grown attached to this mortal, so I can spare you this task because only a nightmare will wake her now."

Jay glared at Phelan. "And this seems to be your speciality these days, doesn't it, *Ikelos*?" he said bitterly.

"Don't call me that. You never have before," Phelan whispered in a sombre tone. "You know I don't accept that or any of the others as my own. Not all of us are happy to take the names *they* give us. They cannot possibly understand who we really are, and they could hardly label two brothers with the same likeness—it simply does not make a good story. Phobetor, Icelus, Ikelos, God of Nightmares—so many names and different ways in which tales of us are told. However, you know the very first mentioning of these names we are dubbed, predate when you and I were even born. Even if they were inspired by the visions of oracles, the stories that go with them don't reflect the real truth. The Oneiroi love to tell a story as much as any mortal. Of course these names would be assumed ours and stick with us throughout Aneiros. They represent the perfect balance most Guardians seek. It simply makes for a good tale, Brother.

Yes, I can create a perfect nightmare, but you know as well as I do, so can you. We *all* have to wear the mask of evil sometimes, but it does not mean it is who we really are, and it does not make us monsters. Please, don't doubt that or me, Jay. Let me wake Aarie. Let me do this for you to keep you both safe."

"I told you, you *can't*, you'll kill her, and I won't let you. Do you understand me? I know the difference between her and a shadow. I am still a Guardian and, as you well know, I have been for a very long time. I know what I'm telling you is the truth without any doubt. I have not just simply lost my mind!"

"Are you sure? Because I'm not sure I recognise my brother anymore," Phelan snapped, as Jay glared at him with burning fury. Phelan sighed glumly. "Look, I don't want to argue with you. We *never* argue, Jay. Do you realise, I don't think we have had a single bad word since you were a small child. Now, I believe you would fight me with all your strength—and to what end, I dread to think—for *her*. Tell me, am I wrong?"

Jay blinked, moving his gaze back to the table, saying nothing in return. His head sank slowly into his hands as he took a deep breath, holding them there as if to hide from the world. Jay pushed them back through his hair, leaving them there. For a moment, he became a lifeless statue. His eyes glazed over. He closed them, bringing a hand back to his face as if nursing a pain within his mind. He breathed heavily. Jay hadn't felt this helpless since his mother had first passed. This suffering was intolerable, and he knew he could not hide it from his brother.

"I don't doubt your skills as a Guardian, Jay," Phelan said in a softer tone than previously. "The whole of Aneiros would never doubt them, but I think she has clouded your judgment. I saw the way you looked at her, and all that talk before about you never wanting a Semper Sodale—there was a time when that was all you ever wanted—and it's because of her, isn't it? Because she's mortal, and you have feelings for her, don't you?"

"It's *more* than that, Brother," Jay said as his eyes opened and glanced back to Phelan. "I can't describe it to you because you simply wouldn't believe me. So maybe I really have failed as a Guardian, and I'm sorry, Phelan, but I don't know what to do. Aarie can't help coming here, and I know she will return. And yes, Brother, if you try to hurt her again or send your wolves for her once more, I'll have no choice but to protect her. I'll have no choice! Do you understand? So you tell me, what do I do now?" Jay's voice wavered as he seemed on the edge of shattering.

"I never sent my wolves this time, Jay. I was not amongst that pack, and those were not Guardians sent at my order. Do *you* understand more clearly now? If I did not send them, then someone else must have. Either that or dreamwalkers seem to have a feud with this mortal of yours. Maybe her transition is not to their liking, who knows, but what I do know is that other's know about her, and now, as you so boldly and quite literally swooped in to save her, there are witnesses. It is just a matter of time before word spreads. That means if you don't undo what you have done, both of you will pay the price. Do you want that for her? Because I'm not willing to lose my brother over this," Phelan said firmly, leaning forward on the table towards his brother.

A new wave of turmoil seemed to enter Jay's mind as he grimaced, rendering him momentarily unable to answer.

"Jay, you have to make her leave, and soon. You can't keep her here anymore. The wolves or other Guardians will eventually get to her. You know that you can't protect her forever. Even if they don't get to her soon, it is just a matter of time before she becomes a dreamwalker. If those wolves were dreamwalkers, then my guess would be that she will become a blood demon. You know most of them have done lately, and wolves do not attack their own kind. Jay, you couldn't possibly want that for her either? No one would want that for anyone they care about. She would not be as you know her, she'd be a monster, and you would have to destroy her yourself. She can't be far off transition if she can already transport herself from one place to the next. I can see this pains you. I don't take any enjoyment in seeing you like this or having this conversation with you, but you know she has to leave. You must know now that someone has to wake her, don't you?"

Jay took a deep inhale of breath. "I know, Phelan. I don't want it to be true, but I know it."

"Then let me do it for you. You need not suffer anymore with this."

"No, I told you, Phelan. You can't do it. You *will* kill her."

"But Jay—"

"—It has to be me, Phelan. I have to do it. Aarie trusts me. I am the only one that can give her a true nightmare without killing her. If it is me, she will know there's no one coming to save her, and there will be no reason for her to want to be here in the first place. It could only ever be me."

"And you are sure you can do that to *her*? If you give her a nightmare, you know what that means—she won't remember much of this place or you, not for very long. It will all just be some fading horror she once dreamt until she has blocked it out completely. You'll no longer be her guardian angel—you'll be the demon that haunts her nightmares. She will hate you and fear you until she has forgotten you. Then, she will never return here again. Are you prepared for that?"

"I have to be. It is as you said. I have no choice. I either make Aarie leave, or her death is inevitable, and it will be my fault. This is the only way I can protect her now."

"Yes, but this is also for the best, Jay. In time you will see—"

"—Phelan, please don't say anything else. Your words will not help me. Neither will time, especially after what I must do," Jay said as his mind wandered. "Do you know, after you left me this morning, I came back to find her having a nightmare. I think it was about me, Phelan. She vanished from this place straight afterwards because of it, and I thought she might never return again. But she did, and you can't imagine how glad I felt that she had returned, that she *wanted* to return to me. Now, I think she believes I no longer want her here because she stands between my duties as a Guardian. She thinks I value that more than her. I made her think that. I heard her heart breaking, Phelan, and I said nothing to stop it because I knew I could do nothing. The worse thing is, now I have no choice but to do what I must do and completely shatter what's left of her heart in the process. Now, I really *do* wish she had never returned because she will finally see the monster that I truly am, and I'm not sure I can bear that.

So, don't tell me that in time I'll be okay. When Aarie leaves here for good, I know a part of me will die. All I'll have will be the knowledge that she'll be out there somewhere, alive and safe and away from all of this," Jay said before sitting back in silence. His brother did not respond, but his words still echoed in Jay's mind, making his thoughts all the more unbearable.

She will hate you and fear you until she has forgotten you.

Chapter 12
The Ball

The fire had died out long ago, and a chill sent a shudder down Aarie's spine as she slumped back onto the sofa. She had wandered around the house and sat alone in many of the rooms throughout the day. Now she resided here once again. Aarie chewed an uneven fingernail as she glanced up at the black clock on the wall. The clock had been a recent addition to the living room, and Aarie took note that it looked like any ordinary clock from her world. It also appeared to be set by the time in her world. She wondered if it would become redundant soon. Her foot tapped frantically, making the sofa shake slightly. A rhythm of multiple beats for every second that the clock ticked by. Footsteps abruptly interrupted the rhythm. She turned and jumped due to Jay's sudden appearance but immediately eyed him with pure relief. He had been gone so long. Hesitantly, she got to her feet, stumbling against the coffee table; her limbs seemed to have gone limp, sending her coordination slightly off-balance as she moved towards Jay.

"Are you okay?" Jay asked, taking hold of her hands to steady her.

"Not really... I mean, physically, I suppose I'm okay, but I was worried about you," she admitted, frowning as she took in his harrowed expression. "What happened? What did your brother say? Will you be okay? Are you still in danger?" she panicked.

Jay's expression immediately softened in response to her many questions.

"Aarie, I don't deserve your worry. Promise me you'll look out for *you* in your own world before you think of others. Don't let anyone take advantage of your kind nature. Think of yourself first."

Aarie's heart sank as it had done earlier. The tone of Jay's voice seemed so final, as though he knew he would have no part in her future. "So, is it as you said? I have to stop myself coming here soon or someone... dies?" she said fretting.

"We have been granted a little time, and my brother will not interfere in finding the best solution to keep you from coming here. He is trusting me with that, but, in the meantime, he will not hurt you. He promised me that much, and I know his word to me would never be broken."

"I'm not talking about me—I'm talking about you!" Aarie said. "Are you safe? 'Cos I swear, if I come back, you don't need to protect me—I'll hide. Just deny you've ever seen me if anyone finds me. Whatever happens to me, you don't need to suffer. You don't need to be in danger. You don't even have to be in contact with me or feel any responsibility—"

"—Aarie, stop! Enough!" Jay interrupted, raising his voice. "You should be talking about you, and what's best for *you*! I don't want to hear you sound like you'd give up your safety—possibly even your life, so I don't suffer. Do you even know how much *that* itself would make me suffer? I never cared about what happened to me because *that* would be worse. You don't seem to place much value on your short mortal life. Not as much as you should. I need to know you'll be okay when you're not here. I won't be able to be there for you, and I need to know it. I can't be unsure about this forever, dammit!" he shouted.

Aarie was immediately silent. She had never heard Jay shout before, but even though he sounded angry, she knew it wasn't directed towards her. His right hand rubbed his eyes, and Aarie glanced down at his left hand as it still lovingly held hers.

"Maybe you should listen to your own advice too... then I may think about it," she whispered, glumly.

There was a brief silence. Jay's fingers tightened gently around hers, and her gaze flicked back to his. He searched her face as though exploring all its intricacies—each curve and movement. His features had softened again, and his irises were their usual bright sapphire blue. His mouth stubbornly twitched as he gave in to the subtlest of smiles.

"I will if you will first," he whispered.

"Then we have a problem. Maybe it's something we have to do at the same time," Aarie mumbled, trying to hold onto the moroseness that had shaped her face; it felt wrong not to reflect at least a small fraction of the overwhelming sadness that loomed inside of her. However, her eyes had already laid upon Jay's face and the gentle smile on his lips. She let out a brief sigh as she let a subdued smile of her own, creep onto her face.

"We still have some time," Jay concluded. "Who knows how long it will take for you to stop coming here. We don't know for sure. We can worry about the technicalities of it another time—the next time you come, perhaps. For today, just this one evening, maybe we shouldn't act differently. Can we just forget it all just for tonight? Can we just make the most of what's left of this day as if you never left this morning? I'd like one more evening with you as it was before all of this. Can we have that?"

Aarie's mind wandered briefly to that distant carefree moment. "I'd like that," she admitted, though doubt immediately tugged at her. "But what would your brother say?"

"He wants to meet you. In fact, he's invited us to a special annual evening at the house tonight. Music, wine, fine food—that kind of thing."

Aarie's forehead creased. "What? I don't understand. One minute we're awaiting his firing squad and then the next, we're out celebrating. I don't understand. Jay, what do you mean? I don't believe he wants me here. When he found me, he—He doesn't *want* me here, trust me. It must be a trap. I don't think I should go."

"I thought we were going to forget our worries this evening?" Jay said.

"I can't. Besides, you said to start looking out for number one. So, here I am doing that. I think Phelan may want me dead, and also, I don't want you fighting your own brother to protect me."

Jay laughed, dismissively waving a hand. Aarie thought it was out of character for him, but she ignored the thought as he spoke.

"My brother didn't want to fight me. That's why he's inviting you. He doesn't want you dead—he didn't know you could be hurt, that's all. He wants to meet the reason I've broken every law in Aneiros, and for one evening, he wants us to be happy since we may not have many left together."

Aarie did not reply.

"Please just give me this one evening, Aarie. I'm asking you because I think I really need it. Think of it as me taking my own advice after all. Besides, you know I would never take you anywhere if I thought my brother was going to hurt you."

She hesitated, but she knew she could not say no. After all, this was probably the last chance they would have a full evening together, and for once, she would not have to hide.

"Okay then. We will have this evening," Aarie replied. "I will go, but when you say 'special annual evening', does that imply smart dress? Because if so, I can hardly go dressed like this?" she said, gesturing to her muddied white dress.

"Hmm... well, there are *some* perks to being Oneiroi, you know?"

"Remind me, what those are again," Aarie glumly said.

"A new wardrobe always on hand in case of emergency," Jay replied, wafting a hand in a circular motion like a fairytale wizard.

Aarie glanced down as her white slip dress transformed into a luxurious red, silk gown. A subtle parting at the side revealed a slight glimpse of her ankles and lower leg between the delicately embroidered seams. She gasped as she twisted around. Alongside its magical appearance, the dress's exquisite detail and tailoring were breathtaking. On any other occasion, it would have sparked an instant explosion of reactions from Aarie, but the current mood threatened to extinguish any. Despite this, she wanted so much to give Jay this evening, and she knew she needed it too. *One last full evening as if nothing had changed*, she thought. She would not be the one to spoil it. After all, there was no denying, this was a beautiful dress, and Jay awaited a response with his usual infectious smile.

"Do you like it?" Jay asked.

"It's incredible, Jay. Is this how you manage to dress so immaculate all the time?"

"Sometimes. Well, only in emergencies, actually. Like, for instance, when certain attractive mortals unexpectedly drop in at all hours of the day, prone to ask an unlawful amount of questions."

Aarie smiled. Only Jay could possibly make her smile like this when she felt so sad inside. For a moment, she was hopeful that it would be easy to pretend all was okay. He would make it easy. For one last evening, he would be *her* Jay. He would make her happy, make her feel alive, and for some reason still make her so positively and excitingly nervous.

"But this isn't real, is it?" she said. "What I'm seeing is just an illusion, right? I mean, you can't have just undressed and then re-dressed me really fast or something like that, can you? Not that I mind. I mean... I *should* mind, but I didn't notice if you did, so I guess I don't. Erm, that came out all wrong." She cleared her throat, blushing red and cringing at her words.

Amusement was evident on Jay's face as he held her gaze in silence for a brief moment. "It's just an illusion, Aarie. When you wake, the illusion will not travel with you."

"Well, it really is beautiful. But wait, does that mean I'm still in my muddy dress?"

"Yes, I'm afraid so."

"So, what happens now?"

"We have a couple of hours before we need to be at the house," Jay replied. "If you want, you can shower and clean your actual dress, if it will make you feel better. The dryer here will clean and dry it in minutes. You can borrow some of my clothes until then if you want?"

Aarie nodded. "Yeah, that will feel much better. Thank you."

******

Aarie's dress was already dry and hung up in her room, but there was something about feeling the fabric of Jay's shirt against her skin that made her delay getting dressed. It only came down to her thighs, and she tugged at it slightly, conscious that it was shorter than she had first thought. Her legs were bare, but her skin still held the warmth from the hot shower she had taken. She stood barefoot now, staring out of the french doors that overlooked the lake. The little rowing boat bobbed up and down in the darkening water. She didn't know why she had come into this room, but it felt like it was to say goodbye.

Jay walked in from the doorway across from her and paused for a moment. She was oblivious that he was there, and for a moment, he watched her. The last remaining sunlight threw tiny lances of orange through the panes of glass, highlighting Aarie's profile as she stood deep in thought. His shirt hung loosely on her but creased in at her slender waistline, defining the shape of her hips. His gaze slowly wandered to the edge of the fabric that rested high on the bare skin of her thighs. He cleared his throat.

"My shirt suits you. Maybe you should go just like that," Jay said.

Aarie turned. Her jaw dropped open as she took in Jay's strikingly flawless appearance. He wore a long luxurious black frock coat style jacket with gold braiding to the left and a row of gold buttons to the right. Its long sleeves had upturned cuffs with matching buttons. Aarie could just make out the familiar symbols engraved on the buttons, and she knew they matched the symbols Jay had on his right wrist. Exquisite swirling black and gold brocades and beautiful embroidery embellished his jacket's cuffs, seams and collar. Underneath, he wore a dark navy double-breasted waistcoat, white shirt and a sapphire blue necktie that matched the colour of his eyes. His hair gently and naturally spiked out to the front from the top and sides with gentle wisps that curled out at his neck. His smart black trousers and polished black shoes completed his look. Aarie thought he had a slight look of an eighteenth-century prince about him as she caught her breath. His eyes seemed alive and as bright and warm as his smile.

"Jay, I didn't hear you come in. I was miles away," she said, realising it was soon time to leave. "I should quickly change. I'll be back in a—" She broke off, blinking as she neared him in the doorway.

"What is it?" Jay asked as she rubbed her eyes. "Are you getting tired?"

"No, I think I just got déjà vu, just then, as I walked up to you. Weird. I guess some things are no different to back in my world. I'd best grab my dress from upstairs so you can work your wizardry wonders on me. You look... really *nice*, by the way," Aarie said, running a hand slowly down the front of his jacket. She glanced up at him, instantly making her heart leap in her chest. It was not good for her to feel like this right now. She turned away, reluctantly forcing herself to leave the room to get ready. Jay's eyes followed her until she was gone.

Aarie hurried through the house and up the winding stairs to 'her room'. *'Nice'? Why did I say 'nice'?* she thought to herself. 'Nice' was not the word she had wanted to say. There were so many things that Jay was, and 'nice' did not capture a fraction of it. 'Nice' did not make her heart skip several beats, nor did it make her nervous or drawn to him. 'Nice' was not why her eyes had lingered longingly at his lips before she left; it was just a pointless, average word that was safer than committing to what you really wanted to say. Then again, she supposed there was no point saying anything else now. It would just make things harder for her to stop thinking of him in the long run. Besides, she needed to get dressed, and this shirt she wore was way shorter than she had first thought. She could not be half-dressed and slobbish around Jay when he looked so excruciatingly perfect.

Fifteen minutes later, Aarie wandered down the wooden staircase. A subtle shade of eyeshadow shimmered from her eyelids, highlighting her eyes and black lashes. A touch of pink coloured her cheeks and accented her cheekbones. She was glad to have kept a modest stash of makeup here that she had brought over gradually during her visits. Her hair was now half pinned up at the back, leaving two soft curls to frame the sides of her face and the rest to flow over her shoulders. Her white dress was pristinely white again as it had been this morning. Luckily, she had managed to find her grey sandals too before making her way back downstairs. Her eyes immediately went to Jay, who was waiting for her at the bottom of the steps. His mouth opened slightly as though to say something, but instead, he just took a deep breath.

"Am I okay like this?" Aarie asked, standing now beside him. "Obviously, after you've worked your magic with the dress and everything."

His brows raised slightly as his gaze still fixed. "Hmm? Sorry, I mean, yes, of course. You look beautiful."

Aarie's dress transformed as it had done before. She noticed that her casual sandals were also now glistening silver evening shoes. Their heels were encrusted with what looked very convincingly like diamonds. She wiggled a foot.

"Thanks," she said.

"Are you ready to go?"

"Ready as I'm ever going to get, I think. Tell me again, what is this annual event?"

Jay swung an arm under Aarie's, linking them together as he walked them towards the cottage doorway. Before Aarie could blink, there was a mild whooshing sound, and they were suddenly walking towards the steps of the large manor house. The moon lit up what was now a clear night sky. A warm golden light beamed through the building's glass entrance, casting a rectangular glowing shape at the top of the steps. They continued their way up towards the four stone pillars and the ivory arch that framed the doorway. Aarie looked around and then back to Jay, still awaiting his answer.

"My parents always had this annual event. It was originally to mark the anniversary of their marriage, or more accurately, their Semper Sodales official ceremony. It became a family tradition after that. Tonight it will just be us, my brother and a group of trusted family friends."

"But I thought I'm not supposed to be seen by anyone else? Doesn't that endanger you—I mean, both of us?"

"You are my guest. They will assume you are Oneiroi, Aarie," he said.

Aarie frowned nervously. "Erm, I'm not sure I will be *that* convincing. Your brother knew straight away."

"You will be just fine. Phelan only knew because I had lied to him and because he accidentally nearly scared you to death. So, are you ready?" He stopped to turn to her.

"Yes."

"Hold up. There was something I forgot to do," Jay said, reaching into his jacket pocket. He pulled out a rectangular black box and opened it. Aarie involuntarily gasped as the box revealed a diamond-encrusted necklace. She had never seen this amount of gleaming diamonds on a single piece of jewellery before. Tiny beams of reflected moonlight shot out like starbursts in every direction, and there was no doubting that these were real. She stood speechless.

"The finishing touch," Jay continued. "To be that little extra Oneiroi convincing."

Before Aarie had a chance to speak, he gently took hold of her waistline with both hands and turned her around. He lifted her hair aside as he placed the jewellery around her neck. The necklace slipped down in place, perfectly framed by the dress's sweetheart neckline. Aarie spun around to face Jay, touching the jewels that now hung from her neck.

"It's beautiful, Jay. I've never seen anything like it before."

"I've never seen anything like you before," he whispered as his eyes bore deep into hers.

His were their brightest blue, yet somehow Aarie thought they seemed darkened by a sadness that emanated deep within. She blinked as Jay's hands came around her waist, gently pulling her nearer to him. Her arms rested against his chest as his face came close to hers. She still wasn't used to how being this close to him affected her heart rate. His own heart beat fast against her arms, in time with hers. He seemed to be studying the details of her face like he was trying to memorise them, and she wanted to say something, but the words just wouldn't come. Aarie worried that being like this would only prolong her agony and wondered if he knew he was making it harder for her to ever put him out of her mind. She would never be able to stop herself from coming here to save them both if she did not move now. There was also something new in the way he held her: a deep longing in his eyes. She took note that the blue of his irises had not flickered in the slightest. At that moment, she needed to know what he was thinking and feeling.

"Jay, what are you doing?" she blurted out in a hurried whisper.

"What I wanted to do the first time you came to the cottage. Aarie, if you remember anything from tonight, I want you to remember this, more than anything. Please, just remember this moment."

Jay cupped Aarie's face with both hands and leaned his head down towards her. An unmistakable sadness dampened his eyes. Before she could comment, his lips were on hers and hers moving against his. He pulled her even closer, and her arms wrapped around the back of his neck. Her hands ran through his hair as she pressed him firmer against her. A sudden rapture spread throughout every vein in her body, sending her heart racing and her mind spinning. *How could she ever not remember this moment?* She never wanted it to end. Though she knew it would be impossible to keep him from her mind again, for this one moment, she did not care.

A shadow broke up the stream of light from the doorway as a figure walked passed. Jay abruptly broke away from their embrace. Just at that moment, a crack of thunder echoed in the distance, followed by a series of white flashes that forked the night sky. Thick clouds now approached, threatening to block out the moonlight.

"We'd better go in," Jay said, seemingly startled. Taking hold of Aarie's hand swiftly in his, he gestured towards the door with the other.

Just like a switch had been flicked, the moment was gone, though it embedded itself in Aarie's mind. Jay's kiss lingered on her lips. The heat still flowed in her veins, but they walked on, under the ivory arch and through the doorway. Stringed orchestral music greeted her ears as Aarie entered a grand hallway. Her head tilted up towards the enormous crystal chandelier that hung in the centre of the ceiling. The black and white mosaic tiles of the floor beneath it depicted various creatures and symbols that she did not recognise. Several large doorways lined either side of the hallway. A grand stairway with an ornately carved bannister wound out of sight up ahead. Aarie glanced into one of the rooms to the left as they neared it. Dozens of people gathered there in ballgowns and exquisite eveningwear fit for royalty. Their luxuriously embroidered garments and expensive jewels glimmered from them, matching those she wore herself. Jay had been right; there was no obvious difference from the way she looked to the way they did. But she doubted their hearts were racing as much as hers right now. A lively hubbub of chatter echoed from the doorway as they stepped past it. As they continued to walk on by, it began to fade, gradually becoming muffled.

Another doorway came into view. This time, the music that travelled through the house was louder, and Aarie knew this was the room from which it flowed. As they turned and entered the room, her eyes widened at the sheer size of it. It was a ballroom.

The centre of the room was alive with movement, laughter, chatter and the warm melody of a waltz. Ballgowns and jewels glistened as couples twirled and stepped in perfect time with each other. Another larger chandelier hung in the centre of the room as dozens of feet softly stepped and glided on the polished floor beneath it. The music came to a gentle slow, followed by a brief silence, and then a roar of cheers and applause. A chorus of laughter and chatter filled the room. Couples dispersed into the throng of onlookers around them until the whole place was filled from edge to edge with merry guests. There was something very familiar about this room. Aarie knew she had never been here before, but somehow something sparked recognition in her mind. She hesitated to move as Jay tugged slightly on her hand to lead her into the room. He glanced back to her as she lingered at the door. She had paled, and her gaze appeared momentarily distant as if in thought.

"Are you coming?" Jay asked.

Aarie glanced up, allowing her eyes to skim over his face and stop at his lips. She wondered if their kiss lingered in his mind as it did in hers. However, there was something else also whirring in her mind now, something that made her freeze in the doorway. She blinked, then nodded her head at Jay, trying to push all thoughts aside.

"Yes, I'm coming." As soon as she spoke, her mind wandered back to those thoughts. Regardless, Aarie followed Jay swiftly through the crowd as silk fabrics and various embroidered textures, brushed past her skin. Many guests turned and smiled towards Jay as they acknowledged him passing by. They held their smile as their gaze landed on Aarie beside him and then moved on back to their conversations. Jay brought her out of the crowd to a more spacious corner of the room. There was a scuffle behind her, and she turned her head. The guests in the room had all brought out masks that they held to their faces. Some were shaped like strange demons, and others were a mixture of spiked patterns that wound over their eyes. Large horns, pointed beaks, spikes and sharp, angry shapes decorated their faces as they laughed and conversed in, what Aarie thought to be, an eerie manner. Jay had not mentioned this would be a masquerade ball, and though it was a surprise, it also triggered another wave of déjà vu.

In that instant, she realised that she *had* seen this place before, and now she knew exactly where. A shudder ran down her spine. She looked across the room at a masked figure she knew would be stood in the opposite corner—a man of similar height and hair colour to Jay. The same blue eyes glared at her from behind his mask. It was Phelan. Her troubled gaze went back to Jay.

"Jay. Please, I want to leave. Please, can we just leave?"

Jay turned to her, acknowledging the distress in her voice. "What? Why? We just got here."

"And in five minutes, you're going to ask me to dance. Tell me if I am wrong?"

Jay debated something for a moment. "Well, it is a ballroom, Aarie." He shrugged.

"But in a moment, everyone will dance a *specific* dance, one that you are sure I do not know the steps to. Then you will laugh as I will watch you dance with the brunette across the room in the green dress."

Jay stood, confused and speechless for a moment. His features became rigid and serious as he took in the matter-of-fact tone Aarie had spoken in. He glanced across the room at the girl in the green dress, then back to Aarie. "That is ridiculous. Why would you say that to me?"

"Can we just go, please?" she pleaded once more.

"Tell me why you said that?"

"Because it's going to happen now, isn't it? But Jay, there's one thing you don't know."

"And what's that?"

"I *do* know the steps to that dance. I've always known them. I don't know how or why I do. I don't even know why in my dream I pretended not to know."

"In your dream? What dream?"

"The one I had this morning before I left."

Jay's face grimaced at the memory, then his eyes widened. "Show me. Show me the steps, Aarie. Let me dance with you."

Jay's tone was firm, and she knew he would not let her leave now. She swallowed and then nodded as she took hold of his outstretched hand. The two of them walked to the centre of the room, leaving the crowds on the outskirts. Aarie took a deep breath as she positioned herself a step apart from Jay, who watched her intently.

As the music started, her right arm raised, mirroring Jay's. Their forearm touched as they stepped in a circle, and their eyes followed each other. As the music picked up, Jay's arm came around Aarie's shoulder, and his hand gathered hers. Together with perfect synchronisation, they stepped to the rhythm, feeling the music with their bodies. Their arms raised up as Aarie whirled around and then back into his arms. Their bodies moved closer together, entwining briefly. Their hearts raced against each other, and their gazes held firm. Round and round they whirled to and from each other. Gliding, spinning and stepping until the music began to slow. Their breath was now slightly staggered. Jay stepped forward, holding Aarie's weight as she leaned back into a graceful finale pose. The music seemed to change to a discordant clatter of notes that made Aarie shudder as Jay slowly lifted her back up to him. His eyes frantically searched hers. The sadness that Aarie had seen hidden behind them earlier, engulfed them now.

"What happens now, Aarie?" Jay whispered, with a voice that seemed a mixture of agony and uncertainty.

She stood up straight, breaking away from him gently as his arms fell to his sides. Her eyes had welled up, and she hesitated to answer. Instead, her gaze went now to someone behind Jay, causing her body to tremble. Jay acknowledged her distress, but on awaiting her answer, he did not turn to greet his brother, who stood beside him.

"Is everything okay here, Jay?"

"Give us a moment, Phelan," Jay snapped.

"Oh, come now, Jay. You've not introduced me to your guest yet," he said, glancing to Aarie.

She involuntarily stepped back as her eyes flitted between both of them.

"I believe you've already met. I just need one more moment, Phelan," Jay insisted.

Phelan edged forward. "Maybe it is about time I introduced myself properly, Jay," Phelan replied, resting his arm on Jay's shoulder. "And seeing as you seem unwilling—"

Jay turned abruptly, nudging his brother's arm away. "Phelan, what are you doing?"

Phelan frowned. "Maybe it is you and I who need a moment?"

"Maybe so," Jay replied, gritting his teeth slightly. "Aarie, I'll be back. Don't go anywhere," he called back as he walked away with his brother.

Her eyes followed them to the far corner of the room. They seemed to be arguing, and she was alarmed by the rage that seemed to distort Jay's face as he shouted at his brother. With the music playing once again, she was unable to hear anything that was being said. For a brief moment, the crowd around her caught her attention due to their sudden stillness. The people seemed to be frozen in time like statues, but then, with a strange juddering motion, they began to move once again as though she had imagined it. Her confusion lingered there for a second, but her concern swiftly moved back to Jay and Phelan. They seemed to be in a standoff with each other.

"I can handle this, Phelan. What are you doing? You agreed you would leave this matter to me," Jay yelled.

"You are compromised, Jay. You were ready to break your word. I saw how you were with her when you danced. I don't think you have it in you to do what we agreed. That's why you changed the plan. You taught her the dance, for pity's sake!"

"I didn't! She already knew it. Tell me, if she is just another mortal, how did she know it? I didn't change the plan, Phelan—she did!"

"That's impossible," Phelan hissed.

"She has defied the impossible on many occasions."

"So what happens now, Jay? This doesn't change anything. She is still in danger of becoming a dreamwalker if you aren't both sentenced to a fate worse than death before then. I won't let her leave tonight, Brother—for your sake! So, you need to make your choice. I will keep my word to you if you keep yours to me."

"I will. Phelan, I know what has to be done. I just needed a moment, that's all. You can't imagine what that felt like out there. It's not just the dance. I think she knows what is to come. I think she knows, and yet she still danced with me. And that dance of all dances!"

"Then let me help you, Jay. I can do this for you. You don't even need to be here torturing yourself," Phelan said, reaching for his brother's arm.

Jay looked down at his brother's arm on his. Then, with a burst of rage, Jay lifted Phelan off his feet by his throat, pushing him against the wall.

Phelan struggled. "Jay, it makes sense. Why won't you let me help you?" he said, half choking.

"Because if anything goes wrong—if she dies—I'll hate you forever. I don't want that, Phelan. It has to be me. Right now, I need to give in to the rage that I'm feeling for you if I am to succeed. Forgive me for this, Brother, but I will keep my word."

And with that, Jay threw Phelan against the wall. His hands came up in a blur of speed, striking a heavy blow to Phelan's face, then slashing a deep wound across his brother's chest. Phelan groaned in pain but seemed unwilling to retaliate. Instead, he glanced up at Jay with a smirk as he wiped away the blood from his face. Jay stood before him with eyes as black as coal, his face now pale with dark veins that streaked the sides of his hairline. Sharp razor teeth lined his mouth as he glared back at his brother with pure menacing hostility.

"Please don't fight because of me!" Aarie shouted, appearing suddenly from behind Jay.

Jay transformed back to his usual self, though his face and hands were covered with his brother's blood. Jay wiped it off onto his waistcoat as he turned to face her. Aarie's eyes widened as she took in Phelan's wounds and the blood on Jay's clothes.

"We are just having a brotherly chat. Nothing to concern yourself with," Jay snapped.

"Just let me leave, Jay. You don't need to see me again," Aarie pleaded.

Jay's gaze became a harsh glare, and it startled Aarie. "I can't let you leave, Aarie," he declared, grabbing her arm with sudden haste and bringing her stumbling towards him. He began pulling her to a doorway, away from the eerily still crowds. His pace quickened as he reached the hallway, bringing her to another smaller room. Once again, he tugged on her arm.

"Stop it. You're scaring me, Jay," Aarie shouted.

Jay pulled her into the room and then closed the door. It looked like a study; books lined the shelves of one wall, and a large desk stood in a corner. Two large brown leather sofas sat to the back of the room where Jay gestured for her to sit.

"In your dream, what happened next, Aarie?"

"I don't want to say," she replied, taking a seat on the sofa the furthest away."

"Then, I'll have to make you," Jay threatened as he moved away from the door and towards her.

"You won't hurt me. I know you won't."

"You *know* I won't?" he said in a mocking tone. "But that's just *it*, Aarie —you don't *know* anything about me. Not really. As amusing as our time together has been, my brother informs me that it is time for my little experiment to end."

Aarie frowned. "Experiment? I know you don't mean that. He's put you up to this, hasn't he? Is he controlling you somehow?"

"Controlling me? Aarie, there are very few people that can do that. Now tell me what happens next!" Jay shouted.

She flinched at the hostility in his voice. "Things have changed. I wasn't in this room. I was in a dining room, but you were as you are to me now. Jay, please, I'll just leave. I promise I'll try to stop coming here. Don't do this."

Jay closed his eyes briefly as he took a deep breath. They snapped back open with more hostility in them than before. He loomed over her, and she recoiled, moving back on the sofa.

"Don't do *what*, Aarie?"

"Nothing. I know you won't hurt me. You wouldn't. You're just trying to scare me to make me believe you're a monster so I won't want to be here, but it won't work, Jay. I don't believe you'd hurt me."

Jay kneeled down on the floor in front of her, resting his hands on her knees. As he did, the illusion of her long gown vanished, revealing her short white slip dress. She jumped at the sudden warmth of his hands on her bare skin. It made her uneasy as he ran a hand along her thigh.

"You know nothing about what I would do. You know nothing of the real me because I never told you any truths," Jay said coldly as his eyes bore into hers.

Something sharp scratched against the skin of Aarie's arm, and she glanced down to see Jay's fingernails had transformed into sharp claws. She gasped, but before she could pull away, Jay slashed his claws across her arm in one blur of motion. A cry of pain escaped her lips as she pulled back, cradling her wounded arm towards herself. A rhythmic pounding erupted from her chest as her heart raced. Aarie paled as the gaping wounds bled out, sending a burning pain through her whole arm. She was unaware of what point her cries of searing pain had changed to sobs of grief, but her tears fell as her wounds bled. Aarie looked back up at the man she had held close only minutes ago. Terror filled her eyes now. It filled her heart and her mind, but she continued to stare at him because she could do nothing else. Her face contorted with emotional and physical pain as she gave in to the sobs.

"Was everything a lie then?" Aarie whispered. "And outside, what I felt, was that not real? Or was that part of your *experiment* too?"

"As I said, I never told you any truths, Aarie. You were simply the means to learn more about mortal emotions. I should really thank you. You have taught me a great deal of your kind."

"I don't believe you. I can't, Jay," she whimpered.

"Just like you didn't believe I would hurt you?" Jay tutted, mockingly waving a finger from side to side. "But it doesn't matter. I really don't care what you believe anymore. Although I have to say, it has been very entertaining to see what you can believe, but then, mortals are always so gullible. Did you really think there was a future for *us*? Your life is a small flicker in time to me, do you know that? It's such a tiny insignificant moment—then gone. What is that in the face of eternity?" he scoffed.

"So, it is true. I am mortal, and you were always... the opposite," she said unevenly as her lips quivered. "I really *am* nothing to you, aren't I? And you really had me well and truly fooled. Everything you ever said to me—was it all just a sick twisted game to you?"

"Don't feel disheartened," Jay quickly replied. "It is what I do best. I fool mortals. It is what we all do. To get in your heads, we have to study how you are. It's how we learn to create the perfect illusions. As your ridiculous emotions and feelings are so hard to grasp, my brother thought it good for me to spend more time studying them. Though, now I think he is a little annoyed with me for being too convincing because it's something he has not managed to do himself yet. My brother doesn't control me, Aarie. He didn't bring this thing to an end—he started it! I am the one who decided to finish it. Phelan brought you to me so that I would learn from you, and you were just too good an experiment for me to pass up. But, as interesting as you were in the beginning, I tire of this game of pretence, and I tire of *you*. It is time for you to leave."

Aarie flinched at his over-enunciated words, feeling every syllable like a dagger in her chest.

"You're a monster, Jaydon Onuris—if that's even your real name," she hissed. "But not only that—your experiment failed. You really haven't grasped the true meaning behind mortal emotions because you could never do this if you had. Maybe you're fated to be an emotionless monster for all eternity. I don't want to remember anything about you or this place. I hate you, Jay. I HATE YOU!" she screamed, almost choking on her words as she spat them out. Her shattered heart felt like it lay in a million pieces as sobs ripped out from her uncontrollably.

Jay shifted to the sofa and perched close beside her. He unexpectedly cupped her face, holding it there. The way he did, mimicked the way he had done so lovingly, earlier. She trembled as his face came so close to hers. For a brief moment, she thought she saw the same sadness in his eyes from earlier, but all hope and trust in him was gone.

"Did you ever wonder why I looked away from you when my eyes darkened, Aarie? Well, I may as well let you into that secret now. My eye's darkened when I was so close to you because you have something I crave, something that runs through your veins. I didn't want my experiment to end too soon because you were admittedly more interesting than most mortals, but I don't have to hide anything now. I think deep down you already know the truth, Aarie. I think you may have seen it when you dreamt of me this morning. So there is really no reason for me to pretend anymore. You see, I can only be what I am, and for you, Aarie, unfortunately, that is your worst nightmare."

Aarie struggled to move from Jay's clutches as the blue of his irises transformed into black, soulless pits. His face structure became more angular, and the crunch of reshaping bones sent shudders down her spine. Shadows emerged under his eyes as dark veins crawled down the edges of his face. His hair became wildly dishevelled, tangled and harsh like barbed wire. Everything familiar about Jay was gone. This was a stranger, and he was just as menacing as he had been in her nightmare. An eerie grin spread upon his face as he opened his mouth to reveal sharp razor-like fangs.

Aarie screamed, and he lunged towards her, ripping the necklace from her throat. He grabbed her by the back of her shoulders, thrusting her toward himself. His fangs sank deep into the side of her neck.

A gurgling cry escaped Aarie as her arms flailed in the air, desperately trying to grab at Jay's wrists. She tore at his sleeves but lost her grip as a cuff button came loose in her hand. It was no good; he was too strong, and the pain was like fire on her skin. Time seemed to slow down, and this struggle felt like an eternity. Her arms struck him over and over until they felt bruised and weak. Her heart beat wildly, though she knew it would soon slow as she had started to become lightheaded. She was almost glad of it because it dulled the pain. Her mind began to drift as her body tired of fighting.

'Please, just remember this one moment', he had asked her, *but this was not that moment anymore,* she thought. *Had that moment ever really existed?*

The bitter irony of it all was that, though this place was real, at the same time, nothing had ever been real. It had all been a lie, and there would be no one to save Aarie from anything now. There was no reason for her to hold on. Her body gave up as her eyes closed. A heart surely could not beat much longer when it was this broken.

Aarie's body went limp in Jay's arms as he stood and she slipped into unconsciousness. Her pulse slowed, and he desperately pulled her closer to him. He quickly covered her wounds with his right palm, which he had slashed open. His self-inflicted wound bled into hers, sealing the gaping wound in her neck.

"I'm sorry, Aarie. Forgive me," Jay whispered into her ear as her body began to disappear in front of him.

Phelan had already come into the room and had witnessed the whole scene. He urgently hurried towards his distressed brother. Jay turned around sharply to face him and then stepped back. Aarie was already gone, and it was just the two of them now.

"Phelan, I have to go with her," Jay insisted. "She wouldn't wake. She just wouldn't wake. What have I done? She's lost too much blood. If I don't go, she'll die!"

Phelan's face paled with concern. "Jay, you can't!"

Jay snarled. "Brother, don't make me fight you. If she dies, it will destroy me. Do you hear me? Just this once, I have to go. I did this to her. I did as you asked, but I can't let her die. This is a matter of life and death."

Phelan froze as he stared at his brother's agonised expression. He could do nothing now but watch Jay slowly vanish before him.

Jay found himself in a dark bedroom. Lighting from the street lamps outside streamed through the blinds at the window. Aarie's unconscious body laid on top of her bed, and he hurried towards her. He reached for a sidelight on her bedside table, then switched it on. He didn't need it to see her, but somehow it felt better not to feel like he was creeping around her in the darkness.

The claw marks along Aarie's arm and the gashes on her neck were like red beacons that tortured Jay's soul. He had quickly tried to heal them with his blood before she had vanished. It had been enough to stop the bleeding but not enough to undo the damage. As he bent down beside her, the shame of what he had done sent an agonising chill through his body, but he had no time to waste. Pressing his mouth against his wrists, he sank his fangs painfully deep into his own skin. He placed his gushing wrist over Aarie's mouth as he gently opened it to let his blood trickle in. Her body twitched slightly as the liquid ran down her throat. Jay held his wrist there for several more moments, watching her wounds slowly fade before his eyes. He listened to her heartbeat as its pace strengthened and started to pick up speed. As Aarie began to stir, Jay moved quickly. He waved his arm over her, causing a golden glow to scan over her like a transparent golden sheet of light. The blood that soaked her clothes and bed seemed to lift off and disintegrate from sight, removing all proof that anything had ever happened to her. Jay switched the light off quickly, and just before her eyes began to open, he stepped back into the shadows, then disappeared.

Chapter 13
Insomnia

Aarie sat up immediately, gasping as she clutched her throat. Her eyes flitted around her bedroom to make sure she was alone. The room was silent except for the low rumble of the occasional car passing on the street. Her mind ran over and over images as her thoughts filled with Jay: the moment they had shared on the steps, the dance that had a hidden meaning, Jay's transformation, the blood, Jay hurting her, and Jay almost killing her. So many things made her believe she had never really known him. He was a monster to her now. The sudden feeling of loss was almost unbearable. It was like losing something as precious as the air she breathed. Her chest felt like it was being crushed, and she clung on tightly to her sides. A quiet sob broke from her as she gently rocked herself in the darkness. She couldn't contain the sadness that seemed to grow inside her. It filled her to the very core of her being, and she quickly broke down completely. Tears streamed down her cheeks, and there was nothing that would comfort her now. She wondered if there was anything that could comfort her ever again.

Hours seemed to pass, and the early morning light began to creep through the blind. Aarie was curled up on top of her bed with her arms wrapped around her knees. Her eyes were bloodshot and swollen, her body numb, and she wondered if she had slipped into a state of madness. She ran a hand along the skin on her neck. Then she glanced at her arms. There was no pain, no wounds or signs of any injuries, yet she had a clear memory of them. So many memories filled her mind of the strange and wonderful world and of Jay. She had usually woken up believing them to be just dreams, but lately, her sleeping self had told herself over and over to believe in them. She had even spoken to Angela about Jay. However, apart from her feelings and memories, there was no real evidence that any of it had been real. She wondered if it had all just been in her mind after all. Maybe she had just gone mad and was crying over something that never really existed in the first place.

A memory came flooding to mind. It was a memory of the first time Jay had held her in his arms properly. She had told him how she feared waking up to believe him to be nothing but a dream and never seeing him again. Now, she didn't know if it was better that way or if it even mattered. After all, if it weren't a dream, then it had been all lies anyway. What she had thought was there between her and Jay had never been real. Dream or not, he had lied about everything. He was a monster who had toyed with her for his amusement. He had hurt her and took pleasure in it, and if that weren't bad enough, he had fed on her blood to the point of her losing consciousness. She wondered how she had not seen the kind of monster he really was, but even as she thought this over and over, something in her heart still denied it. It didn't make sense for him to have done all of this to then just heal her afterwards. Her mind wandered back again to the most obvious and rational explanation—none of it had really happened.

******

The wind blew fiercely, scattering the last of the pink blossoms into the air and stripping the branches lifeless and bare. Thousands of maple leaves had fallen too, coating the wet earth a deep shade of crimson. The rain washed them downhill, creating thick glistening streams of violent red as though the ground bled out from a fresh gaping wound. The gale whistled and roared as it swept through the treetops behind the stone cottage. The leaves there had browned in colour and seemed to crumble and fall away as the wind whirled around. The rope bridges swung and creaked wildly while a lonely figure stood on one of the higher wooden platforms within the trees.

Had anyone been there to see him, he was sure they would not recognise him as Jaydon Onuris; he barely recognised himself anymore. He stared ahead at the grey clouds as they darkened over the mountains in the distance. Rain fell down on him, soaking his bloodstained white shirt through to his skin, but he didn't seem to notice. His shirt sleeves were rolled up, and he clutched his right wrist to himself, holding it in pain. Looking down, he opened his right arm out in front of him and forced himself to see what he could no longer deny was there. A new looped symbol had appeared on his wrist with a violet glow that made it unmistakable. Jay knew only too well the meaning behind this symbol. His face contorted with the pain that now ripped through his chest. He sank down to his knees as if his legs had suddenly given way. For the first time in his life, he felt hopelessly and agonisingly broken.

******

Aarie thought back to the struggle when Jay had held her forcefully and drained the blood from her neck. She shuddered but carried on searching her mind for some kind of clue in her memories. She wanted clues that would prove she hadn't lost her mind. Images surfaced of her frantically trying to break free but not having the strength. She had felt her life slipping away and had grabbed at Jay's arms and torn at his sleeves. Regardless, nothing she remembered proved any of this had happened.

Aarie sat up on her bed and dropped her legs over the side as she contemplated getting up. The others would be awake in a couple of hours, and she couldn't face them today. There weren't any words she could say to them to hide how she was feeling. She lifted herself off the bed, but as she put her feet down, something dug into her heel. A hard object stuck into her skin and made her tipple back onto the bed, rubbing the pain in her foot. Aarie glanced down at the floor to see what it had been, then froze. A glint of light reflected off a small golden object. She focused on the item and the tiny details engraved on it: patterns weaved into the shape of a moon and stars.

Aarie gasped out loud. She bent down, taking it in her hands to examine it closely. There was no mistaking it; it was Jay's button, and her blood was on it. This was all the proof Aarie needed. She wasn't insane. However, it also proved that Jay was real. She could not remove him from her mind, especially thoughts of him holding her and kissing her. *Him kissing her.* Even now, her body swooned at the thought. She didn't understand why he had waited all that time to kiss her on that particular night. *What did it matter the reasons why?* she asked herself. *It wouldn't change anything.* But deep down, she knew why. The loss Aarie felt wasn't because she couldn't go back to the magical dream world, it was because she had lost *her* Jay, not the monster she knew him as now. Aarie knew that soon after meeting him, she had fallen completely and blindly in love with him. Even though she told herself he was a monster who had hurt her and never cared, she could not fathom why he had healed her. Jay must've cared enough to heal her. Aarie could not get herself out of the confusing emotional turmoil she was in, but there was one thing she *was* sure of; she was very much afraid of him now.

Aarie stood up, wiping away the tears as they began to fall again. Reaching into her wardrobe, she grabbed a large travel bag and threw it on the bed. Hastily she stuffed it with clothes and other belongings she would need for a few days. She couldn't be around her friends right now, not for a little while at least. Her dad wouldn't ask too many questions if she went back home. All she'd have to hint at would be boy troubles, and he would probably give her space. Though, if he knew the truth, it would be a different matter. Nothing sparked her dad's anger and protective side more than worrying about the safety of his daughter. But she would never tell him the truth, or anyone else for that matter. *Who would believe her anyway?* She didn't fancy being locked up for being crazy. Aarie zipped up the bag and quickly got changed into some jeans and a hoodie. She stepped into her trainers and grabbed a jacket on the way out of her room. After tiptoeing through the house and down the stairs, she hurried out of the front door, closing it behind her as quietly as she could manage.

She would catch the train and then get a taxi home from the station. Hopefully, by the time she got home, her eyes would not be as bloodshot and may have dried at least. This is what she told herself as the tears still poured and soaked her cheeks. Pulling up her hood, Aarie wondered what she looked like to passers-by. Luckily, it was early morning, and not many people were about on the street yet. She hurried on with her head down.

Breakfast.
Student Union

Adam carried his breakfast tray and then set it down on the dining table where Angela and Jamie were already seated. He pulled out a chair opposite them, then sat, giving a silent hand wave to them as he tapped his phone and pushed it to his ear. The Cafeteria echoed with the low murmur of idle chatter as other students sat eating their breakfast. An answering machine tone beeped in Adam's ear, followed by another as he ended his call. He slammed down his phone on the table, frowning in the other's direction.

"It's been two weeks! She's not answering any of my calls. I'm telling you, something's really wrong. She's never gone this long without speaking to me."

"But she's texted you, right?" Jamie asked.

"Yeah, she's texted us all, but that's not the point. When have you ever known her to just up and leave for this long? Or for any amount of time in fact, and not answer calls?"

"Never," Jamie agreed. "But maybe she needs space, Adam. We know where she is, and she's answering texts, so what's the problem? Let her tell us what's wrong in her own time. If she wanted us to know now, she'd tell us. If she's not back soon, I'll go check on her in a few days, okay?"

Adam pulled a face. "*You'll* check on her? Maybe I should go. In fact, maybe I should go today. I *am* her best friend, after all."

"Whatever. You're not the only one who cares about her, Adam. I think you need to give her some space."

"Jamie's right. If Aarie wanted you to know, you would already know," Angela piped up.

"And do *you* know?" Adam asked.

Angela didn't reply but looked away.

Adam leaned forward. "You were here that weekend, and you spoke to her before she left. You *know* why she left, don't you?" he concluded.

"Look, Adam, it's like I said. If she wanted you to know, you would know."

"Come on, Angela," Jamie cut in. "If you *do* know something, we should all get to know. We all care about her, and it might stop us worrying."

"Yeah, I agree with Jamie," said Adam. "There might be something we can do or a way we can make things better. Come on, do you really think she'd be angry at you for sharing it with us?"

Angela grumbled. "Oh okay, but you're not gonna like it, Adam."

"Well, now I definitely need to know," Adam replied.

Angela continued. "Okay. So, she told me how she'd been seeing this guy called Jay. She seemed really happy about it—I mean, proper into him

—but she said it was complicated and seemed worried it might just come to an end. It's where she's been sneaking off to every other night."

"She denied sneaking off anywhere," Adam insisted.

"I know. Aarie still denied it to me too, but she wasn't in her room the night before I saw her, and she admitted staying over at his—"

"She did?" Adam interrupted.

"Nothing happened *apparently*. My point is, I was meant to meet her later in the day after I went to see Lori, but she'd already gone. I assumed she'd gone to see him again. Anyway, she came back really late that night, and I heard her crying, Adam. She was *really* crying, and I've never heard her cry like that before. I wanted to knock on her door, but I'd been drinking that night with Lori's friend, Gem, and trust me, I was in no fit state to comfort anyone. She's a bad influence that girl. I really hoped to speak to Aarie in the morning, but she left so early. I saw her rushing down the street from my window. She looked awful. God, I really wish I had knocked on her door that night. I know she's gone because something's happened between her and this Jay guy. I think they've split up or something. I texted her about him, and she just said she didn't want to talk about him ever again. If you'd heard her talk about him before, Jeez, you'd know she was in love with him, and I mean properly in love."

"Did she actually say that?" Adam quizzed.

"No, but a girl knows these things."

"Do you think the bastard hurt her?" Jamie asked.

"I don't think so. Well, not physically, anyway. And the way she described him, I don't think he was a bastard. Maybe he was ill or had to leave the country. I don't know. I'm just guessing now, but I don't think you should go storming down there to see her. She just needs time."

Adam's lower lip jutted out slightly into a sulky pout. "So, you don't think she'd be up for coming out tonight? It is my birthday, and she's never missed that before."

"Jeez, Adam, why do you always have to make things all about you? Aarie clearly has other stuff on her mind than your birthday. She must be really having a hard time," Jamie said in a huff.

"I just think it would do her good to have some fun, you know, forget this loser. He clearly didn't know what he had if he broke her heart."

"Maybe she broke his," Jamie replied.

"Well, whatever happened, it would do her good to be with friends. I'll text her the details, and if she wants to come, she'll come. If not, I guess I can't do anything about that."

Adam started tapping away at his phone as he began a text to Aarie. Seeing as Angela was already scrolling through her phone, Jamie decided to get his phone out too. His fingers also tapped in a quick message to Aarie.

Jamie:

Hey Gorgeous, how are you feeling? It would be good to see you out tonight. Mainly 'cos I don't really wanna be stuck with this pining loser who calls himself your best friend. Please save me!

But joking aside, I know you must have stuff going on with you, so I understand if you can't make it. No pressure, just really hope you're okay. Let me know if you wanna chat about anything. You know I always have ears for you.

Love Jamie. x

Adam:

Hey, me again. (sorry). I know you're not answering calls & that probably means u don't wanna talk but worried about u. Please give us a ring if you can. U can talk2me about anything, whatever u have going on. Anyway, I know it's not a good time to ask again but, in case u wanna come out tonight 4 my birthday, here are the deets:

7:00ish drinks & food at home

8:00 Faversham 9:30 Mission

(CALL ME!...please.)

xXx

Angela:

Hey Chick,

just seeing if I can persuade you to come out tonight? It may be good to get out and have some fun. Let your hair down. Here to chat if you need me. xx

Jamie:

P.s would you mind much if Adam was not quite as intact as he was when you last saw him? I've decided I definitely like him so much LESS when you're not here. :-/

Miss you.

"Are we all texting Aarie at the same time?" Angela said, glancing at the others.

"Yep, looks like it." Jamie grinned.

Angela tutted. "Great. Just what she will want—another bombardment of texts."

"Well, she should just pick up her bloody phone, then we wouldn't have to," Adam moaned.

"So what's the plan anyway, you guys?" Angela asked. "Who's out tonight? Is Meira coming out, Jamie?"

"Who's Meira?" Adam asked.

"Just some girl I met," Jamie said nonchalantly.

"So are you two a thing?" Adam quizzed.

"We're just friends."

Angela scoffed. "Right—*whatever*. Like you could be just friends with her. She's way out of your league, but she looks at you like the sun shines out of your backside." Angela turned to Adam." She's proper fit like a model or something. She's gorgeous."

"So?" Jamie huffed. "I am perfectly capable of having friends who just happen to be attractive girls. I'm friends with Aarie, aren't I?"

Angela frowned. "Ahem, what about *me*?" she interrupted, fluttering her eyelashes. She nonchalantly brushed a hand through her fiery auburn hair as her big sage eyes played at gazing sultrily into his.

Jamie smirked. "Okay, I suppose you too."

"So, is she coming, this Meira?" Adam asked.

"Yeah, I think so. I think she must've really clicked with Aarie 'cos she seemed disappointed when I said I wasn't sure if she was coming. I didn't even think Aarie had chatted to her much the last time she came out with us."

"So, if she's hot, and you two are just friends, does that mean I can buy her a drink?" Adam raised an eyebrow.

"No," Jamie grunted. "I thought you were pining for Aarie, anyway?"

"I am. I mean, I'm not *pining* over her, but maybe I should try to move on. She clearly doesn't feel the same way. I didn't even know anything about this Jay guy. Even if she is single again, I'm not sure she'll ever see me *that* way. God, sometimes I think she looks at *you* in less of a friend zone way than me."

"That's because I'm way better looking than you, matey. Can't blame her for having good taste." Jamie chuckled.

Annoyance swept over Adam. "What's *wrong* with you? Why are you always saying stuff like that?"

"Oh, come on, it's just a joke," Jamie scoffed. "Get over it. You're too easy to wind up."

"Oh, Fuck off!" Adam spat. "You're always frigging flirting with her. Why do you do it? You know how I feel about her—"

"—You don't *own* her, Adam," Jamie snapped. "I can do whatever the hell I want. I'm not gonna change who I am because you started fancying our hot friend. It's just our thing, and it's just a bit of fun. The only person who gets to tell me to quit it is her. So, if you don't like it, then maybe *you* should just fuck off!"

"Boys! *Boys*!" Angela shrieked, holding her hands up between them both. "What's gotten into you two?"

Adam leaned back in his chair, glaring at Jamie across the table. "He frigging started it."

"Grow up, Adam," Jamie said.

Angela leaned forward. "Come on, Jamie. It's his birthday. Well, it will be after midnight. You know he's just upset Aarie's not here."

"We're all upset, Angela, but we're not *all* being dickheads about it."

"Jamie, quit it," Angela warned. "Look, say sorry to each other. You know I don't like bad vibes between us. Bad energy—it's not good for you, you know. It's bad for the soul."

"You what?" Jamie grimaced. "God, you've been hanging around that Lori too much. You'll be trying to cleanse our souls with joss sticks and read our frigging palms next."

"Jamie, just do it, and you too, Adam. Otherwise, I'm gonna tell Aarie not to bother coming back for a bit 'cos you two are acting like a pair of knobheads, and it's the last thing she needs to deal with. Alright?"

"Fucking hell, Ange. Who died and made you police of bad energy?" Jamie laughed. "We're men—we swear, tell each other to fuck off, then we go out and have a beer together later—it's just what we do!"

"So, you're still coming out tonight then... knobhead?" Adam asked Jamie, stubbornly unready to smooth out his frown.

Jamie picked at his fingernails. "I suppose so. But only 'cos Aarie would kick my arse if I didn't," he replied in a sulk.

Angela tutted again. "God, great apology guys. Can't wait for tonight's drunken version. Yay," she said sarcastically.

Chapter 14
Dark, Dark Soul

"She's not coming. I knew it. God, maybe I really should've gone to see her this morning. She really can't be right if she doesn't wanna be here tonight," Adam worried.

"It's still early. There's still time," Jamie said optimistically.

"It's quarter to ten," Adam replied.

"Yeah, and the club's open till four. It's early. Meira's only just arrived. I'm gonna meet her at the bar," Jamie replied, as he swung the club main room door open for Angela and Adam to go through.

"Don't forget your ticket!" shouted a short, plump woman who sat behind the cloakroom counter. Angela hurried back to the dimly lit entranceway as Jamie waited. The woman leaned over to pass her what looked like a yellow raffle ticket with a number on it. Angela scampered back through the door.

A cloud of fragrant smoke filled the air, illuminated by multicolour beams that streaked across the invisible ceilings of this otherwise dingy club. The pulsing drumbeat of the music boomed through the room, thumping against their chests like it had replaced their own heartbeat. Their hair vibrated and tickling their face as their eyes adjusted to the contrast of darkness and blinding strobe lights. They were greeted at a distance by Lori and Meira, who were squeezing past a queue at the bar. The two girls waved to them over the crowd, holding up full glasses and bottles of beer as they hurried forward.

"Hey, we got you guys drinks. The bar's absolutely packed," Lori shouted over the music as she reached her other friends.

"Thanks," Adam shouted back, passing a beer to Jamie and grabbing one for himself.

"We're gonna head to the other room to grab a booth, so we'll see you in a minute," Angela said to Adam and Jamie before she and Lori swiftly disappeared amongst the crowd.

"Hey, this is Meira. Meira—Adam," Jamie said with his arm around a tall oriental girl in a blue satin top and dark jeans. Her slick black fringe and shoulder-length hair framed her face perfectly. Angela had been right about her looks, and Adam's eyes widened at the stunningly attractive girl who leaned towards him.

"Hey, nice to meet you," they both said at the same time, smiling awkwardly.

A hand tapped Adam on the shoulder, causing him to turn around. He appeared slightly annoyed to be pulled away from this girl's attention, but his annoyance immediately melted away at the sight of the one girl he had really wanted to talk to tonight.

Aarie.

Adam flushed as his eyes took in every inch of her: the brown curls that fell loose against her shoulders, her smokey eyes, her full lashes, and her vibrant red painted lips. She looked different tonight. The fitted black dress Aarie wore hugged her slim figure, and Adam's jaw dropped as his eyes wandered over the curves of her body and the skin of her bare legs. She was so much taller in her high heels. His eyes shot back up to hers.

"Aarie!" Adam finally said. "You look—wow... and you came! I'm so glad you're here. I've missed you, and I was so worried."

"I know. I'm sorry," Aarie replied. "But I would never have missed your birthday. So, here I am."

Adam threw his arms around her, carefully hovering his drink over her shoulder. Her arms came around him too as Adam sighed contently.

Jamie tapped Aarie's arm, making her glance up. "Hey, you. We almost thought you were gonna be a no-show." Jamie smiled.

"Well, I had to come back. I was beginning to worry about Adam's physical safety if I left the two of you alone any longer." She grinned, gently breaking away from Adam.

"Come here then," Jamie said, reaching in for a hug but then lifting her straight off the ground. Her arms went around him. "You had us all so worried," he said into her shoulder as he gently placed her back down.

"I know, but I'm back now for good and ready to have some fun. So, what did I miss?"

"You missed drinks, but here, have mine. I'll get another in a bit. Hey, you've met Meira, haven't you?" Jamie asked, turning to Meira now."

"Hey, yeah we met a few weeks ago." Aarie smiled, leaning in nearer to Meira. "Hi. Are you having a good night?"

A warm, friendly smile spread on Meira's face. "Yeah, so far. I've only just got here too, but I like the music. It's cool that you could make it. Jamie said you had some bad news or something?"

"Oh, it was nothing really. I was just feeling under the weather," Aarie lied. "I'm fine now, though."

Adam draped an arm around Aarie's shoulder. "Hey, the others went to the next room. We should go to meet them. They'll be glad to see you're here."

Aarie nodded. "Lead the way," she replied.

Adam grabbed her hand, pulling her through the busy crowd as Jamie and Meira followed. They came into a brighter lit room with leather booth seating areas and another bar. Vintage lamps hung on long cords from the ceiling. Dim orange spirals of light whirled in the centre of their bulbs, casting an ambient sunset glow throughout the place. The door closed behind Meira, instantly cutting off the booming underground drum and bass from the other room. A more relaxed electronic beat replaced it.

Adam pointed to one of the larger booths in the furthest corner of the room. "There they are."

"Aarie, you're here!" Angela cheered, hurrying to give her a big hug.

"Yep, I made it," Aarie said, smiling. "You look amazing by the way. I love the dress. Is it an Angela Bennett original?" she asked, struggling for breath as Angela squeezed her tightly.

"Of course. I only just finished it yesterday. I might make another in sage green to match my eyes," Angela said, pulling on her slinky grey dress. "But enough about that—you look bloody gorgeous, Aarie! Wow. Come and sit down. We're sat just over here," she said, moving back to the table.

They all shimmied into the booth. Glasses and bottles already cluttered the table in front of them as they rested their drinks down. Aarie sat in the middle of Adam and Lori. Angela, Jamie and Meira sat across from them. Another group of Adam's friends wandered in just after them and moved to sit in the booth opposite theirs. They threw high fives to Adam, who reached up to greet them all as they passed. He got up and followed them to their booth, stopping to chat to them for a while.

Lori turned to Aarie with a beaming smile. Aarie really liked Lori. She was one of those people that you felt like you had known for years even though you had only met them a few weeks ago. She had feline blue eyes, platinum blond hair, and tiny pointy ears that stuck out from her messy style ponytail. It made her look like some kind of cool pixie girl, Aarie thought as she smiled back at her.

"How are you, Aarie? Heard you had bad news or something?" Lori said.

"Yeah, so everyone keeps saying—like someone *died* or something," Aarie replied with a laugh. "But I'm fine, honestly. I've just been under the weather and not sleeping that well lately, that's all. I just thought I'd spend a few days at my dad's. It was really nice to spend a bit of time with him, but it's good to be back too."

"That's nice. You know, if you're not sleeping, I have some good herbal remedies that work wonders. They work well for hangovers too." She grinned.

"Do they stop nightmares?" Aarie asked.

"They can sometimes. Why, what kind of nightmares are you having?"

"Well, I don't really want to go into it too much, but just random stuff. It just whirls around my head over and over, and I just can't seem to push it out when I sleep. If I could, I'd try not to sleep at all at the moment."

"Oh, that's not good," Lori said as her brows creased. "This may sound strange, but just humour me, okay? Give me your hand."

Aarie laughed. "Are you gonna read my palm and tell me my future? 'Cos Angela told me you do that sometimes."

"I do. Mainly when I'm drunk... so it doesn't tend to work that often." She laughed.

Aarie's brows raised. "But only because of the drink, right?" she joked.

137

"Of course. Anyway, no, I'm not going to read your palm, but I did want to try something. I have a weird gift. Maybe I can help figure out why you're having nightmares."

"I doubt that," Aarie humourlessly laughed. Lori ignored her and took Aarie's hand into her own, creasing her forehead as she concentrated.

"I want you to focus on whatever it is you have nightmares about. Focus on it really hard, and then I may be able to see and analyse it. Some people have problems with this part because they don't remember most of their dreams, not properly. Also, they don't take me seriously, but just try your best."

"Well, believe me, I remember mine clearly," Aarie said as images instantly surfaced in her mind. Lori's eyes scanned the air in front of her as though trying to see something invisible. Aarie didn't want to think of her nightmares right now, and she also didn't believe Lori had any gift. However, Lori was nice, so Aarie did as she was asked. Aarie wondered how her night had already brought her back to what she had been running from. Images of Jay became clear in her head, and she focused hard on him.

He had seemed so gentle and kind in the beginning. His blue eyes and gentle smile had always looked genuinely kind from the first night they had met, to when he showed her his home, and even as he slept beside her. However, the stranger that hurt her did not have kind eyes or a kind smile. They were dead eyes and deadly jaws, and she had been just something for his amusement.

Lori gasped, then let go of Aarie's hand, abruptly pushing it away. "What was that, Aarie?" she shrieked.

"What was what?"

"The monster! Jesus, is that what your nightmares are of? And who's the man with the blue eyes,"

Aarie's mouth dropped open. "You saw Jay?" she asked, in disbelief.

"Jay? Is he your boyfriend?" Lori asked.

"No, he's... he's no one to me anymore."

"Did he hurt you? Is that why you're seeing him as a monster in your dreams?"

Aarie's heart sank at the thought, and she wanted to change the subject before the night was ruined entirely.

"No. Look, sorry, I know you mean well, but I don't want to talk about him tonight. It's just a stupid dream. Maybe it's to do with my accident I had in the summer. Post-traumatic stress or something. I don't know."

"Hmm, could be, but it's just so strange that your dreams are so clear. They're like real memories of your life. No wonder you're not sleeping," Lori said, fascinated.

"I'm simply amazed you could actually see what I was seeing," Aarie said astonished but also wanting to change the subject. "You really have a gift, Lori. To be honest, I didn't believe you at first, and if there's someone who should have believed you about something unusual like that, it should've been me. I'd like to talk to you about it another time, I really would. It's incredible. But maybe just not tonight, okay? Jay is a sore point right now."

"Oh right, you two split up, huh? I get it. Okay, enough said. Let me get you a drink," Lori said, sitting forward to get out from the booth.

"Too late," Jamie interrupted as he came to the table carrying as many drinks as he could carry. The bottles and glasses clanged together as he placed them on the table. He lifted a glass over to Aarie. "Your drink, Miss Stone." He smiled, then glanced up at the others. "You guys might have to grab whichever's yours. I can't remember who wanted what," he said.

A while later, Adam came back over from the other table of friends and sat back down next to Aarie.

"How's my favourite girl doing?" Adam asked, seemingly slurring his words.

"Trying to catch up with you guys," she replied, taking a large swig of her spiced rum and coke.

"Well, drink up guys, 'cos I think it's time we head back into the main room for a dance."

"Did you hear that, everyone? The birthday boy says it's time to get on that dance floor. Woo-hoo!" Angela cheered, ruffling Jamie's hair, to his annoyance.

Aarie lifted her drink up, and within a few long gulps, her glass was empty. She let out a satisfied sigh as she wiped her mouth, then set her glass back down.

"I'm ready when you are," she said.

"Alright, my girl's ready to party!" Adam boomed, then downed his drink. "Let's go!" he said, seconds later. He grabbed Aarie's arm, helping her out of the booth as Angela, Lori, Jamie and Meira followed behind. The other's guzzled their drinks faster, mouthing that they'd meet everyone else in five more minutes. Adam led the way to the next room.

The thumping beat vibrated through their chests and drummed in their ears as they entered the main room again. As they joined the swaying crowds on the dance floor, their bodies moved in time to the captivating rhythm. A fresh dose of alcohol coursed through their veins while the buzz of the night felt electric. The lights, the music, and the carefree motion of the crowd—everything was exhilarating. Aarie could finally be free to forget her troubles and simply get lost in the night. She stared up as beams of light streamed above her head. Closing her eyes briefly, she smiled, and she danced.

Aarie had now been dancing for hours. Though she could feel her hair slightly sticking to the sides of her face in the moist air, she hadn't tired of moving to the rhythm. It felt so good just to let herself go and have fun despite the rising temperature of the room. The heat and the alcohol in her blood made her cheeks rosy pink. Her arms raised up high above her head as she swayed and twisted her hips slowly in a hypnotic trancelike manner to the beat. The song was not one she knew, but Aarie liked the beat and wanted to enjoy the moment, thinking of nothing else.

However, at that moment, some arms came up from behind her, resting on her waist. She tensed, but before she could turn around, a familiar friendly voice spoke.

"It's just me, Aarie," Adam said, letting Aarie relax once again.

It felt good to have someone who cared about her, hold her close. Adam and Aarie had always openly hugged each other and showed friendly affection towards each other, but there was something different in the way he held her now. He gently swayed behind her to the rhythm of her hips, slowly pulling her closer. A memory flickered in her mind, of dancing with Jay at the ball. She thought of Jay's warmth against her as he pulled her body close to his. *How could that or their kiss outside the manor house not have meant something to him?* Drifting into her thoughts, she leaned back into Adam, subconsciously pulling his arms around her tighter.

"Are you having a good night?" Adam asked, breaking her from her brief reverie. She paused, taking in how close they were dancing together, and it caught her slightly off guard.

"Um, what? I mean, yeah. Are you?"

"Yeah." He smiled, resting his chin gently against her hair. "You look beautiful tonight," he said softly in her ear. "I know I said it earlier, but you do. I'm pretty sure most of the men in this club haven't been able to stop looking at you all night. I haven't." His voice was so gentle and had an unfamiliar tone that Aarie had never heard before.

Aarie didn't reply. Instead, she glanced down at her arms that held his tight around her. *This was okay, wasn't it? He was her best friend, after all*, she thought. Then again, she knew from his tone of voice and touch that this meant more to him than that.

"I think I'm a little drunk," she confessed, hoping that Adam wouldn't read too much into them dancing together. She loosened her grip, then glanced at her watch. Time had flown. She turned abruptly within his arms to face him.

"It's two o'clock." She smiled gingerly. "Happy birthday." She stretched out and rested her arms on his shoulders, putting a little more distance between them. "You're officially nineteen."

"Thanks." He smiled but then was studying her face. "Aarie?" he said hesitantly. "There's something I've been wanting to say to you, or more accurately, to ask you."

"Please don't ask about why I left," she said quickly.

"Oh, okay, but it's not that. It's probably not a good time for this either if I'm honest, but if I don't just say what I want to say now, I'm scared I might never have the guts to say it." He clung on to Aarie's arms, which were still on his shoulders, and then glanced down at them. "How do you see me, Aarie?"

Aarie noticed how he avoided her gaze as he spoke, and she was almost afraid to answer. "Adam, I don't understand what you're asking me?" she lied.

"I care about you a lot, Aarie. You know that, right?"

"Yeah, of course I do. You're my best friend. I care about you too."

"But it's more than that, Aarie, and the way you look tonight—it's been driving me crazy. I need you to know that I think I'm in—"

"—Adam stop," she quickly said before he could finish his sentence. "We've had a lot to drink tonight, so please, don't say any more. Earlier, you asked me if I was okay, and I said I was, but I'm *not*. I'm really not. I don't think I will be for a while. I'm confused about stuff I don't want to talk about right now, and I'm a little drunk. I think we both are, and I don't want either of us to say anything we're gonna regret in the morning. I really need my best friend right now. I can't lose you too, okay? I just don't think I could handle that."

Adam glanced away as his cheeks flushed red. "You're right," he said. "I shouldn't have said anything. I didn't think. I'm sorry. You've got enough on your mind, and I *am* very drunk. Now is probably the worse time. Aarie, I don't want to have ruined anything between us—"

"—You haven't. You don't need to apologise. You probably won't even remember this in the morning. Look, we're having a good night, so there's no reason to end it worrying about anything. We're good. Nothing has changed from ten minutes ago. Okay?"

"Okay," Adam sighed.

"I should probably get us some water from the bar," Aarie said.

"I'll go get it."

"No, it's alright, I'll go. I need to go to the ladies room anyway while I'm up that way. I'll be back in a few minutes, so stop worrying already," she assured.

"Alright," Adam replied, but Aarie was already disappearing into the crowd.

The bar was still busy, so Aarie guessed she would be a while. She let out a long exhale of breath as she pushed passed the moist dancing bodies around her. She hadn't really needed the ladies room or the water, but Adam's drunken words had surprised her. Consequently, she thought it best to give them both space and a few minutes to think.

An arm reached out from the crowd and tapped Aarie on the shoulder, stopping her in her tracks.

"Hey," Jamie said.

"Hey, where's Meira?" she replied.

"Oh, I think she went somewhere with Lori. They'll probably be back soon," Jamie replied nonchalantly before changing the subject. "So, you and Adam looked pretty close over there, didn't you?"

"How do you mean?" Aarie asked.

"I thought you were about to cop off with him at one point."

"Don't be ridiculous. It's Adam. We were just dancing."

"Like *that*? You know, he's probably likely to read something more into it than you think. He's got a thing for you, just to warn you. It's probably not a good idea to lead him on if you're not interested in him that way."

Aarie's brows puckered up. "What? I didn't lead him on. He's my best friend. What do you mean he has a thing for me? I thought he was just drunk!"

Jamie frowned. "Come on, Aarie. You shouldn't play with people's feelings like that. You're a good looking girl. Don't play dumb and tell me you don't know that. You know perfectly well how men look at you. You *must* do, and it's not right to string Adam along. As much as he can get on my nerves sometimes, he doesn't deserve to be made a fool of. I just thought better of you that's all," Jamie said bitterly.

Aarie's mouth dropped open. She scanned over Jamie's scowling face, and it stung. He had never spoken to her like this, and it appeared he hadn't finished yet either.

"Maybe I just don't know you as well as I thought I did. After all, I never took you for someone who'd go around sneaking out at night, throwing yourself at some loser like you were desperate. You're an adult, so it's fine, but just because you let this Jay guy use you and break your heart, doesn't make it's okay to use your friends as a rebound to patch things up —"

Aarie's hand came up almost as a sudden reflex to the painful sound of Jay's name. The palm of her hand struck Jamie's face with a rasping slap. She froze, acknowledging the shock on his face and feeling the shock of her own rage. Her lip trembled slightly, but she briskly turned and began to move through the crowd. Jamie grabbed hold of her hand quickly before she could leave.

"Aarie, wait! I didn't mean that. You know I didn't mean it. Shit. I'm really sorry. I'm no good at this... not with you."

She turned, avoiding his stare. "Good at what—telling me what you really think of me? That you think I'm *that* type of girl! But above all, you think I'm a crap friend who is too absorbed in my own problems to notice anyone else's feelings?"

"I never said that," Jamie insisted.

Aarie's lip quivered again as a lump seemed to build up deep in her throat. "But you wanted to. And maybe I *am* a bad friend. I didn't notice how Adam felt, but I should have because it's so obvious now, especially with the way he's been acting around me all this time. I was just so wrapped up in things going on with me, that I never noticed, Jamie. But I would never intentionally lead him on. As for Jay, not that it's any of your business, we never... Look, it wasn't like that, okay! You don't know anything about us. How can you even think I'm like that? Is that what

Adam and Angela think about me too? I need to go and tell him I'm sorry," Aarie said as her voice wavered and a tear rolled down her cheek.

Jamie immediately put his arms around her, then pulled her to him. "Wait, don't go yet. I'm sorry. I didn't mean to upset you, and I didn't even mean what I just said. No one thinks that about you, especially not me. I'm sorry. I had no right to say any of it."

Aarie let Jamie's arms wrap around her. Part of her wanted to pull away, but as she felt her tears coming, she leaned her head into him so he wouldn't see.

"You must have meant every word, Jamie. Otherwise, you wouldn't have said it. I don't even know where this all came from, but you always speak your mind," she glumly said against his chest.

"No, I don't. Not always. Not when it comes to you," he replied.

"You keep saying that, but what does that even mean? You sounded so angry and so disgusted with me. Why would you—"

"—I'm not angry, Aarie. I'm jealous!" he blurted out.

Aarie looked up at him, hastily wiping her eyes. "What?"

"Can't you see? I'm jealous. God, I'm jealous of Adam, of all people. Seeing him holding you like that—all I could think is that I wanted it to be me. I'm jealous that he's recently decided he fancies you and has plucked up the courage to tell you. He's done in a few weeks what I haven't been able to do for years. And more importantly, I don't just fancy you, Aarie. It's more than that. I was trying to tell you how I felt that night we went out together... before Adam ruined the moment. He wasn't the only one acting like an idiot that night. I know I was too. But the reason I have been an idiot to him lately is I'm afraid that you might pick him.

As for this Jay guy—you can't imagine how jealous I am of him. I didn't even know he existed until today. It kills me to think he could've taken advantage of you or just used you and hurt you. I don't even know what happened between you two. I can only let my imagination run stupid, and I'm sorry." Jamie wiped a tear away from Aarie's cheek as she stared back at him. "Say something Aarie, please. I feel terrible for what I said to you. I didn't mean it or mean to tell you all of this like *this*. I just couldn't help it, but I could never think bad of you. For some reason, I seem to become an idiot when it comes to telling *you* how I really feel. Maybe I'd be better without words," he said, holding her face in his hands as he leaned forward.

"But what about Meira?" Aarie asked, unsure she should remain this close to him.

"Meira is just a friend."

Aarie's eyes focused intently on Jamie's, and there was no mistaking the desire within them. His body pressed against hers, and she wasn't sure why, but she didn't want to pull away as he brought his face to hers. She swallowed. Her eyes traced over Jamie's face, landing on his lips. Strangely, she couldn't stop imagining what they would feel like on hers, and at that moment, she realised that she didn't want to just imagine them anymore. As Jamie leaned in, she pulled him closer to her.

His kiss was soft and gentle at first but soon moved with more urgency as he drew her nearer to him. The thump of his heart beat against her hands as she leaned them on his chest. She was surprised at how natural this felt, and if she let herself, she could so easily get lost in the desire to be loved. The scent of his skin was so familiar, yet being like this with Jamie filled Aarie with the strange excitement of exploring new territory. He held her with so much affection, but Aarie could not help her mind wandering back to Jay and their kiss in front of the manor house. The swoon of it still filled her mind. *How had Jay managed to convince her that he loved her completely if he did not have the kind human heart that Jamie had?* It seemed like both of their hearts beat for hers. Regardless, something didn't feel right, and she couldn't ignore it. Her hands moved quickly over Jamie's, pulling them away from her face as she broke away.

"Jamie, I can't do this. Not now. I'm sorry. I don't want to hurt you, but I can't lie. I'm in love with someone else," she admitted.

"This Jay guy?"

"Yes."

"But he hurt you, didn't he?"

Aarie didn't reply, but she knew her silence told Jamie the truth.

"I would never hurt you, Aarie."

"I know, Jamie. I don't want to be in love with him anymore, but I can't help the way I feel. I thought he felt the same way, but it turns out I can't know what real love is, and I'm just tired of feeling like this." Somehow, this night kept pulling her back to this misery that she wished would just end. "I'm not ready to start anything new, I'm sorry. It's too soon. I'm too confused right now."

"It's okay, Aarie. I'm sorry. I know it's bad timing, but just tell me one thing—I felt something just now when we kissed—I can't have just imagined it, can I?"

"No, you didn't, but I don't know what it means, Jamie. I can't think straight. Please, just give me time to think things through. I don't want to ruin anything between us. Then there's Adam too—this night is really making our friend circle complicated, and I just can't think about all these things right now. I'm sorry."

Her brows knitted together tightly as she stared at him. She thought of all the times she had looked upon his face over the years. This confident boy had been such a big part of her life. *How had she never noticed this spark that was clear in his golden hazel eyes now?* His tousled hair seemed unaffected by the moist air of the club; perfect butterscotch wisps and spikes gleamed like gold under the flashing strobe lights. The ever-changing light of this room could not distort his undeniable good looks or hide the warmth in his presence. He had such a kind heart, and she never wanted to break it.

Jamie finally nodded in response to Aarie's words, giving her hand a gentle squeeze in his. "Okay, you're right, and I don't want to ruin anything either. Whatever happens, I don't want to lose our friendship. I just needed you to finally know how I feel, that's all."

"Okay." She nodded, deep in thought. "Look, I'd better go now. Adam's probably wondering where I've got to with the water I said I'd get."

"Let me get the water for you both. I'll come and find you in a few minutes. You should probably get back to him before he gets withdrawal symptoms or something." Jamie tried for a smile, but he was noticeably glum once it faded.

Aarie pursed her lips, wanting to say something more meaningful, but she couldn't think anymore. She just needed a few more minutes of space again, so she agreed. "Alright. I'll see you in a bit then," Aarie said as she began moving away. "And Jamie, I'm glad I know how you really feel now, so don't regret telling me."

Before Jamie could respond, Aarie was already pushing back away through the masses of people around them. His fingers traced over his lips where her kiss still lingered, then he smiled as his eyes followed her until she disappeared into the crowd.

Aarie reached the area where she had left Adam, but he was nowhere to be seen. Meira caught her attention, waving across the crowd to her. She was on her own too, so Aarie quickly made her way to her.

"Hey, Meira. Where are the others?" Aarie shouted over the music.

"The guys all went upstairs to the rooftop to get some fresh air. They sent me down to get you."

"Oh, Jamie went to get some water. I'll go tell him, then we'll come up."

"It's alright, Adam just went to get water too, so they'll see each other and then meet us."

"Oh, okay," Aarie agreed.

As they made their way up the narrow stairwell near the back of the club, Aarie could feel the air getting cooler. It was refreshing to get away from the hot, sweaty atmosphere of the main club room for a little while. Aarie pushed a steel door open, and a cold breeze rushed past her face. As she stepped out, her eyes scanned the dimly lit seating area. It was empty, and the tables were covered with rippling pools of water as the rain came down. It was already dampening her hair and soaking into her dress.

Aarie turned around in confusion as Meira slammed the door shut. Aarie jumped back, startled. Meira stepped towards her with an emotionless expression, and Aarie was forced to back into a wall.

"Meira, what's going on? I don't understand. Where is everyone?"

Meira's blank expression wavered slightly. "I'm sorry, Aarie. I want you to know that it's nothing personal. I think you're probably a great person. I know Jamie thinks so. I had hoped to make this quick and swift in the dream world. When the Oneiroi stepped in, I thought they had taken this awful but necessary task out of my hands. However, you seem to have survived even the Oneiroi, which by the way, is very impressive. Trust me, I don't think they like anybody who isn't Oneiroi."

Aarie frowned. "What? What are you talking about?" she asked. "How do you know—"

"—You've met me before, Aarie. In a dream." Meira's eyes shimmered at that point, changing from dark brown to honey gold. "Me *and* my pack."

Aarie shuddered. "The wolves," she whispered, staring into golden eyes like those that had haunted her dreams. One more pair of golden eyes moved out from the shadows of the deserted seating area. A low snarl rumbled deep within the wolf's throat as it stopped a short distance away from them. Aarie's attention shot back to Meira. A sharp metal object shimmered in the dim light as Meira held it and took another step towards her. Aarie was backed up against a wall and had nowhere to run. Meira lunged towards her with incredible strength and speed, pinning her down.

"Close your eyes, Aarie. I don't *want* to do this, but I have to. I wish there were another way. I'm sorry, but I will make it quick, I promise," she said with a contrite tone.

Everything had happened so fast, and Aarie felt like a rabbit trapped in headlights. If she had been drunk at all earlier, she seemed to have significantly sobered up now. The adrenaline that pumped through her body had seen to that. Her eyes fixed on Meira, unwilling to close while a knife in Meira's hand drew nearer. Aarie was trembling, but there was something other than just fear working its way through her veins. This person that Aarie barely knew—this thing in front of her—had caused her to feel weak in Jay's world. Aarie hated feeling vulnerable as well as the fact she'd been forced to rely on Jay to save her. Jay, the man who had only protected her in order to prolong his cruel experiment. Aarie's fists tightened. Something inside her exploded and swept through her body, replacing fear and desperation with an all-encompassing fiery wave.

Rage.

Meira flew backwards as Aarie struck a forceful blow to her face. Aarie struck her again, this time kicking her to the floor. The knife in Meira's hand clattered along the ground as shock washed over her. Meira brushed herself off quickly, rubbing her bruised face in the dim light.

Movement in the shadows caught Aarie's attention, and she assumed it was the other wolf, but the silhouette that stood there now was no animal. Although there was something unfamiliar about him, she knew his presence all too well. Her anger slowly subsided as Jay stepped out from the shadows.

Aarie gasped involuntarily, stepping backwards as her head shook in disbelief. His deep blue eyes flickered to hers from within a hooded long black coat. Leather straps fastened the garment against his chest as another strap crossed over one shoulder and led around to his back. Various weapons were attached to it, and she could make out the hilt of a sword peering over his shoulder. The cut of the coat opened out at his hips to reveal a belt that hung heavy around his waist with more weaponry. Sharp, scaled armour covered his shoulder blades and arms. He wore black as he had often done before, but there was something more deadly and dangerous in how he dressed now. He was dressed as though for one purpose only—to kill. His eyes flitted now to Meira and the other wolf beside her as he pulled his hood back.

"Oneiroi, we're on the same side," Meira shouted to him. "The blood demons know about the girl. They're coming for her, but we won't let them get to her." Meira's voice wavered as Jay approached. "We're going to stop this before it's too late. I know she has to die."

"And that is why we are NOT on the same side," Jay shouted with a searing malevolence.

At that moment, the wolf to Meira's side leapt forward onto Jay. Jay reacted instantly, pulling them both into a tumble to the ground. Leaping up again, he lunged forward, flinging the enormous wolf into a wall like a small rodent. It yelped and stayed on the ground where it fell. Meira quickly glanced towards Aarie, who had managed to get a short distance away from her. Grabbing the fallen knife off the floor, Meira leapt towards her in a few brisk strides. Before Meira could reach her, Jay swept Aarie out of the way with one swift movement of his body. He held her out of Meira's grasp with one arm. With his other arm, Jay pulled a sword from the holster strapped to his back. He swivelled it around, then held it towards Meira, who stood defensively with her eyes fixed on him. A rustle sounded behind him where he had left the other wolf. Briefly releasing Aarie, Jay kicked out at Meira with one firm lightning-fast blow that sent her tumbling to the floor. Scooping his arm around Aarie again, he shielded her from the other wolf that got to its feet.

Just then, the metal door flew open, and Adam stood at the top of the steps. Utterly bewildered and incredulous to the scene that laid in front of him, he shouted out, "Aarie? What the hell's going on?"

Aarie immediately turned to him, mouthing his name, but only a whisper came out. Jay glanced down at Aarie and then back at the wolf. Hastily pushing her in Adam's direction, Jay sent her into a run. He shot an urgent and commanding glance towards Adam.

"Get her out of here. Now!"

Adam wasted no time when he saw the size of the wolf; it stood several feet tall and was only metres from Aarie. He grabbed her hand, and they ran towards the stairway to the club. Adam threw one last glance back towards Jay and the wolf that was now upon him, then he and Aarie disappeared down the stairwell.

Jay plunged his sword deep into the wolf's chest. A yelp turned into a gurgling sound as its eyes slowly closed and its body went limp. The claws that had fiercely clung to Jay's chest, now relaxed. He pushed the creature to one side, then got to his feet.

Meira stood in front of him now, half transformed into a wolf. Her golden eyes narrowed as she snarled, revealing sharp canine teeth. She took an attack stance, holding sharp elongated claws out in front of her. Jay's blue eyes darkened until they were their deepest black. His jawline reshaped with a set of razor-sharp fangs as he hissed back at her. She leapt at him, throwing several swipes of her claws in his direction. He ducked and turned, avoiding all of them. With one thrust of his arm, he lifted Meira up off the ground by her throat, then threw her to the side. She fell to the ground, clutching her throat as she stared up at him. Before she could move, he was upon her, holding her down on the floor with his weight. His sword raised above her throat.

"I don't understand?" she cried out desperately. Her voice faltered now as her body trembled. She seemed no longer the menacing creature from a moment ago, just a frightened teenaged girl. "Please, I thought this is what the Oneiroi would want? I never wanted to hurt the girl, but it's the only way. I thought I was helping us all," she pleaded, but the blade was on her throat now, and she closed her eyes, afraid this was the end.

Several moments passed, and the blade slipped away from her skin slowly.

Meira swallowed. "You're Oneiroi..." she whispered, opening her eyes. She peered up at Jay, whose stare had never left her. "...but, you came to this world to *save* the mortal. Why?"

"I have my reasons." Jay glared at her.

"But if the other blood demons get to her first, this could be the end for so many."

"I won't let that happen," he replied.

Meira studied him carefully as she could do nothing else. His black eyes fixed on her as she acknowledged the multitude of weaponry attached to him. Jay did not need it to fight her; his Oneiroi strength was enough, yet he had chosen to arrive in full Oneiroi battle gear as though at war. He had done so as a visual announcement and warning. He had killed Meira's pack member so quickly and effortlessly. It would not take much for him to kill her too if he wished. However, his grip on her loosened.

"Why all this for one mortal girl?" she asked nervously.

"She is *not* just one mortal girl," Jay replied with complete disdain. However, after a brief pause, he moved the blade from Meira's throat, drawing it back into its holster over his shoulder. Shifting his weight from Meira, Jay crouched beside her. "...not to me," he added as his facial features began to transform back to their usual appearance. He heard the intensity of his own voice as he spoke of Aarie, and he knew a slight violet shimmer tinged his irises now. It seemed to trigger immediate recognition and understanding within Meira. She glanced quickly at his wrist as a violet glow shimmered from within the darkness of his sleeve.

"Semper Sodales," she gasped and then slowly sat up on the floor. "She's yours, isn't she? That's why her blood is special to the blood demons."

Jay didn't respond except for a deep inhale and exhale of breath as he stared at her.

Meira continued. "I've never witnessed it before, but I know of it. That's why you had to come here, isn't it? And it was *you* who saved her before, back in your world, wasn't it? I thought you had meant to take the matter into your own hands, but that wasn't it—you were simply saving her because you knew she could be harmed in her dreams. It all makes sense now. You're Jay, who Aarie spoke of earlier, and she's your Semper Sodale," Meira said, almost sympathetically now.

"So, you understand now that I will do *anything* to keep her safe," Jay replied. "If I *have to* destroy you and your whole pack, I will do so. I don't want to, but you *know* that if it has to come to it, I will," he said with no malice in his voice, just a regretful matter-of-fact tone.

She nodded.

"And the blood demons? Will you kill them all too? 'Cos I'm not sure you can keep her safe from all of them forever," Meira asked.

Jay leaned forward. "Then help me. I don't want war with you or your wolves. You and your pack needn't die for this. Help me keep her from them, and I will keep you and your pack safe."

"Oneiroi offering to keep wolves safe? Don't we mess up your perfect world and threaten this one? I thought we were abominations to your kind?" she said bitterly, referring to the common opinion of many Oneiroi.

"I'm not like most Oneiroi, and they don't all speak for me. If I saw you that way, it would make Aarie an abomination too, wouldn't it? So, I think we both know that is not what I believe, at least, not anymore. Oneiroi, dreamwalkers and mortals—maybe we're all meant to be. Maybe none of us could exist without the other?" he said thoughtfully. "So do we have a deal, Meira?" he continued, holding out his right hand to her.

It was the first time he had said her name, and Meira was clearly surprised that he knew it. As she reached out to shake his hand, his sleeve crept up his arm, revealing the skin of his wrist more clearly. Below the shimmering violet looped symbol was another marking that laced his skin; dark patterns wound into the shape of a moon and stars. Meira gasped, as she recognised these symbols too. All Oneiroi and most dreamwalkers knew of symbols like these.

"You're First Blood of the first realm—a direct descendant of the ancient families. Which means... you're Jaydon Onuris. You're royalty!" She said incredulously.

"I was never one for titles," Jay nonchalantly replied. All anger had gone from him now. "...but as much as that is true, so too is my word, and I give you my word, if you help me keep Aarie safe, I will do all I can to protect you and your wolves from the blood demons and the Oneiroi."

Meira nodded and slowly shook his hand. Jay sat back, relaxing his weight onto his elbows with his feet outstretched. It gave the appearance that he had let all his guard down, but in reality, it would only take a split second for him to snap back into fighting mode if he needed to. However, he had done this to put Meira more at ease. She glanced down again at his wrist and to the intricate markings that branded him royalty. They were still on show as his sleeves had rucked up at his elbows. Her eyes reflected the light from the violet looped symbol as it pulsated in the dark.

"How long have you waited for your Semper Sodale?" she asked.

"A long time," he whispered.

"Jesus, I just attacked royalty," she blurted out, as though just letting it sink in. "I'm sorry I attacked Aarie. I'm so lucky to be still alive, aren't I? How did you stop yourself from killing me?" she asked, horrified by her actions.

"I'm still debating it," Jay said dryly, but on seeing a brief twitch of despair on Meira's face, he added, "but I guess we made a deal now, so a deal's a deal. Besides, I think Aarie might be a little angry with me if I killed one of her best friends' girlfriend." His face softened with a subtle smile, but then it disappeared as fast as it had come. "Though, I'm not sure she's in the best spirits to see me here anyway. Maybe she never will be again."

"I don't think that's true," Meira replied. "After all, you can't just switch something like that off, can you? I thought Semper Sodales Seals are kind of a done deal?"

"Aarie doesn't know I bear the mark. I don't know if it's the same for mortals or if she can even bear the mark herself. This has never happened before," he said, subconsciously reaching to touch the looped symbol around his wrist. "Besides, there are some things one cannot forgive. What I did to wake her was unforgivable." He flinched at the memory. "I can't forgive myself. I don't expect her to."

"I'm sorry we chased her. I thought I was saving my kind and hers. It's the only reason why my wolves did what we did," she said sincerely.

"I know. That's the *real* reason you're still alive," Jay said honestly. "If it means anything, I'm sorry I killed your wolf friend. He left me no choice, but I took no pleasure in it."

"Joe—his name was Joe, but I wouldn't call him a friend exactly. He was a bit of a jerk if I'm really honest." Her passive tone surprised Jay. "He insisted on coming with me tonight," she continued. "I think he was planning to overthrow me as pack leader, eventually. There was always something nasty about him. I think he enjoyed hunting Aarie. I think he wanted to watch her die more than he wanted to stop the blood demons getting to her. I probably would've had to put him down myself."

"Well, since you put it that way, I'm not sorry at all." Jay dusted off his hands and got to his feet. He offered a hand out to Meira, who was still sat on the ground.

"You're *alright*, Meira. You're not what I expected to find when I got here."

She took his hand as he pulled her up to stand. "You're not what I expected of an Oneiroi Guardian either. I'm glad. If I'm honest, I'm still a bit overwhelmed by who you are. Aren't you like *mythical* or something?" she asked with a hint of awe.

Jay laughed.

Just at that moment, a drunken teenager stumbled through the doorway in the far corner. It was Jamie. He seemed unable to see them in the dark shadows.

"I'd better go. I should make sure Aarie got home safe," Jay whispered. "I trust this charming chap is safe in your hands? In fact, I must insist that he is. I feel he may be quite important to Aarie," he said, gesturing to Jamie.

"What should I say to him? How do I tell him what I nearly did?" she despaired, glancing up at Jay, full of guilt and regret.

He rested a hand gently on her shoulder. "Don't say anything. Not until I've seen Aarie. I don't think he needs to hear any of it yet. Just make sure he gets home, and leave the explaining to me. It's probably best that Aarie and the others don't see you till I've spoken to Aarie."

She nodded. "Tell Aarie, I'm sorry, and I'm glad she packs a good punch. I suppose, hanging out with Oneiroi Guardians means a girl's bound to pick up fighting skills, right?"

"She didn't pick it up from me. I've never seen her fight like that before, but yes, I will tell her," Jay replied.

Meira walked over to Jamie, who was propped up against the door, pulling out his phone from his jeans pocket. She turned back to Jay, but he was already gone.

Chapter 15
The Truth

Adam held on tight to Aarie's hand as they ran from the rooftop stairwell, into the main room, and then onto the crowded dance floor.

"What *was* that? What the hell is going on, Aarie? And that guy—who was he?" Adam blurted out breathlessly

"Jay. He's back, and so are the wolves. They're after me!" she cried out, terrified. "Meira, she's one of them. She tried to kill me. We need to get out of here. Where are the others? Do you see them?" Aarie shouted.

"There they are," Adam replied, spotting Angela and Lori, who stood near the entranceway holding a couple of coats.

Adam and Aarie pushed through the crowds as fast as they could until they reached the others.

"Angela, Lori, we've gotta go. Now!" Aarie urged.

"Hey, you don't need to tell us. We're waiting for you guys," Lori said tiredly.

"Where's Jamie and the others?" Adam hastily asked.

"I think Jamie went home already. He said he was feeling a bit rough. The other's all left half an hour ago. Why are you guys running? Someone chasing you?" Angela smiled but instantly stopped when Adam and Aarie's distressed faces did not ease up. "Okay guys, what's going on?" Angela worried.

Adam edged out of the door. "We have to get out of here and back home—now! We'll explain when we get back safe. Now let's GO!"

They had all bundled into a taxis outside the club. Adam watched Aarie's pale face staring out of the cab window as it drove into the night. She had said nothing since they got in the car, and her body trembled against Adam and Angela. Lori sat worried in the front. Angela glanced at Aarie and then to Adam, whose eyes met hers. They shared a brief look that seemed to voice unspoken words that they both understood. They stayed in silence until they arrived at home.

The house door slammed shut behind everyone, and Adam hurried to lock it.

"Jamie? Are you Home? Jamie?" Aarie shouted, running up the stairs and halfway back down again as everyone stood in the hallway. "He's not here!" she panicked.

Adam stepped forward. "Aarie, calm down. You know what he's like. He always wanders off. He likes to walk and get fresh air," he said calmly.

"Can someone tell us *what* the hell is going on?" Angela implored, looking from Adam to Aarie.

"I'm not sure what I just saw, but I've got a feeling *we're not in Kansas anymore!*" Adam said with a hint of hysteria.

"What?" Angela said, none the wiser.

"Aarie?" Adam said, looking at her for an explanation, but she had no words. "Well, this is the version of events I saw," Adam continued. "Feel free to elaborate or correct me if I miss anything out, Aarie, 'cos I'm just going to come out and say this," Adam spurted, keeping the same hysterical tone as more words began to tumble out of his mouth. "Right. I went to look for Aarie 'cos I had seen her and Meira head to the rooftop earlier. Anyway, when I got there, there's a wolf. An *actual* giant wolf! And I mean seriously, it was huge! It looked like it was about to rip Aarie to shreds, but instead, it starts fighting with some crazy guy, *who*, by the way, turns out to be the mysterious Jay. Yes, apparently he is back, and judging by the size of that wolf he was grappling with, I'm not entirely sure he's human! Oh, not to mention, Meira is also one of the wolves who tried to kill Aarie. I guess that makes her some sort of werewolf then. Hope that all makes sense to you, 'cos I'm struggling with it just a little bit," Adam said with a humourless laugh. He sat down on the bottom step of the stairway and glanced back at Aarie, who was staring at him from two steps above him.

"Have you gone mad?" Angela said as her glance flitted between them both.

Lori stepped forward and put a hand on Angela's shoulder. She glanced from Angela to Aarie.

"No, Ange. It's all true, isn't it Aarie?" Lori whispered. "Back at the club, I tried to do a reading from Aarie. We were just messing about really, but I saw something. I thought it was just snippets of dreams and nightmares. I saw wolves chasing her, and then I saw Jay. He was in all of the visions I saw, but then something happened to him. His face... he changed. He *wasn't* human. Oh my God, Aarie—it was all real, and he hurt you so bad. There was so much blood."

Adam's face was a mixture of concern and anger when he glanced back at Aarie.

"Aarie, is this true? Did he physically hurt you?"

She reluctantly nodded as her eyes began to well up.

"I'll kill him!" Adam spat.

"No, Adam. You don't understand. I don't think he *meant* to. He's saved my life so many times like tonight. I don't know why he did what he did, but he healed me. I woke up fine as though nothing had happened. I thought I was going crazy for so long."

"Are you defending him?" Adam said, confused and angry.

"No. I just don't know what happened or why he's here. I've never seen him *here* before."

"What do you mean 'here'?" Adam quizzed.

"He's not from this world. Sometimes when I fell asleep, since the accident, I dreamt of a place. It was dark at first, and things lurked in the woods. Wolves would always appear... until Jay helped me. I thought I was just dreaming at first, even though it all felt so real. I wanted it to be real. Then the wolves found me again. They nearly killed me—"

"I don't understand. How did they get to you in your dreams?" Adam asked, completely bewildered.

"I don't know. It was like I travelled to another dimension—" Aarie broke off as she noticed everyone staring at her incredulously now. "Do you see why I never told you?" she continued "It sounds like I've completely lost my mind, doesn't it?" she sobbed.

Adam reached for her, but she stood and began to run up the stairs.

"I just need to be on my own, just for a little bit, okay?"

The others began to murmur something, but she was already disappearing into her room. She closed the door behind her.

As she turned around, she instantly jumped back, startled. Jay was already there waiting for her. She tried to turn away, but he caught her gently with both arms.

"Aarie, please listen. I'm not here to hurt you," he urged.

"Let go of me. LET GO OF ME!" she cried out, struggling with all her strength to get free.

"Please! Let me explain before you run out of the door," he implored, hurrying to get his words out as she struggled in his arms. "I'm sorry, Aarie. I never wanted to hurt you. I didn't have a choice. I thought it was the only way to save you. Everything I ever said to you was the truth except what I said in that room that last night. That was the lie, Aarie. I'm not the monster from your last dream. Please, please believe me," he said, letting her go as his last words turned into a desperate pleading whisper.

She stopped, then turned around slowly to face him as the door flew open, just narrowly missing her.

"Aarie?" Adam gasped as he came rushing into the room, immediately glancing at Jay standing by her. He positioned himself in front of Aarie. "Are you okay?" he asked her without taking his eyes off Jay.

"Yes," she whispered.

"How did he get in?" Adam said.

"I'm not here to hurt Aarie. She's in no danger from me," Jay interrupted.

"Are you sure about that?"Adam snapped. "'Cos from what I hear, that's not quite what happened the last time you saw her."

Jay flinched. "I need to speak to Aarie."

Adam frowned. "Yeah well, I'm not leaving her alone with you. I certainly don't trust you, and I don't care whatever the hell you are!"

Aarie had never heard Adam speak like this to anyone. Her eyes went back to Jay as he began to take a few steps closer, stopping right in front of Adam.

"Adam—" Aarie said, breaking off as she placed a cautious hand on his arm to urge him to back off.

"I'm not afraid of him, Aarie," Adam said without turning.

Jay seemed to tower over Adam now, though he showed no malice towards him. He paid attention momentarily to the trembling hand that tugged at Adam's arm, then met Adam's glare.

"I'm glad to hear it," Jay said. "because I'm not one of the things you *need* to be afraid of right now. *They* haven't arrived yet." Jay's calm manner and the way he set his words unsettled Adam. "If you care anything for Aarie, you will let me explain to her what's going on so I can keep her safe. I think you can gather from that little scene back on the rooftop that she is in danger. So please, let me help her." Jay's calm tone was beginning to waver.

Adam seemed to flinch at Jay's intense expression when he said her name. There was no doubting the fact that Jay had saved Aarie tonight. If Aarie was in danger from things like the wolf on the rooftop, there was no way Adam could protect her from them. He turned back to Aarie, ambivalent about the situation.

"Adam, it's okay," she answered before he could speak. "Just let us talk alone for a few minutes. I'll be fine."

"Are you sure, because you don't look sure? You don't have to do anything you don't want to do, and I don't have to leave you alone with him either."

"I'm sure, Adam. Please. You know I need to do this."

"Alright, but I'll be close by. Just shout for me at any time, okay?"

"Okay, and thank you," Aarie replied.

Adam threw one last pained look in Jay's direction before reluctantly leaving the room. The door closed behind him, and for a moment, there was silence.

Aarie glanced up at Jay, who met her gaze. They were alone now, and there was no hiding the fierce pulse in her chest.

"I don't know who or what you really are. I don't know why you did what you did. I don't even know how any of this is possible. Adam said he wasn't afraid of you, but I *am* afraid of you," she whispered. "But I also know you could have just left me here to die that night or tonight if that's what you had wanted."

Jay walked over to the far corner of the room, creating more distance between them. He leaned his back against the wall. Aarie eyed his abandoned hooded coat and the array of weaponry that he had discarded to the side of her bed. She moved to sit on the edge of the mattress, watching him carefully as he glanced back at her.

"How much do you remember?" he asked.

"All of it," she replied. "I thought they were just dreams at first, even as they grew more real. Everything felt real in my heart, and because of that, I thought I was losing my mind. Even after *that night*, I couldn't be one hundred per cent sure it was all real until I found your jacket button. I tore it off your sleeve when you—"

Jay flinched again as she broke off. He looked onward distantly as though seeing into his mind's eye, then he slowly slumped down on the floor. His head sunk into his hands as he took a long deep breath, pushing his hands through his hair.

"I've made a mess of everything, Aarie, haven't I? I know I've destroyed everything we ever had together, and I'm sorry. I'm *so* sorry. I don't expect you to forgive me because I can't forgive myself, but I need you to know I did it because it was the only way to wake you. I thought it was the only way to save your life, Aarie. I will never lie to you ever again, I swear to you. You *need* to know everything now, so I will start with the truth from the beginning.

My family and I are Guardians of the Oneiroi world—Aneiros. I know I've told you that, but I never fully explained what it means. Aneiros is what some would call a dream world or more accurately, a parallel world that some mortals gain access to through their dreams. Most mortals, however, never reach it. Only a rare few make it there during deep sleep for reasons no one really knows. They usually appear as a shadow in our dimension. You could say a shadow of their soul crosses over temporarily, but they are not really there. Like the man you saw the third time you came.

Within dreams, we cast illusions and transform our appearance to guide the shadows away from the knowledge that our world exists and that we exist. We do it to keep them safe, Aarie. We break the link they have to our world because, by returning too often, their minds can be lost forever or worse—part of the dark things from our world can come back with them as part of them. We usually sense the early stages of shadows becoming real and stop it before it's too late.

However, when you came to our world on the night of your accident, you were only a shadow for a brief moment. Our world was already real to you by the time I found you, and you were dying, Aarie.

When you came the second time, all I could think of was how glad I was that you had not died in your world and that you had returned. I could not make you leave, though I should have because that is what a Guardian is supposed to do, and maybe if I had done it straight away, I would not have had to hurt you as I did. You see, the longer mortals are in our world, the harder it is to wake them from it. That's why we use nightmares— because they are normally more effective at waking mortals instantly, keeping them away long enough for them to forget. Most mortals never return after a nightmare. When you came, it was my brother who found you first. He was one of the wolves you saw, and the others were his illusions. You should have woken when you fell down that hill, but instead, you transformed from a shadow and became real. As you were real, your wounds from your own world became your wounds there.

Aarie, when my brother found out about us, he gave me no choice but to make you leave, or he would've woken you himself. I knew that would probably kill you, so I would never allow it. Nothing I could say would persuade him to change his mind because he feared for my life. He feared for it because the wolves that chased you through the desert were not his wolves, as I had first assumed. He worried that they were other Guardians who had witnessed your presence and me saving you. They could have been. You see, there are other Guardians who would benefit from the downfall of my family. They would gladly make an example of me for breaking the law because it would weaken my family and my realm.

There are different realms of Aneiros. Within them, the Guardians follow different methods to deal with shadows. My realm and another believe in casting dreams first, using nightmares only when necessary. The third realm, however, is less tolerant of mortals and create only the darkest of nightmares. The difference in opinion of which method is the correct one has divided Guardians for centuries. It is what keeps the different realms on the brink of war.

To put it simply—I have enemies, Aarie. Enemies who would have gladly used this as an opportunity to have me destroyed. I would suffer the worse death that can come to an Oneiroi Guardian, and it would bring great shame to my family. Worse still, you would die a hundred deaths within your mind before they killed you slowly. They would most likely have kept me alive to watch it first, as a lesson to others."

An icy shiver ran down Aarie's spine. "But they weren't Guardians. It was Meira's pack," Aarie said.

"I know that now, but even if we had known that they were dreamwalkers—wolves like Meira—it wouldn't have changed anything. Word amongst dreamwalkers can so easily spread amongst our worlds and back to those Guardians. Phelan was not willing to take the risk with my life, and I wasn't willing to take the risk with yours.

I hurt you Aarie because it was the only option I had that meant you lived. I had no choice but to create your nightmare, one that would wake you up and stop you coming back to my world forever. I had to break your link. I never meant to hurt you as I did, and I never believed I would have to. I thought if I made you hate me and broke your trust in me, you would have no reason to want to be in my world. I thought you would wake up straight away. I was trying to protect you. I just didn't expect to nearly have to kill you myself to save you."

The words seemed to stick in his throat like knives as he paused, hanging his head low in shame. "But you trusted me too much—so much that you didn't believe I would hurt you. It's what stopped you from waking, right up until almost the end. What's worse is that I know it was my fault that you trusted me so much. On the steps that night, I shouldn't have—" He paused, struggling to string his words together as he recalled their embrace on the steps. "I *made* you trust me, and I'm sorry. I was selfish. I just wanted to say goodbye. I wanted to believe you might remember that part of me if you remembered anything. I couldn't stand the thought of you just hating and fearing me. I was never meant to come back here to this world with you. You were supposed to wake up unharmed. You were meant to forget my world eventually and finally be safe."

Aarie could almost feel the pain in Jay's expression as it contorted his face, reflecting his inner agony. She could not move her eyes from his as he continued to speak.

"But another cruel twist of fate means that everything I did was for nothing because danger found you anyway. It followed you here, and so you're still not safe, Aarie. That is why I am here—to protect you. I know you must hate me now, but *please*, let me at least do that since this is all my fault. I found a loophole in the law that allows me to be here. I can protect you, and it breaks no law. No harm should come to you from me being here now."

There was a long silence. Aarie scanned over Jay's face, analysing every detail she had missed with all her heart, but he did not seem like the same man she remembered. The shadows under his eyes were dark, and his brows creased with the misery that engulfed him, taking away any trace of the smile she had loved. His hair was dishevelled, and his skin was pale and unshaven. Even his blue eyes seemed icy and lifeless. It pained Aarie to realise that he had been suffering just as she had been.

"I don't want to be afraid of you anymore," she stated, breaking the silence. She slowly got up from the bed and came to sit beside Jay against the wall. She wrapped her arms around her knees, trying to conceal her trembling hands and cover her bare legs, which suddenly felt exposed.

"You need to understand what I am," Jay hurriedly said as though needing to unburden himself of the truth. "You need to know, if you're ever going to trust me again, and I'm not even sure you will want to after that.

I'm the thing that haunts people's dreams and plays on their desires and fears. Something that lurks in the pages of mortal fiction, in your myths, folklore and urban legends. A monster, a demon, a shapeshifter—there are so many names I go by in this world, but I am quite literally *your* worst nightmare. So, I guess I lied to you when I told you I was not the monster from your dream." He swallowed as he glumly took in Aarie's reaction. She was pale and clearly frightened by his words, but she did not move from where she sat. "I *am* him when I have to be, and more, but please believe that I thought I needed to be him to save you. Otherwise, I would never have—" Jay struggled to carry on as his brows furrowed deeper and his eyes searched his thoughts. He broke off and looked back to Aarie. "I will *never* hurt you again, Aarie. I swear it. I'm so sorry."

They both were silent for a moment, and Jay clearly worried that he had said too much too soon.

"Show me," she whispered. "Show me my worst nightmare. I want to see him."

Jay grimaced. "What? Aarie, no."

"I need to see him if he is a part of you. I want to trust you, so I need to see him," she insisted.

He stared back at her and then finally gave a reluctant nod. Aarie watched as his deep blue eyes slowly changed to black, and his face paled to an icy grey. His bone structure became more angular, and his face jaunt and shadowed. Dark veins began to creep down the sides of his face as his hair darkened and tangled like barbed wire. Bones crunched and reshaped as his chest grew wider and his fingers grew longer with claws. Aarie gasped as he took a slow intake of breath, opening his mouth slightly to reveal a row of razor-sharp teeth and fangs. The throbbing in her chest filled her ears as she stared, taking in every detail of him. She froze.

"What are you thinking, Aarie?" he asked.

She was surprised that he sounded just like his usual self; a tell-tale sign that he was not the same monster from the dream. She took a long deep breath. Then, to Jay's surprise, she moved closer to him so that the sides of their arms were just touching. Her back was to the wall, but she was still facing him. She let out a long exhale of breath as though she had been holding it in.

"Not too scary after all," she whispered, though her heartbeat still pounded frantically. She closed her eyes, taking another deep breath, and then leaned her head against his shoulder. "I probably wouldn't stop to chat if I had just met you down a dark alleyway, though."

She felt Jay's body jolt slightly as a brief incredulous laugh escaped his lips. Her head shot up immediately, trying to catch what he looked like laughing in this form. His eyes were still black, and his mouth drawn to a razor-sharp smile. His face did not have the same menacing edge now, and she realised he was looking at her the way he had always looked at her. The corners of her mouth twitched as she gave in to a smile, and he transformed back to the Jay she was more familiar with. Aarie leaned her head back into him. His shoulder moved, and she knew he had glanced down at her, but she didn't look back up. Instead, she reached out, resting her hand on top of his by his side.

"I don't hate you, by the way."

Jay didn't reply, but his hand slowly turned over, and he closed his fingers around hers.

Several minutes must have passed as they sat in silence, contently holding each other's hand. Aarie was overwhelmed at how quickly it felt so right to be close to Jay again. The pain in her chest was soothed once more, and for this moment, she wanted to be nowhere else. However, she knew he was here because she was in danger, and she couldn't help her mind from wandering and worrying about what danger that meant for him.

"You said Meira and her pack of wolves were dreamwalkers. What does that mean, and why are they after me now?"

"You don't need to worry about the wolves anymore."

"What happened? Are the wolves dead? Is Meira—" Aarie felt a rush of guilt for being so caught up in her own feelings that she hadn't given a thought to what had happened to Meira or how Jamie would feel when he found out. She gasped as another realisation hit her.

"Jamie! He's still not back yet," she panicked.

"Jamie's fine, Aarie. He's with Meira, and she's fine too. I didn't hurt her."

"How can Jamie be fine with her? She's a wolf, and she tried to kill me."

"She won't hurt him, trust me," Jay quickly assured. "Yes, she's a wolf, but she cares for Jamie. Also, we came to an agreement, and she wouldn't break an agreement with me or any other Guardian. It would put her pack in more danger. He will be fine, I swear to you, and believe me, I didn't take it lightly what she did to you. I nearly killed her for it, Aarie. For a brief moment, I wanted to," he whispered, looking away from her now. "But I knew why she had done what she did. She isn't evil. Everything she did was done because she thought she was saving her kind and helping your world. They were afraid of you."

"Of me? That is ridiculous. Why would they be?" Aarie said incredulously.

"Because there's never been someone like you before."

"That doesn't make sense. I'm just a girl!"

"No, Aarie, you're not. In so many ways, you're not! *They* know. The wolves can sense it, I could sense it, and so can the blood demons."

"Blood demons?"

"Yes. They are the ones who are really after you now. They have noticed you coming to my world. Maybe my involvement stirred up interest too, I don't know. You asked me what dreamwalkers are—well, they're the wolves and the blood demons. When mortals cross over to our world too often and become too aware of things, it can be dangerous. Some become trapped within countless nightmares partly of their own creation. They are often slowly driven insane or are changed somehow. No one knows why, but certain Oneiroi abilities cross over with some mortals when they leave. They then begin to have the ability to come and go between worlds as they please. My brother thought this was happening to you. That's another reason why he urged me to wake you.

Fully transitioned dreamwalkers can reveal themselves as one of two Oneiroi forms—the wolf or the blood demon. Mortals refer to them as werewolves and vampires. The main difference between them, besides their appearance, is their nature. The wolves keep most of the traits of their human selves mixed with the traits of that particular Oneiroi form. The blood demons, however, very rarely hold on to their human personalities. Their human bodies are not designed to cope with this kind of power, and so, they are often driven mad by a constant thirst for blood. This makes them dangerous to people.

The blood demons believe that your blood holds the key for them to be able to have all the strength of the Oneiroi, here in this world. They want full control of their abilities, and they don't want to hide in the shadows of the night. They want the day too. You see, in the day they are left weak because the sun burns their skin, and they are unable to have any life that resembles their old one. They crave more blood and power, but not only that, they can create an army of blood demons. The new blood demons don't even need to have travelled to my world. The wolves have this ability too, but it is more complicated. And they do not often have the desire to create more of their own kind other than through loneliness.

It is written in old prophecies and old stories, of a mortal who possesses the power of the Oneiroi, as I once told you. The blood demons *believe* those stories, Aarie, and the wolves being their sworn enemy, didn't want to take the risk. It would mean their inevitable demise, especially after a recent rapid increase in blood demon numbers."

"And they think that's me—the mortal? Like in the story you told me about."

"Yes, I believe so."

"That is crazy. As I said before, I'm just a normal human girl!"

"That's what I'm trying to tell you, Aarie. No, you're not. Yes, you're human, but the Oneiroi power *does* run through your veins. I know it..." he said, glancing down again. "I know it, Aarie because I've tasted it."

There was a long silence as Aarie considered Jay's words.

"What does that mean?" she whispered finally.

"I don't know. All I know is that the blood demons will never get to you, Aarie. I will make sure of it. Meira has given me her word to help keep you safe from them too. I honestly don't think she ever really wanted to hurt you. She just didn't have a choice before. I have sworn to protect her pack in return."

"Does this put my friends in danger too? What if the blood demons use them to get to me, Jay? I can't let that happen."

"I will protect all of them too, Aarie. I swear, I will. I know somewhere safe we can all go. The sun will be coming up soon, so we'll be safe until the evening. It gives us plenty of time to get there. Everything will be fine. It can be that simple."

"Okay. I trust you, Jay. I didn't think I could ever trust you again, but I do, more than anyone," she whispered, searching his face.

She searched for a trace of anything that could put doubt back in her mind, but she could not find it. Part man, part wolf, part blood demon, part shapeshifter, part fictional being and more; it all meant nothing to her. He was *her* Jay, and his hand still held hers in his. Now, as her fear slowly subsided, curiosity began to move in to take its place.

"Is this your natural form?" Aarie asked. "I mean, is this how you really look?"

"Yes. Pretty much."

"'Pretty much' being yes or almost a yes?"

"Why? Do you not like the way I look? 'Cos, I can pretty much look like whatever you want me to," he replied.

"Yes, of course I like how you look, very much so in fact. I just—" Aarie worried she had offended him but then saw his subtle smile and his raised eyebrow. "You *know* what I mean. I just wondered. But really—you can do that?"

He kept his smile. "Yes, I can do that. And to answer your other question seriously—yes, this is me... pretty much."

She frowned in confusion as he stood up. He reached forward, taking hold of her hands gently to help her up in front of him.

"The Oneiroi have three main forms: the form of the blood demon, the wolf, and our natural Oneiroi form. Okay, this is me. *All* of me," he said seriously.

Aarie's eyes widened in amazement as a pair of pure white wings slowly unfurled from behind Jay's back. They raised up above their heads and hovered around them, encompassing them in a feathery dome. She reached upwards to touch the feathers and gasped in awe at how soft they felt.

"This is really you?" she asked, peering at him from under the feathery arches.

He nodded, analysing her reaction warily. "Yes. We can naturally conceal our wings for practical reasons. Our clothes are made from natural Aneiros fabrics that enable us to manipulate and change them as we change—in case you were wondering.

We can make significant changes to the appearance of any of our main three forms, depending on our imagination. It does have limits—wing shape, texture, facial features, colours, presence—that kind of thing can be changed. These things are usually determined by dream or nightmare, peace or war. We can't alter our mass a great deal, so anything we appear to be that is of greater or smaller size, is an illusion. What you see in those illusions may be happening, but not necessarily how *you* see it. So, back to your question—yes, this is really me in my full, natural form. What you see now is who I am."

"So you missed out something from your list of things that you are."

"How so?" he said worriedly.

"You were always there just in time to save me from the wolves. I guess you were like my guardian angel," she whispered.

Jay seemed to process Aarie's words with great thought before slowly reaching for her arms and gently guiding her nearer to him. He rested his arms loosely around her waist.

"Aarie, I am no angel," he whispered with a rueful smile as his hand came up to brush her cheek. "And I know I have no right to feel the way I do about you after what I did, but I can no longer stop myself. You have to tell me if I am making you uncomfortable or you want me to leave. I can still protect you and your friends but keep my distance."

Aarie leaned her face into his hand, keeping it by her cheek with her own hand. "I missed you so much... like the air from my lungs was taken from me. I don't want you to leave. Any distance is too far," she admitted. It was the truth, and she could not keep it to herself any longer.

Jay took a long deep breath. "I never answered the question you asked me at the house that night. Not truthfully, anyway." They both seemed to flinch at the thought, but he continued. "When you asked me 'if it was all a lie' and if 'what you felt was real?' I honestly don't know, not for sure, what *you* felt, Aarie, but I do know what I felt was real, then and now, in this world and my own."

Aarie uncontrollably stepped closer to him, sliding her arms around his waist. Jay cupped her face with one hand. "Aarie?—" But before he could say anything else, he leaned in gently to kiss her. The softness of his touch was electric. At once, she responded, and their lips met with sudden haste and desire. His hands drew her nearer to him, and hers pressed him closer still as her fingers twined through his hair. Their lips moved in harmony, opening gently, then moving against each other more intensely. A dizzy sense of weightlessness swirled around her head. The thump in her chest filled her body with a heat that pulsed through her veins. The room and the world around them seemed to disappear. All that existed at this moment was them holding each other tight and the warmth of their lips on each other's.

Jay's wings were still wrapped around them when they eventually broke away. They held each other close as their eyes locked and a smile crept on both of their faces. Neither seemed willing to be the first to speak. Jay slowly retracted his wings, and they disappeared from sight, revealing the room around them once again.

"What are you thinking, Aariella Stone?" Jay said, finally breaking the silence.

At that moment, the door creaked open, and a hesitant Adam hovered in the doorway. His eyes landed on Aarie in Jay's arms. Their expressions were intensely focused on each other, and Adam flushed red, sensing that he had walked in on a private moment.

"Adam?" Aarie said as Jay's eyes followed hers.

"Erm, sorry, Aarie. I just wanted to check you were alright. I'll go," he muttered glumly.

Aarie moved out of Jay's arms, acknowledging Adam's unease. "Jamie is okay, by the way. Jay saw him. He's fine. He should be home soon."

"Oh, that's a relief. I should tell the others," Adam said awkwardly as he turned back to Aarie. He glanced back up at Jay, who was still watching him. Adam's look lingered, turning into a bitter glare as his mind drifted.

"I should explain everything to your friends, Aarie," Jay said.

"Okay," Aarie replied.

Adam nodded in agreement. "They're still downstairs. I don't think anyone's going to be getting much sleep around here tonight. They're all freaked out, so it would be good to know what the hell is going on."

Adam was startled by the sound of the front door opening as it echoed from downstairs. They all listened to it shut gently, followed by the sound of keys landing on the hallway sideboard, a few stumbling steps, and then a familiar voice.

"So I guess Jamie's back just in time for the update on events too," Adam concluded.

All three of them made their way out of the room to the stairs.

Chapter 16
First Blood

Angela and Lori were sat chatting in the hallway as Jamie came in.

"Hey," he said, casually nodding to the girls. "What are you doing still up... and on the floor?"

Angela looked from Lori to Jamie. "We were waiting for you. Something happened to Aarie—" Angela broke off, eyeing the others coming down the stairs."

Jamie glanced up, following her worried expression. His eyes passed over Aarie and Adam, then rested on Jay. "Who's he?" Jamie asked with a hint of suspicion in his voice.

"Jay," Lori said, biting her nails.

"Oh—right," Jamie replied, quickly glancing back to Angela and Lori. He seemed to be re-analysing their matching faces of concern with a growing concern of his own.

"So what's going on guys? You all look spooked or maybe just wasted, I can't figure it out," he said nervously, but no one responded. "What happened to Aarie?"

Silence.

No one replied again, and all eyes were down as though everyone was not sure it was their place to speak. As soon as Aarie reached the bottom of the steps, Jamie reached out for her arm, pulling her gently to face him. He laced his fingers in hers as he casually swung his arm down to his side, keeping hold of her hand. His eyes were wide and questioning.

"Aarie, what happened? I looked for you tonight, but I couldn't find you. Are you okay?" he asked with a surprisingly gentle manner for Jamie.

She swallowed; she knew everyone's eyes were on her now. "Something happened back at the club with Meira. Jamie, she..." Aarie struggled to look at Jamie.

"She *what*, Aarie?" he asked.

"How well do you know your girlfriend, Jamie?" Jay said abruptly, moving towards them.

"What?" Jamie said, bewildered as he tore his gaze from Aarie's and then looked over her shoulder to Jay. "My Girlfriend? What do you mean? Aarie, what's going on here?" he asked, perplexed and seemingly annoyed by the stranger asking him questions.

"I mean, do you know Meira's a werewolf?" Jay replied before Aarie could answer.

"A what? Firstly mate, Meira is not my girlfriend, and secondly, is that supposed to be funny?" Jamie frowned in confusion.

"He's telling the truth!" Adam cut in. "She tried to *kill* Aarie tonight, Jamie."

"What? What is going on here, guys? Is this some kind of practical joke, because, well done, you all got me, but it's still not funny."

"It's no joke, Jamie," Aarie said, looking him in the eye. "If Jay hadn't been there, I would be dead now."

Her words appeared to make Jamie flinch. "Aarie, I don't understand what you're telling me? Are you trying to say the two of you had an argument and got into a fight? People say and do things they regret when they're drunk." His face seemed a mixture of pain and confusion as he reached out to touch the side of her cheek.

Adam seemed to shift uncomfortably beside Aarie and Jamie. He scrutinised over the way Jamie gazed at Aarie and how he was at so much ease around her. It was clear that Jamie loved her just like all of them did. Her friends would do anything for her and couldn't bear to see her hurt, but Adam wondered what they looked like to an outsider—like friends or a couple? Adam felt a slight twinge of jealousy towards Jamie, though he knew he shouldn't; Jamie was always like this with Aarie. Surely it didn't mean anything other than friendship. Still, he wanted to be the one touching her cheek right now. He wondered if Jay was reading just 'friendship' from Jamie's body language.

"No," Jay said, answering Jamie's question to Aarie. "She's trying to tell you that Meira is literally a werewolf and that she tried to kill her."

Jay's voice was not unfriendly, but it seemed to hold a hint of impatience or annoyance somehow. "I can prove it," Jay continued.

Unsettled by Jay's tone, Jamie let go of Aarie. She moved to Jay's side as he spoke.

"I find in situations like this, seeing is often believing," Jay continued. "Aarie, you don't have to watch this if you don't want to, okay?"

Aarie guessed what was coming, and she shook her head. "No, it's okay." She glanced at everyone else and then gave a slight nod in an attempt to ease their minds for what came next.

"For the record," said Jay. "I'm not here to hurt Aarie or anyone here, so there is no cause for alarm at what you're about to see. It will be over in seconds."

Jay walked to the back of the hallway to put distance between him and the small nervous crowd in front of him. They were all staring at him like he was about to do some kind of bizarre magic trick. He stood up straight, then his blue eyes began to change to a golden honey colour. His body jerked with a sudden cracking sound of bones and muscle. Claws emerged from all of his limbs, and his body arched. Within seconds, a thick white fur covered his body. Now, a giant wolf stood staring back at the frightened eyes that watched him. His gaze passed over the group of friends and rested on Aarie as she stared back with wide eyes.

"What the—" whispered Jamie.

166

There was a gasp and then silence from the others. Before the silence could turn into anything else, Jay transformed back to his usual self and casually scanned the crowd.

"So as you see, werewolves exist, which brings us back to you, Jamie. Meira is a werewolf." Jay glanced at Jamie, taking in his dismayed expression. "She wanted to tell you herself, but I thought it was best if I did it, considering tonight's events," he said, looking to Aarie.

Everyone else was staring at him with opened mouths, but Jamie expression seemed more of despair.

"Why did she try to hurt Aarie? Was it because of me or because of something I did?" Jamie worriedly asked.

"No," Jay replied, regarding him with great thought.

"Then, why?" Jamie asked, this time through gritted teeth.

Hatred was clearly building in Jamie's eyes, and Jay felt a small pang of sympathy for Meira who had seemed so guilt-ridden at the end of their last meeting.

"Before you write Meira off, you must listen to the full story. Things are not simply black and white, good and evil. Meira won't hurt Aarie now. She never really wanted to." Jay looked around at the others again. "I suppose you need to hear the rest of the story to understand what happened."

******

They had all made their way into the lounge, and Jay had talked through everything that he had explained to Aarie earlier. He had told his story to the small group of friends as they muttered between themselves with gasps of horror and disbelief. There had been a long silence after he had finished talking, then shortly after, the room erupted into a frenzy of questions. Adam pushed past everyone to get to Aarie, leaning in with a hint of urgency in his eyes.

"Aarie, can I speak to you, alone?" His eyes flitted across briefly to Jay, then back to Aarie.

"Yes, of course," she replied.

She made her way out of the door, and Adam followed, closing it behind him. Muffled murmurings came from the living room through the wall. Aarie waited for Adam to speak as he paced back and forth.

"What is it, Adam?"

"When I saw you on that roof tonight, and then when we got back home—I've never seen you that scared, Aarie. It's understandable, I mean, I've never been that scared either, but then I realised something. You've had this whole massive thing happen to you. All this craziness has been happening to you for weeks, and I had no idea about any of it until tonight. You should have been able to talk to me about it, no matter how crazy it made you sound. I should've been there to look out for you 'cos that's what friends do. But I wasn't. I know I probably haven't been a great person to talk to recently, and I know that's my fault, Aarie. I'm aware that I've not been a very good friend to you lately."

"Adam, that's n—"

Adam waved a hand to cut Aarie off before she could defend him. "No, it's true. I've not been acting myself. I never used to be like this, and I know you remember that. I've been so... distracted lately. I've been acting strange, self-centred and even clingy. I know it, and I'm sorry. I want things to be how they used to be when you could tell me anything. I want to be that person again. I want to start afresh, Aarie. Starting with me looking out for you, listening to you, and not just thinking of myself. So, I want to ask you if you are okay with everything that's going on?"

Aarie took a moment, remembering the boy that had comforted her when her mother had died all those years ago. He had listened, brought laughter back into her world, looked out for her, and been there no matter what. She had seen a glimpse of that boy she remembered when he had stood up to Jay earlier, despite his own fear. That boy stood here in front of her once again, and she realised that she had really missed him.

"Yes, I'm fine. At least, I think so," Aarie finally replied. "There's been so much going on, I haven't had time to let everything sink in."

"But you're not afraid now... of Jay, I mean? You trust him? Because, if you are afraid and want to get away from all of this, it's not too late. All you need to do is just say. We'd all be with you, whatever your decision."

"No, I'm not afraid anymore, Adam. He is here to help. I know that's the truth, and I wouldn't say it to any of you if it put you in danger."

"Okay. It's just, I know he saved you back on the roof, Aarie, and I'm grateful for that, but please don't forget that he hurt you too. I don't completely understand what is going on between the two of you. I don't know him, Aarie, so I have to trust your judgement here. I just want you to be careful, alright? You don't owe him anything because he saved you. So, if you ever change your mind about needing his help, you can."

"I know that Adam, and I will be careful, I promise. Yes, Jay hurt me, but I understand why he did it now. Adam, you need to know that Jay has saved my life many times, not just tonight on the roof. When he told you about how I first came to his world, he left out an important part. He didn't just heal some small wounds that I got from running from the wolves. He was the reason I woke up fine after the accident. The unexplainable quick recovery that happened to me—that was after I first found his world. He saved my life that night for the very first time.

I know I don't owe him anything, and he would never ask for anything, but there is no doubt that I would have died a long while ago if it weren't for him. So yes, I trust him and am grateful to him, but also, I know we need his help now, Adam. We're *all* in danger—don't doubt that. So please, let him help us all."

Adam considered Aarie's words as he stared off into his own thoughts. He took a deep breath.

"Alright, Aarie. I just wanted to make sure *you* were sure about all of this. If you do need to chat about anything else later, when you've had more time to think about stuff, I'm always here, okay?"

"Thanks, Adam. I really appreciate it," she said, pausing a moment to look at him. "It's good to have the old you back," she added as a gentle smile crept on her face.

Adam's mouth hitched up to one side. "Yes, well, I guess that other Adam guy was beginning to get on my nerves a little. Do me a favour, if you see him again, tell him to sod off," he muttered. "I suppose we should get back to the others now," he concluded as Aarie nodded in agreement.

Aarie and Adam wandered back into the subdued atmosphere of the living room. Angela, Jamie and Lori sat at a table in the corner of the room, briefly falling silent as they glanced up at the pair approaching. They quickly went back to murmuring among themselves. Jay stood alone, arms folded, leaning against the furthest wall in the room with his head down. He could almost have been a statue. With a lift of his head, his eyes followed Aarie's through the room. His lips parted as words eagerly waited on them. Adam briefly glared at Jay, then pulled out a chair to sit with the others. Aarie stopped in front of Jay, tilting her face up to his. His rigid stance relaxed immediately, and his folded arms dropped to his sides.

"Hi," Aarie whispered.

"Hi," replied Jay

"You okay all the way over here?" she asked, eyeing the distance between him and her friends.

"I didn't want to frighten anyone, at least not more than I already do."

"You don't frighten me, not anymore."

"I know, and you don't know how much that means to me. I know I don't deserve anything from you. Aarie, you really don't owe me anything. You know that, don't you?"

Aarie wondered if he had heard her conversation with Adam, but then remembered that he could hear her heartbeat from a considerable distance.

"I know, Jay," she replied, wanting to say so much more, but she could feel the other's eyes on them both, so she settled for leaning on the wall beside him. His eyes still followed her to his side.

"Okay, you're making me nervous now," she said without turning.

"In a good way?" he asked as a gentle smile tugged at the corners of his lips.

"Always," she whispered, fighting a smile of her own as her eyes scanned the table in front of her. They landed on Adam, who kept clandestinely glancing up at them both. She felt Jay's hand reach for hers, loosely playing with her fingers at her side. Her fingers laced through his as she slid nearer to him to conceal their hands from the others.

"So what's the plan now?" Adam piped up abruptly to address Jay and Aarie. "Do we run, hide, leave? What are we supposed to do?"

Jay looked up as Aarie released his hand from hers. "We need to leave as soon as we can. You should all get some rest. The sun is coming up now, so you'll be safe. They won't come till nightfall, but we should leave later this morning. I know somewhere you'll be safe," Jay assured them all.

They all turned back, chatting amongst each other as the mention of Meira came up from Jamie. Jay turned back to Aarie.

"You should get some rest. You must be tired," he whispered.

"Like you wouldn't believe," she admitted.

"I should speak more with your friends. I know they have more questions, and I should answer them. I need to explain more about Meira too."

"Alright, well, I'll go get ready for bed, but I'll be back in a little bit 'cos I really need to speak to you before I sleep," she said, unwilling to leave him just yet.

"Okay." Jay nodded before she slipped out of the door.

A few minutes later, Aarie quietly wandered back into the room in pyjama bottoms and a t-shirt, trying not to make herself noticed by Adam and Jamie. They seemed to be muttering among themselves while Jay answered more questions. Angela and Lori had already made their way up to bed.

Aarie curled up on the sofa, pulling a throw over herself as she nestled her head into a cushion on the arm. She glanced up at Jay, who had turned and smiled.

"I'll just rest my eyes for a bit," she mouthed almost silently in response. Gently she closed her eyes to stop the stinging of tiredness as Jay turned back to continue talking. She hadn't intended to sleep yet, but, like always, as soon as she closed her heavy lids, her mind drifted off. She tried to focus on the voices in front of her, but they gradually became a faint muffled sound.

"I want nothing more to do with her," Jamie muttered to Adam across the table. "What would I say to her, anyway? She tried to hurt Aarie. It makes me shudder thinking about if she had succeeded. What kind of person or thing can do that? How could I trust her again?"

"I don't know, Jamie. I don't think I can fully trust anyone who tried to hurt Aarie." Adam shot a deliberate glance at Jay, who looked back at him. "But, that's the least of our worries, Jamie. It's the other *things* that we need to worry about, so I've been told."

Aarie mumbled something incoherent, and Jay looked back at her on the sofa. She had given in to exhaustion, and her hands cradled her head as she slept. Jay watched affectionately, wondering what she was dreaming of and where; he knew she could no longer go back to his world. He wondered if they would be regular mortal dreams or just a collection of thoughts from

170

the day's events. Jay hoped, whatever the case, they would be pleasant dreams, no longer tinged with darkness and lurking monsters.

"Do you care about Aarie? I mean *really* care?" asked Adam, breaking Jay from his thoughts.

Jay turned around to meet both Adam's and Jamie's stare. "Yes."

Adam glanced at Aarie, who was now deeply asleep. "That girl there is important to us. We don't want to see her hurt again. I don't know what there is between you two, but I know she trusts you. If you can keep her safe from these monsters you say are coming for her, then I guess we have to trust her judgement and trust you for her sake. But I swear if anything happens to her—"

"I won't let it," Jay said firmly before Adam could finish.

"Yet you trust Meira?" Jamie frowned. "After what she did? How can you be sure she wouldn't try again?"

"Because she gave me her word."

"Just her word? That's all?" Jamie asked.

"It's not the same as normal promises people make to each other. A wolf would never make a deal with *me* that they could not keep."

Jamie's brow creased. "Because you'd kill her?"

Jay paused momentarily, weighing up Jamie's tone before he spoke "Because she would bring an Oneiroi war down on her pack. All that she was trying to protect in the first place would be lost. Neither of us wants that."

Jamie's mixed emotions about the subject were evident on his face.

"Meira is not a monster, Jamie," Jay continued. "What would you do if you thought the human race could potentially be wiped out? All your family, your friends and every living person you care about. If you believed there was only one way and that one sacrifice could save them all, would you take it?"

Jamie didn't reply. He stared down at the table, considering Jay's words in silence.

"But she was wrong, wasn't she?" Adam worried.

"Yes, she was wrong. She thought there was no other choice," Jay replied.

"But if the blood demons do get to Aarie, could that mean the end for everyone?" asked Adam.

"No one knows what that would mean, not for sure."

"But you say Aarie is different from other people?"

"Yes, but it doesn't mean the blood demons are right. They are just after what they are always after—blood and power. They might not even really believe Aarie holds the key. They always find ways and excuses to keep their cruel games new and interesting for themselves."

"But what if they *are* right?" Adam continued to ask.

"They will *never* get to her to find out," Jay stated.

"Good," Adam said with the same conviction Jay had spoken with. For one brief moment, the pure hatred in Adam's eyes seemed to subside.

There was a rustling sound behind them as Aarie stirred in her sleep. Jay walked over and then bent down next to her. He pulled her throw over her a little more before scooping her up gently into his arms. She stirred again but did not wake as he carried her towards the door. Jay stopped to glance back at the two boys. They both sat with their mouth slightly ajar as if about to comment or possibly object, but before they could, Jay spoke.

"Aarie should rest properly. I'll take her upstairs to sleep. You two should probably do the same. We may have to leave before the afternoon, and the sun is already coming up."

"Jay," Jamie said in a serious tone, causing Jay to pause. "The last time you left her, you nearly broke her. Do you understand? She trusts you, but if you break that trust again—" Jamie broke off suddenly as Adam shifted uneasily in his chair. Jay nodded without needing Jamie to finish, then left the room.

The early morning light was streaking through the blinds of Aarie's room, filling it with a warm golden glow. Jay lowered Aarie down gently on the bed, then pulled the throw over her. Her eyes flickered open and went straight to him.

"I'm sorry, I tried not to wake you," Jay whispered. "I thought you could probably do with your bed rather than the sofa. I know everything that has happened is a lot to take in, and you seem exhausted from it."

"I don't think the copious amounts of alcohol at the start of the evening helped much either," she smirked. "That and the fact that it's now early morning."

He smiled back, nodding. "I'll leave you to sleep then. We can talk later."

"Wait. Where will you go? Will you sleep too?"

"I don't need to sleep tonight, but I'll be close by."

"Stay," she said, reaching for his arm. "At least for a little while," she whispered.

Jay sat at the edge of the bed pondering at her anxious tone, and then he nodded. He eased off his boots and laid back against the pillow beside her. With arms by his sides, his face turned to hers. For a few moments, their eyes explored each other's in silence, their faces inches from each other.

"I thought I would never see you again after that night," Aarie finally said.

"Did you want that?"

"Part of me tried to believe I did, but no."

Her eyes shifted from his and focused on the marks on his right wrist by her side. Running her fingers along his skin, she began to trace over the black patterns. She had seen them many times before, but her tired eyes studied them now, wondering their true meaning. She had thought she had seen another marking earlier, but there was nothing there now.

"What do they mean, the markings on your wrist? Sometimes they're there and sometimes they're not. You never told me what they are apart from they seem to open doors."

"I was born with these," he said, eyeing the black patterns and symbols. "Everyone in my family has them. You could say it's like a birthmark."

"It looks so intricate. Like it was designed with black ink rather than a birthmark. Do all Oneiroi have these?"

Jay paused before answering. "No, just certain bloodlines. Direct blood descendants of the original, ancient Oneiroi families. We are called *First Blood*."

"First Blood? What does that mean exactly?"

"All First Blood have strength nearer to that of the original Oneiroi Guardians. It means that our blood is almost as pure as the first of our kind. Only three such families have these kinds of marks."

Aarie's eyes widened at that. Although she could barely keep her eyes open now, her mind raced with questions. "How long have the Oneiroi been around?"

Jay took a deep breath then exhaled. His left hand reached to brush her cheek gently as he leaned closer. "A long time, Aarie. *I've* been around a long time—if that's what you are really asking me? I am not as old as my brother. I am the youngest son, and though we hold a similar power to the originals, we are not them. The Oneiroi are our people, but the Oneiroi Guardians live to protect our world and yours. Guardian numbers are not like the numbers of your world—we are of very few in comparison. So, for each one of us comes great responsibility, especially for First Blood. Time doesn't move the same for us as it does for you. We can get so engulfed in our purpose and duties that it can make our world seem like one endless dream to ourselves. When you came to Aneiros, it was like I finally awoke from that dream and became part of the real world for the first time. When you thought you dreamed, I thought I finally had a reason to stay awake.

I have lived for a thousand years, Aarie, but I have never really been part of the living. Not until you came. Time never really mattered to me until now." He paused, studying her face for any change before he carried on. "Guardians are immortal, and forever is a long time. Sometimes we grow tired of our world, and when it feels like it holds nothing for us, we choose to 'sleep' for a long while. This can last for anything between decades to centuries at a time. Our minds shut down, and we rest. Though we do acknowledge the passing of time, it can feel like the blink of an eye when we wake. I chose to sleep for one hundred years, only to wake just short of two decades ago. You cannot imagine how a world can change in that time. We pick up fragments of past and current events through the minds of shadows. However, when we first awake from this type of sleep, it's like being a child all over again. Though we still have our old memories, everything in the present time is new, and there are so many things to learn. Therefore, part of me knows I've been around a long time, but a large part of me feels like my life started when I woke again."

He paused, acknowledging her furrowing brow. "That was probably also a lot to take in, and I was supposed to be letting you sleep. Have I frightened you again?" he worried, trying to decipher her new expression.

"Yes," she said, taking a deep breath.

"I'm sorry—"

"—Only because," she interjected, "I don't know *why* you're here? You must have met so many people and seen so many extraordinary things. You could do anything you want. I can't even imagine why you would go to all these lengths to help someone so... so *ordinary* and mortal like me. I feel like it's just a matter of time before you realise your mistake and leave again. I know you said you found a loophole in the law now, but all I've done is cause you trouble—inter-dimensional trouble, at that. If it's through guilt or a sense of responsibility you feel for me because you're a Guardian, I won't blame—"

"—I've just told you that I'm a thousand years old, on top of the fact that you already know I'm every kind of monster, and the thing that worries you most is that you may have caused me *trouble*?" A gentle laugh escaped through Jay's smile. "Sorry, you're right, 'Inter-dimensional trouble' is the worst kind," he beamed. "But maybe I like trouble." He reached for her hand. Intertwining his fingers with hers, he brought them to him and placed a kiss against her knuckles. "And you're anything but ordinary, Aarie. How you can even think it, baffles me. I saw you punch a werewolf in the face tonight. You kicked her halfway across the roof! It would've been quite exciting to watch if I hadn't been worried about your life and thought you hated my guts at the time. The fact that you don't hate me and that you can even bear to look at me after what I did, makes you the most extraordinary creature I've ever encountered. I don't deserve to be here with you now, and it is me who worries that *you* will change your mind and ask me to leave. I think half of your friends would give anything to be more than friends to you, and yet you fail to see how special you are."

Aarie made a sound as though to protest, but before she could, Jay continued.

"As for guilt—yes, I feel guilt. I can't erase what I did. You can't imagine the shame I feel for what I did to you. I'll always feel it. I made a mistake, and not just because I hurt you, but because any plan that involved me not ever seeing you again was *always* doomed to fail miserably. I realise now that I would have eventually found an excuse to come to this world to find you and ask you to forgive me."

Aarie stared back at him, speechless. She didn't know where to begin. All of Jay's words were whirling around in her head. No words of her own would come out, but she leaned her face against his chest, wrapping her free arm around him. She took a deep breath, taking in the familiar scent of him: the alluring sweet coppery smell of his skin blended with the fresh pine meadow scent that clung to his clothes. Comforted by the gentle rhythm of his heart and the warmth of his body, she closed her eyes. He brought an arm around her, keeping his other hand locked in hers. Aarie wished to tell him that she *never* wanted him to leave because it had hurt so much before. However, her eyes would not will themselves open. Exhaustion was taking its toll, and it was so easy to drift away, feeling the warmth of his body against hers. Her grip gently loosened on his hand as her body relaxed, and her breathing steadied.

"Goodnight, Aariella," Jay whispered as he closed his own eyes.

Chapter 17
Semper Sodales

Jay stood by Aarie's bedroom window, peering through the blinds. The sun had come up hours ago, and it was now late morning. It was October, and the trees in the street below were beginning to turn a golden brown colour. An old couple walked hand in hand, laughing to themselves. For a moment, Jay wondered at how long they could have been together and what memories they would've shared. *Did their time together feel like a blink of an eye?*

A sudden gasping sound behind him immediately dragged Jay away from his thoughts. He spun around to face Aarie, who now sat up on the bed. She hunched over herself, clutching her arms around her body as if she were in pain. She cried out, confirming it.

"Aarie, what is it? What's happening?" Jay panicked as he rushed to her bedside, then lifted her head up gently. Her eyes were closed as she cried out in pain again, pulling away uncontrollably.

At that moment, Adam barged into the room, having heard her screams.

"What did you do? What did you do to her?" he yelled, horrified as Aarie seemed to be having a seizure.

"I did nothing. I didn't do this!" Jay protested with fear evident in his tone as he reached back towards Aarie.

"Aarie, can you hear me?" He lifted her face up to him as her eyes began to open.

Jay was startled as a pair of violet eyes peered at him through half-closed lids.

"Something's wrong, Jay. It hurts," she mumbled before passing out. Jay caught her by her arms and lowered her back on the bed, frantically checking her pulse. Something caught his attention at once. Intricate black markings laced the skin of her wrist, but they instantly vanished before he could study the pattern. A shimmering glow of violet began to form above where the black marks had been. Jay stared at the looped symbol that matched his own.

He gasped, stepping back in shock. "It's not possible."

"What is it? What were those black marks?" Adam panicked, as he moved in to check Aarie himself. He stared at the glimmering purple shape that remained on her wrist, then turned to Jay, who was now inspecting a matching mark of his own. "What is it? What's happening to her? Is she dying?" Adam shrieked. "What do those markings mean? What did you do to her?"

"I didn't *do* anything. The black markings must have always been there —"

"What are you talking about? I've know Aarie most of my life, and she's never had anything like that on her wrist. You must have done this."

"She was born with them. We just couldn't see them before," Jay replied, lifting up his own wrist to show his marks vanish and then reappear. "Only a few of my kind have them. Aarie is not dying—something just triggered a change, and they became visible. She is human, though, so I don't know what this means or how this is possible."

"And what about this glowing mark," Adam asked, eyeing the still present symbol on Aarie's wrist. "Was that always there as well? You have it too, so what is it? Something was hurting her, and it must be to do with that."

"I don't know. I don't have all the answers. There's never been someone like Aarie. She's the first of her kind."

Adam saw the looped mark on Jay's wrist pulsate as though it breathed. Jay grimaced as though he too was now in pain as he sat down beside Aarie and reached for her.

"You're lying," Adam accused. "I think you know exactly what that is. Tell me!"

Jay inhaled deeply, then sighed. "She's in pain. I feel it, and I can't do anything about it." Jay turned back to Adam. "The violet mark is a symbol that normally only appears on the skin of some Oneiroi. The symbol comes as a pair. We call it the Seal of Semper Sodales. It is extremely rare, so much so that some of the Oneiroi don't believe it exists at all."

"What do you mean 'it comes as a pair'?"

"I mean there's a reason Aarie found her way to my world and why I came back for her. Our souls, our blood, and our entire being call out to each other. We are two halves of one set. I didn't do this to her—she was born this way, as was I. The violet mark only appears after Oneiroi soul partners meet and a solid bond is formed. It is meant to be a sign that their bond is sealed and their souls linked for all eternity. Except, Aarie is human —mortal. This has *never* happened before."

Adam glared at Jay with a burning hatred. "That is ridiculous. I don't believe you. She's not *your* soulmate if that's what you're implying. I would know. You come here, and you barely even know Aarie, yet now you think you've got some kind of claim on her already. I've known her most of my life. I know things about her that no one else knows. I have memories that no one else has. I won't let you hurt her again. I think you need to get away from her. Now!" Adam shouted.

Jay stood to face Adam. "I don't want to fight with you, Adam. Aarie cares about you, and she wouldn't want it, but I'm not leaving her side," he said bleakly.

"This is your fault! None of this would have happened if you had never come into her life," Adam shrieked, shaking as rage swept over him. He lunged forward suddenly, shoving at Jay.

Jay stood firm. "I can't leave—"

Before he could finish, Adam threw a heavy punch towards Jay's Jaw, splitting his lip with a knuckle. Jay glowered at Adam but did not respond with any violence. Adam blinked in disbelief as Jay's wound healed before his eyes as though it had never happened.

"There is *nothing* you can do to make me leave her side right now, do you understand, Mortal?" Jay snapped as his body tensed.

Something seemed to erupt inside Adam, and he threw the whole weight of his body into another punch that aimed at Jay's face. Jay caught his arm this time, spinning him around in an arm lock before Adam knew what had happened. Adam struggled as both of his arms were being held behind him, but he knew he had no chance to break free; Jay was far too strong and fast.

"I am patient, but I am no saint," Jay snarled as a warning in Adam's ear. "I'm not leaving her because I don't know what all of this means for her yet. The power that runs through her veins is active now, and I don't know if her body is strong enough. If this is the case, she may need me around. Do you understand? I won't leave her."

Adam reluctantly nodded. Jay let him go, pushing him away hastily. Adam spun around to face Jay, whose eyes were now pure black, his face had paled, and sharp fangs were visible.

Adam swallowed. "And if she is okay—if this nightmare is ever over and she is safe again—what happens then? How can you possibly think she is better off with you around her? Look at you—you're a monster. She doesn't belong with you. Can't you see you're killing her," Adam said bitterly.

Jay studied Adam carefully, slowly transforming his eyes and face back to their normal form. He stepped away and then sat back beside Aarie, checking her condition.

"I have no claim on Aarie. She is not a possession that can be owned. I simply told you the truth," Jay said calmly as he glanced back to Adam. "I have never had this mark before. I'm not an expert on it, and I don't know if she will respond to it in the same way as Oneiroi do. I would never ask or expect anything of her. Aarie doesn't even know of my seal. I never thought it was possible for her to bear the mark herself, so I never told her. I would never burden her with such a thing, knowing of her mortality. I only told *you* because you needed to know I didn't do this to her, and because... I know you love her. It is only fair you should know," Jay said as Adam turned away. Jay continued. "Whatever made this possible, it is the reason the blood demons want her."

Several moments of silence passed, but finally, Aarie began to stir. Her eyes opened, and she looked to her side.

"Jay?" she whispered.

"I'm here. Are you okay, Aarie?" Jay asked, touching the side of her face as she tilted her head up at him.

"I think so."

"Are you still in pain?"

"No. It's gone. What happened? I—"

At that moment, Aarie noticed the violet glow that pulsed on her right wrist. She glanced towards Jay's right wrist as his hand moved from her face. She gasped, recognising the symbol from the pendant Jay had worn around his neck. It had been his father's Seal of Semper Sodales pendant.

"We need to talk, Aarie," Jay said. "Are you sure you feel okay? There's something I need to explain to you."

Aarie's eyes met his for a moment, and she could have sworn a glint of violet glowed within them. Something instinctive made her reach for his arm, gently raising it up with hers. She slid her palm to his, positioning their shoulders level and their hands as though they were about to take part in a gentle arm wrestle. She studied her mark on her wrists as it aligned with Jay's. Then, holding their arms there, they stared in astonishment at each other. The same violet shimmer reflected in each of their eyes. Aarie's heart fluttered in her chest.

"What are you thinking, Aarie? Do you feel what I feel?" Jay whispered with a pained expression. His voice was a mixture of both hope and fear, but before Aarie could answer, movement caught her attention from across the room.

It was Adam.

Aarie spun around immediately, taking in his expression as he focused on both of them. *What did this look like to him?* she thought.

"Adam," she said, releasing her hand from Jay's.

"Are you still you, Aarie?" Adam asked as his forehead creased with worry.

"Yes, of course. Why would you say that?" she said, though she already knew. She had seen her own violet eyes reflected in Jay's. Briefly, she glanced back at Jay. Having not answered his question, she immediately wanted to hold him again, but she couldn't while Adam's eyes were on her. She moved off the bed towards Adam as concern shaped a frown on his face.

"Aarie, I don't trust him. I need to say it because I'm scared for you. Think about everything that has happened since you met him. Now there are those marks on your arms... and you're eyes. Something's happening to you, and I think it's because of him being here. You were in pain because of him. Again! We've always looked out for each other, so I can't stand back and watch this without saying anything. We don't need him to keep you safe. We can go somewhere for a while until those things stop looking for you. We can even leave the country for a bit—"

"—Leave the country? Adam, what are you talking about?" she asked. "Why are you saying all this?"

Jay stood up. "Because he's in love with you, Aarie," he blurted out, staring in Adam's direction as the room fell silent.

Adam looked down. "I'm not ashamed to say it's true, Aarie." He swallowed as his eyes flicked back up to hers. "I love you, Aarie. It's why I've been acting so crazy around you lately, and I'm sorry. I just wish I had had the guts to tell you weeks ago. Maybe if I had, you would never have left the coffee shop alone that night or crossed that road at that time. Maybe none of this would ever have happened."

"Adam..." Aarie whispered, sympathetic to the inner pain that was plain on his face. She knew she loved him. He had always been her best friend, so of course, she did. It hurt her to see him suffering. "I don't know what you want me to say?"

"That you'll come with me, even if you don't feel the same way about me. It can be just as it was before, without all this impending doom, monsters, nightmares and worrying that you might explode or something. This shouldn't be part of your reality, Aarie. It's his, not yours. He's not even human!"

Jay stepped forward, seeing the conflicting emotions on her face. "Aarie, if this is what you want, I won't stand in the way. You could have a normal human life. All I ask is that you let me protect you from what's coming. Once I know they can no longer harm you, I will leave, I swear, if that is your wish."

Aarie turned to him immediately. "Leave? Jay—" she gasped, catching his hand. The same flutter in her chest sent her pulse racing through her veins as her skin touched his. She briefly closed her eyes, then let go of his hand. She shot back to Adam. "Nothing can be the same as it was, Adam. I'm sorry. I can't go back to pretending things aren't real when they are. Something has changed. I can't hide that. I don't know what this all means yet, but I'm still the same Aarie I've always been," she said, glancing down at the violet mark on her wrist again. Her eye's marvelled at it as the looped shape pulsated like a heartbeat, but she was still aware that Adam's eyes scrutinised her every move, so she quickly hid her wrist from sight. Her head snapped back up. "Please trust me when I say that I *know* we can trust Jay. We have to all leave together and go somewhere until this is over. You're my best friend, and you know I love you. I can't risk any of my friends getting hurt because of me. Please, I need you to trust me on this," she pleaded.

She moved closer to Adam and then put her arms around him. Adam instinctively wrapped his arms around her too. He leaned his face on her shoulder.

"Alright, Aarie. I trust you. You know I do. I just want you to be safe and to know you're okay. These marks—are you still in pain, or do you feel anything strange?"

Adam slowly pulled away from Aarie, holding her by her shoulders to see her reply.

"No. I'm fine now. I feel the same as I always did. So, you will come with us, won't you?" she worriedly asked.

"Okay, Aarie. You know I'd do anything for you. We all would. So, I suppose I'd better gather some stuff together if we're heading off soon. I'll make sure the others are ready too. I suppose I should leave you two to talk through this stuff," Adam said, waving a hand at the mark on her wrist.

"Thank you," she replied as Adam broke away.

Skulking off to the door, he threw one last glance at her before leaving the room. Aarie sighed as the door closed. She turned to face Jay, whose expression was unfathomable.

"Aarie? I meant what I said. I can leave after this is over. You only need to ask. You owe me nothing, and you can be free of my world forever," he said with no hesitation, though the tension in his jaw and the pain in his eyes as he spoke, revealed it cost him gravely to say it.

"Jay..." Aarie began, closing the distance between them. "I can never be free of your world. I have a feeling that somehow it's always been a part of me, and I don't want to be free of it. This mark—I don't understand what is happening to me, but I feel something, Jay, and I know I will *never* ask you to leave."

"But you said you love him."

"Yes, I do love him. We've been best friends since we were children—of course I do, but I'm not *in love* with him, Jay. Adam knows that. I didn't answer your question before because he was here. I know he has feelings for me, and I didn't want to hurt him."

"What are you saying, Aarie?"

"I'm saying that when I'm around you, I feel complete. Every part of me feels that it's right. I feel more alive than I ever have, and so, when you talk about leaving, it feels like it would simply destroy me. But somehow, I sense that it's the same for you to say it. I wanted to tell you how I felt last night, but I think I literally passed out... and not from alcohol, it turns out." She smiled. "But even if I hadn't, I was scared to admit how I felt just in case you didn't feel the same."

She reached her right hand to take his as she had before, sending the same flutter in her chest. This time she did not try to calm it. Instead, she let it take hold of her. Her pulse raced, spreading heat through all her veins. Their eyes locked together now shimmering violet once again as she spoke.

"I'm saying that I love you, Jay. I'm in love with you, and I always have been. I'm not afraid to say it now," she whispered, glancing down at their glowing violet symbols. "I'm not afraid because now I know I feel as you feel."

Jay let out a deep exhale of breath as though he had been holding it in. An instant wave of emotion poured into his face as though he had finally let all his guard down.

"I love you too, Aarie. More than anything I've ever loved in the whole of my existence. I've wanted to tell you for so long."

Before they could say any more, Jay brought Aarie's face to his. At once, his lips were on hers and hers on his. Driven by impulse. Untamed. Urgent. Aarie's arms wound up Jay's back, sliding under his shirt and feeling the warmth of his skin. He groaned gently at her touch, moving his kisses to explore her neck as he whispered her name. Aarie pulled Jay closer to her until they found themselves against the wall. She could feel the weight of Jay's body pressed against hers, hear the sound of their heartbeats quickening, and see his eyes full of the yearning she knew would be in her own. Her hands worked down the front of his shirt, undoing buttons as they ran over the skin of his chest. Their mouths moved back to each other with more desire than before.

At that instant, the bedroom door opened, and Angela walked in. Her eyes immediately flew to the scene of Aarie and Jay, who were clearly oblivious to her intrusion.

"Uh-hum," Angela coughed, immediately startling and breaking up the couple. "Sorry. This is awkward." She blushed, though amusement was clearly on her face. "Lori sent me to check you were still alive, Aarie. She wanted to make sure you didn't need rescuing or something, but I'm not entirely sure who needs rescuing from who, as you both seem to be devouring each other," she smirked, eyeing Jay's undone shirt as she glanced back to Aarie.

"Angela! Does no one knock these days?" Aarie blushed as she and Jay straightened themselves up.

"Well, since impending doom and scary monsters became a reality— no. Besides, Adam said we were leaving soon, is that right? Or do you guys want a few more minutes to *think* about it." Angela grinned, suppressing the urge to giggle.

Jay cleared his throat. "Yes. I mean, yes we should leave soon," he mumbled, seemingly caught off guard for the first time.

Aarie glanced at him. *Was he blushing too?* she thought.

"Okay, just give me time to get showered and get a few things together, then I'm good to go," Aarie agreed, looking embarrassed. She ducked around Jay, quickly grabbing a towel and her dressing gown off the back of the door. Before she left, she threw one look back at Jay; their gaze held a new electric sense of wonder. Then, she reluctantly disappeared around the door.

Angela stepped further into the room. "Well, I see Aarie's clearly not too worried about you being a danger, so I'll put Lori's mind at rest." She paused for a moment studying Jay as though weighing him up. "You'll take care of her, won't you? That is if we all survive whatever is coming for us.

She's been through a lot lately, and she deserves to be happy. I have to admit I haven't seen her this happy for ages. Well, maybe not when the wolves were trying to kill her last night... and when you nearly killed her the other week. Though, I know you've explained all that—that you weren't really trying to kill her, and you actually saved her, and... okay, that came out wrong."

Jay's forehead creased with a mixture of horror and amusement as Angela continued.

"My point is, before all this other stuff, when she first told me about you, I could see you made her happy like she is now. But I don't want her to take off again. So, just take care of her, okay?"

"I will. I swear on my own life."

"Right, well, my mind is sort of put at ease for now, but I don't think there's anything I can do to convince Adam, I'm afraid. You may have noticed that he can get a little crazy when it comes to Aarie. You two might want to be a little more subtle around him. Let's just say, he cares *too* much sometimes, if you know what I mean?"

"I know what you mean, and I don't think we'll be in danger of being best buddies any day soon either," Jay replied.

"Has he said something to you?" Angela worried.

"Do you mean before or after he punched me in the face?"

"Ah—he's an idiot. I'm sorry about him. So, did you guys fight? Neither of you looks hurt, but you're not gonna wolf out or something like that if he does something stupid again, are you?"

"Hmm, let me think. It does depend on how many times I'm supposed to let him punch me in the face. Surely that can make the best of people wolf out just a little bit?" Jay smiled. "But no, I guess we didn't really fight. I won't let that happen in the future either."

"Thanks. I think he'll take the hint about Aarie one day, hopefully soon, for all our sake."

"And Jamie? Do I need to tiptoe around him too?" Jay asked, raising an eyebrow.

"What do you mean? Oh—I know, that scene last night when Jamie came back—you caught that, huh?" Ange asked, and Jay nodded in response. "Oh, you don't need to worry about Jamie. He's always like that with Aarie. I used to think he had feelings for her too. Maybe he does, I don't know. I never know what that boy's thinking half the time, but he's too much of a realist to get caught up in unrequited love. I think the fact that he has never made a move on Aarie means he definitely wouldn't now. I think it would hurt his ego too much for her to turn him down, but it doesn't stop him from flirting now and then. She's really hot, you know. Well, clearly, you know."

Jay laughed.

"Anyway," Angela continued, "I'd better hurry up and get my things together too. Sorry again for barging in before," she said, turning to make her way out.

"Angela," Jay said, stopping her just before she left. "I can see why Aarie likes you."

"Thanks. I can see why she likes you too." She smiled. "Though clearly, there are some reasons more obvious than others," Angela said, waving a hand in the direction of his unbuttoned shirt. She let out an impish giggle and then casually slid out of the door.

Jay stared at the back of the door, thinking to Angela's previous words. He knew he had been right about Aarie's male friends from the time she had mentioned them both arguing. A twinge of jealousy had hit him then. *Was no man in the universe immune from her allure?* Jay thought to himself now. However, he was glad he was not immune because she had chosen him.

Chapter 18
Safe Zone

The methods of Oneiroi transportation were not something anyone could easily accept as possible. Inevitably, it had sparked numerous questions from Aarie's friends earlier. Those vaguely answered questions arose again in everyone's mind as Jay appeared from nowhere once more. This time, Aarie and Adam were with him. Jamie, Angela, Lori, Meira and her pack friend, Max already sat waiting in a brightly lit lobby of a disused hotel. A large circular chandelier hung from the centre of the ceiling like a giant halo. It's many lights reflected on the marble floor below it. Dust sheets covered chairs and tables, though it did not seem like the hotel had been out of use for very long; the lighting all still worked, and although the decor needed a fresh coat of paint, it didn't seem too dated in style.

"What is this place, Jay?" Aarie asked.

"An old hotel that is currently out of use," Jay replied. "I know because I own it."

"You own it?" Angela gasped as the other's eyes widened too. "But this place must have cost millions!"

Aarie interrupted. "Jay, what do you mean you own it? I thought Guardians couldn't come to this world? You said 'life and death situations only', remember?" Aarie asked, puzzled.

"We can't. Not just anywhere we please, and not without caution either. We have to create safe zones in preparation for any such occasion. These are places mortals or others will not be likely to see us. The land around this hotel is private and runs for hundreds of acres. I have security guarding the perimeters of the outer walls, and they are not permitted to enter. This place is a stopping point to enable Oneiroi Guardians to pass through to this world unseen. Think of it as a place to keep a watchful eye on this world from a distance. It's a way for Guardians to keep mortals and both our worlds safe from danger."

"And how long has it been that way?" Aarie asked.

"Two weeks."

"Two weeks?!"Adam gasped. "That's ridiculous. No one can buy up a hotel this size that quick and have it on lockdown."

"I move fast, and the owner was already selling up," Jay replied.

Aarie thought back to two weeks ago. It had been when she had awoken from his world one last time. She pictured Jay coming to this world, purchasing this hotel and making a new gateway to her world just as he had closed her gateway to his. She thought back to what he had said to her the other night.

...any plan that involved me not ever seeing you again was always doomed to fail miserably. I realise now that I would have eventually found an excuse to come to this world to find you and ask you to forgive me.

She knew now that he had been trying to find a way back to her as soon as she had left.

"Are you okay, Aarie?" Jay asked, snapping her out of her reverie.

"Yes," she whispered. "So, what happens now?"

"We just wait, I suppose. No one knows of this place, Aarie. It's new. You will be safe. Think of it as a holiday if you like. I have made sure the first floor rooms are kitted out with all that you and your friends may require for the next week."

"Ha," Angela laughed, astonished. Adam shot a glare at her, and she pulled a face back. "What? You have to admit, that is pretty impressive," she said, smiling. "Even without the teleporting thing. We're basically on holiday, and we don't even have to suffer jet lag!"

"Angela, Aarie's life is in incredible danger and so is ours—this is not a holiday!" Adam griped.

Jamie tutted. "Oh, quit moaning Adam. What can we do, anyway? We might as well enjoy our time here. It is the mid-term break, after all," he said.

Meira and Max sat a little distance from the others. Max was a slim and gangly looking teenager of seventeen. He looked a lot younger because of his thin frame and slightly blemished complexion, but he seemed kind. Aarie threw a gentle smile his way as her gaze landed on him. Jay had assured Aarie that it was good to have extra help to keep her safe, but Aarie knew it was also so that Meira had someone present who didn't seem like they hated her now. A hint of pity struck Aarie as their eyes briefly met. Aarie un-pursed her lips, forcing a half-smile, then quickly looked away.

"So, anyone up for exploring? We can do that, right?" Jamie said, turning to Jay.

"Yes. You can do whatever you like. Just don't leave the hotel, and you should be safe. It's that easy," Jay replied.

Jamie took out a camera from the rucksack on his back. He snapped a photo of the hotel lobby and then one of Aarie as she stood oblivious.

Jay cleared his throat. "I trust you will be wise enough not to take photos of anything that may get yourself or Aarie in trouble with the Oneiroi," Jay said firmly as a fact rather than a polite reminder.

Jamie nodded, but a smirk began to appear. "So, no nude selfies then," he joked. Jay did not respond, but Jamie continued. "And you—do you count? Obviously, looking like you do now and not, you know, wolfish or whatever," Jamie said, raising the camera to snap a picture of Jay. "Can you be photographed? Do you appear on images? Or do you come out invisible or showing your true form or something?"

Jay tutted. "This *is* my true form, and of course I appear, but that doesn't necessarily mean I want to," Jay said, casually putting a hand up in front of the lens.

Aarie stepped forward. "I don't have a single photo of you, Jay. It would be nice to have at least one. Is that allowed?"

Jay turned to Aarie, capturing the puppy dog eyes she gave him. A gentle smile escaped him, and it was obvious that he could not refuse that face.

"Okay," he said. "For the first time in mortal history." Jay nodded, removing his hand from in front of the lens. His eyes did not move from Aarie as Jamie took his picture.

Jamie studied the digital image captured on the screen of his camera. "So, let me get this straight—you're the first Oneiroi Guardian to be captured on camera... and captured by me?" Jamie asked, sounding pleased with his achievement.

Jay turned abruptly to Jamie with a serious expression. "I'm not the first, but I have *never* allowed for my image to be captured in this world. The image must go to Aarie alone. And for all your sakes, please do not refer to me as Oneiroi outside of these walls to anyone. These are not things that sit well with my kind, loophole or not."

Jamie raised a hand to give a military-style salute. "Yes, sir!" Jamie said.

He moved past Jay, snapping more pictures of the grand stairway. Angela and Lori followed him, swinging their rucksacks on their backs. They walked either side of him as they neared the stairway up ahead.

"Jamie?" Meira called, causing him to turn. "Can I speak to you in a little while? Not now, but later tonight, when you've had time to settle in and stuff. Please, it's important?"

Jamie muttered something to Lori and Angela before turning back toward Meira.

"Alright, I suppose so. I'll come and find you later, Meira," he said, before turning back and wandering off with the other two girls. Max and Meira whispered something to each other, then picked up their rucksacks and made themselves scarce. Adam had already wandered off somewhere, leaving Jay and Aarie alone in the lobby.

"Do I get to explore too?" Aarie asked, raising her eyebrows at Jay.

"You get the full guided tour if you like?"

"Jay? Did you really buy this place for Oneiroi Guardians to use as a safe zone, to keep mortals safe?"

"Yes and no. I may have exaggerated a little. By 'Oneiroi Guardians' I meant just me, really, and by 'mortals', well, I meant mainly just you." He smiled. "But we do have safe zones, Aarie. I just created a new one just for you, that's all."

"Just after I left?"

"Yes."

Aarie stood gazing up at the man she could no longer live without, and she now knew it was the same for him. "If I survive this week, I'd like to know how you managed to do all this—this hotel and this land—I'd like to know how you persuaded someone to sell it so fast. I'm not even sure paperwork on properties like this can be sorted out that fast, let alone finding the funds to do it. There's so much I don't know about you. But for now, I'd like to keep that a mystery. There's only so much 'wow' a girl can take in one day. It's too much that you are so good at everything and that you're so incredibly..." she trailed off, staring at his lips. She glanced around quickly, taking in the open space around them and wondering if her friends were in eyeshot.

"Man of mystery, I can do," Jay said.

She smiled back, linking her arm in his. "Okay. Full guided tour it is then."

Meira & Jamie's meeting

Jamie and Meira stood beside a large window that was positioned halfway up the main grand staircase to the second floor. The moonlight streamed in from the clear night's sky outside, and Jamie glanced down at the well-maintained gardens below. He wondered if they had also been taken care of in preparation for the group's arrival. His eyes scanned across the empty car park that would probably never be used again. The pruned trees and freshly cut grass around it stretched out as far as he could see. Jay had been right when he had told them that no person could look into this hotel; the land around it seemed to go on for miles up and over the hills. The clear, serene view in front of him was such a contrast to how his mind felt right now.

Jamie turned to face Meira. "Did you get to know me just to get to her, Meira? Is that the real reason you ever bothered with me?" he asked.

"No. Maybe it is the reason we met, but it wasn't just like that, Jamie," Meira replied. "The more I got to know you, the more I cared about you. It's what made all of this even harder to deal with. Look, I'm really sorry, Jamie. I want you to know that."

Jamie frowned. "It's not me you need to apologise to—it's Aarie," he scolded. "And somehow 'sorry' is not enough anyway. 'Sorry' is what you say when you have a row or when you accidentally trip someone up. It's NOT what you say when you try to kill my closest friend—someone who is so *important* to me, Meira."

"I made a mistake," she replied. "I thought I had no choice, Jamie. I'm not some evil plotting villain. I thought my family and friends lives were at stake. I thought the world was at stake. Please, I don't want you to hate me. I like you. I mean, I *really* like you as more than just a friend. But you hate me now, don't you?"

Jamie sighed. "I don't know, Meira. I don't want to. Jay explained everything to us all. I know why you did it. I get it, and maybe I don't think you are evil, but I can't forgive you. It's Aarie we're talking about here, and you nearly killed her!"

"You love her, don't you?" Meira asked.

"Yes, she's one of my closest friends."

"I saw the two of you kissing in the club. You looked like more than just friends then."

Jamie glanced down to avoid Meira's stare, but within seconds, he lifted his head back up and glared at Meira.

"You don't know what you saw, Meira. It wasn't what you think, and you can't tell anyone else, do you hear me?" he warned angrily.

"I would never say anything to anyone, but I know what it was like, Jamie. I heard the whole conversation. Wolves have good ears," Meira glumly said. "You have to know that you don't stand a chance with her now Jay is here. You will never have her, and she will never want you like that. But I *do*. I know what I did was wrong, and I wish I could change it now, even knowing what risk she poses to the world. I want you to forgive me, however long that will take you. I want you to know that there is someone that cares about you more than just a friend."

"I know I don't stand a chance with her, Meira. I know how she feels about him because she told me. I know she kissed me last night how she wanted to be kissing him. I'm not stupid. I may have had a brief glimmer of hope then, but now he is back, I know he is all she wants. At least for now anyway... until he manages to screw things up again."

"You don't know, do you?" Meira whispered. "They never told you, did they?"

"Know what, Meira?" Jamie demanded.

"There must be a reason he has not said. I don't know if it is my place to say," she mumbled, turning away.

Jamie spun her round to face him. "Tell me, Meira. You owe me that at least. If there's anyone who can be trusted with important information about Aarie, it's me."

"They're Semper Sodales. That means soul mates in the Oneiroi world. You cannot complete with their bond now that it is sealed, and it is indeed sealed. I caught a glimpse of Aarie's Semper Sodales mark earlier. She tried to hide it, but I saw it. I guess they must not want others knowing yet because it confirms that the blood demons are right about her. Her blood *is* different."

"What do you mean, 'soul mates'? That's ridiculous."

"Is everything you have seen and heard these past few hours not ridiculous? However, it is all true, and so is this. He will never screw things up, Jamie. You could never make her as happy as he can because that is what comes with being Semper Sodales. He will also never let you have her. I was so lucky not to die by his hands for nearly taking her away from him.

An Oneiroi Semper Sodale's devotion does not usually come with such mercy for someone trying to take away their other half."

"Is that why you are so afraid of him? Because he almost killed you? Are you saying he would kill me?"

"I'm not afraid of him—only enemies need to be. He would never hurt me unless I tried to hurt Aarie again. He would never hurt you because it would hurt Aarie. He's not a murderer. Max and I are not here just because we made a deal with him or because we're afraid of him. We are here because we respect him. Not many of the Oneiroi would make us this welcome amongst them, especially after what I did, and he is more than just an Oneiroi Guardian—he is one of their leaders. He's First Blood. He's royalty to them. Aside from the king who is at currently asleep to their world, he and his brother rule the first realm of Aneiros," Meira revealed.

"A prince? You're frigging kidding me now. Is this some kind of twisted fairytale joke?"

"I would not joke about this. Does this seem like a good time for me to be joking with you?" Meira asked.

Jamie grimaced. He turned back to the window and stared off into space, getting lost in his thoughts. A humourless laugh escaped him.

"Sodding hell, Aarie," Jamie whispered to himself. "A sodding rich, royal soulmate who can conjure up anything and be anywhere and anything you want him to be. Only *you* could have that high a standard."

Meira fidgeted awkwardly beside him.

"Look, Meira, you're right. I have feelings for Aarie. I always have. I know I can't have her. I missed my chance, and if those two really are soul mates, maybe I never really had one anyway. God, my mind feels so ripped to shreds right now."

"I'm sorry to be the bearer of bad news. I never meant it to be like that," Meira whispered.

"Yes, you *did*, and maybe I needed you to wake me up anyway. Otherwise, maybe I'd be clinging to some stupid shred of hope for God knows how long. God, maybe if he knew how I really felt about her, he *would* kill me." He glanced down at Meira, whose mouth had glumly pursed shut as she stood in silence. "I don't hate you, Meira. I suppose I would like us to try to be friends again. It will take time to forget what happened, but I would like to try for that at least, okay?"

"Okay," she replied,

In the distance, a moving dark shadow caught the corner of Jamie's eye through the window. He moved closer to the glass as the shadow began to waver on the distant horizon. Gradually, it seemed to extend outwards, getting wider. He squinted, trying to focus on the growing shape, only to realise that it was not one shape but many. As they continued to increase in numbers, they appeared to carpet the hilly landscape like a mass of ants rapidly drawing nearer. Meira's eyes followed Jamie's worried stare. They both gasped as the moving shadows became hundreds of humanoid figures.

"That's impossible!" Meira cried out. "They must have somehow known we would be here."

"What? Who?" Jamie panicked.

"The blood demons—they're coming, and there must be hundreds of them!"

"How is that possible?"

"I don't know, but they're coming fast. We have to go warn the others—now!" Meira grabbed Jamie's hand. Then they both ran down the stairs.

Chapter 19
Oneiroi King

Adam had been exploring the secret passageways behind an old theatre stage as an excuse to have some time alone to think. He had not bothered to find the light switch and was using a dim phone light to guide him around. A glimmer of light could be seen coming from beyond the stage in the distance. He made his way to the stage side curtains and then peered to the left towards a bright yellow glow. The light was flooding into a balcony from an open door that led to one of the upper floor corridors. Aarie leaned against the balcony railings, looking out over the hotel's empty ballroom. It sat in front of the large stage from which Adam stood.

This room must have once been used to house small theatre productions, evening balls or dining functions with live entertainment. It was dusty in areas and seemingly empty, but apart from that, the whole building looked like it had only been out of use for a short amount of time. It was fairly dark now except for the occasional dimmed wall light dotted around the ballroom. They highlighted the multiple doorways that stood around the edges of this space. It was as though the room was awaiting a performance to start on stage, though no tables or chairs were out. There was just a clear dance floor. No lights lit the stage either; that was just a black rectangular space.

For a moment, Aarie glanced in Adam's direction, and he smiled at her. She did not smile back, and he realised she could not see him. His phone torch had gone out, and he stood in the shadows of the stage side curtains. He was about to call out to her when someone came up behind her from the open doorway. Adam watched, sinking back deeper into the side of the stage to make sure he could not be seen.

Jay drew his arms around Aarie's waistline from behind and placed a kiss on the side of her neck. Aarie gasped, mildly startled, then laughed. She turned and reached up to kiss him. Slipping her hand into his, they stood together looking at the empty room for a second.

As Aarie realised it was a ballroom, a flashback of the night at the manor house arose in her mind. She and Jay had danced in each other's arms, but things had taken a turn for a horrible end. Jay turned to her suddenly. His face seemed tense, and she wondered if he was thinking of that same night. She gazed backed at him as if sensing his worry, then leaned into his shoulder.

"I'd like to dance with you," Aarie whispered, "as though it were the first time I've danced with you."

Jay's face relaxed as a smile crept in. "Then, my love, who am I to refuse a beautiful lady a dance," he said, theatrically taking her hand and kissing it. In that instant, he leaned in and gently scooped her off her feet and into his arms. She giggled, then gasped as a pair of glorious white wings unfurled from his back and shot up above their heads. A moment later, they were gliding down towards the ballroom. Jay gently set Aarie down on her feet as his wings swiftly disappeared from sight.

They stood a short distance apart. Raising their right hand and bending their arm, they kept their wrists parallel to each other's and their shoulders high. A glowing violet light shimmered from their wrists as their marks reappeared on their skin. The glow reflected onto the dance floor around them as though creating their very own spotlight. They stood for a moment, eyes meeting, remembering the tune from the first time they had danced together. Then they were taking steps in a circle to the memory of that tune. The violins hummed a warm, joyful melody, and the gentle rhythm of a cello kept their footwork in time. Jay pulled Aarie closer to him, placing one hand around her waist, and the other in hers and out to the side. Aarie rested her free hand on the back of his shoulder. They glided back and forwards, then spun around, feeling momentarily weightless. Round and round in each other's arms, they danced in perfect unity. It was as though they were finely tuned in to each other's movements. Their bodies swiftly shifted to and from each other and then back together, entwining as though one. Their pulses raced even as the music slowed. This time, there was no cacophony of discordant notes or painful dread that lingered in Aarie's mind. There was just a slowing harmony of notes as Jay spun Aarie one last time and then leaned her back to finish the dance. He gently pulled her back into his arms.

"This dance means more than just a dance, doesn't it? I feel it," Aarie said breathlessly. "We're linked to it somehow, aren't we?"

"Yes. It's the Dance of Semper Sodales, Aarie," Jay replied, still holding her close. "All Oneiroi are taught the steps from a young age, but it is believed that all who are destined to become Semper Sodales, instinctively know it. I realise now, that's why you always knew the steps.

Aarie, I need to talk to you about the mark on your wrist. I need to explain to you what it means properly. I didn't get the chance to earlier, and there's something else too. There was another mark I needed to mention—"

Before Jay could finish, a distressed voice echoed through the hotel.

"Aarie!" Jamie shouted.

The interruption snapped them out of their private moment, causing the rapid disappearance of violet light that had lit up the area around them. They looked up bleakly towards the light coming from the corridor behind the balcony.

"That's Jamie," Aarie said. "We'd better see what's wrong."

Jay nodded before Aarie turned away to shout out a reply. "We're in the Ballroom, Jamie. Where are you?"

There was no reply. Then silence.

A moment later, the ballroom filled with the creak and clatter of multiple doors being flung open. Jay and Aarie spun around as several figures hastily entered through the many entranceways that surrounded them. Jay protectively pulled Aarie near to him as he focused on the figures approaching. His eyes narrowed. He recognised them. They wore dark clothing similar to his own and were armed with weapons. They were Oneiroi Guardians.

"Guardians, why are you here? I sent no order. What purpose have you here?" Jay demanded. His tone was firm and commanding as though he had authority over them.

A deep voice came from one of the shadowed doorways nearer to them.

"They are not here under your order. They are here under mine."

Jay's face softened slightly. "Father?" he said surprised. His voice was a strange mixture of rejoice and concern. "When did you wake?"

Aarie's questioning eyes moved up to Jay's as she mouthed the words, "Father?"

He squeezed her hand gently in his, but he could not answer her now. A tall man moved closer towards them in the centre of the room. Aarie could easily make out the family resemblance; he had the same dark ash brown hair and radiant blue eyes that shone, even in this dim light. However, he did not look much older than Jay, though he held an older presence about himself.

"You sound pleased about my return, yet your eyes hold a great wariness of me that I have never seen before, Son. It concerns me. Did you not wish me to wake?"

"Of course I am pleased to see you. You're my father, and I've missed you," Jay said sincerely. "I've wanted to wake you myself so many times these past weeks. But you're *here*, and with all of these Guardians so unexpectedly. It worries me why that would be."

A distinct warmth had emanated from Jay's father on meeting his son, but as his brows now pushed together, the softness in his face was replaced with a more stern expression.

"You do not know why?" asked his father incredulously. He scornfully eyed Aarie beside him, then acknowledged their hands within each other's. "You stand here protecting this mortal girl—and who knows what Oneiroi secrets you've spilt to her and her band of mortal friends—and you do not know why I am here?" His voice began to shake as anger crept into the lines on his face.

"I have not broken any law, Father. I know how this situation appears, but I ask you to trust me. Please. As you have always trusted me in the past."

"But Jaydon, you have broken every law. The only thing that saves you now is that you are *my* son!" he shouted as his eyes scrutinised Jay.

"Father, please. You know I must have a good reason for what I do. You *know* me."

"I know that time can change a lot of things, even half a decade."

"What are you saying to me?" asked Jay, pausing as he scanned the many faces around him. "You have come with all these Guardians—do you no longer trust me that you feel you need to bring protection against your own son?" Jay's voice wavered in disbelief.

He had let go of Aarie's hand and subconsciously moved towards his father, who had turned away from him as if in disgust. Jay had paled, his face now a picture of hurt as he fell silent. He hesitantly reached a hand towards his father's shoulder. His father turned back to him, patting Jay's hand where it now rested, with fatherly affection.

"They're here to bring you home, Son. We need to talk, just you and I, but I know you will not come if I simply just ask you. Am I wrong?"

Jay took a deep breath and exhaled. "Father, there's something you don't understand—"

"—No, Son! It is *you* who does not seem to understand! Phelan filled me in on recent events. I want you to come home now of your free will and just with me. Please, don't force my hand to give these Guardians an order. Please come with me peacefully so we can talk, Son. If you have a good reason, then tell me. Explain to me so I can understand this madness."

"And if I come, no harm will come to Aarie and her friends?"

"The Guardians will not touch them, on that you have my word."

"Okay. I will come with you," Jay said, defeated.

Aarie stepped forward. "No, Jay. Please, you can't," she said in a quiet voice.

Jay turned and went to her immediately. He reached for her hand as he spoke.

"I have to, Aarie. I'm sorry. You will be safe here for a while. Meira and Max will protect you and your friends while I'm gone. I'll return as soon as I can, I promise."

Jay's eyes searched hers, and she knew they both wanted to say more to each other, but the watchful eyes of the Oneiroi were on them. Jay let go of Aarie's hand and abruptly turned, moving towards his father.

"Okay, Father. Let us go and talk," said Jay.

As he drew nearer to his father, the pair of them seemed to just vanish into thin air. Moments later, the figures around them also disappeared one by one.

Aarie stood alone, blinking after them in the dim light.

"Aarie?" Adam called, stepping out from the darkness of the stage. He came down the side steps towards her. "Are you okay?" he asked.

"No. He's gone, Adam."

"But he said he was coming back, right? He wouldn't have said that if he didn't mean it," Adam replied.

One of the double side doors of the room burst open. Jamie, Meira and the others marched in, looking pale.

"Aarie, thank God," Meira blurted out in distress. "They're coming! We saw them in the distance from the window upstairs. We don't have much time before they get here."

"If you mean the Oneiroi, they've already been," Aarie replied.

"The Oneiroi? No, Aarie—the blood demons. They're coming—" a sudden acknowledgement broke her off mid-sentence. "Wait a minute. Where's Jay?" Meira asked.

"The Oneiroi took him. They were here, and they left just a minute ago," Aarie announced, looking panicked.

"What do you mean they 'took him'? They can't *take him* anywhere. He's bloody royalty. No one would dare,"

"Well, Jay went with them, but they didn't give him much choice. His father kept talking about breaking laws and that they needed to talk. He brought a whole army with him, so Jay couldn't refuse. Jay can't protect us now. And what do you mean 'royalty'?" Aarie asked.

Meira's mouth dropped open. "His father's here? Then he must have awoken. This is not good," she muttered.

"Meira, what do you mean, 'royalty'?" Aarie repeated.

"Jay's family are direct descendants of the ancients, Aarie. His black markings on his wrist are the symbol of their family bloodline. They are royalty. Jay and his brother led the first realm of Aneiros while their father slept, but their father is the king, and he has returned. His name is Erebus Onuris."

"First Blood," Aarie whispered.

"Exactly." Meira nodded. "And though the Oneiroi class them all as royalty, Jay's father has authority above any of his sons. That means, if he has put that authority to use, this is not a good sign or a good time for it either. We have no time to leave this place, and we no longer have an Oneiroi Guardian of such high status to deter the blood demons from entering this building. I don't want to alarm anyone, but there are too many of them to take on. There must be hundreds of them heading this way, so I suggest we hide—and fast!"

"How did they find us?" Adam asked in disbelief.

"I don't know, but something tells me that the Oneiroi's fleeting visit seems a hell of a coincidence. Maybe Jay's father is not in agreement with Jay's recent activities and has taken the matter into his own hands. Whatever the case, we have to go!" Meira replied.

Before the band of friends could move, a figure appeared from the darkness of the stage. His body seemed to shift with inhuman speed as it slid forward in a haunting way.

"Oh, please don't go. You'll miss all the fun, little wolf," a sinister voice taunted as a pale face could now be seen in the dim light of the ballroom. His pale blond hair seemed to blend into his skin as did his piercing ice grey eyes, which scanned over them. He grinned eerily, revealing sharp fangs at either side of his mouth.

More blood demons poured into the room through the many surrounding doors. Within seconds, the friends were surrounded by a thick wall of unfriendly faces, hissing and baring their fangs in a strange frenzy. Adam grabbed hold of Aarie's hand and pulled her closer to him as Jamie, Angela, Lori and the two pack members, huddled together with them back to back. Meira's and Max's eyes glowed the same honey gold. Their hands, now a set of long sharp claws, were set out in front of them as a growl rumbled deep in their throats.

A tall, slender woman appeared at the blond blood demon's side. Her long, straight black hair was parted in the centre and hung loosely tied to one side. Like a flow of black ink, it seemed to blend into her long, slick black dress that clung to her slender frame. Her dark makeup and thick lashes seemed to merge with the colour of her eyes, creating sleek black shapes on a pale face. She lifted her arms out to the side and flicked her wrists as if she were gently waving away flies.

"Darlings, don't frighten our guests," the woman said in a surprisingly soft French accent.

The crowd of blood demons that surrounded the group fell silent and stepped back. The woman moved forward, focusing on the two wolves.

"Wolves, we have no quarrel with you. You need not bare your claws at us. There'll be no bloodshed between us dreamwalkers. I am a modern woman in modern times, and this vampires versus werewolves nonsense has gone on long enough. We are sisters and brothers. Therefore, we should be united as one family."

A blood demon from the crowd snorted as though in disgust, stopping the dark-haired woman in her tracks. She abruptly turned, then went to stand in front of the blood demon responsible, eyeing him with vicious scrutiny.

"You do not agree?"

"I wish you no disrespect, my Queen, but they are werewolf scum. They are not my brother or sister," he spat.

The woman spun around in a blur of motion, thrusting her hand into his chest. Letting out a terrifying screech, she bared her full fangs, then pulled her hand back, revealing a sharp object. She turned back towards the group of friends as the blood demon behind her burst into black dust. She casually walked on.

"I'm sorry about him," she said, sounding sincerely apologetic. "Some people are so old fashion, and that behaviour simply will not be tolerated."

She moved towards Max in the blink of an eye and then gently reached to touch his cheek. He flinched, and the group was startled at how fast she had moved. They all tensed at her proximity.

"Come now, wolf. Put away your claws. If I meant you harm, you would be dead already. I believe in honesty, so let's all relax, hey?"

She moved her hand away from his face. After stepping a short distance from the crowd again, she turned back to look at them all. Meira and Max had transformed their claws back to their hands, and their eyes were no longer golden. The dark-haired blood demon seemed to smile in approval as her eyes fell on them.

"My name is Alyssandra," she announced. "Now, I am a civilised woman, and though there are some blood demons amongst us who tarnish our reputation, we are a civilised people. I am not a mindless monster like the Oneiroi would have you believe, but I will not fill you with illusions. We do require blood to live, and so we feed. Lucky for you all, we have already fed. So, as long as you cooperate, no one will be harmed. Sorry, I will correct myself—no one will be harmed except for Aarie." Her eyes focused now on Aarie, who flinched at the sound of her name on this blood demon's lips.

"You can't have her," Angela shouted.

"Oh, I can, and I will, my dear, but as I said, I am not a monster. I know she is your friend, and this is a hard decision for you to give her up. As a token of apology for this whole situation we are in, I am granting you all your lives and free passage out of here unharmed, but I must *insist* you leave the girl."

Chapter 20
Sufferance

Huge copper doors closed behind Jay and his father, Erebus, as they entered a large, softly lit room. Tall bookshelves lined the walls either side of them and ornate patterns decorated the centre of the marble floor. They matched the ones on Jay's wrist, though Jay's were now concealed. The high ceiling arched into a glass dome, revealing the clear night sky. A large panoramic window bowed out to the right of the room and overlooked a city. Through the glass, spiralling domes and spires of gold and silver shimmered in the night as tiny squares of light flecked the walls they sat above. Two moons shone in the sky like giant eyes watching through the window as they cast a cold white light onto Erebus's face.

Jay stepped to his father now. "You have to let me go back," he despaired. "Whatever laws you think I've broken, please trust me when I say that I have not. I have a good reason for being there, and I just need more time to do what I set out to do. I need to get back. Lives are at stake."

"You mean the mortal girl, don't you? And now also her band of friends." Erebus's disapproval was evident as he spat out his words and glared down at his son. Jay broke away from his father's eyes as they seemed to burn into his, forcing him to look to the ground.

"Yes, but she is not simply a mortal girl as you say with so much disdain—"

"—Jay, do I need to remind you that you are an Oneiroi Guardian? But moreover, you are MY SON! You of all people know the rules more than any other, yet you meddle with these mortals and dreamwalkers and break every rule. Have you lost your mind? Have I slept so long I no longer recognise my own son?"

"I am still him, but I admit something has changed. I don't aim to cause any dishonour to our family or The Oneiroi. When have I ever failed you? What have I ever done for you to doubt my word now?"

"You have feelings for this mortal, Son." Erebus sighed sympathetically, but his voice still held a stern edge. "Phelan told me about her, but I can see it in your eyes, and I fear it has clouded your judgement. I don't hold you here for my own entertainment. I see it causes you pain, and I'm sorry I have to do this, but I need to make you see sense. She is just a mortal. Her life is no longer than a brief glimmer of time. Your feelings will pass as she will fade, as they all fade to dust before long, though, it is more likely she'll become a blood demon before then. More to the point, if I let this go on, who knows how much damage you could do? You risk the knowledge of our existence and so much more. You have already revealed so many of our secrets to these mortals. And, mingling freely with the likes of the dreamwalkers—what's next, Jay? You cannot simply do as you please. We all have responsibilities!"

Jay frowned. "And what about happiness? As a Guardian, do I not get to have that? Do I just simply get to bring misery to others in the form of nightmares?"

"Son, listen to yourself. Of course you can have happiness, but she cannot bring you that, not in the long run. What good is it for you to get so attached to something so temporary? There are laws, and there are others that would be too willing to see you punished for these crimes."

"How did you find me, Father?" Jay wondered suddenly.

"Through my pendant around your neck, Jay. The one your mother gave to me. It was sealed with her blood, and so I can find it as I could find her. You were missing, and your brother was worried you had done something foolish with yourself. That is why he woke me. He did not betray you. He was just concerned for your life as I am, Jay."

Jay swallowed. "Let me go back. Please. I swear I will return here if that is what I must do, but please, let me go back. The blood demons are coming for Aarie soon. I promised I would keep her safe."

"Son, they're already there, but she's practically one them so what does it matter?"

Jay turned back to his father immediately. "What do you mean 'they're already there'?"

"Just that—they arrived as we left. It is why I wanted a speedy exit before we got caught up amidst a blood demon horde."

"No, that can't be. You don't understand—Aarie's not one of them. They want to kill her! I have to go back—now!" Jay frantically despaired.

"Son, I can't let you go back," Erebus's said with a tone of deep sympathy and regret. "If they're really there to hurt her, then it's probably already too late. I'm sorry, but there's too many of them. She may already be gone."

"Why would you say that?" Jay said horrified as a sudden realisation hit him. "You knew they were coming for her, didn't you? You knew, and yet you took me from her anyway? How could you do this to me?" Jay asked as this truth crushed him all the more.

"Son—"

" —Please! I've never asked for anything, but I am begging now—let me return one last time!"

"Son, there's too many of them for you to fend off alone. I will not risk losing my youngest son for this. I'm sorry, but she may already be dead!"

"She is NOT dead!" Jay yelled at his father. "And you don't seem to understand what you've done. You may have *already* lost me!" Jay cried out in exhausted desperation as he sank to his knees in front of his father. He flung his upturned right arm out in front of him. He unconcealed his black markings on his wrist, revealing a more recent shimmering violet mark above them. "Do you see now? She cannot be just simply another mortal because this could not be possible. I *know* she is still alive because I feel her. But if the blood demons kill her, I am as good as destroyed anyway, so whether you wish it or not, you will have lost me because I don't think I can live without her."

His father stood in horrified astonishment. "How is this possible?"

Jay shook his head. "I don't know, but I have not broken any laws, Father. All I am guilty of is protecting my Semper Sodale. This is the one thing that can be held above all laws. The law grants me the right to be there for this, especially when Aarie appears to have attracted the deadly attention of so many dreamwalkers. I asked for no help from any other Guardians. I tried to handle this with minimum attention being drawn to it. I know I have revealed my presence to mortals, but how can I have avoided that when my Semper Sodale is mortal? And, because she is in danger, her friends are too. Father, if the prophecies are true, she is not only my Semper Sodale but also the key to something that the blood demons have gone to great lengths to acquire. If not for her and my sake, that fact alone should be important enough to let me return."

Jay's father stood considering his son's words deeply. He stepped forward and put his hand on Jay's shoulder. Jay's lifted his head in hope.

"I didn't tell anyone of my mark, not even Phelan, because I never thought Aarie could bear the mark herself, and I thought no good could come of it. I even forced her to leave this world in the worse possible way. I have done everything I could to stay true to being your son, but I cannot let her die. I know it is forbidden to get attached to mortals, but she is no ordinary mortal. She is my Semper Sodale, and she does bear the same mark. I cannot ignore that now. So, I ask you again to let me go back. Please, Father. If I die trying, it will be mercy you have given me."

"Stand up, Son. I'm sorry for what I have done, and for the pain that I've caused you. I didn't know. How could I have known? She's human. But I should have trusted you. I made a mistake. Despite this, I still cannot let you go to defeat the blood demons alone."

Chapter 21
Dreams Of Dying

"What do you want with her?" Adam asked Alyssandra, although he knew the answer.

"What do most blood demons want? Mainly blood, but in this case, we only need *her* blood. She will not suffer for long, my love. I see you care about this girl, and so I can promise you that we will make it as quick as possible."

"You can't have her. We won't let you have her," Adam angrily shouted as he gripped Aarie's hand tightly.

"Hmm, you won't *let* me? Do you think that you have a choice in the matter?" Alyssandra asked.

It was Jamie who replied. "We won't let you have her!" Jamie firmly repeated. "And if you don't want to anger the Oneiroi Guardians, I suggest you let her and all of us go while you can."

Alyssandra's eyes narrowed as she stared back at Jamie. "Is that a threat, young boy?" she asked, but continued before Jamie could reply. "If by 'Guardians' you mean Jaydon Onuris, I can assure you, he will not be coming to your aid, so do not be too quick to be brave," Alyssandra said, provoking a mix of panicked expressions from Jamie and the others. "Oh yes, I know all about Jay. I also know about the punishments his kind have for their own when it comes to medaling with mortals. He will be lucky to walk away with his own life. I doubt very much he will be in any position to come to your rescue quite so soon."

Aarie shook her head in denial. She gasped as though unable to breathe. Jamie and Adam moved closer to guard her. Angela and Lori moved nearer too with Meira and Max, creating a circular barrier around her. Meira's and Max's eyes returned to their honey colour, and their claws extended. It was clear that neither of them was giving up without a fight.

It was Angela who spoke up now. "We won't give her up. She's our friend. We're family, and we'll never let you take her from us."

"Don't be fools." Alyssandra cautioned. "You don't have a choice. Don't let yourselves and each other needlessly die alongside her. You *will* all die, and we will still have her."

But as the band of friends stood firm and defiant, anger crept onto Alyssandra's face.

"I will not offer this option to you again. Blood demons can be very rash and impatient, and I will not be the one to hold all of them back for you when they tire of waiting. I need you to make a quick decision, for it will soon be taken out of your hands. Then you will all die."

There was no response from the group of friends as they stood strong around Aarie. A low snarl erupted from several of the blood demons within the crowd. Aarie looked around at the black eyes surrounding her as they stared at the group of friends with pure hostility. She glanced back to Alyssandra, who now harboured a deadly scowl. Abruptly, Aarie yanked her hand out of Adam's, forcing her way through her friends as she ran out towards Alyssandra.

"You can have me! No one will fight you, just don't hurt them," she cried out.

"Aarie, no!" Adam shouted. But it was too late; Aarie was within the blood demons reach now. She turned to look back at Adam as a tear ran down her face.

"Adam, please. If you love me, don't let me see you and all my friends die because of me. Please, promise me you won't fight. You said you would do anything for me. Please, do this!"

"Aarie, I can't," he replied.

"Promise me!" She yelled, almost choking in desperation. "*Please*, before it's too late."

"I promise, Aarie," Adam reluctantly said. Tears filled his eyes as he watched the girl he loved walk toward the clutches of a monster.

Alyssandra reached out her hand as though to greet Aarie, but as she did, Jamie shouted from the broken circle of friends behind them.

"Please, stop! Just take me instead. Don't hurt her. *Please*—just don't," Jamie pleaded.

Alyssandra turned, eyeing the teenager and the friends around him. Aarie stood, shaking her head as she mouthed his name. Tears streamed down her cheeks.

Something seemed to catch Alyssandra's attention as she examined the small band of friends at this moment. "It is *you*," she gasped.

The friends looked at each other in confusion. Acknowledging this, Alyssandra sighed.

"The prophecy refers to 'The barrier of mortal flesh—the protector and defender of the power that lies within'. It is all of you. The prophecy mentions you all. I always thought it referred to just one mortal, but you were always meant to be here right now, protecting her with your lives. This is a rare quality in mortals these days, and believe me, it is with great regret that I cannot give her back to you unharmed. We cannot have just any blood. It has to be hers and hers alone," Alyssandra said, sombrely turning back to Aarie.

Hesitantly, Aarie held her hand out to Alyssandra, who had once again reached for hers. The blood demon gripped Aarie's immediately, shaking it gently as she kept it in hers.

"I am Alyssandra Roux, and you are, I believe, Aariella Stone." She smiled so softly that Aarie was confused about how to react. Her hand trembled in Alyssandra's as she finally nodded.

"It is courageous and admirable to save your friends with such a selfless act. I give you my word they shall not be harmed, and so, the protectors become the protected."

"Please, let them leave now. I don't want them to see this," Aarie whispered so quietly that only Alyssandra heard her.

"Very well," Alyssandra looked up over Aarie's shoulder. "Let the mortals and their wolves leave. See they *do* leave and that they are not harmed, and I mean not in *any* way. I will know if my orders are not followed out as I say now, so please, see it is done."

A small crowd of blood demons ushered the group of friends out of the room. Adam and Jamie turned back, trying desperately to see Aarie over the shoulders of the blood demons that forcefully moved them along. However, they were gone within seconds, and the doors closed behind them.

"It is done. Now come, my dear." Alyssandra said, letting go of Aarie's hand.

Alyssandra walked to the steps at the sides of the stage, then sat at the top of them. Aarie looked to the blond blood demon, who was beside her now, gesturing for her to follow Alyssandra. Aarie followed and then sat down beside her at the top of the steps as indicated.

"Seeing as I am going to die, please tell me why you have come for me? Why do you want my blood so badly? What do you believe it can do?" Aarie shivered at the thought.

The blond-haired blood demon strode towards the bottom of the steps. "It will give us the power of the Oneiroi in this form with no weakness. We will no longer hide in darkness away from the burning sun. We can walk amongst mortals in the day. We will feast on their blood for pleasure, as and when we please. Not because we need to, but because we want to. As our numbers grow, we will finally rule over mortals and take our rightful place as the rulers of this world."

Aarie sank backwards involuntarily. Her heart pounded, and her body trembled.

"Charles, you're scaring our guest. Stop it immediately," Alyssandra snapped.

Aarie frowned at Alyssandra. "You're about to kill me any moment now —there is nothing that you can do to stop me from being afraid. You said before that you weren't monsters, but how can you believe that if everything Charles says is true? Is this an act for my sake, or are you really oblivious to your own evil?" Aarie asked.

Alyssandra looked at Aarie thoughtfully and with such a kind expression that it shocked Aarie.

"Child, do you know how old I am?" but before Aarie could answer, Alyssandra answered her own question. "I am over 2000 years old. I have seen many things, many awful things, and not a single one has ever dulled my view of how awful they are. I have accepted they exist, and sometimes they are a necessity. It does not mean I enjoy them as so many of our kind do. I am what I am, and I have had enough time to accept that. So, I may have told you a small lie before..." She leaned in so that her lips were at Aarie's neck.

Aarie shuddered as Alyssandra's hands wrapped around her shoulders. With one swift movement, she sank her fangs into Aarie's skin. Aarie's body tensed as the pain shot through her neck, but she did not cry out. As soon as the pain came and the blood flowed, Aarie felt dizzy and drifted into a strange dreamlike state. She could hear a voice as if it was in her head. It was Alyssandra who talked to her now.

"When I said blood demons are not monsters, I meant I am not a monster, or at least I do not want to be anymore. I have searched the world for another like me, but in my whole existence, I have found only one other. All of the others lose their minds through bloodlust and hunger for power at some point. I fear it could happen to me one day, but I won't let it. I won't allow monsters to take over this world. I will be free, and I will free your world from our poison. Charles and the others are not old enough to know the true meaning of the prophecy, but I know it. The only solace I can give you is that your friends will be safe, and your sacrifice will save all mortals.

The other like me—she is the one who first told me of you. It is because of her that I will not have you suffer all you could incur. The only kindness I can give you is that my bite will numb most of your pain."

Alyssandra pulled away, wiping a single drop of blood from her mouth as she cradled Aarie's dazed body in her arms. Aarie felt as though she had been drugged.

Was this the 'kindness' Alyssandra spoke to her of? she wondered.

Charles was now beside her and knelt down baring his fangs. "How sweet does she taste, my Queen?" He grinned.

"As sweet as cherry wine," Alyssandra replied. "Now drink. All of you drink, but only a small drop each. Do not kill her in haste and carelessness. There has to be enough to go around everyone."

Charles took Aarie into his arms. He drew his fangs back and sank them into the puncture wounds already on her neck. Then he fed. Aarie's eyes widened, fighting the drowsiness as the pain shot through her neck once more. The pain had been numbed slightly by Alyssandra's bite, but there was still pain. She tried to move away, but he was too strong.

One by one, the blood demons came to draw their mouthfuls of blood, passing Aarie around as if she were a rag doll. She wanted to be strong, and she needed to hold on for Jay; he would feel her death, and she couldn't bear that thought. Aarie fought hard to resist the drowsiness, but it was impossible. Her body was getting weaker, and she eventually had no choice but to give in, slipping into unconsciousness.

Aarie's heart began to slow, and her skin paled. The blood demons slowly filtered out of the room until the number of lingering blood demons dwindled to around a dozen. A few more gathered around her, drawing blood now from her arms, wrists and hands. Her body laid motionless as they continued to feed.

In that instant, the room flooded with blinding golden light as the ceiling spotlights switched on. The main entrance doors of the room flew open with force. Several Oneiroi Guardians marched in, heavily armed with weapons. Jay led the group into the room. His eyes were a menacing black as he took his blood demon form. It was the true face of Oneiroi war, and there was no doubting that Jay was not here peacefully. A pair of wings arched from his and all the other Guardian's backs, making a clear distinction between them and the blood demons within the room. Unlike the white-feathered wings Jay had revealed to Aarie, these were as black as night, and the feathers looked more like armoured scales. This was Jay as Aarie had never seen him. His father and Phelan marched hastily beside him as they moved toward the crowd of blood demons in the centre of the room. Startled by the number of heavily armed Oneiroi Guardians, the blood demons backed towards the wall at the opposite side of the room. Jay's black eyes frantically scanned the room.

"Where is she?" he roared ferociously, baring his fangs. He did not need a reply. His eyes had now landed on a crumpled figure that lay between four blood demons on the stage. The blood demons moved away from Aarie as they saw Jay. Their mouths dripped with her blood.

At once, Jay leapt into the air. His wings helped him cross the distance in an instant. Anger flared in his eyes as he reached the top of the steps with a sword in his hand. He drove the blade into the chest of the first blood demon he came to, dodging another as it lunged at him with a blade of his own. Jay grabbed the blood demon's arm and broke it before it could strike him. He seized the blood demon by the throat, instantly crushing it bloody in his hand, then slashed his blade deep across its chest. He pushed its splitting torso aside just before it exploded into dust.

Two more dark-haired male blood demons bared their fangs at Jay as they leapt at him. Jay's black wings towered above them as he caught one mid-air, then threw him back to the ground. In a blur of black scales, Jay spun around as his blade decapitated the other blood demon with one fluid motion. The blood demon on the ground clambered to get up off the blood-soaked stage, but Jay was above him too fast. Jay kicked him back to the floor and jumped up, driving his sword into his chest as he came crashing down with the full force of his weight. The body beneath him disappeared into ash as all the others had, leaving the sword pierced through the stage floor. As Jay knelt there now, he looked ahead to the small bloodied body in front of him.

Aarie.

Blood streaked from punctures and gashes to her neck, arms and wrists. A pool of blood formed around her; it soaked into her clothes and matted her hair. Jay's heart sank as he took in this lifeless figure that looked like it had been torn to shreds; his Aarie.

He stood immediately. His black wings lowered as he hastily pushed them behind his back. They shed their colour in one swift transition from black scales to soft white feathers. His facial features softened, and his blue eyes returned as he hurried to Aarie's side. He knelt down and gently pulled her body to him. His hand reached to find a pulse from her neck, but he could feel nothing. His own heart pounded with pure terror and desperation.

"No. No, Aarie you can't be dead, I still *feel* you. You can't be dead. Please, stay with me."

He lifted his left wrist and bit into his skin so hastily that blood sprayed over his face and dripped over Aarie. He pressed his bleeding wrist to her mouth, opening it slightly and then trickling the dark red liquid into it. His violet mark on his right wrist seemed to pulsate slightly, but its shimmer had already begun to fade. Jay reached for Aarie's right hand, turning it upward to try to find her seal on her wrist. Her marks had been concealed, but they slowly began to reveal themselves to him. He feared it was because her life was slipping away. Her black markings that he had only briefly seen once before laced her wrist now. Something about their patterning triggered a clear recognition in his mind, but there was no time for this now. His attention swiftly moved to the violet mark above it. It no longer held a glow, and his heart felt like it was slowly being crushed. Placing his right hand in hers, he aligned their violet seals against each other's, trying desperately to feel some remaining connection.

There was nothing.

A memory flashed up in his mind. It was a memory of the first time he had brought Aarie to the cottage and shown her around 'the wooden palace within the trees', as she had called it. His world had instantly been brought to life with her smile, her presence, and the way she had always made him feel. She had seen him in a way no one else ever had, and she had made *him* see everything around himself with new curious eyes. He looked at the girl who had won his heart so completely, as she laid lifeless in his arms. He had always known she was mortal but had never brought himself to admit that one day, she would be gone. He never wanted it to end like this or so excruciatingly soon. Any day within forever would always be much too soon. Regardless, it seemed that day had come. Jay could no longer feel any trace of his Semper Sodale's life force now.

Aarie was dead.

Jay's face tightened and contorted with his pain. His feathered wings lowered gently around the two of them, and he slumped down on the ground, pulling Aarie's unresponsive body closer to his. While holding her, the room fell silent, and he closed his eyes.

The blood demons and Guardians down below were frozen in a silent standoff as they watched the scene on the stage. The blood demons had seen the violet mark on the wrist of the king's son, and they knew its meaning. They stood watching in fear of what that meant for them. They had fed from Jay's Semper Sodale to the point of death, and the price for such a crime was in turn death.

The king rubbed his eyes as he mournfully watched his son holding Aarie's lifeless body. Jay sat unmoving with his arms around her and his head to hers as though he had died too.

"Son, she is gone. You have to let her go," The king said sombrely, but there was no reply.

A blood demon stepped forward from the crowd. "Erebus, we did not know she was your son's Semper Sodale. Her mark was concealed," he said, looking to Jay's father fearfully.

"We know what you thought!" Phelan shouted before his father could speak, and he drew a long blade from the weapons belt strapped to his back.

"Kill them, kill them all!" Erebus roared.

He and Phelan lunged into the crowd of blood demons, slicing across them, and sending a wave of exploding black dust into the air. The rest of the Guardians joined in combat immediately. The room became alive with swords, claws and flailing limbs, screams and wails, gushing blood and clouds of dust. In a blur of black and crimson, the room was silent once again.

It only took seconds for the Oneiroi to dispatch of the small crowd of blood demons that they had found remaining in this room. The hundreds of others that had been here earlier were nowhere to be seen. Jay's father had already made his way to his son's side on the stage. He reached to touch Jay's arm. Jay half-opened his eyes but did not move from his position. Two more Oneiroi Guardians walked in through the main door with a group of people following behind them.

"We found the other mortals a short distance from the building. It looks like they were unharmed, but the majority of the blood demons have already fled."

Aarie's friends urgently shuffled in behind the Guardians. An unearthly scream came from Angela as she caught a glimpse of her friend's battered and bloody body in Jay's arms. Lori moved her arm around her, pulling her to look away as Jamie collapsed uncontrollably to his knees at the same sight. Adam shook his head in denial as his eyes blurred with tears. He pushed past the Guardians in front, running to the stage. He was immediately stopped by Phelan at the top of the steps.

"I'm sorry, I can't let you any further," Phelan said sympathetically.

He had the same blue eyes and hair colouring of Jay, and Adam instantly knew that he was Jay's brother.

"I need to see her. You can't stop me seeing her. I have to—*please!*" Adam pleaded, trying to push past.

"That's enough," Phelan said firmly, grabbing Adam's arms and silencing him immediately. "You don't understand, mortal," Phelan whispered now. "When a Guardian loses his Semper Sodale, it can be regarded as a fate worse than death—to live while half of your soul has died. This is a dangerous time for Jay. What happens now can be the difference between a slow recovery or slip into madness and inevitable death. She is gone, there is nothing you can do for her now, I'm sorry. But Jay—we can still save him. I'm afraid I can't let you be near her right now, do you understand?"

The real world seemed to have been stripped away, revealing a nightmare filled with only grief and the haunting sound of his own heart breaking. Adam had known what he would find when they all came back to this room, and though he refused to accept it, Phelan's words had made it seem more final. Adam had barely coped after Aarie's accident at the beginning of summer, but this was pure agony. At least when he had held her bleeding on the road then, there had been some hope that she could still survive. He didn't even have that now. He couldn't even be close to her. Adam looked towards Jay, who clung to Aarie as his father tried to speak to him. Jay did not respond to his father. He just stared lifelessly through half-closed lids. This was not the Jay that Adam remembered. Jay did not look like the monster Adam had wanted to believe he was. The scene before him looked more like something from a biblical painting, depicting a winged and seemingly angelic creature holding the bloodied figure of his best friend in his arms. Jay's face was pale and drawn with sorrow. But there seemed more than grief taking hold here; to Adam, Jay looked like he was dying. Adam wondered if what Jay had told him of Semper Sodales had been the truth after all. *Was it really possible that their souls had been bound together?* Adam glanced at Aarie in Jay's arms and then at Jay's torn wrist wounds that had been self-inflicted in the desperate attempt to revive her.

Adam thought back to the scene of Jay and Aarie dancing earlier. He had seen how they had been together, and he knew that Aarie truly loved Jay. She had said it in the way she had looked at him. It had been so hard for him to watch, but he could not deny that Jay had cared so completely for her too. Jay was like a shadow of his earlier self now, despite the enormous white wings that seemed to create a bed of feathers around him and Aarie. Jay was suffering as he was suffering.

"Phelan, please, let him pass," Jay said. He did not appear to have moved, but his eyes focused on Adam.

Unwilling to deny his brother anything right now, Phelan stepped aside and let Adam pass. Jay's father stood and moved next to Phelan to allow Jay time to speak with Adam.

Adam hurried to Aarie's side, kneeling by Jay in silence. He was so grateful to be near her though he knew it was too late. Adam reached for her arm, which hung loosely on the ground, and then held it. Her skin was cold already, and Adam sat horrified as he saw the thick blood that covered her neck, soaked her grey t-shirt and trickled red vines down her arms. It now coated his hand. He felt sick. He had once thought that it would be unbearable for her not to love him the same way he loved her, and to have to watch her fall in love with someone else. He was wrong. This was unbearable, and all he wanted was to have his best friend back. There was so much blood, and his mind wandered over all the horrific things that Aarie must have endured. Adam looked to find where the blood had flowed from but could not see any marks on her neck. No gashes or bite marks gave a sign of what had happened. There was nothing, just blood.

"I don't understand," Adam said suddenly, letting go of her arm and staring down at the blood on his hand. "There is so much blood, but where are her wounds?" he asked.

Jay immediately sat up, lifting Aarie's face to see the side of her neck where the deep puncture wounds and gashes had been only moments ago. He wiped the blood with his sleeve, revealing smooth, unmarked skin beneath. She was still cold and had no pulse. Jay gently kissed Aarie's cheek, then held his face to hers as he whispered to her. "Aarie, I can't live without you." He closed his eyes once more as a single tear rolled down his cheek. Adam felt a pang of guilt for intruding on Jay's grieving, though he was grieving himself and his own cheeks were moist with tears. Jay had not answered his question, and Adam was certain it was because any hope had melted away.

Several silent moments passed, and Adam questioned if Jay was still alive as he had remained motionless for so long. Adam wondered how long it would take for Jay to accept Aarie's death and how long it would be before he let her body be taken from his arms. He wondered who would be the first to dare do it because it seemed that no one ever would. The torturing silence continued, giving in briefly to the escaping sobs that echoed through the ballroom. Adam's own grief seemed to choke him silently, and he realised he needed to accept the truth himself. Aarie was gone.

Chapter 22 - Prophecy
Aneiros Dream Lily

The 'Flower of The Oneiroi': a mirror of our immortality
and the chosen's treasured light.
When a troubled night is upon us, it seems as though
the lilies are lost forever from this world.
When three realms are divided between dreams, nightmares and sleep
itself,
a dreamer walks amongst us, holding the key to the forbidden world
and a promise of new beginnings.
The lost Aneiros Dream Lily is carried.
Its power is unleashed into the darkest corners in the darkest hours,
bringing light to all darkness and dreams to a world of nightmares.
This returned light cannot be ignored,
for it is not just light but hope and freedom to all.
It is the key, the heart, the strength of the Oneiroi.
Guarded by a living barrier of mortal flesh:
the protector and defender of the power that lies within.
It allows a heart to beat and the light to shine as darkness tries to return.
A mortal heart knows it cannot beat without all it is made of,
and mortality cannot defy its limitations in a time that is too short.
Walls stand firm because only with the bravest of hearts shall time be
kind.
Yet, be it impenetrable, no fortress can undo fate.
Thus the lily's light will once again be doused from the world,
giving new freedom and strength to those banished from light's power.
A mortal heart dies as petals fall.
Roots remain strong, and nourishment comes
from the blood that brought them home.
'The Flower of The Oneiroi' stays true to its name.
Thus, another bud blooms and its light returns
brighter and stronger than ever.
Petals of crimson emerge as a reminder of the beating heart
that was sacrificed so that it may return home once again.
The memory of a mortal dreamer will live on in the Aneiros Dream Lily
and in the light that was returned to Aneiros forever.
A symbol of hope, strength, prosperity
and new beginnings that lead to a divine future.
And as darkness has his companion,
Aneiros will too be bound together in peaceful unity.

Jay's eyes flew open. He gasped, and his body shifted. Adam seemed startled by Jay's sudden movement but stared as a violet glow coloured Jay's eyes. Jay glanced at his right wrist as a faint yet definite shimmer of violet illuminated his skin once again. He looked at Aarie's wrist. Her mark seemed unchanged to the human eye, but Jay saw a subtle dull violet shimmer. As Jay moved the strands of hair from Aarie's face, he thought a flicker of movement ran across her eyelids but was unsure if he had just imagined it. Jay stood abruptly, lifting her within his arms. His gaze still fixed on her face as he watched for any subtle changes that would bring her back to him.

"What is it?" Adam anxiously asked.

"She's not dead," Jay whispered incredulously.

Adam seemed to cling on to Jay's words, though doubt was evident on his face. "How can that be? She was cold. I felt no pulse," Adam said. After glancing once again at the violet that illuminated Jay's wrist and eyes, he appeared to re-evaluate the situation. "Are you certain?" Adam asked with new hope.

"I feel her," Jay replied. A subtle smile broke through the agony that had masked his face only a moment ago. "I feel her," he repeated with even more conviction.

Adam witnessed a movement across Aarie's eyelids once more. His hands came up against his temples, and he let out a humourless laugh in disbelief. "She's alive. She's really alive!" he cried out, turning to see Jamie and the others, who were near the edge of the stage. Gasps and sobs of joy and relief spread amongst them as they witnessed a brief but definite movement from Aarie's hand. Her fingers twitched, and Jay took them in his as he turned to Adam and the others.

"I have to take her away from here. I can't let her wake here, not on this stage like this, not with all this blood around her. This is where she died, Adam. Maybe only for a few moments, but she *did* die, and I don't want her to wake up here. She may also need more of my blood to help her recover faster. I'm sorry, but I have to leave. I can't let her suffer any more than she has already," Jay declared.

Adam's face dropped, and Jamie and Angela muttered objections in the background; they were desperate to see her alive and well for themselves. Adam shot a pained look at them and then back to where Aarie stirred in Jay's arms. The pools of blood on the stage around them haunted Adam's peripheral vision. Jay was right; this place looked like a scene from a massacre. Adam momentarily closed his eyes tight, then snapped them open to face Jay once more.

"Do what you have to, Jay. Just bring Aarie home safe. Please. We're trusting you," Adam said.

Jay nodded in reply. As he stepped past Adam, Erebus and Phelan approached.

"Son, please know that you are *both* welcome to return with us, especially while Aarie recovers. This truly is a miracle, and we will see that she will have the best care. I can't express how relieved I am that she will be okay, that both of you will be okay. Please, come home with us. We have so much to discuss, and it has been a long time since we have spent time as a family again. Aarie is now part of that family, Son."

It felt strange for Jay to hear his father say Aarie's name, and for a second, Jay shuddered, thinking of the last words his father had said about her back in Aneiros.

"I can't, Father," he replied. "Aarie has to wake somewhere familiar to her. She needs her own home, but perhaps when Aarie is well, we will return to you," Jay whispered.

Phelan leaned forward. "Jay, I feared the worse for you, Brother. You wouldn't believe how glad I am she is going to pull through. Trust me that I really mean that. When Aarie wakes, please let her know that she is always welcome in Aneiros. She is your Semper Sodale—of course she is welcome," Phelan said, briefly resting a hand on Jay's shoulder.

Jay glanced at Aarie's friends, then back to his brother. "Phelan, Aarie's friends..."

"I'll see to it they get home safe," Phelan replied before Jay could ask. Jay walked past his brother and father, then stepped to the side of the stage. He vanished from sight, leaving the other's staring after him.

******

Jay switched on the bedroom light of Aarie's room as he carried her gently towards the bed. Aarie moved in his arms and slowly opened her eyes.

"Jay?" she whispered. "You came back."

"Aarie." He smiled, though his smile was tinged with sorrow. "I thought I had lost you forever, Aarie. You can't believe how good it is to hear your voice and to feel your warmth again. My Aarie, you're really here."

"And so are you," Aarie said. Her hand reached up to touch Jay's damp cheek as she acknowledged the pain that was still etched on his face.

Her mind flickered back to earlier with Alyssandra and the rest of the blood demons; to the pain that had struck her neck, arms and wrists repeatedly; and then to the eventual nothingness she had slipped into. Her memory was hazy, but she knew what had happened to her by the end of the night. She knew that Jay had been aware of all the pain she had felt. Aarie could feel his agony and relief now. Reaching up, she tried to pull Jay to her, but she did not have the strength. Instead, Jay's arms wrapped tighter around her, and she leaned against his chest. The warmth of his body and the sound of his heartbeat was as comforting as always.

"It was so dark, but I could feel you. I knew you would come back," Aarie whispered into his chest.

"I was too late. I felt your heart stop, Aarie. Even if only briefly, I felt every moment of it like an eternity. This should never have happened. I'm so sorry. Please forgive me."

"There's nothing to forgive, Jay. This was not your fault. You're here, and because of you, so am I. Thank you for coming back for me."

"You don't need to thank me—"

"—Yes, Jay, I do. You've saved my life so many times, and I'm not sure I've ever thanked you."

"I can't live without you, Aarie. If you did not exist, there would be no point to anything for me anymore. I can't stand the thought of you getting hurt in any way, but the thought of me living without you is unbearable. And so, I feel everything I have done has been purely a selfish act for the sake of self-preservation. It is why I will never leave you again. I'll always protect you, I swear it, Aarie. I'll never leave you again," Jay repeated.

"I love you," she said.

"I love you too. So much more than I thought could ever be possible."

Aarie took in a long inhale of breath as they held each other close. It seemed like there had never been enough time for them to be together in each other's arms. The night had briefly brought the terrifying prospect of never having any time ever again. Neither of them seemed willing to let go, and they clung to each other in silence, appreciating this moment together.

Eventually, Aarie lifted her head and turned, only just recognising her bedroom around her.

Jay pre-empted Aarie's next questions. "You're safe. Your friends are all safe too. They know I brought you home to recover, and they'll be here soon too."

"Are you safe too, Jay? Are you safe coming back for me?"

"Yes, my father knows of our seals now. My mark was the loophole in the law that I told you of yesterday."

"And the blood demons—what happened to them?"

"They're gone for now. The Oneiroi won't tolerate events like tonight, Aarie. It is dangerous for dreamwalkers like them to be left free to roam this world, especially after what happened. The other Guardians will find them all soon."

Aarie lifted her head up and wriggled slightly. "Jay, I think I may be able to stand if you ease me down."

Jay did as she asked, carefully setting her down. She took a moment to steady herself, and as Jay hesitated to let go, a strange impulse struck her. It was like hunger, but Aarie had no appetite after her ordeal, yet her body definitely seemed to crave something. She felt lightheaded and slightly dazed, but she ignored it. Something else had already caught her attention. Across the room, she caught a glimpse of her reflection in the mirror and moved towards it. Her bloody clothes, matted hair, and arms were streaked with dried blood, like wild vines crawling all over her. She gasped at the sight. It was like something from a horror movie, but then, that is what the night had turned into when Alyssandra and her blood demons had set about her. Shuddering, she closed her eyes, trying to block the thought from her mind. Jay came up behind her.

"Aarie?"

"I'm okay," she replied.

As he came closer, the strange impulse hit her again. This time she knew what was causing it—blood. She could smell Jay's blood and hear his heartbeat. It was his blood she was craving. She knew her body had already tasted it. It was still on her lips, and she wanted more. A terrifying thought came over her as she failed to block out the images of the blood demons in her mind.

Quickly, she turned to Jay. "I just need to get out of these clothes and have a shower. I need to feel like me again and get rid of all this blood."

"Are you're sure you're okay? What you went through tonight is a lot for anyone to deal with. You look pale."

"I'll be fine," she replied, though she knew it wasn't entirely true. "I'll be right back."

She leaned against the wardrobe, then grabbed some nightclothes and a fresh towel from a chest of drawers next to it. Slowly, she made her way out of the door.

Jay leaned against the chest of drawers. He rubbed his eyes, trying to forget the night's events and erase the images from his mind. Alone now in the room, his gaze fell on a pinboard full of photographs hung on Aarie's wall by her bed. He walked towards it and looked closely at the montage of pictures. They looked like a mixture of old and new as some looked slightly worn and faded at the edges. Aarie's face smiled back at him from most of them along with the faces of her friends. One of the pictures showed Aarie as a small child of around seven years old, holding a little boy's hand. He had familiar dark brown eyes and brown hair, and Jay immediately recognised him as a young Adam. He examined the other images one by one, seeing Aarie and her friends grow up from small children to their present-day selves before his eyes. There was a newer photograph of Aarie with her friends holding a birthday cake for her. The cake had a number eighteen iced on it. Jay reached for the photo and pulled it gently off the pinboard to get a closer look. The icing on the cake also spelt out June 14, and the picture had evidently been taken this year. He ran his fingers over the date and smiled to himself.

Jay sat down on the bed, still looking down at the photograph in his hand as Aarie came back into the room. He turned around as Aarie closed the door. She stood still, facing away from him as her damp hair hung over her trembling shoulders. Jay realised that she was leaning against the door to support her weight. He got to his feet immediately, sliding the photograph onto the bedside table.

"Jay, stop. Don't come any closer to me. Please," Aarie said.

"Aarie? What is it?"

"I lied before. I'm not fine. I think something's wrong with me."

Jay moved towards her despite her words, and his arms came around her shoulders to support her weight. She reluctantly turned around but hid her face behind a curtain of damp hair. His hand gently lifted her chin to face him. Her eyes were now black as they searched his desperately for answers.

"Jay, what's happening to me? Am I turning into one of them? I have these feelings—cravings. Jay, I don't think I should be around you at the moment—"

"Aarie, you need my blood," he said quickly. "There's nothing wrong with you. You're not turning into one of those monsters. You don't even need blood to survive—your body just knows it will help you. Aarie, you died back there, and I think when you came back, it activated the rest of the Oneiroi power that laid dormant in your veins. That new power needs you to be at your full strength to thrive. Otherwise, it will feed off your energy and slow down your recovery process. This confused state, lack of energy, and more importantly, this thirst I know you're feeling now—it happens to all Oneiroi. It is normally during childhood when our power naturally gets activated, and these cravings happen. The cravings also happen when you are gravely wounded. In your case, I think you are feeling the intensity of both of these factors. You should drink, Aarie."

"Are you saying I'm becoming Oneiroi?"

"No, I'm saying part of you was always Oneiroi, Aarie, though part of you is human. I don't know how it is possible—I just know that it is so."

Aarie shook her head as if in disbelief, but the thirst Jay talked of was undeniable. "You healed me earlier with your blood, didn't you?" she asked.

"Yes."

"And you want me to drink your blood now?"

"I know the idea may feel strange to you, maybe even repulsive after what has happened to you tonight and in the past, but I don't want you to suffer anymore, Aarie, and I certainly don't want you to worry about this craving around me. It is not unfamiliar for Oneiroi, and so your bite does not repulse me or frighten me in the slightest."

"My bite? You want me to *bite* you?!"

"I can do it for you if you wish, but I know what you crave. It is completely natural for you to want my blood, Aarie. You are injured, and I am your Semper Sodale. I want you to recover."

"And you want me to... bite you?" Aarie asked nervously.

Jay softly sighed as he took hold of Aarie's hand and gently pulled her to sit on the edge of the bed beside him. She looked anxiously at him.

"I don't want to hurt you, Jay. That night at the house—"

"—That's what you're worried about—hurting me? Aarie, it won't be like at the house. That was the only way I could wake you from my world. I was not trying to be gentle, and that really was not the same thing. You understand that, don't you?" Jay worried.

"I know. I do. I'm sorry I brought it up. It's just I don't have a lot of good experiences surrounding the whole biting thing at this moment in time, so I don't know what to think. I'm confused. You have to explain how this all works, Jay. I'm scared. When you told me *that night* about craving my blood, was that part true after all? Will I crave blood from now on?"

"That part was only half true, Aarie. When my eyes darkened, I felt the craving, yes. It is another reason the Oneiroi distance themselves from mortals. This craving, however, is usually very mild and very easy to ignore. For me, this was not the case whenever I got too close to you, and it makes sense why that was now. I was affected in such a way because we were always soul partners. Our blood calls out to each other as our very souls do. But for Semper Sodales, it's not a predator and prey thing, Aarie—it is a symptom of intense attraction. I just wasn't sure because it doesn't ever happen between mortals and Oneiroi. I had never felt like that around *anyone* before, and as you were mortal, I worried that I could accidentally lose control and really hurt you. When I gave you your nightmare, I used this truth to make it believable. It was the only way you would wake. I twisted it because you had to believe that I didn't love you and that I *would* hurt you.

Apart from when we get injured, the only other way to trigger something similar to this thirst is to trigger aggression. Aarie, you won't have to worry about craving blood all the time. You will never have the bloodlust of the blood demons, and you will never have to worry about hurting your friends or anyone else, if that's what you are thinking. You will only ever feel this particular way around me, and more so if you are injured. I am not human, so you don't need to worry about losing control or hurting me. If anything, it has quite the opposite effect on me, if that makes any difference? It's hard for me to explain it to you without showing you."

Jay moved closer to her and then leaned in as though to kiss her. She was confused about the direction in which this conversation had gone, but she couldn't help leaning in too. Just before their lips met, he pulled away briefly.

"Aarie, do you trust me?"

"Yes, of course I do, completely."

At this, his eyes slowly darkened to black to match hers, and though she saw the change, she still saw her Jay and leaned in to kiss him. Her hands moved to the back of his neck as their lips parted against each other. Aarie pulled Jay closer, and they fell back against the bed, their lips colliding. One of his hands knotting into hers as he held it against the pillows. His lips moved swiftly and softly to Aarie's neck, sending her pulse racing. She gasped as the pressure of his kisses increased, sending a tingle down her spine and her mind into a sudden state of ecstasy. Her chest heaved as her breathing quickened and her face flushed with colour. Abruptly, Jay stopped kissing her neck and moved his face to hers to look at her.

"Did I hurt you, Aarie?" he whispered.

Aarie noticed that his lips were tinted red, and he wiped what she realised was her blood from his mouth. She knew he had done this purposely so that she would see it.

"No. Quite the opposite, actually," she said surprised as she tried to steady her breathing. Her face was thoughtful as she looked at him now. "In fact, why did you stop?"

Jay laughed gently as he placed another kiss along her jawline. "Because I'm not the one who needs blood, remember?"

Aarie took a moment to register what Jay was saying, then leaned forward as though to sit up. Jay sat up on his knees, moving his weight to the side of Aarie to let her up. As he did, she playfully pushed him back on the bed. He looked at her in surprise but smiled, wrapping his arms around her as he pulled her back to him. Their lips met once again, but this time, Aarie was distracted. Jay's pulse raced against her body, and she was very aware that she craved his blood more than before; it was what drove her now. Maybe it was the sight of blood on his lips, she wasn't sure, but her instincts seemed like they wanted to take over. Her mouth moved to his neck, softly kissing his skin. His pulse thumped against her lips, and her jaws automatically opened, revealing a set of sharp fangs. Gently, she applied pressure through a kiss. Piercing his skin, she let a flow of warm liquid run into her mouth.

A gentle groan sounded deep in Jay's throat as his arms held her close. Her body tingled as though she could feel a new lease of life flowing through her veins. She held onto him tightly as the blood continued to flow, and the same rapture hit her as before when Jay had kissed her. It felt like she could let this moment go on forever, but as soon as she thought it, her mind began to worry that she had drunk too much.

Would he stop her or would he just slowly slip into unconsciousness, blissfully unaware? She quickly drew away from Jay's neck, relieved to see his wound healing up right before her eyes. His heartbeat was fast and still strong. She sat up abruptly, turning as she dropped her legs over the side of the bed and wiped her mouth. Her head sank down into her hands as a sudden rush of dizziness hit her. All the confidence and natural impulse she had felt a moment ago, started slipping away. The reality of the evening began to creep back in. Jay moved to her. He rested his hands on the sides of her arms as he gently kissed her shoulder. "Are you okay?"

"I—I don't know. Everything feels strange. I don't quite understand what just happened? Everything's happening so fast. I haven't had time to adjust or let any of it sink in. I don't know what any of this means, Jay.

What's happening to me? What am I?" she asked, turning back to him. Her anxious eyes had returned to her natural chocolate brown.

"I'm sorry. We haven't had the chance to talk properly about everything. Trust me, things are going to be okay, even if they seem strange right now. There are so many things I need to tell you—some things that I've only just learnt about you, but first, I need to talk to you about the violet mark on your wrist. You know I have it too, and I know you feel this new connection between us. It's the reason I felt your life fading before I had even reached you tonight. It almost consumed me to know I was not fast enough. I know I've told you briefly about the Seal of Semper Sodales once before, but I need to know how you really feel about it, Aarie. There is only so much I can know through our link."

There was a moment of silence before Aarie replied.

"I've got so many questions, but I don't know where to begin, Jay. If I'm honest, I'm scared to find out some of the answers."

"Oh," Jay whispered, seeming a little disheartened as he moved back to lean against the headboard. He looked down at his hands as he considered his next words. "Aarie, I don't want this to be something that scares you, so please, just tell me whatever's on your mind."

Aarie sat back beside Jay against the headboard and glanced up at him. "I was born in *this* world, and I am getting a pretty strong picture of how most of the Oneiroi see people from this world. I know that your family can't be thrilled about your Semper Sodale being just a mortal girl. I could see the disgust in your father's eyes when he looked at me just before he made you leave—just as it was in Phelan's at the ball."

"That's not true. They didn't know what you were or what you are to me, Aarie—"

"It doesn't matter. You're an Oneiroi Guardian, and *royalty* at that, and I'm... I don't even know what I am. What I'm trying to say is, I don't understand why you want to be with me. It doesn't make sense to me that you do, and so, I find myself wondering if you would still feel the same way if you didn't have your mark? Does being your Semper Sodale mean you don't get the choice?

I don't want you to think I'm not sure about how I feel about you. I know how I feel about you. Even before I had my mark, I knew. I just want to know that when you kiss me, it's because *you* want to kiss me, not because you are bound to me by some supernatural force that's out of your control," Aarie said, searching Jay's sapphire blue eyes.

"Aarie, it's true that by nature, our souls called out to each other in the beginning. There was a link that brought us together. Some of the Oneiroi believe our souls are a matching set that is powerfully drawn towards each other. We call them soul partners. It's why you found your way to my world, and why I couldn't ignore your presence or your suffering that first night. I think your soul knew you were dying, and so did mine.

The violet seal has to appear on both soul partners to be complete, but once it is, the soul partners become Semper Sodales forever... usually, that is," Jay said hesitantly pausing before he carried on. "We become aware of that invisible force that links our souls, and because of that, we can feel things that the other feels. Not everything is clear at first, but it grows clearer with time as we become more in tune with each other. Everything we feel is real, Aarie, our seal just magnifies it. But you need to understand that this seal didn't make me love you. You did. You're the only one who's ever made me feel this way. You made me feel like I wasn't just a monster, for the first time in my life. I felt like I had been living in the shadows for so long, then all of a sudden, you brought light to my world. You made me feel human, and I wanted to be human, to be mortal, for you. If I could have, I would've changed for you. This mark on my wrist didn't do that to me, and I didn't have it then anyway. It's true that the Seal of Semper Sodales only appears on two people whose souls are connected by some unfathomable force, but for it to appear, a bond needs to form first. That bond is *love*, Aarie. You cannot force it or fake it. If it is not there, the seal never forms, and the force that connects the souls fades eventually. It is the reason Semper Sodales are rare—most never meet in time, or when they do, they simply don't get on."

Jay reached to cup Aarie's face in his hands. She gently bit her lip as his eyes locked with hers. "I fell in love with you, Aarie. So, when I kiss you, it's because I'm in love with you. But also, I *want* to kiss you because I'm so ridiculously attracted to you. Oneiroi Guardian or not, I'm still a man, and I'm not blind."

"And do you want to kiss me now?" Aarie asked.

"Yes," Jay replied, unable to stop a smile spreading on his face. He leaned in and kissed the woman who owned his heart.

It would be so easy for both of them to get lost in this feeling of bliss, held in their Semper Sodale's arms, but there was something now that seemed to play on Jay's mind. He broke away gently.

"Aarie, there's more I need to tell you before we let ourselves get distracted. Your friends will be here soon, and I want the chance to explain this properly to you before then. You wanted to know what's happening to you and what you are."

"Yes. Yes, you're right, I did, I mean, I do," she said as her cheeks flushed slightly. She leaned back against the headboard. "I'm ready. Okay, I need to know everything."

"You know how I said you were born part Oneiroi? Well, I'd like you to try to unveil your marks on your wrist, and I do mean 'marks', plural. When your violet seal first appeared, so did a black marking like mine. It unveiled itself so briefly that I did not get the chance to see it properly. At first, I thought you had it because you were the first of your kind like my family are the descendants of the first of ours, but I was wrong. The black marking became visible again when you died Aarie, and this time, I had the chance to recognise the pattern. You know how I told you that only very few Oneiroi have markings like these?" Jay asked.

Aarie nodded.

"Well, only my family and two other family's have marks like these. One of those families is believed to have died out a long time ago by many of the Oneiroi. They were known as the Adara family. Aarie, you have the markings of that family."

"What? I don't understand. What does that mean?" Aarie gasped.

"It means that not only do you have the Oneiroi power in your veins, one of your parents must have been an Oneiroi Guardian, and a direct descendant of the ancients. It means that you were never mortal, Aarie, or at least, you can't be now. Your power is definitely active, and no one can take an Oneiroi form without the side effect of immortality. When your eyes changed and you drank my blood, that was part of your first Oneiroi transformation.

It makes sense, Aarie. Our souls would not have sought so hard to find each other if one of us was fated to one day roam the rest of eternity without the other."

"Are you trying to tell me I'm immortal like you?" Aarie asked.

"Yes."

"That's impossible! I'm sorry, I can't believe it—"

"Aarie, I know it's a lot to take on board, but please try to reveal your marks and see for yourself."

Aarie focussed hard to imagine seeing new marks on her wrist. As she did, black swirls appeared that flowed into the shapes of wings and flames. She gasped as she studied the marks, tracing over it with her fingers. She had seen these marks carved into one of the three tree trunks at Jay's cottage.

"Do you believe it now?" Jay asked.

"I don't know. How can this be possible? Is just doesn't seem real, Jay."

"I know, but what other explanation would you have for everything that has happened to you?"

Aarie's forehead creased in utter bewilderment, and she could not think of any explanation.

"But it just doesn't make sense, Jay. My parents... my dad is just *my dad*, and I can tell you now, he is no Oneiroi Guardian. Besides, he's fifty-five and looks fifty-five, which looks a lot older than *your* Dad. So, I guess that proves he's not immortal."

"Not necessarily. We can look like whatever we want, remember? Anyway, how about your Mum?"

"My mum died when I was a child, Jay. I can assure you, she was very much mortal," Aarie whispered, glumly. She had just realised she had never mentioned her mum's death to Jay, and it felt strange now.

"Aarie, I'm sorry. I didn't know."

"It's okay, I never told you. It was a long time ago. I guess it is something we, unfortunately, have in common. I was just six years old. Anyway, back to your question—this means my mum was mortal, which only leaves my dad. You can't really believe he is an ancient Oneiroi Guardian, can you?"

"Yes, I'm sure of it!"

"And if it is true, not that I believe it, but what does that make me to your family?"

"I don't know exactly, Aarie. Our two families were good friends in the beginning. My father used to talk about the old times when I was young, but I know something happened between all three families many years ago. My father knows the truth, but he has never told a living soul. I think he believes my mother died because of the distrust that still lies between all three realms and their leading families. This includes the Onuris family, the Adara family and the Alinoy family. They each rule, or ruled, over one of the three realms of Aneiros. Up until now, I believed the Adara family had died out, as many of the Oneiroi still believe. Though, it is a mystery what happened to the two last remaining members. They have not been seen or heard of for centuries, but their realm still runs as though they simply sleep. However, everyone else believes this is not the case."

Jay paused as he seemed to get lost in his thoughts. He turned back to Aarie suddenly. "My mother was my father's Semper Sodale, and her death almost drove him near to madness and his own demise for many years. It's why he chose to sleep—to recover..."

He was looking at Aarie with such pained eyes, and she acknowledged it instantly. Her hand slipped into his, knotting their fingers tightly together as she thought of the pain she would feel if she ever lost Jay. She knew he had felt this pain earlier when he held her lifeless body.

"I'm sorry, Jay."

"There's no need to apologise. But Aarie, there's something I've just realised. My mum died twelve years ago."

"Twelve years ago? That's around the same time *my* mum—"

"—I know, Aarie. It seems too much of a coincidence, doesn't it? There has to be a link. Two deaths within two ancient Oneiroi families in the same year—it just seems too unlikely not to be linked."

"But if you think our Mother's deaths were linked, are you saying you think our families are enemies?" Aarie asked, looking horrified as she saw Jay's answer already written on his face. "I can't believe that," she said in response. "My mum died in a car crash, Jay. It's what my Dad always had me believe. There can't be a link."

"Aarie, after everything that's happened to you and everything I've told you, can you really believe that there's no possibility that it could be linked?"

Aarie glanced down as if it hurt to look him in the eye. "Apart from nearly everything in my life being a lie, what does it mean for us, if what you are saying is right? If our families are enemies, will they ever accept us being together? Being part human was one thing, but now I could also be the daughter of your family's enemy. Will they force us to be enemies too?" she anxiously asked.

Jay lifted her chin to him gently. "No. It doesn't change anything for us as long as you don't want it to. I would like their blessing, but I don't need it. If they are enemies, that is their choice, not ours. Anyway, we don't know anything for certain, Aarie. We could be wrong. I am just simply trying to piece things together. Whatever happens, things will be okay as long as I have you. I know that, and that is all that matters," he said, kissing her hand as he kept it in his. "You believe that, don't you?"

Aarie nodded, then leaned against him. "Yes," she replied, certain now that he would always be there for her as she would be for him.

The temporary effects of Jay's blood were wearing off, and she felt slightly drained of energy once again. She no longer craved Jay's blood, but she knew she probably needed to sleep.

"So what happens now?" she whispered against his chest.

"You should rest," he replied, stroking her damp hair. As he did so, the leftover moisture from her shower slowly evaporated, leaving her curls soft and silky once again. "When your friends get here, I can tell them that you are still recovering and may need to sleep until the morning if you like? Though, I can't guarantee they will be able to wait that long to see you. I know I wouldn't be able to."

Aarie couldn't help but think back to earlier that evening, and the last time she had seen her friends. She let out a long exhale of breath.

"The blood demon's queen said my friends were written in the prophecy—something about them being the wall of flesh that protected me. My friends bought me time, Jay. They stood up to the blood demons, and they wouldn't give me up to them. Because of that, they bought me the few extra minutes I needed to survive until you returned. They would've died trying to protect me, but I would never let them do that. I gave myself up to the queen, and she let them go unharmed. If they hadn't done what they did, I'm not sure I could have kept my heart beating for any longer. Without all of you, I would not be here. I have to speak to them before I sleep, to thank them for what they did."

"Then I should speak to them too," Jay said. "If you did not come back, I do not know what would have become of me."

Aarie tightened her arms around him, and he rubbed her back gently.

"Okay," she whispered sleepily with her eyes closed. "And tomorrow, I should go to see my dad and talk to him. I'm not sure what to ask him. There's a possibility he will just think I've lost my mind, but I need to figure out the truth."

"I agree. I'll come with you."

Aarie's eyes blinked back open as though Jay had said something that had completely caught her off guard. Her mind wandered, conjuring up images of two important but very separate parts of her life juxtaposed for the first time.

"Hmm—what?" she gasped. Before she had time to think more about this, she heard voices echoing from the hallway downstairs; her friends were back home safe.

Chapter 23
The Three Realms

After a traumatic evening and an emotional reunion with her friends late last night, Aarie had surprisingly slept like a baby. She did not remember falling asleep or having any of the nightmares she had worried she would have. Aarie had woken up in the late morning in Jay's arms; she suspected this had been the real reason behind sleeping so well. After waking, she had convinced herself that she was prepared to face whatever unknown hurdles were about to come her way.

Aarie's hands now trembled as she fumbled through her satchel for her house keys. She stood in the driveway of her family home as Jay stood close. His curious eyes took in the place in which his Semper Sodale had grown up: a detached stone cottage surrounded by a luscious country garden, now full of vibrant autumnal colours. Maples, magnolia and cherry blossom trees were dotted around a large garden pond. Jay took note of how their spring flowers still decorated many of their branches even though it was not the correct season for them in this world. The air was clear, and there was no sound of traffic nearby, just a pleasant sound of birdsong. The afternoon sun lit up the sky with a golden orange tint, complementing the hues of the garden.

The stone gravel crunched underfoot as they moved towards the doorway. Jay immediately recognised the cottage's duck egg blue door from one of Aarie's photographs in her bedroom.

"What did you say to your father?" he asked, staring ahead at the house.

"I said I was coming home for a quick visit and that there was someone I'd like him to meet. Which is true, though quite terrifying."

"How so?"

"Well, my dad's always been quite protective when it comes to me and boys. I've never really introduced him to anyone that I've really cared about before, and I'm afraid he'll see how, you know, how much I really do care... and then freak out. He's the only family I have, Jay, and I've just realised how much I want him to like you."

"Well, I'll be on my best behaviour, I promise. I'll be the perfect gentleman—what can he not like?" Jay smiled.

"Okay, well here we go," Aarie said, turning the key.

She opened the door, and Jay followed Aarie into a large hallway, closing the door behind him.

"Hello? Dad, it's me. Are you home?" Aarie called out into the empty entrance hall.

Her dad emerged from one of the other rooms. Aarie was immediately startled by the cautious and serious manner in which he approached. She realised that he was holding something by his side. A glint of silver caught Aarie's eye, and she froze, noticing the large sword in her father's hand.

"Dad? What's going on? Please, tell me why you have that in your hand," she asked, standing firmly in front of Jay.

Aarie's father glared at Jay over her shoulder with clear hostility. "Aarie, you need to move away from him."

She drew in a short breath, shocked by the harshness of her dad's voice. "No," she gasped, panicking suddenly as her dad—for the first time in her life—seemed unsettlingly menacing. "Wait. Dad, stop! What are you doing? This is Jay. He's—"

"—I know who he is, Aarie. He has his father's eyes. You don't understand what he is, and I won't let him hurt you. Please, get behind me," he urged desperately, gesturing for her to come to him as he edged closer to the pair of them.

Jay met Aarie's father's glare. "Aarie knows perfectly well what I am, though I cannot say the same for you," he said defensively, but quickly tried to soften his tone. "I don't know what being my father's son means to you or what you think I am here for, but I would never hurt Aarie. We are just here to talk."

"Dad, please, he's telling the truth. I know about the Oneiroi, and now I know it's also true that you lied to me all these years, isn't it? Are you a Guardian?" Aarie's voice wavered as she heard her own words yet still could not believe she was saying them.

"It's true, Aarie. I am Oneiroi, but you have to believe me, you may think you know this boy, but he is not a boy, and I think he is here to kill us both. I believe they killed your mother, and I won't let them take you too."

"Enough!" Jay shouted. "I had nothing to do with Aarie's mother's death, and I am most definitely not here to kill Aarie. She's my Semper Sodale!" Jay reached for his sleeve to unveil his shimmering violet seal.

Lyle's eyes flitted immediately to his daughter. "Aarie, is this true? How can this be?" he said with an audible gasp as he lowered his blade. She lifted her jacket sleeve to reveal her matching violet symbol on her wrist.

"It's true, Dad. Jay's not here to hurt either of us. He's saved my life so many times already. Please, can you put the sword away because you're really freaking me out."

Lyle stared in astonishment at the violet seal on his daughter's wrist. He re-sheathed his blade, then leant it against the wall.

"Okay, Aarie. Let us all talk," he said at once, gesturing now to both Jay and Aarie to come into the living room.

Aarie and Jay sat together on a grey sofa against the wall as Lyle came into the room and sat in an adjacent grey armchair. There was a brief moment of awkward silence, filled only with the quiet ticking of a clock that stood on the stone fireplace to the front of the room. The golden orange of the afternoon sun flooded in through a large bay window, casting a slight shadow over part of Lyle's face. His gaze passed over Aarie and Jay beside her, landing on their hands that were tightly knit together.

Jay gently cleared his throat, breaking the silence. "Mr Stone, please forgive my outburst earlier. The subject of Aarie being hurt is extremely unsettling for me, especially when I'm being accused of being the one responsible."

Aarie was surprised by the polite manner in which Jay spoke, though she had heard him talk to his father in the same way.

Jay continued. "I had hoped for our first meeting to go a little better than it has so far. I'd like to make a better impression from this point on. It is important to Aarie, and so it is also important to me. I don't know what happened between our families in the past. My father has never told me of the details. I know there have always been feuds between the three families, but I also know our families were good friends once. I would like to start back from that point."

Lyle's expression was controlled. "Jaydon, your father believes I killed your mother, and I believe he had Aarie's mother killed to get even. I doubt very much that our families can ever be friends again. I don't doubt your good intentions for my daughter's sake—I know how the Seal of Semper Sodales works—but your father wholeheartedly believes I am your mother's killer. Don't tell me you don't want to strike me down to seek vengeance for her," Lyle said sombrely.

Jay's jaw tightened now as he stared at Lyle. A flood of mixed emotions visibly seemed to reshape his face. He briefly glanced at Aarie as her hand gently squeezed his.

Jay focused back on Lyle. "Then explain to me what happened, because I don't believe that *Aarie's* father would do such a thing."

"And I didn't," Lyle replied as his eyes studied Jay's expression closely. "But I was there. I held her as she died in my arms. I was covered in her blood when your father found us.

A long time ago, before she and your father were bound with the seal, we were once in love. I still cared for her even when we parted ways. I would never have done anything to hurt her, but your father believed I killed her through jealousy. We were once set to be chosen partners, but she and your father started showing signs of being soul partners. When their seal was made, there was nothing I could do but let her go.

At first, I did not understand what Semper Sodales were as they are so rare. Your father was a close friend, as close as a brother, and I loved them both. Their feelings for each other felt like the ultimate betrayal, but later, I learned the truth of Semper Sodales, and I could not deny them this happiness. They did not betray me, in fact, they had stayed apart because of their love for me. I realised I had to give them my blessing, knowing that they could never truly be happy without each other anymore.

I left Aneiros and came to this world. It is forbidden to do this, but because of my situation and who I am, an exception was made. An agreement was put in place. The Alinoy family were always happy for a chance to gain more power in my absence. So, between them and your father, the law permitted me to leave to create a new life for myself here as long as my real identity remained hidden from both worlds. I never returned, not noticed anyway, until the night your mother died, Jay.

I returned to Aneiros then because I had received urgent news that my assistance was required by your mother, Nyxantia. She believed she and your father were in danger from someone, but needed to confide in someone outside of Aneiros. However, when I arrived, it was already too late. She was gone.

The rage of a Semper Sodale's partner after they have gone is stronger than any bond between friends, even those who were once like brothers. When your father saw me holding the body of his dead Semper Sodale, there was nothing I could do to convince him it was not me. I had not seen him in centuries, so he did not know me anymore, and there I was, holding the woman he had taken from me many years ago. But it was not me. Your mother's killer may still be out there, Jay, and I can do nothing.

Though I have existed here for many centuries, I only truly decided to settle here when I met Aarie's mother. We were happy for many years. She was mortal, so I knew we could never be Semper Sodales, but if there is anything close for mortals—soulmates perhaps—then I believe that is what we were. It was the first time I felt part of any world again. When Aarie was born, my one and only child, I swore to protect her always. I told Anne what I am long before we were married," Lyle said, turning to Aarie now. "She knew everything about me, but we chose not to tell you, Aarie. You showed no signs of being Oneiroi, and we thought it best to keep you safe from that world. I'm sorry we lied to you, but we thought it dangerous for reasons you probably understand now. Aarie, you don't know how many times I've worried that one day I will lose you as I have your mother, simply to the natural mortal ageing process. But, if you two are Semper Sodales, does that mean you can change form now? Are you truly Oneiroi after all? Have you been blessed with immortality?"

Aarie struggled to answer her father's questions as he looked at her now with such hope and talked in such an unfamiliar manner. She turned to Jay for help. It was Jay who answered.

"I think part of Aarie's power was first activated when we became Semper Sodales, but then fully when—" Jay paused, looking back to Aarie hesitantly.

"He should know, Jay. It could be important," Aarie said.

Jay nodded, then turned back to Lyle. "Aarie's first transformation happened last night. She is no longer mortal if she ever was. The rest of Aarie's power was triggered off when she died yesterday. It happened only for a few moments, but her heart did stop."

Lyle's eye's widened with concern. "What? How did this happen?"

Aarie sat forward. "Blood demons, Dad. A lot of blood demons. Somehow they knew about me. They knew I was different, and they wanted my blood. They believed I was part of some Oneiroi prophecy that meant they would have more power without being weakened by daylight. I'd be dead now if it weren't for Jay."

Lyle gritted his teeth. "They'll pay for this! No-one touches my daughter and lives."

Jay lifted his head. "I'm working on it, trust me. But if the blood demons were correct, then they have succeeded, and who knows how dangerous that could be in the near future. The ones I got to, did not leave this world pleasantly, and neither will the others," Jay said in such a vicious tone, it surprised Aarie for a moment.

Lyle came to crouch on the floor in front of Aarie, then reached his hand to her arm. "I'm sorry I did not protect you better. I had no idea they knew you were different or how to find you." He leaned in to hug her, and her arms came around him too. "Aarie, there are so many things I've always wanted to tell you but couldn't. Now I can. I will tell you anything you want to know." Lyle looked over at Jay as he embraced his daughter. "Thank you for keeping her alive."

"There's something else," Jay replied. "I hid Aarie and her friends in a location that no one other than my Oneiroi Guardians should have known about, but somehow the blood demons knew where she would be. Not only that, but they must have known that my father would come to bring me back to Aneiros, giving them enough time to get to Aarie. It's too much of a coincidence that they came at the exact right time. Is there someone amongst the Oneiroi that would want to hurt Aarie?"

"Apart from your father, you mean?" Lyle said, sitting back down in his armchair.

"He wouldn't do that to me."

"Wouldn't he? Tell me, why did he come for you, and why did you not take Aarie with you?"

Jay hesitated before answering. "He thought Aarie was mortal and that I had broken the law, so I was asked to come back peacefully to talk. I did not have any other choice but to leave her. He didn't know she was my Semper Sodale at first, and he doesn't know she is your daughter. He brought me back with his army to stop the blood demons in the end."

"And did he know the blood demons were on their way already?"

Jay didn't answer, but doubt was visibly spreading in his mind.

"I'll take that look as a 'yes'," Lyle said. "Could it be that your father had a sudden change of heart about condemning my daughter to a pit of filthy blood demons because he realised he was condemning his very own son too?"

"No—" Jay wanted to protest, but he couldn't as he was no longer sure. His father *had* known the blood demons were coming and had not been willing to let Jay go back for her at first. "I don't believe he would purposely do that. He thought Aarie was one of them, and he thought we had broken the law. He may have seen that they were coming, but he didn't know what they would do, not at first. *Why* do you think so little of him?" Jay whispered.

"You're his son, he would know you would forgive him for letting a cherished mortal die, eventually, but not your Semper Sodale. There's nothing fiercer than that type of rage, remember? Do you not feel a little of that rage towards the blood demons who got away and those who caused this to happen in the first place?"

"I will not simply turn on him. He's my father!" Jay snapped.

"But he's also a grieving Semper Sodale. Even time cannot heal those wounds. Aarie is my flesh and blood, and he knew it would hurt me. He thinks he's avenging your mother's death, after all. I have no proof, but I believe he killed my Anne, Aarie's mother," Lyle said, briefly pausing to look in Aarie's direction. "I'm sorry I lied to you again, Aarie. There was no way to explain to a small child what I really believed had happened," he said, before continuing to address them both. "Not long after Jay's mother passed away, I came home late one night to find a crumpled note pushed through the door. It was stained with Anne's blood. She had written it in a hurried scrawl, saying she was scared and that there were monsters amongst us that we were oblivious to. She wrote that Aarie was no longer safe and to be wary of the Onuris family because they would come for her one day. Jay, she mentioned *your* family in her last message to me, and I never saw her again. I rushed around the house that night looking for her and Aarie in complete dismay. When I got to Aarie's room, I found her tucked up in bed underneath a blood-stained duvet. I immediately feared the worst, but when I uncovered her, she was unharmed and asleep like nothing had happened.

You ask me why I think so little of your father, Jay—because I cannot explain what happened to my wife. I have no other explanation. He is the only one who had a reason for doing this. The night he found his dead Semper Sodale, I fought so hard so I would return to my family, but also because I did not want to kill my old friend. I knew how it had looked to him, but I did all I could to convince him of the truth. In the end, I told him that there was no reason for me to have committed this murder because I had a family of my own and that I would never put them in danger. I thought this is why he eventually let me go with no interference from his army. But when Anne disappeared, only months after, I realised that this was a fate worse than a quick death—to lose your soul mate and fear for your child's life. If this was your father's doing, he had taken out the ultimate revenge. Maybe he had been driven to madness by grief, I don't know, but I know Anne would never leave Aarie or me this way unless forced.

You know what the worse thing is? She asked me for forgiveness for being helpless because she had no power to stop what had happened to her. I don't even *know* what happened to her. My mind can only imagine the worst, over and over. Your father must have done this, and I could not fight him for Aarie's sake. My wife was innocent, Jaydon, and he took her from me."

Jay looked down, considering everything Lyle had said to him. His forehead creased as he ran a hand through his hair. Finally, Jay looked back at Lyle. "He wants us to go back to Aneiros to discuss matters. How can I bring Aarie if either of us has *any* kind of doubt that she will be safe?"

"I can't say I am happy about Aarie being in your family's company, but I don't believe he would hurt her now. Don't you see the irony? His own son is my insurance that my daughter is finally safe from him."

Jay sat thoughtfully for a moment, rubbing the tension from his brow.

"This has to stop, this feud between you two. It's been too long. My mother wouldn't have wanted this. When I go back, you need to come with me. Explain to him what you have explained to me. This insurance you talk about, it surely extends to you too. You're Aarie's only family, so it would hurt her gravely for you to be harmed, and therefore it would hurt me."

"Don't be so sure that your father wouldn't be willing to hurt you, Jaydon. Killing you or driving you to insanity, maybe not, but what is a little pain in the face of eternity? After all, if Aarie had not been your Semper Sodale and your father had let her die, wouldn't it still have hurt? Or if you had refused to go peacefully, what do you think would have happened to her?"

Jay stared ahead, deliberating Lyle's questions. His mind was conflicted, and he knew Aarie could feel his anxiety and emotional pain now. Her eye's reflected the same pain and concern.

"Jay? You don't believe your father could have had anything to do with my mother's death, do you?" she asked.

"I don't believe he would hurt an innocent. I *have* to believe that, Aarie. Otherwise, what does that make me? But at the same time, I can't forget that he *did* know the blood demons were already on their way to you. I begged him to let me come back when he told me, but it wasn't until I showed him my mark, that he allowed it. Though, as I said, he thought I had broken the law, and this was proof that I had not. I want to believe my father thought he was protecting me from the blood demons and Oneiroi law. I don't want to think he would deliberately try to hurt you, Aarie simply because of who your father is. I need to ask him the truth about everything, in person. I don't want to believe he is capable of this, but if he is, then I don't know what else he could do."

"Even I am surprised that he would work with blood demons to get to me," Lyle said.

Jay ignored Lyle's comment. "I need to speak with him immediately, Aarie. I need to know the truth, no matter what that is. My father asked for both of us to come. He welcomed you, and I want to believe that was sincere, but what if I'm wrong? I don't want to leave you again either, so you have to tell me what you want to do?"

"I want to come with you. I need to know the truth too. Whatever happens, Jay, it still changes nothing between us, remember?"

Jay knotted his hand tightly in hers without saying a word. Jay got to his feet, and as Aarie was about to stand too, Lyle quickly looked up.

"Jaydon wait. Before you both go, could I talk with Aarie alone for a moment? We have never spoken about Oneiroi matters before, and a lot has happened recently. I just need a few minutes."

"Yes, of course," Jay replied. With one last glance to Aarie, he left the room, closing the door behind him.

The room fell silent again for a moment, except for the clock ticking. Lyle came to sit beside Aarie on the sofa.

"Aarie, are you okay? I look at you now, and you look the same to me—my same little girl. You know you'll always be my little girl, no matter what, but I know so much has changed since we last spoke in person. The Oneiroi, the blood demons, me and my past, and everything—it's so much to handle. I just want to know for sure you're really coping."

"Yes. I mean that, Dad. I know we have lots to talk about, and I'm glad I'll get that chance now. The thing with the blood demons is not something I want to think about or talk about at the moment, and it is a shock to find out that most of my life has been a lie, but I'm glad that I know who I really am now."

"And Jay, does he make you happy?"

"Yes, but I guess you already know that because *this* isn't possible if he didn't," Aarie said, lifting her wrist briefly to show her mark.

"I never imagined that I would ever talk about the Oneiroi with you. I thought that part of my life would always have to be kept hidden to keep you safe. I always imagined just being an overprotective dad, trying to scare off undesirable mortal boys who'd try to court my daughter. I would never have guessed that you would have a Semper Sodale, Aarie. I didn't think it was possible, and now you do, I don't even know how to react.

But, Jaydon Onuris—of all the boys in the universe you could have picked—I mean, technically he's not even a boy. You know that, don't you? In fact, do you know how old he is, Aarie?"

"Yes, Dad, I know. But I'm eighteen—I'm an adult. After everything, are we really having *this* conversation?"

"I'm sorry, but as I said, Aarie, you're my little girl. Mortal or not, I still want to protect you. Look, I know you two are Semper Sodales. I know the deal, believe me, I do. I know you think you're an adult, but to me, you're still a child and very impressionable, and he's, well—he's old! I'm just saying you two don't need to rush into anything. You have the whole of eternity. I'm just asking you to be careful—"

"Dad—stop! I don't think I like where this conversation is leading." Aarie said as her cheeks flushed red. "Besides, what about you and Mum? She was only a few years older than me when you two met, and I'm pretty sure you were a lot older too."

"That was different. "

"No, Dad, it wasn't. Look, you know as well as I do, age is not the same with the Oneiroi."

"Aarie, you've barely had a serious boyfriend in the past, and now you have a Semper Sodale. One who just happens to be a royal Oneiroi Guardian, whose father... Look, I'm just asking you to think things through before you give up everything for him, Aarie—your home, your life, your friends and possibly even me."

"I would never do that! This is stupid. I don't want to fight with you about this. It's pointless. You know that *nothing* you can say can change anything, Dad."

After everything that had been discussed, Aarie's hopes of her dad being pleased for her were shattering. Her heart sank. "If you really think Jay's dad had something to do with Mum's death, I know it's hard for you to see him here, but whatever is the truth, it wasn't Jay's fault. Dad, I'm sorry if I've disappointed you in my choice, but I... I just really hoped you would like him, because he's important to me."

Aarie stood up to leave, but Lyle reached his arm out to her.

"Aarie, wait. I never said I didn't like him. I know how it looked when you first came in, but I honestly thought his father had sent him to kill us then. It doesn't matter what happened between his father and myself. I know the Seal of Semper Sodales does not lie. I *know* what you feel for each other."

Lyle got up off the sofa and walked across the room to stand by the window. He let out a long exhale of breath and stood still for a few moments with his hand rubbing his creased forehead. He turned back to Aarie, hesitating before he spoke.

"I'm sorry, Aarie. I don't want to upset you. It was just a shock seeing you with him. All of this is a lot for me to take in too, especially when I had tried so hard to keep you hidden from his family, thinking they would be a danger to you. I thought I had kept you safe from my world, but it seems to have reached out and found you anyway. I don't even know how you two met, and as your father, I suppose, no one will ever be good enough for you in my eyes, no matter who they are."

"You said his name—Jaydon—like you know him. Have you two met before?"

"No, but I know of him. I may have left Aneiros, but I still visit from time to time, avoiding detection. I make sure to keep in the loop of most happenings there, and most Guardians of Aneiros are familiar with whom Jaydon is. His name and so many others he is known by, have reached this world in some form anyway.

His realm and mine were close allies a long time ago, and though that was a time before he was even born, I know that he is well respected by the Oneiroi of both realms today. You see, our two realms have always shared the same core beliefs in Guardian methods of dream casting regardless of his father's and my feud. But, as my realm's Guardians are loyal to me, the closeness between our two kingdoms may never be fully bridged again.

You should know my realm still exists, Aarie."

"Your realm?"

"Yes. There are three realms of Aneiros you need to be aware of— Horngate, the first realm of Aneiros, led by the Onuris family. Jay and Phelan take rule alongside their father, Erebus.

Firestone is the second realm. This is our family's realm. Your real name should have been Aarie Adara, had you been born in Aneiros.

Ivoriark is the third realm, led by the Alinoy family. Orin Alinoy is their king. Of all the realms, this is the one you must be most wary of.

The Guardians of Firestone are still loyal to me, and I to them, so one day I will eventually return. I still have a duty, even if the other realms may not recognise it or have forgotten my name. I am still a Guardian, and I have never abandoned that. I have kept a close eye on this world and lived as a mortal. In doing so, I have gained an invaluable insight into what it is to be one of them, to care about them and this world, and to have an understanding of mortal minds. You will not yet understand how important that is to Guardians, and I wish to explain it to you more when we have more time. I must pass my knowledge on to my Guardians in Aneiros one day. My absence from them will eventually reap some benefits for them. As much as this world is home, it is in my blood to want to know what is going on in my world. Now I see it is in yours too," Lyle said, analysing Aarie's current expression. Although she was curious about his words, her glumness had not left since his brief outburst.

Lyle sighed. "Aarie, I didn't mean to sound like I was disappointed in you—because I'm not. Half of the things I said before, I didn't even mean. I just don't know how to react to any of this because it's happened so suddenly. If I were to be completely honest with you, it's hard for me to say the truth. I know he's a good match for you. I know he can protect you better than most other Guardians because he's First Blood. If it weren't for him, you would already be dead, and for that, I am grateful to him more than you can imagine. As far as Guardians go, there are very few that could live up to Jay's impeccable reputation, if you must know."

"You say that like you have *respect* for him."

"Yes, Aarie, I do now I know he can't possibly have had anything to do with your mother's death. Jay's skills as a Guardian are renowned amongst the Oneiroi. You should probably know that his mastery of dream casting has become somewhat legendary amongst the Oneiroi. Though dreams are his realms speciality, he and his brother are also much known for some of the most effective and fearsome of all nightmares, Aarie. I don't know how much Jay has explained to you about our world, but for a Guardian, both sets of skills are invaluable.

He's royalty, Aarie, and technically so are you. As I am First Blood, so are you. If ever there was a perfect match amongst the Oneiroi, it is the two of you. I know it more than you even know yourself, but I don't want you to lose yourself in everything. Our families are not on good terms at present, and I just want you to make sure you know what you're getting into before you make any big decisions. You might find yourself in the middle of a war, and you might be forced to make choices you're not ready for."

"Choices? What do you mean? What choices?"

"If I'm right about his father, Jaydon won't be able to forgive him easily, Aarie. I saw his face when doubt appeared in his mind. I don't know what that means for Jay if it is the case. To be at war with your own family when you're royalty can mean to give up everything as a Guardian. I just don't want you getting hurt in the crossfire. You may need to choose a side.

I know you're not two immature teenagers. I wish it were that simple. Even without the matters of our two family disputes, you're both *royalty*. That alone will draw the attention of many, along with certain expectations and responsibilities. There is an uneasy peace that lies between all three realms at this time. A difference in opinion on how to deal with shadows has always separated ours and Jay's realm from the Alinoy's realm, Ivoriark. That divide seems to grow each year. Many amongst the Oneiroi have become less tolerant of mortals, but none more so than the Alinoy family and their Guardians.

So, to be a central figure amongst the Oneiroi with your origin, will be controversial. I know Jay can handle that, but are you ready for that?" Lyle said, regarding Aarie thoughtfully. "Look, you and Jay haven't had enough time together for you to understand all of this fully. I just want you to take care of yourself by taking your time to adjust to everything. That's all I ask. Can you do that for me?"

"Yes. I promise," Aarie replied as she got up to move closer to her dad.

Lyle reached his large arms around the tiny frame of his daughter and embraced her. Her own arms came around him too. Aarie realised that apart from today, she had not hugged her dad properly for a long time, and she held on for a moment longer.

"We met in a dream," Aarie said. "You asked me where we met—it was in a dream. After the accident, Jay was the miracle that saved me, Dad. I kept finding myself in Aneiros not long after that. I thought I was just dreaming or losing my mind for so long. Then, when dreamwalkers tried to get to me in Aneiros and this world, Jay helped me again. He followed me back here to keep me safe. So, now you know how we met." Aarie finally broke away gently, taking in her father's thoughtful expression. "Before I go, Dad, I'd like to see the real you. You're not in your natural form now, are you? You look older than you really look, don't you? And your wings— do you have wings?"

Lyle nodded. "Yes, Aarie, you are right. I've lied to you for too long," Lyle said, stepping back to create space between them. "Okay, Aarie, this is the real me..."

Aarie stepped back in astonishment as her father began to get younger before her eyes. His greying brown hair darkened to a rich brown, and his face smoothed out the traces of time. A pair of large white gold wings unfurled from his back so fast that they caught a glass vase that had been on the windowsill behind him. It tumbled over the edge onto the floor with a heavy thud of shattering glass. Aarie and Lyle barely seemed to notice it as they stared at each other.

"My real name is Lelan Adara. This is who I am, Aarie."

Aarie's eyes widened in awe. Her father was truly magnificent to look at. His wings arched out above him, fluttering slightly. He held his wrist to the side to reveal the mark that matched her own; it was the mark of their family's royal bloodline.

"You're incredible," she whispered.

The room door opened slightly at that moment, and Jay worriedly looked in. Both Aarie and her father's eyes shifted instantly to the door, somewhat startled. Jay's gaze moved over Aarie and then to her father, whose enormous wings began to fold back behind him. Lyle stood with a still grace, watching Jay's reaction to his present appearance.

Jay cleared his throat. "I didn't mean to intrude. I heard glass breaking and... wings unfurling. I just thought—"

"What? That I might be attacking my own daughter?"

"No—I... I don't know what I thought. I was just anxious. Last night's events left me unsettled. I apologise. I should have knocked. I'll leave you to it," Jay said, looking unusually uneasy and flushed.

"Last night, meaning the blood demon attack?" Lyle asked, prompting Jay to nod silently in response. Lyle's eyes softened. "Don't apologise for wanting to protect my daughter, Jaydon. I would hardly judge you for that. But you need to know I would never hurt her in any way."

Jay nodded again, slowly turning to leave the room. Before he could, Lyle spoke again.

"You may as well come in now. I know you heard most of our conversation anyway. These walls weren't built to block Oneiroi hearing, and it is hard to switch off your mind and ears when someone you care about is involved."

Jay's eyes met Lyle's, startled by his understanding tone and accurate assumption of him.

"It wasn't my intention to eavesdrop," Jay replied, throwing another apologetic look towards Aarie then back to Lyle.

"Dad—" Aarie began.

"—It's okay, Aarie. Just one moment," Lyle said softly, as he waved a gently dismissive hand in her direction to cut her off.

236

"Hmm. So, Jaydon, it would appear you are very important to my daughter. I know how the seal works, so I know it works both ways. We didn't get off to a good start on our first meeting, and that is mainly because of me, so I would like to make amends." Lyle moved nearer to a baffled Aarie, and took hold of her wrist, gently lifting her hand out.

Looking up in Jay's direction, he gestured for Jay to come closer, which he did immediately. Lyle reached out his free hand for Jay's, and Jay offered his as though to shake hands. Instead, Lyle lifted Jay's hand and placed it on top of Aarie's, leaving it there as he stepped back.

"Take care of my daughter, but also take care of yourself too. Your wellbeing is her wellbeing now."

"I will," Jay replied.

"And please, both of you, don't let your new connection rule your emotions or judgement in the future. I know that will be hard as it is strange and new to you both. Jay, you know what it feels like to lose that connection first hand now, so it may be even harder not to act on impulse if you think Aarie is in danger. Be aware of that."

Jay nodded in agreement. "I hope that one day, our families will become the good friends I know they once were. I will do everything I can to find the truth behind what happened to both Aarie's mother and my own."

"I know you will." Lyle smiled sincerely. "You take after her, you know —your mother, that is. I see a lot of her in you now—more than I did at first. Whatever truths you may find out, please know that there will be no war from my side now. I would not act on any of my beliefs, knowing it would cause Aarie pain to do so."

Aarie shared a brief glance with her father and mouthed the words 'thank you'. Jay clasped her hand now in his and swung it down gently by their side.

"I know you're keen to find answers, so don't let me keep you any longer," Lyle said.

"Thank you," Jay replied, then turned to Aarie, "Are you ready?" he asked, taking hold of the sides of her arms gently.

"Yes." She nodded.

Jay's arms wrapped around her back as he brought her closer to him. "I want you to concentrate on what you feel as we travel. I will take full control of the travelling part because you don't know where we're going, but I want you to take note of what you sense I am feeling. You are no longer linked to Aneiros like the shadows, but because of your Oneiroi transitioning, you will be able to travel there whenever you please now. I want you to practice in case there is a time you need to travel back without me, okay?"

"Okay," she replied.

Jay gave one more glance to Lyle, who stood watching them. "We'll return soon, I promise."

Lyle nodded. Jay's grip tightened around Aarie slightly, and she could feel the same strange tingling that she had when they had travelled this way earlier. She closed her eyes and concentrated. They slowly faded, becoming more and more transparent until they were no longer in Lyle's living room.

Chapter 24
World Of The Oneiroi

"We're here. You can open your eyes," Jay whispered.

Aarie shot a glance at Jay, then anxiously around her. Pivoting on the spot, she took in her surroundings. A majestic garden stretched out ahead of her for as far as she could see. Luscious green lawns carpeted the ground as paths weaved in various patterns at the edges. One long pathway divided the green carpet straight down the middle. Her eyes followed it past marble fountains and shaped hedgerows, past blossom trees and maples, under spiralling crystal archways, and onwards until it seemingly came to an abrupt end. Trees lined either side of the path, blocking the view beyond their branches. However, as Aarie's eyes moved back to the centre of the pathway, she could make out a blur of white and golden light. It was as though nothing but cloud sat beyond those trees. Aarie turned to her left and realised nothing blocked the view of the side edges of this long ornate garden. Yet, once again, she could not see anything other than the same strange blurring of white and golden light that made the garden appear to come to an abrupt end. Only a low stone wall stood at its edges.

Curious to work out what she could see, Aarie hurried towards the edge. As she did, a white mist seemed to thin and drift away, revealing towers and spires in the distance. She gasped as she reached the wall and gripped hold of it firmly. The wall only stood up to her waistline, and below was a drop so far down that it disappeared into what Aarie now knew were literally clouds. She knew that this place was not somewhere any mortal had ever walked before; this was indeed a place where only immortals could go.

Aarie turned to Jay, but before she could say anything to him, her eyes fell on the magnificent white building that stood behind him, illuminated by the golden rays of the sun. In this direction, the pathway that divided the garden met with white stone steps. These led up to what Aarie could only describe as a palace. She had never quite seen a building like it; its architectural design seemed to have no era. It appeared to mix past, future and something only of dreams. Large stone pillars lined its central facade, and Aarie's eyes wandered over its hundreds of windows of all sizes, balconies, towers, turrets, spires and glass-domed roofs. She finally came to acknowledge the backdrop that framed it. Hundreds of structures stood on the mountains that surrounded the back of this building. There were smaller towers and spirals of gold and silver, glistening rooftops, archways, pathways, gardens, steps, and bridges that stood alongside these buildings.

Aarie realised she was looking at an Oneiroi city behind this palace. Jay stepped toward her.

"This is my home—my real home," Jay said.

"The cottage—was that not your home?" Aarie asked.

"I guess so, but more of a favourite small retreat I like to enjoy."

"Small? I wouldn't have said *small*," Aarie replied, utterly amazed by Jay's casual tone.

"We're in Horngate City now, the capital of the first realm of Aneiros. This is the official House of Onuris. When you came before, we were in the country. It's what made your presence so unusual in the beginning because no one but my family ever goes there. It is very rare for dreamwalkers to appear near the private homes of royal Guardians, and virtually impossible for shadows to cross the boundary that protects royal grounds," Jay replied.

"So you live *here* most of your time?"

"Yes."

"And this is like your family's *palace*?" Aarie's voice seemed to go up a pitch with every question, and Jay could not help but chuckle.

"I've never called it that, but I suppose, yes, in a way."

"Jay, this is literally a palace in the sky, like the treehouse palace but *a lot* bigger!" she said in awe.

"Well, think of the treehouse as the prototype. I drew many more sketches as I grew up." Jay smiled.

Aarie's jaw dropped. "You designed this?"

"Me and my brother, Phelan, a long time ago now." Jay's smile began to fade as his mind wandered. "I wish we were here under more relaxed circumstances. I wish I could give you a proper tour right now, but I should let my father and Phelan know that we have arrived. We have so much to discuss."

Aarie sensed Jay's anxiety once again. "It's okay, that's far more important. It's what we came to do, after all," she said as he slipped her hand into his automatically.

"Maybe later though," Jay suggested, trying to bring a smile back.

Jay led Aarie up the steps to a grand entranceway between the stone pillars. He reached his wrist up to large golden doors, but before his skin even touched them, they began to open at once. Jay gestured for Aarie to step through and then followed behind her.

They entered a large entrance hall. Painted murals of winged figures, framed with ornate gold patterns covered its walls and high ceilings. Grey marble flooring gleamed under a huge domed shaped light that was caged in a gleaming gold framework. Arched doorways and marble pillars lined all four edges of this vast space.

The sound of footsteps on the marble floor echoed through the room. Jay and Aarie looked ahead at the figure that was casually strolling towards them. It was Phelan. He was dressed in typical Oneiroi Guardian attire as

Aarie had seen him before. His face was softer and not in the slightest bit menacing as she had remembered it in her nightmares. That time seemed so very long ago now as he drew nearer. He smiled to greet them, and Aarie was immediately shocked by the striking family resemblance there was between him and Jay. She had never really noticed before, but he had the same warm smile, deep blue eyes and dark hair, though Phelan's hair was slightly longer. His voice was similar but somewhat deeper as he spoke now.

"Jay, you're back, and welcome, Aarie. I thought you both may have taken longer to return, which would have been understandable after what happened. How are you?"

"Much recovered, thank you," Jay replied

"I am glad to see that you are, Brother, but how about yourself, Aarie? Are you okay?" he said, looking directly at her now with genuine concern. "You looked in such a bad way the last time I saw you. I wouldn't have thought it possible for a *mortal* to recover from something like that so fast."

Aarie's throat and mouth seem to have gone dry, and she swallowed before she replied. "I'm fine, thank you. Thanks to Jay, I am fine."

A wave of nausea came over Aarie as though to contradict her. She leaned back slightly into Jay, feeling lightheaded. She kept Phelan's gaze, trying not to show anything was wrong, but there was something about the way he looked at her now that made her sure he knew something wasn't right.

"Jay, it would appear Aarie may need more time to rest after all," Phelan said at once. "How long ago was her first transformation?" he asked astonished.

Jay immediately moved around to face Aarie and saw what had prompted Phelan's question. Aarie's eyes were flickering a deep gold as she blinked back at him in confusion.

"Impossible," Jay whispered in disbelief. "Aarie, how do you feel? Do you feel okay?"

"Jay, what is it? You're both starting to scare me now," she said. "What's going on? Why wouldn't I be okay?"

"I'm sorry," Jay replied. "It's nothing to worry about... I don't think. It's just your eyes—they're showing signs of the second wave of Oneiroi transition. They're flickering golden right now. It normally takes months or even years for that to happen. It would appear you seem to be in a rush to complete the next stage in a matter of hours."

"Oh, that might explain it—" Aarie mumbled as her eyes rolled back and she passed out. Jay and Phelan reached out and caught her.

"So, she's *not* just a mortal after all, Brother." Phelan smiled, but Jay did not return it. Instead, he angrily shoved Phelan aside as he lifted Aarie into his arms.

"She was never *JUST* a mortal, even when I thought she *was* mortal. Do you hear me?"

Phelan's face dropped. "That's not what I meant. I just meant we were all wrong. I didn't mean any offence by it, Jay."

"I know you didn't, but the way you always speak of mortals, you do just that. All of the Oneiroi do. I sometimes think our world would be better if we were more like *them*. Maybe Aarie would not have suffered last night if it were the case," Jay said, feeling the bitter tone in his own voice. He did not think he blamed his brother or father for anything that had happened to Aarie, but it was clear to him now, part of him did.

"I'm sorry, Jay. Nobody would've wanted to cause you the pain you went through last night or Aarie either. Father would never have allowed it, had he known—"

"—Had he known *what*, exactly?" Jay erupted. "That I was in love with a mortal? Or that she was my Semper Sodale? Because either should have been enough to make you both want to protect her. It should have been enough, Phelan. She wasn't just caused pain—she *died*.

I needed both of you, more than ever before, as my *family* not as Guardians. But I had no one, no one but her. She did nothing to deserve any of this except love me. I have given my all to this world and to my family. And after everything *we've* been through together in our lifetime, how could this happen, Phelan?"

Phelan glanced down, unsure of how to respond. At that moment, Jay's father stepped towards them, and they immediately turned to him. Neither of them had noticed him coming until he was already here, so it was clear he had heard the last of Jay's outburst. Erebus gaze swept over Phelan and Jay, then to Aarie who was unconscious in Jay's arms.

"What happened here? Is Aarie okay?"

It was Phelan that spoke first. "It would appear that Aarie—"

"—She may have needed a bit more time to recover after all," Jay said, quickly cutting Phelan off before he could say any more. "She will be fine. She just needs rest, that's all,"

Phelan glanced at Jay in slight confusion as to why he was keeping Aarie's transitioning a secret from his father. Jay's eyes passed over him for a brief moment, but it was enough to indicate that he had a reason for not bringing the information to attention.

"I see. Then she must rest," Erebus said. "Phelan, please would you see that Aarie is made comfortable. Your brother and I have many things to discuss. I doubt Jay would have come so soon if he did not have urgent matters on his mind."

Phelan hesitated, glancing at Jay and then back to his father.

"I would, Father, but I do not think Jay trusts me right now with his Semper Sodale."

"Is this true, Son?" Erebus asked.

Jay looked down at Aarie in his arms without answering.

"Son, do you not trust me now either? You cannot believe we would do anything to hurt her deliberately, can you? Do you think us to be monsters now? Son, please, answer me."

Jay broke his silence to look up at his father. "I want to believe you. I came here to trust you. I just don't know if I can take the risk... not with her. Maybe I shouldn't have come so soon."

"Son, you are here now. I give you my word as your father, she will be safe. There is no risk from *us*. I swear to you. Does that not mean anything to you? Is my word also worthless now?"

"No," Jay whispered, deliberating his father's words. "Of course, it means something, but I need you to answer one question. When you came to bring me home yesterday, did you know who Aarie's father was?"

"Aarie's father? I don't understand. How would I know that? And why does this make any difference? I have excepted Aarie is mortal. The law is not broken as she is your Semper Sodale—it makes no difference who her mortal father is. But to answer your question properly—no, I did not or do not know. I give you my word on that too," Erebus replied, clearly confused by the question.

"Okay," Jay whispered. He moved toward Phelan slowly, holding out Aarie. "Take care of her. If she wakes before I return, let her know I won't be long and that she is safe."

Phelan stepped forward, gently taking Aarie from Jay. "She's in good hands, Jay, I swear," Phelan reassured.

Jay nodded. "Phelan, what I said before—I'm sorry."

"No. No, you're not, and neither should you be. I won't let you down again. Now go, talk, sort things out here, and I'll speak to you later."

Jay watched as Phelan walked away, carrying Aarie. He disappeared through one of the arches ahead of them. Jay was now alone with his father, who seemed to be studying him carefully as he turned back to face him.

"Shall we?" Erebus said, lifting a hand to gesture Jay to lead the way.

In silence, they both walked through another archway that led to a different hallway with several more doorways. A grand marble stairway, embellished with ornate carvings of more winged figures, wound to the left of them. The pair of them made their way through a large copper door that stood ahead of the archway they had come from. After entering a room, Erebus closed the door behind them. Jay moved to stand by the large window that overlooked the city. His family often used this place for meetings and family gatherings. It was the room in which he had spoken to his father the last time he was home. Jay took in the city in front of him, taking a deep breath before his father spoke.

"I know you blame me for what happened to Aarie," Erebus said, moving closer to Jay. He stopped a few metres from him at the opposite side of the window. "I didn't *know*. I didn't know what she was to you, but more importantly, I didn't know that they would harm her. Not until you

243

were so sure of it. By then, it was too late. What I said to you before I knew she was your Semper Sodale, was unforgivable. Yes, I knew there was something between you both, but I thought you had broken the law, Son. On any other occasion, it *would* have been 'enough' to make me want to protect her for you, I swear it would have been. However, I was out of time and distracted. The Alinoy family had already heard about you and Aarie. They had heard rumours through the dreamwalkers that you had become protective over a mortal. You had been spotted mixing with other mortals and dreamwalkers as though you'd gone completely rogue. Orin Alinoy was coming to gather evidence against you, and if he had gotten that evidence, he would have forced me to bring you to trial, Jay. They would have taken your wings and sentenced you to death. And Aarie too.

I would not have intentionally put Aarie in danger. I just did not want to risk losing my son to an army of blood demons. Above all, I could not risk making matters worse for you in the eyes of the law. I said what I said to try to convince you, Jay. I couldn't bear to lose another member of my family. I'm sorry."

Silence filled the room as Jay stood thoughtfully staring out through the window. He swallowed.

"I don't blame you... or at least I don't *want* to. I was angry before and unsure of whether I had done the right thing to bring Aarie here. I just don't understand, Father—how did the blood demons know we were there? Did you tell them? Were you working with them?"

"No, not exactly. Before, you asked me if I knew who Aarie's father was —I don't—but I know her mother. Or more accurately, I know what her mother is," Erebus replied, and Jay abruptly turned to face him.

"Aarie's mother? But Aarie's mother died twelve years ago... or at least, she went missing," Jay corrected himself as he considered the possibilities.

"No, I can assure you she is very much alive. She is called Annabel Stone, and she visited me a few days ago. Jay, she's a blood demon. She is the one who warned me that the Alinoy family had heard about your contact with Aarie. Being her mother, she worried about what the consequences would be for her daughter."

"But she's a blood demon. Surely she cannot have any concerns or mortal emotions regarding her daughter's welfare anymore, can she?"

"Aarie seems to defy the normal limitations of a mortal, and that strength seems to run in her family. Her mother *does* appear to be holding on to her humanity. She was very convincing on that front, and it is a rare thing. Maybe if one's will is strong enough, then there is a way. Or, maybe it is because as a mortal, she had other gifts. Jay, Annabel was blessed with the gift of 'future sight'. She is an oracle."

"Like the one who wrote the story of the Aneiros Dream Lily—the old prophecy?" Jay asked.

"As the legend goes, yes. Annabel has visions of potential future happenings. Any such visions can be altered if certain interventions are made. She told me of two possible futures she had seen. In the first one, Aarie died at the hands of numerous Alinoy Oneiroi Guardians. Here, she was a mortal who stood no chance to protect herself against their vast numbers. Alongside her, my youngest son would die too, trying to save her. No mercy would be given to you, and you would be stripped of your wings despite your pleas of injustice. Your death would be the most dishonourable and painful way for a Guardian to die. I saw that future for you, Jay, as though it really happened." Erebus broke from his thoughts to briefly glance at his son, whose eyes fixed on him intently. Turning back to look at the city through the window, Erebus continued to explain. "In the second vision, she showed me Aarie lived, and the blood demon armies ceased to grow. The blood demons that existed were no longer a threat to humans or the Oneiroi. In this vision, no dishonour or ill fate would await you as far as her sight could see, and you seemed happy, but most importantly, you lived, Son.

I was told that I had the power to choose which vision would become a reality. I just had to do one thing, and it would be set in motion. Annabel asked me to tell her where Aarie was, to prevent the first reality from ever happening. This is what I am guilty of, Son."

"And you believed her? Even though she is a blood demon?"

"She proved to me her gift of sight, Jay, as she proved to me that she has somehow retained a lot of her human traits. She is Aarie's mother, and I did not believe she could fake the desperation I saw in her eyes. That same desperation had brought her to me, knowing that I could have had her killed. Annabel convinced me that she and Alyssandra had agreed to help protect Aarie like one of their own. I thought Aarie was already close to being one of them anyway. I did not know then that they would allow for her to be hurt as she was. Anne lied to me about that part, but I can't help believe that she knew Aarie would survive and this was the only option she had."

"But how can you be sure she is Aarie's mother?"

"Because she showed me some of her memories. I assure you, she is very much Aarie's mother, and she is alive. Annabel explained that she left Aarie's life because she could not trust her own blood cravings. She feared that she was slowly losing all that made her human, though now it is clear that Annabel has retained more than she ever thought possible."

Jay took a deep breath. "Aarie's mother is alive," he whispered in amazement. "I must tell Aarie as soon as she wakes. She has to know you didn't kill her," he declared.

"She thinks I killed her mother? Why would she think that?"

"I'm not sure if she does, but her father believes it for certain."

"Back to her father again—who is he, Jay? And why do you think I know him?"

"Because you *do*, Father. There is something I haven't told you about Aarie. I only found it out myself yesterday. Aarie is no longer mortal. She is very much Oneiroi, and more than most. Her father is Lyle Stone, but you know him as Lelan Adara," Jay revealed, scrutinising his father's response.

"Lelan Adara?" Erebus gasped.

Jay nodded. "Yes. Aarie was not still recovering when you saw her earlier—she was in Oneiroi transitioning."

Erebus eyes opened wide. "First Blood calling to First Blood," he whispered. "*Incredible*. This has never happened before, Jay. And Lelan— have you spoken to him recently?"

"Yes. At first, he thought you had sent me to kill him and Aarie until I showed him my seal. He thinks you killed Anne as you believed him to be my mother's murderer."

"How can he think that?"

"Is it not true that you believe him to be Mother's killer?"

"No, it is not true, Jay. There was a brief moment of madness when I believed he had. I saw her lifeless body in his arms, so of course, it looked possible that he had killed her. But I know now that he was not responsible. Son, if I truly still believed it was him, he would not have left here that day. He knew that. He must have known. No grieving Semper Sodale would allow it, and I would *never* have taken revenge on an innocent, no matter what. What monster does he mistake me for?"

"I suppose grief can twist anyone's perception. Father, when I came here, I had doubts. I'm sorry, but I did. I never wanted to doubt you, and I never will again, but the grief that I felt when Aarie's heart stopped beating, I can only describe that as temporary madness. I was angry, and I needed someone to blame for everything that had happened. Aarie's father is trapped in that space between despair and not knowing because his wife just disappeared all those years ago. He doesn't know the truth about her transformation. He can't do. It all makes sense to me now. She was never taken. Neither did she abandon her family. Anne simply feared that she would hurt Aarie if she stayed. From Lelan's account and what you described to me, I think she may have attacked Aarie because of her bloodthirst. I don't think she could control it, and she knew she had to leave. Lelan doesn't know this, and maybe she didn't want to admit what she had become. I have to put things right by telling him the truth. Things should be made right between our two families. If you have no qualms with him, he should know. It is time," Jay said.

Erebus nodded. "You are right. I have delayed our paths crossing again. I admit it, but I never knew what he believed. Otherwise, I would *never* have left it so long. I was ashamed of the way I treated him after he gave up so much for me. He was like a brother to me, and I should never have doubted him. I will put things right from this point on."

Jay's forehead creased. "Father, if you don't believe Lelan killed my mother, then who do you really think *was* responsible?"

"The same someone who was helping the blood demon army grow," Erebus replied.

"Who? The blood demon queen?"

"Alyssandra? No, she merely keeps some kind of order amongst them, where possible. As one of their eldest, she is one of the strongest, but she has never turned a single mortal to her dark world. She hates the very nature of her kind, and that is the only reason the Oneiroi let her be. She is the only other blood demon I know of that has held onto part of her humanity. Son, I believe it was the Alinoy family. Though I have no proof, it makes sense now.

The night before your mother died, she told me that an anonymous Guardian had discovered some important information regarding dreamwalkers. She knew the Guardian well and had arranged to meet with them alone, but for their safety and others, she agreed to keep their identity unknown from anyone else. Your mother trusted them, so she never worried she would be in danger. But someone did not want that meeting to happen or did not want your mother to learn what she would. When I saw Lelan with your mother's dead body, I thought the anonymous Guardian was him at first because she trusted him and... I don't know how much Lelan has told you about his past with Nyxanthia but—"

"—He told me of their past, their parting, and why he left," Jay quickly replied.

Erebus nodded. "Well, because of our history, at first, I thought Lelan had betrayed her to get revenge on us finally. When I came to my senses, I knew deep down it could never have been him. He always cared for her, and no Guardian with a new family of their own would start a pointless war like this. His presence was merely an unfortunate coincidence, or maybe Nyxanthia had wanted him there, I don't know for sure, but Lelan was not the anonymous Guardian she had planned to meet. Perhaps she had already met them before Lelan got there or maybe she was killed before it took place.

For years I searched for answers, but there were none to be found. All my unanswered questions, alongside your mother's death, nearly drove me to insanity. If I had not had you and Phelan, maybe it would have done. I knew I needed the deep sleep to recover from this loss, and so, I slept for over half a decade, never finding the answers. When I woke, I swore I would never allow myself to lose any of my family again. I knew I would not survive a second time. All the while, the same questions burned in my head. As the dreamwalkers were one of the last things your mother mentioned, I had begun to think that maybe it was them who had murdered her.

Then, something started to make sense finally. An essential piece of the puzzle was given to me. When Annabel came to me, she explained that the Alinoys are letting blood demons create an army. They know of their increasing numbers and plan to allow them to increase until they are so many that they could eventually destroy the human world. The Alinoy family promote and use the cruellest, most sinister of nightmares they can

247

muster because they do not care if the mortals return home safely. They don't care for our duties as Guardians of both worlds anymore. They want to stop mortals from coming to our world for good. They are turning a blind eye to all of the dreamwalkers that are created in their realm—most being blood demons. Alyssandra believes that their methods of waking shadows are the very cause of blood demons in the first place.

Their realm uses the darkest of nightmares and nothing more, even when unnecessary because they believe it to be the most effective method. Though it is true, it comes with too much consequence. All that dark energy in one realm, surrounding every mortal mind that crosses over—it is no wonder it can't be stopped from crossing back with them, alongside driving those mortals almost insane. Annabel and Alyssandra want no part in this. They never wanted to be part of the blood demon world they were thrown into, but the Alinoy's clearly don't want to stop it. I think that they may be hiding the truth from their own Guardians. I believe this is what your mother was to find out that night, and so they had her killed, Jay," Erebus concluded as his voice wavered.

Jay had paled, sickened by what he had heard. The grief he had buried within himself for many years, momentarily surfaced.

"Son, I promise, if this is true, they will not get away with what they did to her. You know I will not rest until I have avenged her. However, we must bide our time if we are to gather proof. They will be brought to justice.

But, there is more, Jay. Orin Alinoy is the one who spread the word of Aarie and the prophecy to most of the blood demons once he learned of her. I don't know if he really believes in the prophecy himself. Maybe he thought it worked in his favour to cause such attention to her or perhaps he just knew it would hurt you. Whatever his reason, the blood demons believe it now. Annabel and Alyssandra have always known that the prophecy is misunderstood by most. The common belief is incorrect, Jay. Yes, the prophecy speaks of the blood demons losing their weaknesses, but it also means they lose their blood demon nature. This means they will have no bloodlust or will to end humankind. Their conscience will return, and for most, that will be too unbearable to deal with. Some have lived without remorse for so long, and this could lead to their own destruction.

I thought Aarie was not in danger from the blood demons because her blood was not the key they thought it was, but now I see the whole truth of what happened that night. Though Alyssandra and Annabel knew what the true effects of Aarie's blood would be, I *know* they must have seen to it that the others still believed it was the key. They did not tell the others because they would never have been eager to drink Aarie's blood if they had. I realise now, Alyssandra and Annabel must have orchestrated yesterdays events together. They wanted the blood demons to drink Aarie's blood because it would end all that they hated and, in turn, it would keep the mortal world safe.

The Alinoy family want bloodthirsty, mindless monsters roaming the mortal world. They want them to thrive until no mortal blood is left to spill. They will be very disappointed when they realise these blood demons will soon be very human minded creatures. The blood demons will no longer want for destruction unless their hearts were originally ones of pure evil when they were mortal. Above all, they will not seek to make more of their kind. If anything, they may want to hunt the unchanged blood demons down or even the Oneiroi who are responsible for their existence."

Jay lifted his head. "I planned to hunt Alyssandra down along with every single blood demon that was there yesterday, but now you're telling me that Aarie's mother was one of them and that she allowed this to happen to her own daughter. What am I supposed to do? What do I tell Aarie?"

"Jay, I don't believe she had a choice, and I doubt very much she would have been there to witness or take part in her daughter's agony. However, I am sure that she always knew what the outcome of the evening would be. Maybe in *both* potential futures, Aarie died. Although Annabel did not show me her death in the second vision, it must have been there. She had assured me that she and Alyssandra would protect Aarie. I was too emotionally distracted to doubt them, and when I saw you on that stage with Aarie's lifeless body, I thought I had been wrong to trust her. I thought she had tricked me and that I had failed you in the worse possible way. Now, I realise she knew that the night would only bring her daughter the death of her mortality. She did not fill me in on her full plan because I would never have agreed to it. I don't believe she would have come to me in the first place if she was asking me to let her daughter truly die. I saw the desperation in her eyes, and it was the desperation of a parent trying to save her child.

You were forced to hurt Aarie once because you thought it was the only way to save her—this was no different. In doing this, Annabel may have also saved the mortal world.

When you speak to Aarie, you tell her that her mother loves her, and she did the only thing she could do to save and protect her. She *has* done that, Jay, don't you see? If Aarie is transitioning, she will never be the defenceless mortal in Annabel's first vision.

The old story of the Aneiros Lily—the one I used to read to you—it was all true, Jay. It was always meant to become true, just as Aarie's mortal heart was always destined to stop beating. Aarie, you and even her friends are written in that prophecy. That is maybe even why you always loved to hear that story, and why you memorised it when you were so young. For the first time, I know its true meaning. Because of everything you have told me today, it all finally makes sense," Erebus said in revelation. Jay intently watched, realising his father was right and that somehow part of him had always known the story was true.

"Our family's mark—the moon and stars—they're symbols of the night. I am the darkness and the First Blood that brought her home," Jay uttered under his breath. He thought back to a past conversation with Aarie.

What good is light without darkness?

...together, the possibilities are as infinite as the wildest imagination...

Jay thought back to when he had walked in on Aarie's nightmare and how she had known the outcome of the night of the ball before it had happened.

"I think Aarie may have inherited her mother's gift even though she does not realise it yet," Jay whispered in astonishment as his father regarded him thoughtfully.

"Son, there is one thing I must request of you. You must not seek revenge on those blood demons now. They will soon no longer exist as the monsters who hurt Aarie, but they need to survive so that the Alinoy's plan to destroy all mortals fails."

Jay was silent for several moments, but the certainty in his father's voice made him eventually nod in agreement. "Very well, but what happens now, Father?"

"The Alinoy family will soon learn that you have not broken any laws and that Aarie is your Semper Sodale. Your seals are your proof. The Alinoys cannot lawfully do anything to you now. They will have to find another way to weaken us. They do not know that we are informed of their crimes. Alyssandra and her blood demons will testify against the Alinoy's in time, once they have gone through the change. I do not think that the Alinoy's plan to play by the rules forever, which means we will need proof of their crimes by then.

If the Alinoy's wish for Aneiros to be swallowed by the darkness of nightmares, they need control of all three realms. That is the only way they can enforce their methods of controlling shadows. The rapid growth in blood demon numbers and their own armies is a clear sign that they will make a move soon because they know it will not go unnoticed for much longer. When they make their move, we should have our proof ready—witnesses and substantial evidence. Their Guardians will see the truth for themselves, and not the Alinoy's version of the truth. Once we show them in their true colours, we have the right to fight against them with the law, and most likely, their own Guardians on our side.

"And you are certain they would start a war against us?"

"I believe they already have, Son. Starting with your mother's death and now being so keen to make an example of you. I know they want you gone. I have suspected it for a long time."

"But why would they be out to destroy me, Father?"

"Because of everything you represent. The Alinoys are afraid of the threat you pose to them. Their realm is one that believes in only the darkness of nightmares. They are completely intolerant of shadows. Our realm is one that believes firmly in the balance of both dreams and nightmares. We have proven it works. The Alinoys don't strive to keep both worlds safe—they just want to keep shadows out. They hate mortals and all who sympathise with them. Our realm's principles go against theirs. The mortals and Guardians call you the 'God of Dreams'. You're a legend in both world's, Son. Your dreams are so effective, not only do you keep shadows from returning, you inspire them to make their own lives as imaginative as the dreams you give them. It is evident in their stories, their poetry and their songs. How can Orin Alinoy gain complete control of their realm and enforce their methods, when a good percentage of his own Guardians idolise you? It is why he wants to destroy you. He wants to destroy the legend that is Morpheus—the greatest dream caster Aneiros has ever known. You're one of the Alinoy's greatest rivals, and they want to tarnish all you stand for and our realm. Killing you is not enough. They need you disgraced first so that no Guardian remembers your name in a good light. They have waited years for something to pin on you, and this was the opportunity they'd been waiting for. On top of this, Orin Alinoy wants my youngest son dead, as his own son is dead. He wants me to feel the pain of that suffering, but he will have to be disappointed. He no longer has just cause to take you to trial, and we will be ready for any attack. Our Guardians will be ready."

"But that may not be enough, Father. We play by all the rules and obey all the laws, but they might not. We don't know what else they could have plotted. If they have been planning this for some time, we can't know for sure how big their army is or if we have the power to defeat them."

"We have to be enough. It is all we can do, Son. We have to believe that his Guardians will finally see the truth."

"But what if they do already know the truth about the blood demons and they just don't care? It doesn't have to be this way. I could speak with Lelan. I know his Guardians are still loyal to his realm. He as much as told me. His army still runs his kingdom as though he never left this place. After meeting with him today, I know that he planned to return one day and made measures to keep things in order until then. Our families were once allies and good friends. If the Alinoy family have done all the things you accuse them of, then they must be stopped for the sake of all Oneiroi and humanity. They endanger us all. Once Lelan knows the truth about them and his wife, he will want to help. We need to be allies—he is Aarie's father."

"And you think he will listen to you?"

"Yes, I do. If the Alinoy family were already out to destroy our family, then me being with Aarie is a new threat to them. They will want us both out of the picture. Alongside everything else, I do not believe that prospect will sit well with Lelan."

"Nor does it sit well with me, Son. Our realms have always shared similar Oneiroi values, and I am more than willing to become allies once again if Lelan agrees."

"Then, Aarie and I will return to him and explain once Aarie is feeling well enough—"

Jay broke off suddenly, reaching his arms out in front of him as his weight fell against the window. His teeth gritted together as his face grimaced in pain.

"What is it, Son? What's wrong?" Erebus worried.

"Aarie. Something's wrong with Aarie. I have to go to her," Jay replied.

Chapter 25
Aneiros

Aarie woke to find herself laid upon a king-size bed in a spacious room. The ceiling was high and ornately decorated with gold leaf patterns and intricate carvings. A warm golden light swept through the room from a large window to her left. A gentle breeze blew the sheer curtains slightly, wafting the scent of Aneiros lilies from a vase that stood on the ledge. She sat up, trying to get a glimpse of the view through the glass. Aarie could just make out spiralling spires that glistened in the distance, but she was unable to see clearly from the bed. Her eyes shifted and wandered. This room was the size of a lavish apartment she realised, scanning over it slowly.

She jumped back, startled by a man who lingered a short distance away from the bed. He leaned against a wall near the door as though he had been guarding her. He cleared his throat.

"I'm sorry if I startled you," Phelan said. "I had hoped Jay would have returned before you woke, but he should be here shortly. I promised I would look after you until then."

Aarie swallowed. "Where did he go, and where am I?"

"Jay and my father had things to discuss. Nothing to be concerned with, I'm sure. I thought it best to bring you to Jay's room."

Aarie sat up on the bed, glancing at the door briefly as she thought of Jay. She knew he would not be too far from her. She quickly glanced back down at her hands, avoiding Phelan's gaze, though she could see him in the corner of her eye.

"Aarie, I know after our last meetings, I'm probably not the person you want to be stuck in a room with. I promised Jay I would make sure you were okay, and I did not want to let him down again. However, you are a guest and are free to come and go as you please," Phelan said. He took a few steps closer, then stopped, casually leaning back against the wall. "Aarie, I made a mistake. I should have realised Jay's behaviour could only ever have been the result of him finding his Semper Sodale. I should have never doubted my brother. He has never failed any task, broken any law, or let anyone down in his whole existence. Yet, I did not believe him when he said you were not like other mortals. He told me that it shouldn't have mattered even if you were an ordinary mortal and that I should have done all I could do to protect you because he loved you. He was right. I should have done at least that, no matter what happened. I let him down when he needed me the most. But, you need to know that I did not try to make you leave this world just because I thought you were mortal. I made you leave because I thought you endangered my brother's life as well as your own. If

253

you had simply been mortal like the others, it would have been the death of you both. I only have one brother, and I did what I thought was best for him. I was wrong, Aarie, and I'm sorry. Can you forgive me for what I have done? Because I'd like to get to know you and start again."

Aarie was surprised at how much of Jay she could see in Phelan now. He was sincere, and she knew Jay was trusting his brother with her life, so it meant he trusted him completely now. She guessed that this also meant Jay did not believe his brother had any involvement in her mother's death, at least. He was Jay's only brother, and Aarie knew he was a big part of Jay's life as she was now too.

"I'd like to put the past behind us too," she replied. "I'm sorry, I don't mean to be this anxious. I'm just not used to the presence of Oneiroi, except for Jay, of course, and…"

"Yourself?"

"I guess that too, yes, if that is what I really am."

"And you had no idea of your Oneiroi power before yesterday?"

"No."

"And what of your parents? Are they both mortal or is one Oneiroi?" Phelan asked.

Aarie hesitated to answer. She did not want to lie, but she did not want to give up information about her dad without talking with Jay.

"I'm sorry. I didn't mean to pry. I was just curious," Phelan said. "You don't need to answer if you are uncomfortable doing so, but please know you can trust me. I have no reason or will to let you or Jay down again. I know there is something that Jay is holding back, as he did not tell my father of your transitioning when you passed out. My father still believes that you are mortal. So, if there's a specific reason for that or something you are worried about, then I'd like you both to know that you can trust me with whatever that may be."

"Phelan… I can't until Jay is here. He needs to speak with your dad about the matter."

"I see. Okay, I understand," Phelan replied.

Although Phelan did not seem surprised with her response, Aarie could tell he was disappointed that she did not trust him with the information. He had a similar expression to Jay when trying to hide that his feelings were slightly hurt or that he was hoping for a different outcome.

"I would tell you, but I just—" Aarie broke off as she hunched over in sudden agony. Her hands knotted into the bedsheets in front of her as she cried out in pain. A burning sensation ripped through her back, and she gritted her teeth. She watched as her Semper Sodale seal unconcealed itself as well as the black marks below it that wound around her wrist.

Phelan rushed to her side at once. "What is it?"

"My back! My back feels like it's on fire," she cried out.

Aarie was aware that Phelan had seen her black marks on her wrist. She knew he recognised them instantly, but the pain was too much to bear, and she could hardly think straight.

"Phelan, what's happening to me?"

He sat beside her, examining her face and eyes. "Aarie, I need to take a look at your back. Can I do that?"

Aarie's eyes streamed tears from the pain, but she managed a nod in response to him. She turned to the side and leaned forward as Phelan moved behind her. He pushed the back of her vest top down slightly. His fingers traced over her skin, and she tensed.

"I'm sorry, did I hurt you?"

"No, it just hurts generally. What is it?"

"Aarie, have you ever seen Jay's marks on his back?"

"His marks? Oh—yes, not properly, but I know he has something there. I've seen the top part of them. Is that what's happening to me? Do I now have marks there too, like my wrist?"

"Yes, but do you know what these marks mean, Aarie? Did Jay ever tell you?" Phelan asked, staring at the intricate black marks that formed two mirrored shapes on either side of her back. They snaked around the inside of each shoulder blade, almost forming s-shapes as they wound to a point further down her skin.

"Jay told me about the marks on my wrist, and my father told me the truth about what he was, only yesterday. Jay and I haven't had any time to talk through *anything* else. There's never been any time," she said glumly.

"Aarie, the marks on your back indicate that you are already going through the final Oneiroi transitional stage. It's important that you try to stay calm and focus on how you arrived here."

She winced. "What? Why? And why does it hurt so much?" she asked, tightening her grip on the edge of the bed.

Phelan hesitated to answer. "Aarie, I don't know what Jay has and hasn't revealed to you about Oneiroi Guardians, and for something like this, maybe Jay should be the one. He should be here soon. He will have felt your pain."

"Please, just tell me what's happening to me, Phelan. What is—" but before Aarie could finish, her eyes turned black. A wave of confusion hit her. For a brief moment, she did not know where she was or how she had got here. She turned abruptly to see the stranger behind her. But he was not a stranger; she had met him before. He had hurt her once. He had been a monster who had almost crushed the life from her.

Aarie leapt off the bed away from him, but as she did, she had an instant urge to move her limbs, to stretch them out and relieve an uncomfortable ache. It made no sense as she was already stood up and moving. A sudden whoosh sounded above her, and a waft of air brushed past her face. Her limbs stretched out, feeling immediately better. As she looked up to see her mighty white gold wings that had unfurled from her back, there was something strange in how they appeared to her. It was as though she were seeing them for the first time, but she couldn't be sure. She was no longer sure what was and wasn't strange, or what she was even doing here in the first place. All she did know was that the stranger in front of her had wanted her dead. Therefore, he was potentially a danger to her now.

Phelan stepped towards her, reaching out a hand slowly. "Aarie, you need to listen carefully. You need to wait for Jay to come back. You may seem disoriented and unsure of things right now, but you have to trust me..."

As he took another step forward, Aarie lunged at him, knocking him to the ground. He did not fight back or show any aggression. Aarie backed off, full of uncertainty and confusion as another man hurried into the room. The man gasped at the sight of the other on the floor and at Aarie stood over him with fully unfurled wings. This new stranger seemed surprised, but his face softened as his gaze met hers. His eyes and hair colour were the same as the man on the floor, and he was familiar to Aarie. She knew his presence. Her wrist pulsed, and she glanced down at a shimmering violet mark. The new stranger also had a matching mark on his wrist, but as her eyes searched his face, images flashed up in her mind. They were memories of this stranger hurting her, slashing her arm, tearing at her throat, and drinking her blood. A low snarl sounded deep in her throat as she backed up.

"Aarie, it's me," he said gently. "Take it easy. Look at me—you know me. I know you can feel our link," he whispered, lifting his wrist up for her. "We're Semper Sodales. I would never hurt you." He grimaced, thinking back to when he *had* hurt her. "I need you to let me explain what is happening to you."

Jay reached for Aarie's hand, but she pulled it back, instinctively striking Jay's face with her other. Her clawed hand raked bloody red streaks down his cheek, which slowly faded as they began to heal.

"You tried to kill me," she hissed, stepping back.

Jay flinched. "No, please, you have to trust me. What you see in your mind is not how things are between us. That was something in the past, and it didn't happen how it may seem to you now. Please listen," he pleaded, but he knew how this sounded, and it did not sound good. "Aarie, I won't hurt you. This confusion that you're feeling is usually very temporary. You will know what I'm saying is the truth soon, so please let me explain everything to you until then. *I love you.* You *must* be able to feel that?"

Aarie glanced down again at her violet mark, pausing before looking back up to Jay.

"You're lying to me," she whispered as she glared at him." You're trying to deceive me like you did before. I won't let you trick me again."

"No, Aarie, please. That can't be all you remember of us? There has to be something else? Try to remember how you got here and why. We came to find out the truth about your mother, remember? And I did, Aarie—she's alive. She's really alive. Once you are yourself again, we will find her. I promise you," Jay said, taking another step towards her. Aarie tensed as he did so, taking in his words, but there was no change in how she held herself or in the hostility that came from her.

"I remember that you are a deceitful monster not to be trusted. You're my worst nightmare, and I know I hate you, Jaydon Onuris!" Aarie snarled, feeling the full emotions of the words she had said to him on the night of the ball. With claws raised, she lunged forward once more. As she struck out, she sliced Jay's cheek open again, but this time, the bloody streaks did not heal up. Instead, they bled out. Jay did not flinch, but he stood there speechless and wounded. Another man had come into the room to witness Aarie's outburst. There was a definite family resemblance between all three of the men that surrounded her now, and Aarie felt ambushed. She leapt backwards. Then quickly, she turned and jumped toward the ledge of the open window. The warm, gentle breeze from outside blew softly against her wings, and she spread them, feeling it rush through her feathers. For one moment, she wanted to glide through that warm air and away from the danger of this room.

"Aarie!" Jay shouted with urgency.

For a moment, Aarie turned, unsure of everything, but something was pulling her back to the window; the urge to take flight was strong. In that split second, her mind seemed to uncover old memories of feeling the wind rush through her arms as she glided through the air. She knew now that they were not memories of real events. They were old dreams she'd had a long time ago. What she had vaguely remembered as being her arms, had in fact been wings in those dreams.

Had she once seen this moment long ago? Aarie thought. She couldn't be sure. The urge to feel how she had felt in those dreams was taking over her thoughts. It was like an itch that had ached to be scratched for so long, though she had not realised until now. With one quick glance back, she pushed the window open wider and plunged out of it.

"Aarie, no!" Jay shouted in desperation, but he was too late, she had already gone.

Jay raced to the window but could not see her anywhere. Phelan hurried to him, reaching for Jay's arm as he seemed to edge closer to the open window.

"Jay, she will be okay," Phelan said.

"You don't know that," Jay panicked. "I haven't had enough time to explain anything to her. I thought I would get more time, Phelan, so much more time than this. I need to go after her."

Phelan tightened his grip on his brother's arm. "I don't think that is wise. When the confusion settles, she will return in her own time. Jay, she didn't mean what she said to you. You know we all go through this confused state. It won't last," he said, trying to ease Jay's distress.

Erebus stepped forward. "Son, when was her first transition?" he asked Jay.

"Last night."

"Last night? You mean she completed all three transitions in less than twelve hours?"

Jay nodded. "It would appear so. Father, I need to go to her. She has had no guidance. We only found out she was half Oneiroi last night, and now she seems to be a fully transitioned Guardian."

"First Blood is First Blood, Son. Half mortal or not, if the ancient blood runs in her veins, she is as powerful as any royal Guardian. In fact, you and Aarie are now more likely more so. There has never been Semper Sodales both of First Blood. Your brother is right. I assure you, she will be quite safe. I can't necessarily say the same for anyone she believes may hurt her while she is in this confused state. You should let Aarie return of her own free will," Erebus assured.

Jay turned his back on the window. "She didn't trust me. I can never erase that one memory she has of me—the nightmare that I made real for her—and it seems to be all she does remember of me."

"Jay, don't torture yourself over it," Phelan said. "The real Aarie knows why you did it. She understands, and she has forgiven you. Otherwise, her seal would never have appeared. You know that is true. When she returns to her normal frame of mind, she will return to you. It can't last forever—a day or two perhaps or maybe a matter of hours for *her*, who knows, but the worst is already over. She is now a Guardian."

"But she wasn't born like us. What if she doesn't come back or if she is different? What if she can't forgive me now? She's only known me for a matter of weeks, and though the short length of that time takes nothing away from how we feel about each other—what if she doesn't get her memories of that time back? We all know memories sometimes get lost during this confused state. What if she only remembers the bad things between us?"

"Son, I don't think that is likely. She is Lelan's daughter and *your* Semper Sodale. That gives her more strength than most. She will return to you—" Erebus paused as he acknowledged his son's bleeding cheek that had failed to heal. He stepped closer to inspect his son's wounds. "Jay, you should rest. Have you even slept since reviving Aarie?"

Jay glanced down. "No, there's been no time. How can I sleep now?"

"Son, you must keep up your strength. You must have lost a lot of blood. Phelan and I will watch for Aarie's return. You should rest until then. You will be of no help to her if you are sick when she gets back."

"I will, Father, but I must return to Lelan first. While Aarie is gone, I should speak to him of all we have discussed. I need to tell him of Anne. If it were Aarie, I would want to know the truth as soon as possible, and I should tell him about Aarie too. He may know what I can do to help trigger her memories if they do not come back straight away. Maybe she would trust me if she knew he trusts me."

Erebus reached forward. "Jay—"

"—I can't sit back and do nothing!" Jay snapped, but then softened his tone again. "I must do this one thing first, Father. Then, I promise I will return. I can rest then."

"Okay, Jay, but please do. This is a dangerous time for you," Erebus warned.

"I know, and that is why now is a good time for Lelan to return to his home. I will be back soon. Please, if Aarie does return in my absence, between both of you, keep her safe," Jay said.

Erebus nodded, and within moments Jay was gone.

Chapter 26
Forgiveness

Jay stood hovering outside Lelan's front door, once again taking in the garden of Aarie's childhood home. It now seemed obvious this garden was maintained by an Oneiroi mind, due to its colours and arrangement. The unnatural vibrancy and the prolonged life of its blooms spoke of only a Guardian's magic and a will to bring a small element of Aneiros here to make this home. Jay raised a hand to knock on the door. The door opened before his hand could touch it.

"Jaydon, where is Aarie? Is she okay?" Lelan asked.

"She's... fine. Please, can I come in? We need to talk."

"Yes, of course," he replied, gesturing for Jay to come in. Lelan closed the door behind him, and they walked through to the living room. The low murmur of news reporters on the television came from the corner of the room. Lelan gestured for Jay to take a seat, but Jay was not at ease with sitting for this discussion. Lelan tensed as they both remained standing.

Jay took a deep breath. "Lelan, something has come up. I have come to speak to you about Aarie and the blood demons, and—"

"What came up? Why is she not with you? Where is she?" Lelan demanded.

"I would not be here without her if I didn't believe she was okay," Jay assured. "But, something *has* happened, Lelan. Aarie is not here due to her reaching the last stage of Oneiroi transition. She is now a full Guardian and is currently suffering from the final transitioning sickness. She woke in Aneiros, confused and frightened. Then she left Onuris House, but I know she is okay. I feel it, and I know she is strong."

Lelan's eyes widened. "Oh. Oh, I see. This is incredible," Lelan replied, utterly astonished. "This is remarkable, in fact! It has only taken her this little amount of time. Where about's in Aneiros is she now, and why did she leave your side? Did you not go after her?"

"She doesn't trust me, Lelan. In fact, she attacked me. I didn't want to distress her any further. In Aarie's confused state, she doesn't remember me, not how we were together. She only seems to have one memory of me, and that was not a pleasant one," Jay glumly admitted.

"How so? I don't understand." Lelan puzzled at Jay's penitent expression. Then, comprehension sunk in. Lelan's brows knotted together. "*What* did you do? What did you do to her, Jaydon?" he said in an accusatory tone.

Jay swallowed, but he held Lelan's stare. "I made her leave Aneiros like a shadow. She was never a shadow, Lelan. She was *always* real, but still, I used a nightmare to make her leave," Jay confessed as Lelan glared back at him.

"Why are you telling me this?"

"I don't know. Maybe because you should know the truth. Maybe I want someone to hate me like I hate myself... like Aarie hates me now," Jay replied, choosing now to lean against the wall beside the sofa. Lelan regarded Jay for a long moment before casually seating himself in the armchair opposite him.

"Or maybe you wanted someone to understand why you did it. Maybe you wanted my forgiveness even?" Lelan said.

"I know I don't deserve forgiveness. I made a mistake, and I can never undo it. That's why Aarie didn't trust me when she woke. Who knows if she ever will again—"

"—Tell me Jaydon, was it because you're First Blood and she was mortal that you made her leave? Did someone find out about her coming to Aneiros and your involvement together?"

Jay nodded. "Yes, my brother found out. Then wolves attacked her. They weren't our Guardians, and word of my intervention to save her would have spread. I could no longer be sure of her safety."

Lelan sighed. "I know too well what the price is for royal Guardians who break the laws you thought you had broke, Jaydon. I also know what it is for any mortal involved too. If I had been the one to discover Aarie and learn of her involvement with you, I would have given Aarie the darkest nightmare I could have conjured to make sure she left Aneiros immediately. Make no mistake about that. You did what any decent Guardian should do."

"But you don't understand, Lelan. I nearly killed her myself, trying to wake her. I had to come to this world to heal her."

Lelan was silent for a while. "When did your seals appear, Jay?"

"Mine appeared after my return to Aneiros the same night I drove her away. Aarie's formed only yesterday."

"Remarkable," Lelan gasped.

"Remarkable?" Jay replied, confused by Lelan's choice of words.

"Yes, Jay—*remarkable*. Why are you trying to get me to hate you for saving my daughter's life? That is what you did. The amount of pain and will it must have taken for you to do it, knowing how you felt about her, is incredible."

"But she doesn't remember anything else about me now. What kind of a Semper Sodale am I if she doesn't know anything else about me?"

"She will in time, Jay. If she can go through the full Oneiroi transition process in a matter of hours, I'm sure she will recover her memories within no time. Even if she temporarily loses some, you have eternity to create more. She could never hate you, Jay, not really. If she were ever going to, her seal would never have formed, but I think you already know that's true, deep down. I think you just wanted to know I could understand the reasons behind what you did. You probably figured if I could, then she could too. After all, she is my blood. I think you wanted someone to reassure you that you did the right thing and the only thing that you could do in that position. Am I right?"

Jay was silent for a moment as he thought about Lelan's words. "I suppose I had hoped you would understand, as you do, and for that, I am grateful," Jay whispered. "But it's not the only reason why I told you. Right now, I think she could do with a familiar face around her when she does return. There is no way she could have erased her whole life from her mind. You are one face I know she will remember for sure and she will want to see."

"Are you asking me to return to Aneiros with you, Jay?"

"Yes."

"Jay, have you forgotten all we spoke of the last time you were here?"

"No. I have left Aarie, knowing that my brother and my father will look out for her in case she returns in my absence. Do you think I would have done that if I thought either of them had her mother murdered? Or if they had tried to hurt her simply because of who her father was, do you think I would forgive that?"

Lelan's forehead creased. "So, you trust your father now?" he asked.

"Yes, I do entirely. You know I would not have left Aarie there otherwise. My father told me of a great many revelations. *They* are the original reason I wanted to return to you soon. Before Aarie's transition, I had already planned to ask you to come back to Aneiros. Firstly, there is something you must know about Aarie's mother—your Anne."

Lelan, sat up immediately, his eyes widening at the mentioning of her name. "What is it?"

"Her disappearance was nothing to do with my father. He had never even met her before, not until a few days ago. She is still alive, Lelan."

"What? Is this the truth, Jaydon?" Lelan gasped.

"Yes. My father swears it. He had no idea that you were Aarie's father, but he knew of Aarie's mother because she had gone to see him. There is something you need to know about her. She is not how she was when you last saw her. I am sorry, Lelan but she's a blood demon. However, my father insists she has managed to hold on to her humanity, though she has always struggled to fight the thirst. I think that is why she left—she feared that she would hurt Aarie. My father didn't take revenge, and he doesn't blame you for my mother's death. He knows he had a moment of madness when he attacked you, but that's all it was. He always thought you knew that because he let you leave Aneiros that night. He never knew of your wife's disappearance."

There was a long pause of silence as Lelan processed the information Jay had given him. His face was a mixture of emotions that seemed to wash over him. He took a long deep breath.

"Jaydon, what did Anne go to see your father about?"

"It turns out Anne was a natural oracle gifted with the power of 'future sight'. She came to my father, asking him to help save the life of her daughter. In return, I would also get to live. All he had to do was tell her where to find Aarie. She had seen two possible outcomes of our futures, and she persuaded my father to listen to her by showing him her visions. But there is something you need to know. *She* was the one that informed the other blood demons of Aarie's location when my father came for me. He did not know they would kill Aarie until it was too late, but he believes that Anne must've always known that Aarie would survive and that maybe this was the only way. After all, Aarie is more powerful than she could ever have been now, and I cannot be sentenced to death for breaking any laws."

"And where is Anne now?"

"I don't know, but my father believes the prophecy does not mean what most blood demons believe. It will save the blood demons from themselves and their bloodthirst, not give them more power for destruction. I think Anne not only found a way to save Aarie—she found a way to save all mortals from being overrun by blood demons. Maybe it also means she found a way to allow herself to return to you both."

"But don't you and your father want all of these blood demons dead?"

"Not anymore. Soon, they won't be the blood demons they once were, and I would never harm Aarie's own flesh and blood."

"Jaydon, you don't know what this means to me to hear this news, after all these years of not knowing."

"I know if it were Aarie, I would want to know the truth and not a minute later than possible. Lelan, on any other occasion, this would be enough reason for me to come here to you. However, as I said, there have been many revelations, and so, unfortunately, there is still more.

My family need your help. Obviously, I don't want you and my father to be enemies as there seems little point for it now. We should be allies at a time when war may be on the horizon. My father is almost certain the Alinoy family plans to attack our realm in the future. I have come here to ask you to return home to Aneiros, not only for Aarie but also to make our realms allies. Together our families and Guardians are stronger. We can stop any attack in the future for sure. I know that your realm still holds you as their king because you always knew you would return one day. You are just sleeping in their eyes, perhaps?

If I'm honest, Lelan, I believe our *whole world* needs your help in many ways. It has been a long time since the Guardians of all three realms were united. We have all become distrusting and suspicious of each other, consumed with following rules and laws. We are beginning to neglect why we are here in the first place. We are here to keep both worlds safe—*mortals* as well as Oneiroi. Yet, Aneiros is slowly growing to despise mortals, as the Alinoys do. I know it because there was once a time I thought I had also begun to until I met Aarie. Maybe it is the real reason our world has become so dark lately. So unforgiving and bleak.

We have forgotten what it is like to be *more human*, and we have forgotten how to dream, or more accurately, how to let mortals dream. Both of our realms promote dreams as being the first option for dealing with shadows. But lately, even our Guardians have begun to steer closer to methods used by the Alinoy's realm. My brother has been named a master of these darker dreams. I know it is because mortals have increasingly become harder to drive away with dreams, but maybe we are too hasty in deciding what is best for them. Perhaps pretending to be a monster too often can only result in creating a permanent monster within ourselves. Maybe if we were more patient with mortals, we would learn more from them and care more to let them dream.

The mortal world has changed so much, and it is a harder place to understand. Maybe it is time for us to change too. You could help us all do that. You have lived amongst them for a long time, so you understand them now better than any Guardian. I heard your conversation with Aarie, and I apologise, but you were right—you can offer our world so much with your knowledge. Now is a good time for you to return."

"And you believe the Alinoy family are not to be trusted?"

"Yes. I believe it was always them that couldn't be trusted. Anne revealed to my father that it is the Alinoy's black nightmares that are causing the blood demon's rise in numbers. Orin Alinoy knows this and does not care because he wants the mortal world to be overrun with them until it is eventually destroyed. Fortunately, Anne and the blood demon's own queen has helped ensure that the real prophecy will help keep those numbers down back in the mortal world.

My father thinks that my mother was on the verge of discovering the truth about the increasing numbers of blood demons. She did not get the chance to share her findings because she died before it was possible. Her death was made to look like a suicide, but you, my father and I all know she would *never* do that. No Semper Sodale would, knowing how their partner would suffer. We do not have enough solid proof yet, but we believed she was murdered by the Alinoy family. They are the only ones who had the power and a motive. My mother's knowledge would've threatened to expose them for what they are before their plans could take effect, so they had her killed for it. Think about it—which other Guardians could you picture stooping so low? She was loved by so many and was such a gentle soul. Only someone who embraces evil could be capable of her murder. After everything that they've done recently, it seems so obvious. The Alinoys are traitors of the Oneiroi, and they are all murderers. We have to stop them."

Lelan nodded. "Yes. That is the way it appears, but they are not *all* guilty. Orin's wife and their eldest son abandoned their realm on account of differences of opinions within the law. It was shortly after the death of their youngest son. They have never been seen or heard from since," Lelan said.

"And what happened? Did Orin kill his wife and eldest son?"

"Believe me, it is possible, but in this case, I think not. I believe they are still out there somewhere. It is not against any Oneiroi laws to renounce your title or your responsibilities as a Guardian. It may be frowned upon, but no one has ever been physically punished for simply having free will within the guidelines of the law. Orin's family consists now of only him and his two younger brothers, Darrak and the currently sleeping, Rylon."

"And the youngest son, what happened to him? How did he die?" Jay asked.

"Let's just say, he *did* break the law. Orin makes no exceptions when it comes to the laws he set in place," Lelan said, meeting Jay's serious gaze.

Jay grimaced at the thought but nodded in understanding.

"My father thinks the Alinoys are out to destroy me. When they find I have not broken the law this time, he believes it is just a matter of time before they try to pin something else on me."

"It wouldn't surprise me, Jaydon. Do you really have no idea what a threat to their ideals you are? How can they enforce the darkest nightmares upon their realm when half their Guardians look up to you. They see how effective your dreams have been."

"I don't want Aarie to be in danger because of me. I never sought out for the attention I seem to have brought to myself. I have simply done my duty as a Guardian as best I could. Aarie and I are something new, Lelan, and we are the first Semper Sodales to be both of royal blood. I don't know if Orin Alinoy will see that as another threat to his plans, but our very bond could potentially unify the two realms they want to claim. If they already want to destroy me, they could seek to destroy her in order to do that. Please, come back to Aneiros to help me keep Aarie safe. If for no other reason, please help me do that."

"Of course I will do everything to keep Aarie safe. You know I will, but what of Anne? Oneiroi law may have granted a special case for me here in this world, but that does not extend to Aneiros if I return. Am I supposed to forget about her?"

"No, of course not, but you are a king as my father is a king. So, maybe it is time you both changed the old stupid laws! Times have changed, and if there ever was a need, it is now. Two realms together have that power.

If the true prophecy is correct, the blood demons will no longer be the threat to either world as they were, and so we should find her, Lelan. Soul mates should never be parted for the amount of time you have," Jay said wholeheartedly.

Lelan stared thoughtfully ahead for a long moment before returning his gaze to Jay. A subtle smile briefly flickered on his face, and his eyes seemed to hold a new lease of life.

"Okay, Jaydon. Of course I will come with you. Did I tell you that you may be the first boy to turn up on my doorstep, whom I feel is deserving of my daughter's heart? Though, I do wish that didn't come with the dangers that follow a Guardian of your reputation."

Jay raised an eyebrow as he pondered over Lelan's statement for a moment. "I'm not a boy, remember? And I'm pretty sure you wanted to kill me this morning," he said, as a gentle smile crept upon his face.

"Hmm, yes, well, I did eventually ease up. Fathers are supposed to be protective like that... but they can also be wrong. Jay, I'm sorry for what I said about you and your father the last time you were here. I have been wrong all these years. Without Anne, my mind has simply not been what it was. I have been so lost because I never wanted to let Anne down when it came to Aarie, or Aarie herself, for that matter."

"No apology is necessary. You're Aarie's father, and you did what you could to keep her safe. There was no way you could have known for sure without endangering her," Jay said with no hesitation. At that point, a strange wave of nausea and dizziness hit him. Jay stumbled forward, reaching a hand on the back of the sofa to steady himself.

"Are you okay?" Lelan quickly asked, getting to his feet. Jay had paled a great deal in colour since he had arrived. Faint marks were now also evident on Jay's cheek, which had been turned away from Lelan before. Jay rubbed his face, closing his eyes briefly before he replied.

"Yes, I'm fine. I'm just tired. I haven't slept since Aarie... since the attack. I probably just need to rest. Aarie needed a lot of my blood, and there's been no other chance to recuperate. I'll rest once Aarie returns."

"Hmm, well make sure you do. Maybe you should think about resting before then. Aarie's not the only one who has changed, remember? You both share new strengths now, and your body will need more energy until you have fully adjusted. I can look out for Aarie's return for you once we arrive. I think she would prefer to return, knowing you are well and resting rather than return, worrying that you are sick. Also, she may not return for days."

"I know you're right but—"

"—But you are anxious. I know, so we should probably return to Aneiros now. The sooner, the better for your sake."

"And you are sure you are ready to return now?"

"Yes." Lelan nodded as he stepped forward to rest a hand on Jay's shoulder.

Jay nodded in response. Then slowly, they both began to vanish into thin air.

******

Angela took a sip of her coffee and then came to sit down between Jamie and Adam. They were sprawled out on either side of the living room sofa, seemingly staring into space. Angela sat back slightly to address them both.

"So, why do you think they're going to see Aarie's Dad? I know Aarie said that she just wanted to see him because last night was, you know, so horrendously awful," Angela shuddered, "but, do you think that's the only reason? I mean, they're going *together*, and Lyle most likely doesn't even know anything about Jay. You know how he is with anyone new hanging around her. He's bound to be on full protective dad alert when he sees how they are together. Can you imagine it? I just can't picture how that scene is going to play out. Can you two?"

"I don't know why they've gone," Jamie answered, "but she did die, so that surely makes anyone want to catch up with family, doesn't it? What do you make of all this Semper Sodales stuff anyway? Meira explained it to me, but did they mention anything to you guys?" Jamie asked.

Angela shuffled in the seat, trying to get comfy. "Adam filled me in. It's hard to believe, but I suppose it explains why they are as they are when they're together," Angela replied.

Jamie leaned forward to glance past her. "So, Aarie told you about it then, Adam? And about their marks?" he asked.

Adam turned to face the other two as he leaned against the sofa arm. "I was there when Aarie's mark first appeared. Jay had no choice but to explain what was happening to her—I thought she was dying or that he had done something to her. Her mark seemed to hurt her for the first few moments, but then she was fine."

"And you believe it is true—that they are soul mates?" said Jamie.

"I didn't at first. I thought Jay was trying to trick me or her or something. But that was before I saw them dancing together. Before the blood demons or the Oneiroi came. Their marks glowed violet, and for a moment they seemed the same. The way they moved together—I can't explain it—but I've never seen anything like it. They seemed like they were one being. That's when I really saw it for the first time."

"Saw what?" Jamie asked.

"How they loved each other. It was in every movement, every glance, every... everything they did around each other. I know you all probably saw it straight away, and as Angela said, Lyle will definitely see it too. I didn't want to admit it at first because... well, you know why. When I saw Jay holding Aarie last night, thinking she was gone, the pain of it was so unbearable for all of us, but for him, it seemed so much more than that. His brother was so certain that Jay was on the brink of no return, and there's no doubt that he really believed that. I believed it. Jay did not have to let me be close to Aarie at that moment, especially after what I did and said to him that morning. However, he did. I think it was because he knew Aarie would've wanted it and he would never deny her anything. He was broken until she came back, and she came back because of *him*. So, to answer your question—yes, I do believe it is true. I don't know Jay, and though I wanted to hate him, how can I? He makes her happy. She's only alive because of him. None of us could protect her like he can and has. Though, I know we all tried our best last night, and who knows, maybe Aarie was right. Maybe we *did* all help buy her time until Jay got back," Adam said, meeting Jamie's eyes with a thoughtful look as he continued. "Jamie, when Alyssandra took Aarie, I know why you did what you did, and I guess I also know why we haven't been getting on well lately. I think maybe I've always known. I suppose I'm trying to apologise. Sorry for being an idiot these past weeks," Adam said.

Angela's head turned, looking to Jamie as he picked at the sofa fabric. He glanced up, passing over Angela's hopeful expression briefly and then to Adam. A smirk hitched up Jamie's lips.

"Did we *ever* actually get on?" Jamie joked.

Adam rolled his eyes. "Okay, I should have known you'd act like a knobhead when I'm trying to straighten stuff out," Adam moaned. "But that's what this is, isn't it—an act? You're always joking about everything, being so arrogant, and being so... so knobheadish..."

Jamie raised his brows "Ouch. Are you sure this is an apology?" Jamie murmured.

"You just *act* like that, is my point," Adam continued. "But you're not really like that, at least, not where Aarie's concerned, anyway. So, I guess that makes you okay in my book. We have *that* in common if nothing else. Okay?"

Jamie had returned to picking at the sofa fabric again. His smirk and all humour had gone. "Design. We also have design in common—we're both artists," Jamie said, looking back up at Adam. "And computer games, of course," he continued, waving a hand to the stack of games in front of the TV. "And I suppose you're kinda okay, and also not a knobhead... most of the time... when you're not trying to attack me for hanging out with Aarie, that is," Jamie said, picking at the sofa again as his eyes flitted to and from Adam.

"I think Jay might agree with that one," Angela muttered under her breath as she surreptitiously smiled behind her mug of coffee. A smile flickered briefly on Adam's lips too, but he smoothed it out before Jamie could see it.

Angela swallowed another sip of coffee. "So, do you think they'll tell Lyle everything then? 'Cos Aarie still seemed shaken—as anyone would be —but she won't be able to hide that from him," Angela said.

"Possibly, but—" Jamie broke off as Angela's coffee mug jolted upward, spilling the hot liquid slightly into her lap. She rubbed hastily at where the coffee burned, but she seemed too intensely focused on something across the room, to pay it much attention. Jamie and Adam immediately followed Angela's anxious stare.

An enormous pair of white gold wings arched out to the sides, blocking the identity of the person from whose back they hung. The group of friends gasped in both awe and alarm as they stared at the magnificent feathered wingspan before them. The wings lowered, then neatly tucked away. The winged girl turned, causing the group's mouths to drop open.

Jamie stood up. "Aarie?"

A moment later, another Guardian appeared behind her. His dark ash brown hair and sapphire blue eyes were the same as Jay's, but it was not him.

Chapter 27
The Fallen

The thunder roared in the dark, heavy clouds above. Jay and Lelan glanced up as a fork of lightning carved up the grey harassed sky. They were now in Horngate, the first realm of Aneiros, but it was not the pleasant welcome Jay had hoped for. They stood now behind a row of trees at the far edge of The Royal House of Onuris gardens. Only hours ago, Jay had brought Aarie here for the first time. In the distance, spirals of gold and silver could be seen rising behind the glorious white palace. The exquisite arches, towers and glass domes all painted a magnificent architectural backdrop that would have usually glistened underneath the Aneiros sun. However, they appeared dull in comparison to normal under this dismal weeping sky.

Lelan stepped forward towards the central pathway that would lead him through the palace gardens and to the entrance. As he did so, Jay reached an arm out in front of him, stopping Lelan in his tracks. With one cautious glance, Jay stepped forward first, then peered through the branches of the trees in front of them. In the distance, he could make out his father stood on the top of the steps outside the palace entrance. Several dark-winged Guardians appeared to guard him protectively. Jay took in the number of Horngate Guardians that stood close by, lining the front of the palace. They stood firm and expectant as though awaiting an order. Jay's eyes anxiously scanned over the steps before his father. A broad figure stood tall at the bottom of the steps. It was Orin Alinoy. His back was turned, but Jay could make out the Alinoy symbols on the back of Orin's long cloak—a serpent amongst thorns. Orin appeared to be in discussion with his father, and as Jay continued to scan the area, he acknowledged the enormous number of Guardians who were lined in several columns behind Orin. They were armed heavily and complete with dark armoured wings that hung neatly behind them.

Jay gasped. "They're here already," he whispered to Lelan. "Their armed for war, and there are too many of them for our Guardians to take on. We will not have time to join forces or gather witnesses amongst the blood demons as proof of Orin's crimes. That might have been enough to make the majority of Orin's Guardians stand against him, but we can't defeat his numbers as they stand now. We can't win, Lelan. I have to go to help my father. They *can't* do this—no laws have been broken," Jay despaired.

Lelan reached out. "Jay, wait. You can't go to him. You're not at your full strength, and Orin may not care to play by the rules this time. I can help you. My Guardians *will* help. My realm has been expecting me for a long time. I returned to them weeks ago as I have done so every year since I left. This morning, after your visit, I returned again to tell them that I soon planned to return permanently. Jay, before you asked me, I was already planning to come home. You just made it happen sooner. Aarie is of this world too, so there is no longer reason to hide it from her or for me to neglect my world. Come with me to my realm, and we will return here together with my army."

Jay anxiously mulled over his decision before letting out an anguished sigh. "I can't. They are here because of me. If something bad happens to my family while I'm gone, I can't live with that. I have to go to them now. I will reason with them, and I will make Orin's army see the truth. They can't start a war when no crime has been committed. I trust you, Lelan, and I know you will return, but I have to try and stop whatever this is before it starts. The truth has to stall things at the very least. I have to believe that, and I have to go now. Good Luck, Lelan. Whatever happens, please keep Aarie safe," Jay said as he abruptly stepped towards the pathway that would take him to his enemy's army.

Lelan called to Jay as he watched him walk away. "You stay alive, for her, do you hear me, Jaydon Onuris? I can no longer keep her safe without you. You know she will feel whatever you feel, so please, you do whatever it takes to keep her safe too."

Jay turned around briefly to meet Lelan's eyes. "Always," he said before turning back and disappearing behind the trees.

The path seemed longer than Jay remembered, and he realised he had not walked along the entirety of it for many years. Jay also realised that he would not get the time to recover the energy he desperately needed now. As he neared the army, murmurs spread amongst the Guardians. A rustle of iron feathers and clattering weapons swept through the crowd. Many faces turned towards him—surprise, intrigue, anger and hostility—however, amongst most of the faces that presented themselves to him, there was a great level of respect. As Jay approached along the pathway, the army parted in two, leaving a clear path for him to walk through. Jay paused, looking straight ahead, past the walls of Guardians that stood either side of him, and past the glare of an unwanted stranger in front. His gaze met the concern of his father at the top of the steps. His father's eyes flitted uneasily from Jay to the armed soldiers close by. Taking a deep breath, Jay walked on. His gaze lowered and finally focused on the man at the bottom of the steps. Jay had only met this stranger a small number of times throughout his lifetime, and never in this type of circumstance. The armoured cloak, boots, fighting gear and weapons that hung about his body, gave this stranger an unwelcome and deadly presence; it spelt out the intent of war. As Jay drew nearer, Orin lowered his hood. His closely shaven fair hair emphasised the prominent ridge of his brow, his sharp cheekbones and sternly pursed mouth. There was a harsh bitterness in his glaring grey eyes as Jay came to stand beside him.

"What is the meaning of your presence here?" Jay asked, though he already knew the answer.

"To enforce the law, Jaydon. As your father is very well aware, I am a great believer in the law," he said, sharing a brief glance with Erebus, who winced briefly. "The law has been broken on a great many accounts, and I am here to bring justice."

"And what laws do you speak of?"

"Come now, Jaydon. Do not play me for a fool. I know of your involvement with the mortal girl and her band of mortal friends. The whispers of it are all over Aneiros, amongst the Guardians and the dreamwalkers. Do not deny it. I have witnesses. You cannot deny knowledge of her. I know you are involved with her. Or should I say, *were* involved with her until she became blood demon fodder? I have to say, I am a little surprised you let them have her so easily without much of a fight. Then again, perhaps you knew I would not offer her such a quick end after the crimes you have both committed," Orin said as a vicious smirk began to work its way onto his face.

Jay's fists clenched tight by his sides. "If you are referring to Aariella, I make no effort to hide my knowledge of her or to deny that I will protect her life with my very own. Oh, and I can assure you she is still very much *alive* and also very much *not* mortal. She is my Semper Sodale. Therefore, these laws you speak of, I insist that I have not broken any of them." Jay scowled now.

There was a brief silence as their stares bored into each other. Then an eruption of laughter echoed from Orin. "You really *do* take me for a fool, don't you?"

"'A fool' is not the word I would use," Jay said hoarsely. "And though I do not care too much what you think of me, I care that you are here threatening my family and my realm because you claim to have heard *whispers* amongst dreamwalkers. Do you expect *me* to believe that you came here ready for war with your army because of *whispers*? No, I think it is *you* that takes *us* for fools, but if that is indeed the reason you are here, then you have wasted your time. No laws have been broken. There are things that I cannot lie about, and *this* is one of them," Jay said, pulling away his sleeve to reveal his glowing Seal of Semper Sodales.

Gasps emerged from the army of Guardians that stood behind Orin, causing Orin to turn back to them hastily.

"This is a trick. It's a clever illusion, that is all. I *know* that girl is mortal or was mortal, and I know the blood demons killed her," he shouted out to them before turning back to Jay. "She cannot be your Semper Sodale or anything but a mortal who was once on the verge of becoming a dreamwalker."

Jay frowned. "Surely, you know she is no ordinary mortal if you believe she is the mortal written in the old prophecy of Aneiros. After all, you helped spread the word that her blood was the key to those very *blood demons* you mentioned. Or did you just do that to spite me and cause maximum attention to us? Where is your army of blood demons anyway? Have you noticed anything especially unusual about them lately?" Jay hissed with an accusatory tone.

Orin frowned. "I don't know what nonsense you are talking about, and I won't be distracted by it. If the girl is your Semper Sodale, tell me, where is she now? Bring her to me. Show me her matching seal. Prove to me she is still alive, and you are free to go."

"I am free to go anyway. I have committed no crime, and you have no proof otherwise. You know as well as I do, I cannot fake this seal."

"I know it does not prove that SHE is your Semper Sodale. So, where is the girl? My patience runs thin. I suggest you call her out here now unless you wish us to believe that you are simply stalling for time and deceiving your fellow Guardians."

"I cannot call her. She is not here."

"Then where is she?"

Jay could only answer the truth. "I don't *know*."

"You don't know? You don't know?! Are you saying that—a day after your so-called Semper Sodale miraculously survived a blood demon attack —you simply and so conveniently misplaced her?"

"I did not misplace her. She left. Aarie is currently not herself. When I told you she is not mortal, I meant it. She was never fully mortal. Her father is an Oneiroi Guardian, and after the blood demon attack, she started the Guardian transitioning process. She has completed full Guardian transition in a matter of hours. However, as it stands now, she is currently suffering from the final transitioning sickness. The temporary confusion has taken hold of her, and as she is very strong, it is not advisable for anyone to try to force her to come back here until she is herself again. She will return of her own free will soon, but it is best to wait for this phase to pass."

Orin screwed up his face. "This is ridiculous! Do you honestly expect us to believe this? You are a traitor, Jaydon Onuris, a traitor to your kind, and you stand here lying to my face to save your skin," Orin condemned.

"My son is no traitor!" Erebus stepped forward as two of his guards stood close by. "He tells the truth. The girl is no ordinary mortal. She is indeed now a fully fledged Guardian. I have seen it with my own eyes."

"Why would I lie about this?" Jay added. "When Aarie returns, you will see the truth. Would I not choose a better lie?"

"It is the only lie you *can* give to save yourself," Orin hissed. "You would lie to buy yourself time. It is time you need to plot whatever it is that you are trying to plot. You would lie to try to escape the hand of the law and your rightful punishment.

I am no fool, and I will not wait here for what—a day? Two days? A week perhaps? Just waiting for your scheming to make itself clear to us, and by then, it will be too late. No, that will not happen. My Guardians are here to see you punished for your crimes. I suggest you admit your guilt if you do not want your father to suffer the same fate. If you confess, I will show leniency to him for the lies he has told to protect you."

Anger immediately swept across Jay's face. His teeth gritted tightly as his brows fiercely pressed together.

"My father is the king of this realm. Who do you think you are to come here making false claims? I have not broken *any* laws, and my father most certainly will *not* pay for any mistakes that you are currently making!" Jay vehemently spat as his eyes darkened to black.

Erebus edged forward now, a hilt of a sword visible at his waist belt. His eyes passed over the small space between his weaponless son and his enemy. Erebus fixed his glare now on this enemy.

"Why don't you tell your army what you are really here for, Orin?" Erebus shouted. "You are not here for justice. If you were, you would wait. Judging by the rate of Aarie's transition, the wait for her return would most likely be very short. But you do not care for the truth, do you? You just want more power, and you want this realm, just as you have always wanted it. Jay is a threat to you because of all he has achieved for our kingdom. You cannot stand that his existence proves your whole viewpoint on Oneiroi dream casting to be wrong. It puts your very leadership into question.

You should also tell your army the other reason why you are here too. Revenge. You want to take everything from me because you feel I took everything from you many centuries ago. But the truth is, I did not take those things from you. You did that all on your own. I may have discovered your son's crimes, but it was *you* who sacrificed your own son in the name of the law—a new law then, that *you* put forward. No-one made you do what you did. No one was forcing your hand, and neither would anyone have done so."

Jay looked to his father with questions on his mind, but his father did not meet his glance. Jay briefly thought back to the story Lelan had told him earlier of Orin's son who broke the law. Sudden murmurs rose from the Alinoy army around him; whispered questions mimicked Jay's thoughts. However, Jay could not focus on these now. His nausea and fatigue had returned, along with something else. Jay was not sure what, but he knew something was not right as his vision began to blur.

"You don't know what you're talking about, you crazy old fool," Orin shouted in response to Erebus.

Erebus snarled. "Tell them the truth, Orin! Your son's death is the reason why you hate the mortal world even more than ever. You blame them as you blame me. You think if they never existed, your son would still be here. You simply cannot except that your son loved the mortal world, as my son loves it, as all Guardians should in order to keep both worlds safe."

"Enough! The past has no relevance to anything. The law is the law, and no traitor of Aneiros is void of the hand of justice—not *my* son, not your son, or any son of Aneiros. Who am I to lead my realm if I cannot abide by the rules we live by. As the leader of your realm, you should know that. Maybe you think yourself and your family to be above the law? Or maybe time has finally eroded your mind. You should probably sleep a few more centuries until your mind has healed. Maybe if your Semper Sodale had done so, she would not have killed herself," Orin taunted.

"She did NOT kill herself, as you very well know—she was murdered! I will have my revenge on her killer. A moment I feel may be very soon," Erebus snarled once more as his hands twitched close to the hilt of his sword.

Anger shook through Jay's body as he stood between the two kings, but as his focus on his father blurred in and out, he was in no position to make any move. Sweat trickled from Jay's forehead and down the side of his neck as the voices around him began to lose meaning.

"Now who is making false accusations... and, I think, also threats?" Orin tutted as a smirk appeared to add more insult to Erebus's rage. "I will have justice, and your son *will* pay for his and your crimes," Orin boomed.

Erebus drew his sword immediately. "Step away from my son and leave my realm peacefully now. My patience has come to an end. You and your men will leave, or you start a war here today."

Orin let out an amused laugh. "You do not have the power to make us all leave. So tell me, will you sacrifice your Guardians lives too—all of those who stand with you now—for a traitor who disgraces you? You know you do not have the numbers to fight off my army. We outnumber you at least two to one."

"That is not true."

Orin scanned over Erebus's army and grinned. "I think you know it is. At least at this moment in time. How unfortunate that a good number of your loyal Guardians are constantly caught up in such matters of the mortal world rather than defending their king. Where is your eldest son, Phelan? I do not see him here beside you. He has gained quite an impressive name for himself in the field of nightmares. Maybe so much so that perhaps he has decided he no longer belongs to this weak realm. Surely a 'God of Nightmares' is a Guardian whose heart is like my own. Maybe one day, he will stand by *my* side as a loyal Guardian."

Erebus snarled. "Phelan would never stand by your side. Together, Phelan and Jaydon give the perfect balance to our realm. Dreams and nightmares are both necessities, and my sons are masters of both regardless of the names they have been dubbed."

Orin sniffed. "That is a matter of opinion, but that is not why I am here."

Erebus edged closer to Orin with pure hostility that burned within his black eyes. His armoured wings where now present and his sword raised, preparing to make the first move. Erebus came to a halt as Orin took a step backwards, holding a hand up as though accepting to leave. But with one quick menacing glance, a defiant smirk presented itself on Orin's lips. Orin's hand reached out, jerking a seemingly dazed Jay backwards. His other arm thrust forward, sticking a sharp metal blade deep into the side of Jay's back. Jay's eyes flew open wide. His body arched as his arms clutched at his gaping wound. Jay stumbled to the floor as blood spurted from his mouth and wound, spilling onto the white stone ground beneath him.

Time seemed to slow as Erebus's cries cut through the air. Jay's heart beat fast, and with every beat that drummed in his ears, he saw Aarie's face. He felt her, and he knew she felt *this* now. *What have I done?* he thought as it was clear now that Orin never cared what the truth was. All Orin wanted was Jay to be dead and his father to suffer. Now Aarie would suffer too. Jay grimaced as he applied pressure to his wound and then abruptly got to his feet. Armoured wings unfurled violently from his back. Jay spun around, knocking Orin with great force back into the wall of his army. The black wings and blades of the Onuris Guardian's raised at once, awaiting Erebus's signal as they moved in to protect him and Jay.

Orin lunged at Jay once more. Wielding a sword, Orin flung an all-powerful blow towards him. A violent clang of metal vibrated through the air as another blade blocked Orin's sword.

It was Erebus.

"My son is unarmed! Have you lost all honour? Not only do you hide behind the law, but you also cowardly stab First Blood in the back!"

"First Blood is always armed, and your son is no longer a Guardian—he is a traitor, as are you. You will all die here today. The prophecy spells change for Oneiroi. It is time for me to bring that change and for Oneiroi to start looking after our kind as the priority. The mortal world will not be a primary concern any longer. Mortal collaborators such as your son will not taint our kind anymore. An example *will* be made."

Erebus gritted his teeth as he hoisted his sword in the air, swinging it around with one swift movement towards Orin. Metal on metal clanged together fiercely once more. A frenzy of wings and blades erupted, carving through the air as both armies of Guardians leapt into battle.

Many of Orin's Guardians had seemed reluctant to begin this war, but once Jay had been attacked, the violent retaliation of Erebus and his Guardians left them with no choice. Sides had been chosen, and they were now forced to fight beside the king of their realm to survive.

Jay took in the chaos as his Guardians fought off opposing Guardians around him. One of his fellow Guardians rushed to him, handing him a sword as they swung around to force back advancing enemy Guardians. Jay took it. He staggered up the steps to the entrance only to stumble at the top. Breaking his fall with outstretched arms, Jay glanced behind him to see a fair-haired Guardian who stalked him close. Jay pushed himself up and turned, visibly struggling to stand as he frantically rubbed at his blurring eyes. His wings flapped behind him in an attempt to keep him standing upright. The black armour that had protected them earlier had faded along with most of Jay's strength.

At first, Jay had assumed it was Orin who had come for him now, but as he managed to focus, the family resemblance became more apparent. It was Orin's brother, Darrak.

"It is time to die," Darrak taunted.

Jay watched another of Orin's Guardians come closer to stand beside Darrak. Jay blinked slowly as a fever seemed to be sweeping over him. Another bead of sweat trickled down his face as his body shivered, yet he still held his sword firm.

"He appears to be sick, Darrak. Even before Orin struck him, he did not seem well. What if there is truth in his claim?" the second Guardian asked.

Darrak aggressively turned to this seemingly younger Guardian besides him.

"There is no truth in his claim. Do you doubt your king?" he accused.

"No... but Darrak, he can barely stand. Surely it is not right for any Guardian to go like this, especially not *him*. Orin said there would be a fair trial, but he has had none. Surely if any Guardian deserves one, it is him."

"He is no Guardian! He has lost his right to that title and any right to an honourable death. I don't care about his so-called past glories. He is a traitor, and he will now lose his Guardian wings today. Don't make me doubt *your* loyalty too, Guardian," Darrak threatened impatiently.

The other Guardian nodded uneasily and backed up, throwing a remorseful look at Jay, who met his glance briefly.

"I was never meant to get a fair trial," Jay spat, glaring now at Darrak. "Was I? A fair trial would not allow you to have me murdered or have my father destroyed. A fair trial would mean you and your traitorous brothers could not get your hands on this realm and rule the whole of Aneiros into a pit of darkness. But what you don't know is that you still will never rule the whole of Aneiros. Aarie truly is my Semper Sodale, but she is also of First Blood. Her father, Lelan Adara, is making his way here with the Guardians of his realm as I speak. You cannot win, do you see now?

Even if you manage to take this realm, when they both return, all Guardians of Aneiros will know the truth. They will know who is the real traitor, and they will no longer bow to someone who seeks to destroy all that makes the Oneiroi who they are. How could any Guardian follow someone who would be so willing to sacrifice Guardian lives for lies and power? You are no better than the blood demons you create with your black nightmares."

Darrak held a deadly malevolent stare as he processed Jay's words. The younger Guardian abruptly rushed forward, reaching a hand out to Jay in despair. "Look out!" he shouted as another fair-haired Guardian emerged from behind Jay.

Jay shifted slightly as a sword plunged deep into the back of his right wing, piercing through to the skin of his back. Jay let out a thundering roar as the blade was pulled out, once again tearing through his wing. The pure plumage of white flooded red. Jay flung his weight around, knocking his attacker back with a swipe of a clawed hand. He snarled, recognising it was Orin who now stumbled backwards. Darrak flung himself towards Jay, acknowledging that his injuries were taking their toll. Jay blocked Darrak's blade with his own, delivering multiple blows with the last of his strength. The violent clang of metal sounded once more as rage coursed through Jay's veins. He struck out, again and again, forcing Darrak backwards each time their swords met. But as the mass of ragged feathers now hung low from Jay's right shoulder, he stumbled to one knee, delivering one last strike of his sword towards Darrak. It missed. Jay had no more energy to strike another blow, and his wounds bled out furiously. Orin edged towards Jay from behind, throwing a smirk to Darrak, who also closed in.

The heavy grey clouds above disappeared as an inky blackness devoured them completely. The lightning storm still ran rampant, sending violent sparks clawing their way out of the night. Angry flickers of light cast an eerie motion of shadows upon the spires of The Onuris House. This palace was no longer a fairytale setting of dreams; the shadows of this unnatural night had all but swallowed it up. The cries of wounded Guardians below and the spilling of their blood, echoed through the courtyards and towers, delivering nightmares to every corner. The whispers of ghostly laughter seemed to swirl around Jay now as he struggled to stand. Blood gushed from his side, from his back and his torn wing. These wounds would not heal, but he would not give in. He lifted his sword in his hand, then looked between the two Guardians who approached. Orin wiped the blood from the gash Jay had caused on his face. The wound rapidly healed itself. He growled as his glare focused on Jay.

Jay's vision had blurred again, and he could only make out dark shapes approaching him. He clung on to his sword with one hand as his other clutched his back wound once more. Darrak struck fast at the sword Jay held, knocking it clear out of his hand. Jay stumbled against the palace stone floor. Taking advantage, Darrak lunged at him, lifting him clear off the ground. He pinned Jay up against the cold stone wall behind them, and Jay let out an agonised groan as his wounded wing and back pressed hard against it. Jay no longer had the strength to break free, and he gritted his razor-sharp teeth together as he struggled against Darrak.

"This is the *mighty* legendary Morpheus—I am disappointed. I had expected more of a challenging fight. You are pathetic, and you have delivered your last dreams to your beloved mortals. Today, *you* are mortal," Darrak said with venomous hostility. With his right arm, he plunged his sword into Jay's stomach. Jay cried out in agony as Darrak pulled the blade back from his body and watched him fall to his hands and knees. Jay was weighed down heavily as his wings hung low over his sides. His breath staggered as he struggled to keep himself propped up on his hands. The desperate cry of his name echoed from his father's lips in the distance. Jay knew he could no longer prevent the suffering that all those he loved would now face. Nor could he avoid the pain he was fated to endure.

"I'm sorry, Aarie. Forgive me," he whispered with his last breaths.

Darrak focused on Jay's wings. "This is for my bother," Darrak shouted, raising his sword.

At that moment, a ferocious thunder boomed through the sky. The sky erupted into a blinding furnace of golden light. A shower of flaming torches came shooting down around Darrak. His eyes shot upwards to a blazing winged Guardian that sped across the sky. Their wings were unlike any Aneiros had ever seen. Golden flames licked the armoured feathers beneath them, caressing them in a deadly wave of heat and light. The flaming figure glided across the sky, casting golden rays over the palace and the open-mouthed Guardians who were no longer fighting. Instead, the Guardians now stared in awe at the spectacle that illuminated everything in sight.

Darrak gasped as he glanced back at Jay. Jay's face had turned up to the sky, and Darrak took in the violet glow of his eyes.

"Aarie," Jay whispered as his arms gave out, and he slumped to the ground in a bloodied heap.

Darrak raised his sword once again, this time facing the sky. His wings stretched out behind him, ready to take flight. But in a golden blur of movement, he was knocked to the ground onto his back. His sword flew from his hand, clattering to the floor. An unearthly cry came from him while the skin of his face, arms and legs blistered up with deep burns. Darrak's armoured clothing and wings were shredded. He sat up, shuffling frantically backwards as he watched the blazing figure charging towards him.

"What are you?" he cried.

Aarie looked at the pool of blood that flowed from Jay's unmoving body beside the Guardian she had struck. Rage quickly took over. The violet flushed from her eyes, instantly changing to black and then to deep crimson. She thrust her arms forward, sending a mighty ball of fire hurtling towards Darrak. Flames immediately engulfed his body. Darrak's gurgled cries cut off as his body exploded into black dust. A terrified gasp came from another younger Guardian, who stood nearby. Aarie raised her arms as though to send another fireball, but the Guardian kneeled to the floor with his hands up in front of him.

"No, please, I never wanted this. They lied to us. We never wanted this to happen to Jaydon. They lied, and that is why they have left like cowards. Traitors and cowards."

Aarie's arms lowered. Her eyes scanned around, quickly assessing for any more dangers. Orin, who had been close by, was now gone. The two armies below seemed frozen and locked in a temporary truce as they watched Aarie. Many had discarded their weapons out in front of them. Some knelt on the ground as though in surrender or to witness a momentous event. Another Oneiroi army now approached slowly, but Aarie recognised the tall, dark-haired figure who led them. It was her father. She knew straight away that he was here to help Jay and his family. Jay's father was rushing towards her now, and her eyes immediately flew back to Jay. Her irises had returned to their natural brown, and the furnace that had encased her feathers died away. Folding her wings behind her, she hurried to Jay and sat beside him. She lifted his body to her and cushioned his face against her lap. Jay's eyes slowly opened as he swallowed uneasily. He reached up to touch Aarie's face as a pained bloodstained smile weakly shaped his lips. Blood soaked through Jay's clothing and covered his wings. His pulse was fading rapidly. A tear rolled down Aarie's cheek as Jay's hand fell weakly from her face. His eyelids struggled to stay open, but he fought to meet her eyes through his half-closed lids. For the first time, Aarie could not feel Jay's great strength that was always present when she was near him. He needed blood and fast.

Aarie knew after everything that had happened to her, Jay would never ask for her blood nor simply take it. Even now as his heart grew weaker and his thirst ever more agonising, he did not reach for her; Jay could never forgive himself for what he had done when she had been mortal, but she knew he was dying now.

Aarie pulled Jay closer, hastily moving her hair away from her neck. As she looked at him, there was no fear in her eyes except the fear for his life. There was no disgust or any uncertainty in what she was about to do, just love and the sense of urgency to keep his eyes from closing.

"Please, Jay, don't hesitate," she pleaded. "There's no time, so you have to drink. Please, you need to, and I need you to. I am your Semper Sodale, please do it for me."

And with that, Jay's hand sought out hers, softly squeezing it in acceptance. He lifted his face closer to her neck as one arm came up around her shoulder to support himself. Slowly his lips drew back. His fangs reared up and gently pressed down, piercing through Aarie's soft skin to release a warm flow of blood. And then, he drank.

Jay's thirst surged through him, and he gave in to it completely. His arms tightened around Aarie's shoulder and neck, pulling her closer to him. She gasped, but he knew she was not in pain; she was Oneiroi now. His jaws clamped down with more urgency and fierceness as his thirst drove him. The blood flowed faster, bleeding new life back into him.

Jay's black eyes snapped open wide; some movement had caused him to scan ahead from over Aarie's shoulder as he drank. His eyes focused there, though his grip on Aarie did not break. A group of mortals had gathered to the entrance of the palace in front of them. To Jay's surprise, his glance brushed over Aarie's friends one by one, resting on Phelan, who stood close by them. Jamie had instinctively stepped forward towards Aarie, seeing the scene before him. However, he had stopped in response to Phelan's gesture of warning and reassurance.

After a brief, tense moment, Jay's wings came to life once again, rising behind him. With a gentle motion, they lifted Jay's body, pulling him and Aarie up to their feet as he continued to hold her tight in his clasp. His wings were still once more, but they seemed to arch around Aarie as though shielding and protecting her.

Jay released his lock on Aarie's skin, and he took one long gasp of air. His black eyes scanned around, quickly examining the motionless Guardians who had been fighting moments ago. Phelan gave him a nod of reassurance that the fighting was over. After giving one last glance at Aarie's friends, Jay's attention went quickly back to Aarie. The wound on her neck was already healing fast, and he kissed her skin there with the gentlest touch. His face lingered close to hers, feeling the warmth of her skin as he lovingly brushed against it. Jay withdrew back slowly, bringing Aarie's face fully into his view. The natural sapphire blue of his irises had returned but had begun to take on a violet hue as Aarie's eyes had too. His arms had wrapped affectionately around her waist as hers had around his. Their wings now stretched out behind their backs in synchrony as they studied each other closely. The blood that had matted Jays feathers earlier began to dissolve away to nothing, revealing the brilliant white plumage beneath. His heart beat strong, and his strength had miraculously replenished. To Aarie, he seemed different yet still the same, and so much stronger than before. Right now, they both did.

"You saved my life, Aarie. Thank you for coming back to me," Jay whispered.

Aarie lovingly pored over every detail of him, making sure he was okay. "Self-preservation," she replied, painfully relieved to hear his voice.

Jay smiled with his usual infectious smile that Aarie loved so much. She reached a hand to his cheek, tracing where she remembered she had slashed his skin. It was smooth now with no trace of any wounds.

"I'm so sorry for what I said the last time I saw you. I didn't know what I was saying, Jay. I was so confused, and I couldn't make sense of anything. It was Phelan and my friends who helped me remember again. That's why they're here. I wasn't myself, and there was no time to take them back home. Jay, I never meant anything I said to you," Aarie urgently declared.

"I know because you're here now," he said, kissing her hand. "But I meant *everything* I said to you, Aarie. Do you remember?"

"Yes," Aarie whispered, wide-eyed and hopeful.

"Your mother's alive, Aarie, and I will make sure we find her."

Aarie was speechless but nodded as they stared, unable to tear their gaze from each other. At that moment, a wave of violet light swept over the surface of their wings behind them. It spread from the joints at their back, right through to the tips, igniting them into violet flames. The flames flickered over their feathers, undulating gently in a mesmerising and meditative motion as their wings arched higher behind them. The seals on their wrists glowed brightly with the same violet luminescence. From where Aarie's friends stood, their mirrored wings created a blazing circle of violet. Pure elation flowed between the Semple Sodales as they held each other. Despite the audience around them and the lingering armies that had come to a halt, they could no longer fight the urge that took over them now. No other kiss before had seemed this paramount. Jay did not hold back as Aarie realised he must have done when she was mortal. He cupped her face firmly as their kiss held a new fierce intensity. Their hearts beat heavy in their chest, and their body's held tight together as if nothing could ever separate them. Nothing would ever compare to this connection—this heat, this passion and this feeling of complete love.

The flames that surfaced their feathers fully engulfed their wings now through and through. It was as though the feathers themselves were made of the same violet fire. It spread wildly over the surface of their bodies, becoming part of them in their embrace. What had been a circle of flames from the side, had transformed into a full sphere of blazing energy.

All movement around Aarie and Jay had ceased, and as they finally broke away from each other, they were immediately aware of the deafening silence. Their flames died back at once. They shared one last glance before slipping one hand in each other's. The marks on their wrists had unconcealed themselves once more, and they stared down at them. A new marking had combined with their original one, overlapping them and transforming them into something new. They now both shared this same mark.

They finally glanced up, taking in the happenings around them more thoroughly. A number of Alinoy Guardians had disappeared. The many that remained watched them in wonder as though witnessing a miracle. Orin Alinoy was still nowhere to be seen.

Jay and Aarie looked now towards Aarie's friends, whose mouths hung open. Even Phelan beside them seemed lost for words. Erebus was the first to break the silence as his steps echoed against the stone ground.

"Jay? Are you..."

"I'm okay, Father. Very much more than okay." Jay smiled.

Aarie glanced at the worried expression of her father, whose arrival she had not earlier had time to properly acknowledge. "We both are," Aarie assured.

Jay scanned the area again. "Where is Orin?"

Erebus took another step forward. "He left with the few Guardians that stayed loyal to him. Judging from what we all just witnessed, along with the arrival of Lelan's Guardians, I do not think they will be returning anytime soon. Orin knows the majority of his Guardians will not stand by him now. He has lost, and they have seen his true nature."

"And the rest of Orin's Guardians?" Jay asked his father, looking over the silent Guardians who had dropped all weapons to the ground. They watched from the steps below.

"They want peace. They have abandoned their realm. The new world of change that they had hoped for was never going to be brought by Orin and his dark plans. He lied to them, and he will never be able to return without suffering the wrath of that betrayal. They know now that you never broke the law. Not only have you and Aarie proved that but also they know—as we all do now—the part you play in the prophecy. You're both something no one has ever seen before, and they have witnessed the power you both hold. The change they hoped for has already begun. It started here today with the two of you and the Guardians who stand here as witnesses. Never in thousands of years have so many Oneiroi Guardians of all three realms stood together peacefully. Orin's Guardians want to ally themselves with us. They want to join our realm, Jay. Or more accurately, they want to join your realm," Erebus said, eyeing the new royal symbols that laced Jay's wrist. "Your marks cannot lie. You are reborn a new king today, Son. And your queen is already by your side. The remaining Guardians of Ivoriark await for you to decide their fate."

Lelan stepped forward now. "Aarie," he said, curiously reaching for his daughter's hand. She broke away from Jay and held her wrist out to her father; she knew that was what he was seeking. Lelan's eyes widened as he traced the new symbols that wound around her skin. It was no longer just the patterns that wove into the shape of flames and wings as his marks did, but a new layer of detail laid upon it. Lelan knew it was the Onuris mark that overlapped it. As it did so, it was perfectly interweaved to create new symbols within themselves. Lelan gasped as he recognised one of the most renowned of Oneiroi symbols: the Aneiros Dream Lily. Though all Guardians knew of it, no one had ever seen it laid upon a Guardian's skin like this before.

"Aarie... you really *are* the one in the prophecy. It was always you," he whispered in astonishment.

At that moment, a nervous young Guardian stepped forward. Jay's attention went to him immediately. He recognised the Guardian from earlier as the one who had shouted out to warn him before Orin could deliver a deadly blow. Phelan stepped in front of him, blocking his path. The Guardian hesitantly glanced from Phelan to Jay.

"It's okay. Let him past, Phelan," Jay assured, enabling the Guardian to continue another step forward.

"Jaydon, our Guardians wish to speak to you," the young-looking Guardian said.

"And what is it they are expecting of me?"

"They wish to know where we stand. We attacked this realm, evoking war—you have every right to have us brought to justice for this crime. We accept that it is more than deserved because we blindly followed a traitor. He lied to us all, and we almost followed him to your destruction. What's worse is, we had doubts and suspicions that what he told us was false, but we did not act upon them straight away. However, we ask you to consider that he was our king and that many of us were afraid. He was the law of our land, and we thought we had no choice. We know now that we do have a choice, and we would rather be the prisoners of a worthy Oneiroi realm, than soldiers of a traitor's realm of darkness. We choose to stand loyal to your realm, whatever your decision is for our fate."

"Tell me, Guardian, what is your name?" Jay asked.

"Kaleb Phantasos."

"Tell me, Kaleb, why did you help me earlier? Orin might have succeeded in taking my wings if it had not been for your warning."

"Because what he was doing wasn't right. You were sick, and all Guardians should get a fair trial. You hadn't been given a chance to prove your innocence even after everything you have achieved for Aneiros. It wasn't right, and now we know the truth. We know who was the real traitor and that you didn't break any laws."

"And you're ready to pledge your allegiance to my father's realm?"

"If that is still to be the realm in which you choose to reside, then yes. We pledge our loyalty to your family as we pledge it to you."

"Why?"

"Because you and your Semper Sodale are written in the prophecy. Our realm has hoped it to be true for so long. It takes living in such darkness for someone to appreciate the light of the Aneiros Lilly. You cannot imagine what hope you both offer us for a new future. You had already earned the admiration of so many with your skills as a Guardian, long ago. If our king had ever set us free, you would be our natural choice of Oneiroi leader. You should know that a great many of our older Guardians died refusing to come here to bring you to trial. They refused to fight beside Orin if it came to it because it would be against you. They were branded traitors and suffered the most violent of deaths. The rest of us had no choice but to agree to come here. Most of us believed there would be no war because we hoped that you would prove to be innocent and we would simply leave. Now, we know Orin never planned to let that happen."

Jay paced a few steps away from Kaleb, giving his words deep thought. Moments later, he turned back abruptly to face him once again.

"I cannot allow you to pledge your allegiance to me... not until you know who I *really* am," Jay announced.

Kaleb's forehead creased. "I know who you are—we all do. You're Jaydon Onuris, Son of Erebus Onuris. You are The Great Morpheus, The God Of Dreams. The whole of Aneiros knows who you are are."

Jay shook his head. "No. No, you *don't*, and it is crucial that you do before you pledge your life, your loyalty, or anything to me.

Yes, I am Jaydon Onuris, and yes, it turned out, in the end, I did not break our *beloved* laws. But you should know that I would have *gladly* done so. I did indeed fall in love with a mortal girl who came to our world. That darkness you spoke of was how this world had begun to feel to me before I met her. Before I knew we were soul partners, and before I knew she could bear the Seal of Semper Sodales, I would have done *anything* for her. I would have broken *every* law for her. There was a time when I thought I had already done so. I didn't care that she was mortal. It made no difference to me except that her mortality would one day mean I would lose her. In the end, it was her mortality that held me back from casting out all rules and caution entirely. I cared too much for her safety and valued her life too much to keep putting her at risk. So, I made her leave, the way only Guardians can make a shadow leave this world. But make no mistake, she was never a shadow, and the nightmare I delivered made me ashamed to be Oneiroi. I had to risk almost destroying the one thing that I love the most because of the rules of this world. Because *they* would have seen her put to death as though she were nothing but a disease this world needs ridding of," Jay said through gritted teeth as he thought of Orin.

"It never mattered to Aarie what I was, even after what I did to her." Jay continued talking to Kaleb, though his eyes focused momentarily on Aarie. "I feel that she never really knew that she stopped me from permanently becoming the monster I had started to become. Before she came to me, my world was bleak. The dreams I cast were solely becoming nightmares, and all the while, I was losing myself within them. I had stopped caring about mortals, and it seemed less important what type of dream I gave them. I began purposely opting for a darker kind, which meant I did not have to even look hard into a shadow's mind. I did not want to learn much about them—what brought them to our world or what made them the person they were. I didn't want to know any of it, and with that, I felt myself becoming more distant from them. I no longer understood their world or them, and because of that, I began to despise them. I just wanted them gone, and I didn't care about anything they had to show me anymore. I thought they had nothing to offer me because I thought I had seen it all before," Jay broke away from his thoughts to glance back at Kaleb.

"You may or may not see where this story is leading, but I assure you, everything I say has a purpose." Jay smiled. "You see, you called me 'Morpheus, The God of Dreams', but that is a name first given to me by mortals. I gladly accepted the name purely because of that fact, even if it means more here than it does for mortals these days. It was not through vanity or for the grandeur of the title that I hold that name with such affection. I do so because at the time it truly became mine, I cared as much for mortals as I do Oneiroi, and I liked to believe a small part of their world cared enough to create that name for me. Although many names for the Oneiroi claim a place within mortal fiction, this name is mine alone, and it is one that does not simply depict me as the bringer of mortal suffering.

Aarie made me remember what it was like to care for the mortal world again. She made me feel again and made me want to prove to her I was not a monster. I wanted to prove to *myself* I wasn't. I realised the love I had for the mortal world never really left me, it just got lost in the darkness, and she showed me the way back.

Aarie is First Blood, but she was born mortal. It makes perfect sense to me that only she could ever be my Semper Sodale because she is a combination of both of the worlds I love. She makes me the best version of myself, just like the shadow's link to our world makes us truly Oneiroi. Without that link, we are nothing—we have no purpose, and we create no dreams.

You have come from a realm that has spent decades solely casting nightmares, holding Oneiroi lives above all mortals and causing mortal suffering. I have been a Guardian long enough to know that nightmares are unfortunately a necessity in this world, but I also know that so are dreams. Orin lied to you about more than the prophecy and about me being a traitor. He lied to you about the very Guardians he was making you become and about the unspeakable destruction he planned for you to cause in the mortal world. Day by day, he was slowly turning you into soulless monsters, and all the while you were creating more in your image through the shadows you sent back. The darkest nightmares that you were enforced to use were the very cause of the increasing number of blood demons. Orin knew it, and he hid it from you because he wanted it to happen. He wanted them to eventually destroy the mortal world so they would no longer come here. The blood demons will testify to this in time. For now, please take my word that this is the truth. It is my father's belief that your king had my mother killed for finding out this truth long ago. If anything, you can trust her death is not something I would ever lie about.

I would like you to take a look at my Semper Sodale and the mortal friends who helped save her life. In doing so, they saved mine too. Then I would like you to look at your fellow Oneiroi Guardians who would stand by you, and ask yourselves if we are really all that different. I want you to imagine yourself in a world where mortals don't exist and picture what that world looks like without them."

Jay watched Kaleb's reaction as his eyes widened, curiously examining Aarie's friends as if only just realising they were there. He paid attention to their clothing and their lack of wings; it gave away their mortal origin clearly amongst a crowd of armoured winged soldiers. However, they stood firmly together as though guarding each other and watching over Aarie, even though it was doubtful she ever needed anyone's protection again.

Satisfied with Kaleb's inspection, Jay continued to speak. "This world is my world as it is now my Semper Sodale's, but the mortal world is also her world, and therefore it is mine too. I am an Oneiroi Guardian of First Blood, and I can no longer live by all of the laws that currently rule our land. The mortal world has changed me, and now the prophecy has seen to it that the blood demons have also changed. It makes sense that now is a time for changes in the law. You ask to be part of a new kingdom, but I can only be part of Aneiros if new laws are to be made. It is my wish to unburden myself of promises I can no longer keep and rules I can no longer keep from breaking. I can no longer do my duty as a Guardian without those changes.

So, I come back round to my initial statement. When you ask to be part of this realm, and you pledge your allegiance to *me*, I want you to really *know* who I am. You need to know what world I would envisage for the future. Most importantly, I want you to know the kind of a Guardian you are asking to become if you were to be part of that new world, should it ever exist. I have to know that when a loyal Guardian's life is in danger, you will go to the aid of that Guardian just as when a mortal's life is in danger because of our world, you will go to *help* that mortal. Where dreams can be cast, they will be cast, and if that is not to be so, then only as a last resort should their dreams darken to guide them safely home. I am asking you to care about the decisions you make because they matter to you, not because there is a law enforcing it.

When mortals come here, they will dream of wondrous magical lands, of great achievements and their hearts desires, of aspirations that they can achieve, of life without suffering, of life without limits, and of life with all they could possibly want and dream of. They will dream, and then they will leave, taking back the good that is in the hearts of Aneiros and none of the darkness. We will never question why we do what we do because our eyes will finally be open.

Do you understand who I am now?"

Kaleb met Jay's stare with an intent seriousness that gave him an older presence than that which had emanated from him moments ago. "Yes," he said firmly.

"And do you think you and your fellow Guardians are still ready to join me?" Jay asked.

Kaleb stood up firm and proud. "Yes. I give you my word as a Guardian, we pledge our loyalty to you, your queen and to both of your families. If I am not mistaken, that now unites us with most of Aneiros."

Jay smiled. "Yes, it does, and so, it is done—you and your Guardians are welcome as Guardians of this realm. We are all now brothers and sisters as much as we are all Oneiroi. There is much more to be said, but for now, let us look forward to a new beginning," Jay said, turning to face the crowd at the bottom of the steps.

Jay had known Oneiroi hearing would not fail, and the Guardians now cheered for the decision that had been made. Cheers roared through the crowds, not only from the Guardians of Alinoy's realm but Jay's and

Lelan's realm too. They truly were united at this moment. This moment saw the birth of a new kingdom that had been dreamed of for so long. Cheers soon turned into joyous chants.

"To The God of Dreams!"

"The Light of the Aneiros Dream Lily has returned!"

The words echoed through the palace walls over and over. Jay reached out a hand for Aarie. She stepped forward hesitantly in front of the crowd before her. His hand slipped into hers, and he gently guided her closer to him. She stood momentarily bewildered and nervous as she looked at him. Jay smiled at her in reassurance. Gazing at him now, she realised that she would possibly never have to say goodbye to him ever again. A smile rapidly grew on her face as though the happiness that erupted inside her could no longer be contained. She turned to face the crowds below as Jay raised their laced hands in the air, revealing their new matching royal symbols.

Another roar of cheers erupted.

"The heart and strength of Aneiros!"

"The realm of the dreamers!"

Chapter 28
Sunday

Today was masquerading as a normal day. Aarie's dad had prepared an ordinary (although phenomenally delicious) Sunday roast for effect. Aarie knew tomorrow would be much different. Her dad would return to Aneiros as Lelan Adara—a man she felt she had only just met. She had only briefly seen a glimpse of him this past couple of days, but soon she would know him well.

Tomorrow, the search for her long-lost mother, who was now a dreamwalker, would commence. This was a prospect that scared Aarie, but at the same time, it filled her with an immense, overwhelming joy that she could not put into words. Over the years, there had been so many things Aarie had wanted to share with her. Maybe now she would get the chance one day. It hurt to have missed out on knowing her mum throughout most of her childhood, but at least she now had all the time in the world (or two worlds) to make up for it.

For now, Aarie had to focus on what was now her new complicated dual life. She was Aariella Stone: a regular university student who would go back soon with her housemates to live a normal, everyday mortal existence. Then, she was also Aariella Adara: Semper Sodales to Jaydon Onuris, First Blood royalty of the new and apparently eternally awaited kingdom of Aneiros. How that had happened, still baffled Aarie. It was a story that had not and would not sink in for a long, long time. She had barely had the chance to let the reality of Aneiros sink in, nevermind all the infinite ways in which being Oneiroi would impact on her life.

Aarie had tried to blank out the image of Darrak in the last moments of his life. He had left her with no choice but to take his life, though, in truth, it was her new Oneiroi power which had instinctively kicked in and taken any other decision out of her freshly transitioned hands, anyway. Regardless, the guilt would forever linger. Alongside it, she worried about any repercussions it could have. She wanted to forget that Orin Alinoy was still out there somewhere, seething with hatred and possibly already plotting revenge for the death of his brother. She wished Jay was here now. He would take her mind off this, amongst many other worries.

There was still so much Aarie had to learn about Oneiroi Guardians and Aneiros. Though everything that had happened to her seemed like a dreamlike fantasy, Jay had and now would always remain real. He was the one thing that made sense from a world she still didn't fully understand, though she knew there was still so much they did not know about each other. She knew he had a history and, it appeared, a legendary one at that.

A thousand years surely meant many stories to tell and many memories. She hoped one day he would share them all with her, though part of her worried that her short mortal life would seem dull in comparison. She wondered if he would hold some things back. *Would he always be such a mystery to her? Her Man of Mystery.* She smiled at the thought; she didn't care if he wanted to hold back information for a while. Maybe a little information at a time was enough and possibly all she could cope with for now anyway. Besides, they would now have eternity to get to know everything about each other. *As long as Jay hadn't changed his mind*, she began to worry. *After all, he was supposed to be here by now, wasn't he?*

Words surfaced in her mind from a past conversation with Phelan. He had stolen a brief moment to talk to her before she had left Aneiros. His words now offered her some comfort amongst her sudden doubts.

"Jay has searched a long time to find you, Aarie. I should have known that not just anyone would do for my brother. You had to be exceptional, and you are. I can't wait to see the Guardian you will become in the future. My brother has a gift to see things as they really are. He sees the potential and truth in everything before anyone else. Not only does he create dreams, he feels them. He lives and breaths them like no other Guardian I have ever known. It's almost like they became his only way to be happy, and it's because his very soul was waiting for you to be amongst them. I know now that is why the mortals chose him as their God of Dreams—because he always cared to give them a dream, and he always cared because one day one of them would be you."

These words ran over and over her mind now as she waited for Jay to return to her. They seemed the only thing keeping her sane at this moment. She did not know how things would be from now on, and she realised she desperately needed to talk to Jay. They had not seen each other since late last night when she and her friends had left Aneiros. It felt like much longer. Aarie wondered how she would fit into Jay's life on a permanent basis. *Did he want that? Surely, as her Semper Sodale, he wanted that, right?* she thought to herself. Aarie hadn't doubted it when she was with him yesterday, but strangely, being alone made her worry he might have had second thoughts. She wondered what she could possibly offer a 'God of Dreams' and his realm. Aarie had been overwhelmed by the acceptance and the welcome the Oneiroi Guardians had given her in Aneiros. However, she felt they had been deceived into thinking she was something more than she was. Aarie had power now, but she barely knew anything about how to use it or control it. Neither did she know much of Oneiroi culture, history or Aneiros itself. *What good could she possibly be to anyone?*

Aarie sighed, staring through the steamed-up kitchen window. She subconsciously bit at a nail as Adam theatrically cleared his throat for the second time.

"Helloooo, Aarie. Earth to Aarie," he said, standing in the doorway. "Food's ready and on the table. You wanna come sit down? Jamie's on his way. He said he'll be just a couple more minutes or so. Have you had a sign or sensed that Jay's gonna show anytime soon?" he asked as Aarie turned to face him.

"It doesn't work like that. We're not telepathic. I can feel sudden deep emotions or physical pain, but things are not as clear the further away he is. I have no idea if he's coming, Adam," she said worriedly. "What if he's changed his mind?"

"About lunch? I doubt it. There's a lot of tasty meat at stake here." Adam grinned, trying to raise a smile from Aarie without succeeding.

"What if he's realised that I don't fit into his life or that he doesn't want to fit into mine? It's all so real now, and we're from two different worlds... and you saw how the Oneiroi see him. He's *more* than royalty to them. How can I be good enough for him? He could have changed his mind."

Adam took a long hard look at her. "Hey, believe me, no one would be *that* stupid. Yes Aarie, I saw him, but I also saw *you*, and, I don't know much about The Oneiroi, but I'm pretty sure you had all of their attention too. Above all, I doubt Jay would want to lose you after all the effort he went to get you in the first place. I mean, he pretty much confessed to almost giving up everything he was for you when you were, you know, your old human self. The only reason he didn't the first time around was that you both would've died in some hideous way—one that no one seems willing to tell me about in detail, and it's probably for the best they don't.

My point is, he didn't care when he thought you were a completely different species to him. He was as weird as you were in that respect. So, now it's worked out that you're pretty much the same freaky all-powerful vampire-angel-wolf-creatures—it's all surely gotta turn out better than ever, doesn't it?" Adam smirked as his eyebrows raised.

Aarie frowned, though a smile made an appearance. "Freaky vampire-angel-wolf-creatures? Is that what you think of your best friend these days?"

"I said 'all-powerful', didn't I? And anyway, you're like a cool superhero or something now," he replied, giving in to a laugh as Aarie did too.

"But I'm not *weird*," she insisted, still smiling.

"You so are, but I wouldn't have it any other way. It's boring to be normal anyway. I pride myself on being as weird as I possibly can."

"Well, that does explain a lot." She smirked.

"So how long do we give Jay before we can tuck in? I only ask because they're all ravenous back there and it smells so good."

"It does smell good. I don't mind if you all want to start, and I know for sure, Jay wouldn't either. I will wait a little longer, though I think I could eat a horse. I've only just realised how hungry I am," Aarie said.

Adam raised his eyebrows again. "Wow, a whole horse? Well, lucky for you... and any nearby horses, your dad's prepared enough food to feed an Aneiros army. But you don't actually do that now, do you? Eat horses, I mean, or live *stuff* generally?" Adam asked with a peculiar half-smile that made Aarie realise he was at least partly serious.

She folded her arms and said, in the most composed voice she could muster, "I suppose I have to when I'm really, really hungry and the cravings are too much for me to bear."

"Really?" Adam answered gullibly.

Aarie picked up a tea towel from the kitchen side, then flicked it against Adam's arm. "*No*, you doofus. I eat what I *normally* eat!" she said with a laugh, but a moment later, she seemed to give it a more serious thought. "At least I think I do... I've not been Oneiroi for long. Though, I have to say I'm glad we're having a Sunday roast because I've been craving meat like you wouldn't believe. Maybe I'll check with Dad," Aarie whispered as though talking to herself.

"I didn't mean that to sound bad. I just thought, well, it's just the blood thing. I thought, you know, that maybe you were like the—"

"—like the blood demons? You were going to say that weren't you?" Aarie frowned.

"Well, I don't know, maybe. I don't get it, that's all—the whole blood thing between you and him. I know it seems to heal you both—and thank god it does and *did*—but it kinda looks like the sort of thing the blood demons do. I mean, jeez, I thought Jay was going to kill you when he took hold of you as he did."

"Adam, he nearly *died*. I begged him to take my blood."

"I know. I *know*. Sorry to mention it, and I'm really glad Jay's fine now, honestly. It was just all so hard to watch at the time because I don't like to see you hurt."

"He didn't hurt me, not at all, in fact. It's not like that for Oneiroi, and especially between Semper Sodales. It's why he didn't need to hold back. I felt no pain, and if it puts your mind at rest, no, I don't have a craving to drink the blood of live *stuff* or people either, if that's what you're really worried about."

Adam looked pale. "Oh, well that's good to know...and also *weird*...I made this conversation weird, didn't I? Sorry, maybe we should just go back to talking about food."

"But you know I'm still me, right? I'm still Aarie."

"Yes, I know. Queen Aariella Stone The First."

"Actually, it's Aariella Adara."

"Oh, yes, I forgot. I still can't believe your dad's one of them—I mean, one of you. It's funny because he strangely still seems no different to me. Can I still call him Lyle? I have been, so I hope he hasn't minded."

"I'm sure either Lyle or Lelan is fine dependant on the audience."

"So are you going to change your name officially?"

"I don't know. Stone has always been my name. Maybe I'll use both for now. After all, I'll be kind of living a double life for a while—Aneiros one day, uni the next."

"So you are still going to uni?" Adam asked with a hopeful smile.

"Of course I am. Why wouldn't I be?"

"I don't know, I guess I figured you might have more exciting adventures ahead of you now,"

"I have exciting adventures ahead of me here too." Aarie smiled.

Adam leaned forward to place a kiss on Aarie's cheek as he walked passed. "Mwah. I'm glad to hear it. I'm looking forward to the rest of the year with you as a housemate. I'll let the other's know you're coming through in a bit," Adam said, as Jamie came through to the kitchen.

"I hope those kisses are reserved exclusively for royalty," Jamie said, wrinkling up his face.

Adam puckered his lips towards him as he passed.

Jamie shifted backwards in exaggerated disgust. "Touch me, and we're no longer friends," he joked, making Adam laugh before he left the room.

Jamie looked now at Aarie, whose face lit up to see him. "Hey," he said

"Hey," Aarie replied, "I thought you were coming with Angela and Lori?"

"Yeah, I was originally, but I got held up, sorry. Meira came over. I'm not late, am I?"

"You're just on time. Food's ready on the table. Angela and Lori only got here a few minutes ago. They're in the other room with my dad. Angela's still busy giving Lori an update on events."

"Oh, right. Yeah, that's a lot to take in just before tucking into your Sunday lunch," Jamie said.

"Well, I think Ange rang her last night to fill her in with most of it, but yeah, by the look Lori gave me when she came in, I'd say she was still processing things. She's cool with everything though and happy to still be in this new and strange friend circle of trust. She reckons people think she's already crazy, so she's quite happy not to mention anything to anyone else. Anyway..." Aarie replied, breaking off as her mind wandered. They stood in silence for a moment, though their eyes did not move from each other.

"For a moment, I was worried you might have decided not to come," Aarie said finally.

Jamie blinked. "Of course I was coming. Why would I not come?"

Aarie hesitated, looking at the floor. "I don't know... it's just, I haven't had a chance to speak to you alone properly since the night at the club," she replied. "I can't believe it's not even been three days since then. So much has changed."

Jamie leaned back against the fridge, taking a deep breath. "I know."

"Jamie, about that night, I'm sorry, I shouldn't have—"

"—Aarie, you don't need to explain anything to me. You were upset that night, and I was really drunk. I wasn't thinking straight. It was a mistake, and if I'm honest, I'd just rather not talk about it. So let's just keep it at that, okay?" Jamie said swiftly, avoiding her gaze.

Aarie knew he couldn't have meant for his words to sound so bitter, but still, she heard that they did.

"Sure," she glumly whispered.

Jamie glanced up, hearing the tone in Aarie's voice. "Hey. I'm not angry with you, Aarie if that's what you're worried about. I could never be that with you, especially after these past few days. Look, there's just no point in bringing it up, that's all. After everything that's happened, it seems pointless now. I can see that Jay makes you happy. I'm not that much of an idiot to not see that. We've all nearly lost you at least twice in the space of a few months. So, the fact that you're still here and you're happy means more to me than anything else. Besides, I hear some weird prophecy thing says that you two were always meant to be together. *Nobody* can compete with that," Jamie said with a laugh, trying to lighten the mood. "So, we're still cool, aren't we? You're not mad at *me*, are you?" he asked.

"No, of course not. And yes, we're cool. Of course we are," Aarie replied.

Jamie nodded. "Good." He smiled. "So can we go back to being our normal daft selves, and maybe go eat 'cos I'm starving?"

Aarie laughed just as Jamie added, "...and then maybe you can tell me when you're gonna take me flying with you."

"What? *Jamie*," Aarie said, pulling a face.

Jamie shrugged. "What? I mean it. I should get to revel in this awesomeness that has befallen my closest friend."

"You're serious, aren't you?"

"Yes. You can't keep *all* the fun to yourself. This is the most exciting thing to happen in the sleepy village of Thorndale and to our friend circle. So, how about it?"

"I don't know. Jay won't like it, but... I'll think about it. Let me get used to it myself first before I think about *passengers*." Aarie smiled nervously.

"Ysss!" Jamie cheered, clenching a fist in celebration. "So where *is* the man of your dreams, anyway?"

"Aneiros. Jay had to stay to fully recover. My dad and his dad insisted he *did* this time. They insisted that I did too, seeing as I'm technically still in the final Oneiroi transition stage. So, I haven't seen him since we left the palace. We haven't even had a chance to talk through everything yet. Jay said he'd be here soon, hopefully in time for lunch."

"Well, he'd best get here before we eat it all 'cos it smells bloody gorgeous. Anyway, what does a man have to do to get a hug from royalty these days? Come here," Jamie said, holding his arms open.

Aarie stepped into them, wrapping her own around him too. Jamie exhaled a long deep breath as he closed his eyes in their embrace.

"God, it's so good to know you're here, alive and well," he said. Aarie didn't reply, but she squeezed him tighter as they held each other in silence for a few more moments. Jamie finally opened his eyes again to see Jay lingering in the doorway.

"I didn't mean to intrude," Jay said apologetically.

"It's okay, you didn't," Jamie replied, releasing Aarie from his arms. Aarie gently broke away, then turned around.

"You made it," she beamed. "We were just about to go and sit down to eat."

Jamie edged to the door. "I'll go through and let you two catch up," he said, throwing an awkward but sincere smile to both of them before leaving them alone in the room.

Aarie's heart skipped a beat as Jay made his way over to her. His arms went immediately around her, pulling her to him. Her arms wrapped around his shoulders, linking her hands behind his neck to draw him closer. She took a quick breath as though to say something, but before she could, they were already kissing. Electricity surged between them, awakening all their senses and igniting a heat beneath their skin. Jay pulled back slightly, taking Aarie in. He caught his breath as his eyes met hers once again.

"Hi."

"Hi. I missed you," Aarie replied.

"I always miss you," Jay whispered, stealing more kisses between his words. "There are so many things I want to tell you now that I *can* freely tell you, but I don't even know where to begin. I want us to be part of each other's life properly. I know that will be a big leap from where we've been, and you have to tell me how you feel about it. I just needed to say it now, so you know. Otherwise, I feel like I might go insane if I don't. Aarie, I don't want to have to say goodbye to you again now I don't have to. I don't want to spend another night alone."

Aarie subconsciously pulled him closer. "Neither do I. I want to be wherever you are, Jay," she quickly replied before their lips found each other once again. He was all she ever wanted, and at this moment, she could think about nothing else but him.

Lyle cleared his throat awkwardly as he entered the room. Aarie and Jay broke apart abruptly, creating a little distance between themselves.

Heat lit up the skin of Aarie's cheeks as she looked up. "Dad, I didn't hear you come in. We were just about to come through. Jay just got here."

"Yes, so I see," he said, looking at Jay, who sheepishly met his glance. "Are you better rested now, Jaydon?" Lyle asked.

"Yes, very much so, thank you," he politely replied. "Sorry, I'm later than expected. I got held up. My family and I had a great deal to discuss, as Aarie and I also do later."

"Of course. It's been quite an eventful and strange few days for us all. It's one of the reasons I thought it good for me to share one normal Sunday lunch with Aarie like we used to. We don't get to do it as often these days. I thought it would be good for her before she and her friends head back to uni and things change for all of us. I'm glad you could make it too. It will give me more time to get to know you better now you will be a big part of my daughter's life. Anyway, come, sit down the two of you. Lunch is getting cold," he said, turning back to leave the room again.

Slipping a hand into each other's, Aarie and Jay shared a brief glance before following her dad to another room.

When Adam had said there was enough food to feed an Aneiros army, he wasn't kidding. Aarie's dad had prepared a magnificent roast feast in the large dining room. This room rarely got used these days, but today, it's seven diners sat comfortably around its long table. The overflowing tureens of meat and vegetables gave the impression they were expecting many more guests to arrive. The dining room was at the back of the house, and a set of French doors led into a small conservatory that overlooked the garden. Eating in here brought back so many childhood memories for Aarie. Her friends had often come over when they were younger, to have dinner in the evenings or lunches on the weekends. However, a table this affluently presented was mainly reserved for special occasions—birthday's, Christmas, and general celebrations. It seemed quite fitting that they all sat around this table together today; today felt like the ultimate celebration in so many ways. Aarie wondered if that was why her dad had gone to so much effort to cook all of this food. Whatever his reason, she was glad of it and that he was such a good cook; she had not been lying when she had said she could eat a horse. By the time they had finished lunch, Aarie felt like she had eaten a horse's weight in meat and roast vegetables. She was relieved that she was not the only one. Everyone had cleaned their plates after going back for seconds, and for some, even thirds.

The warm, inviting rays of the afternoon sun had cast a glow through the conservatory windows, luring Aarie and her friends outside into the garden to rest their full stomachs. Sitting now on the grass, they chatted amongst each other. Jay had remained at the table with Lyle at his casual request for a friendly chat before they joined the others. Jay glanced briefly across the table, passed the open French doors and to where Aarie sat outside in the autumn sun with her friends. She threw a quick smile in his direction before returning her attention to Angela. Jay turned to Lyle, who sat beside him.

"Lelan—or do I call you Lyle while you are in this world?"

"Lelan is fine amongst all of us. There is no one here to catch us out," he said with a smile.

Jay nodded. "Thanks for doing this today, Lelan. I think you were right. It's just what Aarie needed—to have a day that feels relatively normal to her, without more overwhelming worries and things that are still quite foreign to her. Being around her like this has been great. We never had much time when she visited Aneiros, so it is nice not to feel like we are running out of time for once."

"Jaydon, there's something I want to ask you. I know the two of you have lots to discuss, and I know that much of it will involve discussing Aarie being in Aneiros. Am I right?"

"Yes. What is your point, Lelan? If you are worried about the matters of Orin's whereabouts, I can assure you, I will make sure Aarie keeps a little distance from Horngate City for a while and anywhere Orin may seek her out."

"No. It's not that. I know you will do all you can to keep her safe, and all of Aneiros knows only a fool would try to attack either of you two now. It's just that, I want to remind you that, although you and Aarie may look as though there are only a few years difference between you, as you know, that is not the case. I know she is an adult now, but she is still only eighteen, Jaydon. She shouldn't have to worry about things that mortals her age don't have to worry about. She is not from Aneiros, and finding out you are First Blood is a lot to take on board for anyone. But she is no longer just First Blood, Jay, and neither are you. You are technically a new king, and she is now a new queen. Aarie may not have realised the full extent of what that means yet. In fact, I know she cannot possibly have because I never brought her up as Oneiroi. One day she *will* know everything there is to know, but she is not ready to take on such responsibility now, even if you are."

"I know, Lelan. Of course, I know she's not ready. Up until two days ago, she didn't fully know for sure what I was, let alone what she really was. I have not had enough time to explain how things are in our world. I would never ask Aarie to take on anything she's not ready for. I don't expect her to change who she is. Yes, she is technically a queen, and no-one can ever take that away from her now, but it also means she has forever—if she wants it—to accept that title."

Lelan's brows scrunched together in confusion. "But I heard your conversation. I know you want her to live with you in Aneiros. However, she has a life *here*, even if she wants to build a life there too. I don't want to sound like I don't want her to embrace Aneiros—of course I do, one day when she's ready—but this world has made her who she is, and I don't want that to be taken away from her when she is so young. She has eternity to discover Aneiros, but she only has a mortal lifetime to have the life she has here now. I know how important that will be to her one day, even if she hasn't yet fully realised that herself. Jaydon, I think she would give up everything for you if you asked, but I don't want her to. I'm asking you please, do not to ask her to."

Jay regarded Lelan thoughtfully. "I said I didn't want to be without her. It doesn't mean I want to take Aarie away from everything she knows—her friends, her life, and her world. I simply meant I want to be part of it. I know she wants to be part of my world—*our* world, Lelan. I know Aarie's not ready to be a Guardian yet or anything more than that. It may be years, decades, centuries even, if ever at all. Until that day, her home is my home, as my home was always hers. I want to be with her wherever she wants that to be. It's what I meant when I told Kaleb that I could no longer live by our old laws. My seal and love for Aarie make them redundant for me. I can't live without her, but I wouldn't expect her to abandon everything else she loves because of me. I would never ask her to, Lelan. *Never*."

Lelan did not reply, but his face softened as he took in the sincerity in Jay's face.

"Is everything okay?" Aarie asked as she glanced at her dad and Jay from the doorway. They seemed to have been in the middle of a serious conversation from where she had sat outside. Part of her wished she had mastered how to tune in to specific sounds with her new Oneiroi hearing, but that was something she was just going to have to learn in the future. Their seriousness had alarmed her at first, but their expressions had already relaxed and even warmed.

Lelan looked up and smiled at Aarie. "Yes, love, everything's great. In fact, I was thinking to crack open some Oneiroi wine to celebrate. It's not every week, my daughter finds her Semper Sodale, you know. Come in and join us. In fact, no, we should join you and your friends out in the sun," Lelan said, getting to his feet.

"Erm, okay. Yes, that sounds great, Dad." Aarie smiled back, hearing the genuine cheerfulness in her Dad's tone. "I didn't know you kept some of that here?"

"Yes, well, I was saving it for a special occasion, and none could be more special than this," he beamed before leaving the room.

Aarie raised her eyebrows at Jay. "What *did* you say to him?" she asked, pleasantly surprised.

Jay shrugged as they stepped outside. A moment later, Lelan appeared with wine glasses and a dark Oneiroi wine bottle.

Jay eyed the bottle in Lelan's hand. "Maybe you should make it a small for Aarie's friends. It would appear it is not just a myth that mortals cannot handle Oneiroi wine. After all, *that* is a strong bottle." Jay chuckled.

Lelan cocked his head to the side. "And how would you know this, Jaydon Onuris?"

"Erm... just a hunch," Jay replied with an impish smile.

"You really *did* break every law, didn't you?" Lelan said, studying Jay with curious amusement.

"Not *every* law. Besides, we've already concluded that my seal makes it all void—it's fine."

"You're lucky I like you, and that your intentions towards Aarie are proven to be honest. Otherwise, I might not be so happy to have such an Oneiroi rebel *galavanting* around with my daughter," Lelan joked.

Jay and Aarie shared a brief glance before bursting into laughter. Lelan's eyes shot back to them in surprise; he evidently had not expected his joke to be regarded as this funny.

"What did I miss?" he asked, looking between the two of them.

"Nothing." Aarie smiled. "And you can make mine and Jay's a large glass. I'm Oneiroi now. We'll see who can and can't take their wine," she said with a laugh.

Lelan handed out a glass to each of Aarie's friends as they all gathered around in response to the high spirited trio that had emerged from the dining room.

"Ooh, out comes the wine, that explains why you're all so chirpy all of a sudden," Angela said, taking a small sip.

Lelan stepped forward, lifting his head to speak to everyone. "I'd like to thank everyone for coming for lunch today. I just wanted to say how glad I am that Aarie has you all. It makes me proud to know that she chose such decent people to have around her. Despite me being slightly overprotective on occasion and worrying that you might lead her astray, she proved me wrong—"

"—There's still time," Jamie heckled with a grin.

Lelan smiled, then continued. "Anyway, I'd also like to acknowledge a special event that I feel, due to other events, has been neglected. This event is one of the most sought-after and highly valued miracles amongst the Oneiroi, yet it is the rarest. This event has brought together two soul partners from two different worlds and united them. I would like to congratulate the couple who are so very lucky to have found each other. Jay's and Aarie's origins make their Seal of Semper Sodales the rarest and most miraculous of them all. I would like to make a toast to Aariella and Jaydon, congratulating them on becoming Semper Sodales. So please, raise your glasses with me—to Aarie and Jay. May your future as Semper Sodales be a long, happy one,"

"To Aarie and Jay!" the group repeated as their glasses clinked together.

"Smile," Jamie said, taking multiple snaps of the group with his camera.

Jay gave a disapproving glance at him as he was caught by surprise.

Jamie smirked back. "Oh, *come on*. You're with Aarie now, so that makes you part of the gang. That also means you're gonna have to get used to me capturing all of our lives. Mr 'God of Dreams' or whatever they called you, you pass for human just fine on a camera."

Lelan smiled. "He's got a point, Jay. Aarie is in no danger from being seen with you now. Mortals have no way of recognising who you really are. Believe me, I've had hundreds of pictures taken," Lelan said, casually taking a sip of his wine.

Jay sighed in defeat. "Okay fine. I can live with that. After all, it's only a thousand years of vigilance down the proverbial drain?"

"Did you say a thousand years?!" Adam shrieked.

Jay opened his mouth as though to comment, then closed it again. Lelan broke out into a gentle laugh as Jay looked at him seemingly for help.

Aarie met Jamie's glance and saw a new question burning there. His eyes scrutinised over her Oneiroi symbols at her wrist before returning to her gaze. She looked down, unsure what she would say. Humour briefly faded from Lelan and Jay as they took in Aarie's reaction. Jamie abruptly turned and hurried a short distance away. He leaned over the garden wall as though to step over. Small furrows appeared on Aarie's forehead as her smile vanished.

"Jamie, wait," she said, stepping forward as though to follow him.

Angela edged toward her but stopped as soon as Jamie turned around again. He began hurrying back to the group. A yellow flashing light came from his camera, which he had now set down on the wall. Jamie smiled back at a relieved Aarie.

"Well, if you're going to be kicking around for all eternity, then I'd best make sure you've got plenty of pictures of *me* to remember me by." He laughed, catching his arm around Aarie and Angela as he manoeuvred between them. "Come on, everyone, get in quick!" he shouted.

Lelan and Jay leaned in beside Aarie while Lori and Adam quickly ducked down in front of them all. The light blinked faster. Everyone smiled just as the shutter sounded, and a picture was taken.

The day had been one of the best in what felt like forever. Aarie had finally been able to be with the important people in her life all in one place. They had sat outside talking together for hours until the day had turned to dusk, and then the night had crept in. The garden lamps and heaters had been switched on. Snacks and more wine had come and gone, and still, they seemed content in each other's company. Strangely, they had talked about everything *but* the past couple of day's events. For Aarie, somehow, that felt good. She knew that Jay had chosen not to speak about Oneiroi related things for her benefit as well as not wanting to make anyone uncomfortable with his or her presence. She knew that it was also partly because, although her friends were no longer in danger from other Oneiroi, it was still not good to reveal all of Aneiros's secrets to mortals. This was in case they were ever to appear as a shadow there one day; it was for their own safety as Jay had once told her on their first meetings. However, Jay assured her that the likeliness of them becoming a shadow now was less than one in a million.

It had felt so easy for her to be around her friends and Jay together. She marvelled at the fact that Jay and her friends seemed to get on well, almost as though they had known each other longer than these few days. Her dad also seemed to be putting in more effort to get to know her friends better, even with Jamie to whom he had shared jokes. It had turned out they had a lot in common. Maybe there was something in the air, or perhaps it had something to do with the Oneiroi wine, but Aarie felt pure bliss. She and Jay had been the last to wander back into the house. They now closed the door to the late evening.

Aarie's friends had already made their way over to Adam's house next door to stay over. They had quite obviously made themselves scarce to give Aarie and Jay time together as the day had come to an end. Lelan had retired to the study with a book, Aarie noted, passing the slightly ajar door to see him comfortably seated beneath a lamp.

Jay followed Aarie into her room, and she closed the door behind him. He took a moment to take in the surroundings. The calming warm greys and ivory walls were brought to life with the bright burst of colour within several well-positioned framed prints, stylish lamps, soft furnishings and vases. This room belonged to someone with sophisticated taste and a definite creative flair. It had a similar feel to the one in her uni house, but it was clear that she was still settling into that one. Also, he had never genuinely had a relaxed opportunity to take it in as now. Jay thought one might judge the occupant of this room to be older than Aarie's eighteen years, though evidence of her not so long ago childhood claimed a small corner of one of Aarie's shelves; a small collection of worn soft toys sat staring out from there. Jay smiled to himself, then scanned across to the many fiction books that lined Aarie's shelves. Fantasy fiction, mystery thrillers, tales of adventure, mythology and folklore. His eyes moved over to the desk in the corner. Many pens, pencils and art utensils were neatly packed into compartments and holders. Sketchbooks and layout pads were tidied away to the side. Jay caught a glimpse of a pencil drawing sticking out from one of the books, and though his curiosity clearly tugged at him to take a peek, he resisted the urge. Instead, he took in the view from the window that looked over the back garden and the tall blossom trees that stood close by. His eyes then shifted over to Aarie's bed in the corner of her room where a small dream catcher hung from the headboard.

"Are you okay?" Aarie said, breaking Jay's thoughts.

Pulling her gently into his arms, he let out a content sigh. "More than okay," Jay replied. "I like your room."

"Thanks."

"I keep thinking back to how we met in your dreams. Now, I feel like I'm the one who is dreaming, and if that is the case, I never want to wake up. We always had so little time in Aneiros. It doesn't have to be that way anymore, and it seems too good to be true. I realised something today—we don't have to feel like we have limited time or have to worry that it might be the last time we'll see each other. We have forever. Once you've fully recovered from the effects of transitioning, you'll find you don't even need to sleep as much as you used to. We don't have to wonder when we will next meet, as we can choose to see each other whenever we please. There's the possibility that you may even *want* me to leave you alone for a while—"

"—Never. That will never happen," Aarie said, shaking her head as she smiled.

Jay laughed. "My point is, I don't want to overwhelm you with everything that goes hand in hand with being an Oneiroi Guardian, and furthermore, being a royal Guardian. Those are things most of us get used to from birth. You've only had a matter of days.

After what you witnessed in Aneiros yesterday, I want you to know there is no rush for you to get to grips with any of this. I know most of it still won't even make sense to you, but you have all the time you could ever need to get used to all that is new to you. There's no rush for anything, Aarie. It's so easy for me to forget that you're still young, and I know you probably haven't even figured out what you want from your life here yet. The last thing I want to do is change who you are. I love who you are, and I know I will always love who *you* choose to become. I want you to have your normal mortal life, Aarie—as normal as it can be with me in it. You haven't lived long enough to understand fully how important this time will be to you one day. I don't want to be the reason you have regrets when you think about this time, one day. What I'm trying to say is that being with me doesn't have to mean giving up any of it. You can—"

"—You're right, Jay, and I *do* really want my mortal life. I know I don't get forever with my friends, and that's why I still want to go to university as I had already set out to. I want to be Aariella Stone, a student living in Leeds. Immortal or not, I know I only really get one lifetime as things are now," she said, watching Jay nod in agreement. "But I also need you to realise that one lifetime is all I ever knew I had, up until a few days ago, and back then, I was always searching for something that was missing from my life. That something was always you, Jay. So now I know it is possible, I want you to be part of my life here as much as I am part of your life in Aneiros. There are the obvious things that, to be honest, are way above my comfort zone—all the things that come with being Aariella Adara and the Semper Sodale of such a highly regarded Oneiroi *king*. It scares me, Jay. I can't hide it—it does, even if I don't want it to, but it doesn't stop me wanting to be part of Aneiros with you if only taking one very slow step at a time.

I won't miss out on anything here, Jay, and I *know* I could never regret any part of being with you. Besides, you said it yourself—I won't need to sleep as much as I used to soon. That surely gives me at least an extra eight hours nearly every other day. I have more time than I ever had, so I want to use that time to explore Aneiros with you. If that is what you want too?" Aarie said.

"More than anything," Jay immediately replied.

"But Jay," Aarie continued, "going back to what you said about the rushing thing and me having my mortal life—since we do have forever..." Aarie said hesitantly, "...maybe it would be nice to be boyfriend and girlfriend for a while before we are solely Semper Sodales. *Please* don't take that the wrong way, because there is nothing I want more than to be your Semper Sodale, ever since you first told me they existed, in fact. It's just that, well, apart from the actual words still sounding quite foreign to me, I really want you to be my boyfriend. That word is more familiar and perhaps even more meaningful to me. Nobody has ever made me feel like you do, and I know it probably sounds stupid, but I think the first person to make me feel this way should surely have the right to *that* title before anything else. I'm kind of new to all of this, not just the Oneiroi thing."

A radiant smile spread across Jay's face. "I'd like that very much," he said.

"And I was thinking..."Aarie added, looking up with puppy dog eyes.

"Go on," Jay said as his brow quirked up.

"...I quite liked the mystery thing we had going on. Though it may drive me insane not knowing everything about you, at the same time, I kinda liked it. Maybe I don't need to know everything right away. Maybe every time we see each other, you just tell me one thing about yourself or Aneiros. It will ease me gently into your Oneiroi Guardian life. That way, I won't ever get too overwhelmed by the overwhelmingly epic and fantastical perfection that seems to be every fibre of you."

Jay's lips twitched in amusement. "I don't think anyone has ever quite described me like that before. But does this mean Miss Aariella Stone will only have just the one lonely question for me from now on?"

Aarie laughed. "It does. Do you think you can cope with this new me?"

Jay leaned in closer. "Absolutely. And I'm happy to take everything slow, Aarie," he whispered before pressing his lips to hers. He pulled back with a grin. "But I'm afraid, this time, I definitely get to ask *more* questions about you. I'm not so fussed about the mystery thing where you're concerned—you're far too interesting. So let's start with... what were you like growing up? What was your life like here in this world? What kind of things did you get up to? And basically, every detail about how you became the very person you are right now."

Aarie smiled as she raised an eyebrow. "Is this what I sounded like the first night you met me?"

Jay smirked. "Hmm, pretty much."

"Fair enough." Aarie shrugged. "I'll grab some photo albums. It'll be easier to talk through. Make yourself comfy," she said, gesturing to her bed as she moved towards the shelves. "But be prepared to be bored. Very, very bored."

"Never." Jay laughed as he sat down.

No matter how long Jay and Aarie had together, time still seemed to move faster than it usually did. Several hours had passed, though it felt like only minutes. Aarie turned to the last page of the fifth thick photo album. She and Jay laid on their elbows on the bed, staring down at the pictures in front of them. Aarie had been describing each photo's events from her memories.

"And so in that last one, that's why me and Angela are laughing and Adam and Jamie look so confused. As you've seen, the number of pictures rapidly increased from the point I met Jamie. He wasn't joking about you getting used to having your photo taken," she said.

"You still have the same smile," Jay said grinning as his fingers traced over the photo that sat beneath the plastic album sleeve.

"Do I? Huh, my dad always says I have my mum's smile."

Jay turned. "We'll find her, Aarie. She's out there somewhere, and I'm sure you'll see her again soon."

"It's been so long. I was only a small child the last I saw her. I don't even know how I should greet her when we meet. I've got so many things I want to tell her. There are so many years she's missed out on. I want her to meet you and see how happy I am."

"So, you *are* happy then?" Jay asked.

"Yes, can you not tell?" She smiled, gently nudging her shoulder against him. "Are you?"

"Yes. I don't think I've ever been this happy before, Aarie." He reached out and held her hand in his. "This is something *I'm* new to."

Suddenly, a tree branch scratched against the bedroom window as the wind picked up outside. Aarie glanced up as a chorus of birds sounded within the treetops. The sky had faintly begun to lighten, and she realised that the early morning sun would be coming up soon. Jay got up off the bed and held his hands out to Aarie.

"What is it?" she asked, taking his hands in hers as she stood up.

"I want to show you something back in Aneiros."

"Now?"

"Yes." He nodded. Before Aarie could respond, they were already disappearing.

******

The wind howled underneath the front door of the house. Lelan was still reading beneath his lamp. He sat up for a moment and glanced up at the slightly ajar study door. The house seemed quiet save for the wind, and he realised he could no longer hear Aarie's and Jay's voices anymore. He had been trying not to eavesdrop on them with much success, but Oneiroi hearing still meant he knew they had fallen silent now. This shared Oneiroi hearing issue would possibly require investing in Oneiroi proofing walls in the future.

There was a sudden knock on the front door. Lelan stood up, briefly glancing out of the window, through the blinds. It was pointless though; the front door could not be seen clearly from this room. He got up from his chair with his book still in hand. Wandering over to the hallway, he glanced at his watch and laughed.

"Aarie, is that you?" he called out as he reached for some keys that hung on the wall. He began unlocking the door. "You know, you're Oneiroi now. You don't actually have to use the door to get back in if you don't have your keys. Though at this time, I'm not even sure what you're—" Lelan froze as he opened the door to realise it was not Aarie who stood at the door now. His book dropped out of his hand and came crashing onto the floor. His heart pounded in his chest as he took one long deep breath, then smiled.

"Anne."

Epilogue
Sunrise

Aarie glanced around at the clifftop that Jay had brought her to the first time she had met him. It was night here too. She gazed up at him as he released her hands from his.

"So what did you want to show me? Is it here?" she asked.

"No. I just thought it was more fun getting there like this," Jay replied

"Like what?"

Jay stepped back and then unfurled his wings, extending them behind his back. "Like *this*," he said with a grin.

Aarie couldn't help returning the smile, but before she released her wings, she realised she was wearing a shirt. Luckily, she had a vest top beneath.

"Hmm, I may need to be more prepared for impromptu flights," Aarie said, removing her shirt.

"Oh..." Jay replied. "Sorry, I didn't think. We'll have to sort you out with a few Oneiroi garments, perhaps. I'll show you how to manipulate the fabric. Trust me—it makes this whole thing a lot easier," he said, gesturing to his wings.

"Okay, but I can manage like this for now," she said, glancing over her shoulder as her wings unfurled. She stared up at them almost in disbelief that they were hers. Jay's smile spread across his face as he watched her, and she turned back to him. "What? I'm new to this, remember?"

"I know, and you're doing great so far."

"Jay?" she asked, glancing at his wings. "Do you have the same marks on your back like me? It's how we conceal them, isn't it?"

"Yes, I have them too. The marks can be concealed as well if you need them to be, just like the ones on your wrist. Your Oneiroi wings mean you are a full Guardian, Aarie. First Blood always are, but not all Oneiroi have them. One day soon I'll explain to you what that means. I can't wait to show you this world properly when the time is right, but for now, I'd like to show you just a small corner of *my* world. Are you ready?"

Aarie nodded. Jay bent his knees gently before pushing down and then lifting into the night sky with ease. His wings spread out wide and gracefully beat as he glanced down at Aarie, waiting for her to join him. She took a deep breath, pushed down against the ground, and then jumped up, letting her wings gradually lift her higher. Jay's eyes lingered over her for one moment before he turned and glided through the night. Aarie followed him, knowing where he was heading immediately; she recognised the canyons and waterfalls below. The mild air of the night brushed against her wings as she soared above the vast hilltops, past the blossom and maple trees that followed along the winding river. They passed the front of the cottage, then came to the woods that housed the wooden palace amongst its trees. Aarie could see wooden structures poking out here and there from the treetops. Jay circled up ahead and came to a slow, gliding gently above the highest trees that stood at the edge of the woods. Aarie could now see a wooden platform protruding from the top of the trees. No winding staircase or rope bridge led to it; it stood on its own. Jay now landed swiftly on the narrow structure, glancing up at Aarie as she neared him. She slowed, trying to balance herself as her feet touched the wooden beams. Jay steadied her, and she set herself down beside him. The small surface area of this lofty viewpoint would no doubt be terrifying for a flightless mortal.

They shared a smile before looking out ahead of them. Aarie's eyes widened at the view of the mountains and the valley. From here, the landscape stretched out for miles. The sun had not come up yet, but she seemed to see it all fine—all the distance she had just covered and so much more. The cherry blossom trees looked like miniature pale pink clouds down below. The details of every tree, mountain, waterfall, and forest were magnificent.

A distinct golden glow shimmered across the hills beyond a forest, and Aarie's eyes narrowed on it. It seemed like hundreds of tiny sunbeams scattered on the ground, but as she focused harder, she realised they were flowers, hundreds of them clustered together. For a moment, Aarie held her breath. Then she turned to Jay.

"Jay, this is incredible. This view is better than I imagined it could ever be."

"I'm glad you like it. If you wait a few more minutes, it's about to get even better."

She watched in fascination as he stood wide-eyed, expectantly staring out ahead. Jay's glorious white-feathered wings arched gracefully out behind him as his dark hair silhouetted against them. The sapphire blue of his eyes gleamed brightly as they always did, and they looked now to meet hers. Aarie contently sighed. He was beautiful. She wondered if she would ever get used to how the very sight of him could beat any view, no matter how magnificent. But she was simply staring now. She looked back out ahead.

"So... this platform is not really a 'design flaw' after all, hey? " she said, remembering the conversation they had shared the first time she was here.

Jay laughed. "Well, actually, I thought there was one flaw, at the time I told you that."

"And what possibly could that be? The view from here is probably one of the best views I've ever seen in my whole life."

"Yes, it *is* incredible, but when I'm up here, far away from everything, it can have a habit of making me feel like the only Guardian in Aneiros. I used to feel lucky to have this peaceful place where no one else came... until you visited here that night. Afterwards, I no longer felt privileged to see this, nor was it peaceful. I was simply alone. What good was this spot if I could never share it with you? So, I thought it was flawed by design until now."

Jay raised his wings slightly as he sat down on the platform and dropped his legs over the edge. He looked back to Aarie. "The sun is about to come up."

She settled down beside him, taking a deep breath as they waited together. Aarie realised she had found the missing pieces of her life. The fog had finally been lifted. Or perhaps there had never really been any fog in the first place. Maybe the truth had merely shone too bright for her to see and believe. In the end, it had not been university life that had brought clarity to her. It was not in the city or even in her world. And though her band of friends had and would always play an essential part in her life, it was within the depths of her own mind and soul that she had first found Aneiros. There, she had found the first piece of the puzzle of her life, discovered the magic of The Oneiroi Guardians and, of course, extraordinarily met Jaydon Onuris. Light and Darkness had found each other at last.

What had once seemed like just a dream, was now very much her reality. Purpose had also found her, and amongst it, she had played an essential part in an ancient Oneiroi prophecy. She had helped set in motion change for the future of a whole world. Never had she felt a sense of purpose more astounding than that. However, this incredible change did not take precedence over the little changes she had created in a small corner of her own life. She had finally created *that something* that really meant *something* to someone. Not only had she helped create an unbreakable bond between herself and her closest friends, but she had also jointly created a bond that had changed the shape of two people's hearts forever; she was Jay's Semper Sodale. Amongst many new things in her life, this would always be an important purpose now: to be happy and be all she could be for him as he would be for her. He was her present, her future and her new eternity. She smiled as he drew her closer to him, and they watched the sun slowly rise behind the mountains in the distance. Their great wings arched behind their backs, curling around each other to create a dome of feathers as they sat on the highest platform amongst the treetops of red, gold and green. A deep orange glow shimmered on the cusp of the mountain in the distance. Moments later, a golden incandescence light flooded the sky as the sun hovered at the peak of the mountain like a giant halo.

"Good morning, Aarie." Jay smiled as he squeezed her hand in his.

"The first morning of forever," she blissfully whispered.

Aneiros was now her world just as much as the mortal world. Her heart felt like it had expanded to accommodate the love she had for both. As Aariella Stone looked at the adventure that was now her life, through new

Oneiroi eyes, she knew it was one more incredible and magical than any she could have dreamed.

THE END

Author's Note

From a very young age, the stories I loved the most were the kind filled with wonderful, unknown possibilities and, of course, magic! To let one's imagination explore new worlds with the limitlessness of dreams is the gift of a good tale. As a child, I jotted down many of my own experiences in the form of short stories and took mental notes of interesting dreams. But over time, I forgot or discarded most of them. I left tales untold. After all, I never really thought of myself as a "proper" storyteller. Who was I to write anything down for real?

Nevertheless, I did have at least one story that desperately and relentlessly wanted to be told: this one. The desire to write this story overwhelmed me. So too did the requirements of writing a fantasy romance novel: the extensive effort, time, research, emotional highs and lows, doubts and major anxieties about sharing my own words with strangers. Yet somehow, here it is. Perfect or not, my novel made it to paper! Writing it felt like an attempt to give something back for all the times that a story touched my heart or pleasantly lingered in my mind days after reading it. I hope this tale brings you the same joy reading it as it did for me writing it. May you fall in love with the world of Aneiros and its characters as much as I did.

Love Dalia

Printed in Great Britain
by Amazon

17339495R00182